To Sue +

♡

Margy

Margaret Turner Taylor
February 2024

Do You Know Who I Am?

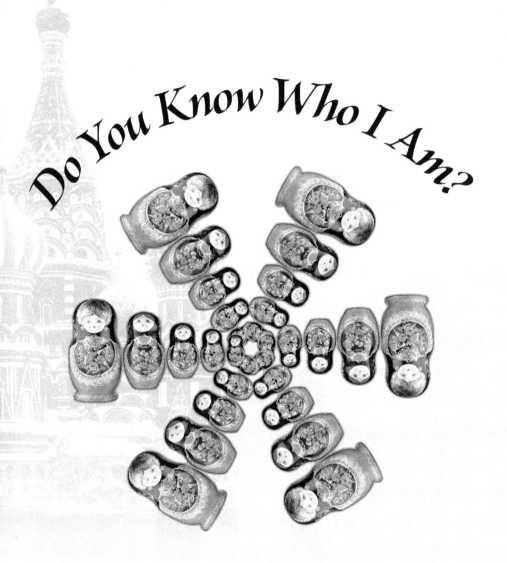

Margaret Turner Taylor

LLOURETTIA GATES BOOKS • MARYLAND

This book is a work of fiction. Many of the names, places, characters, and incidents are products of the author's imagination or are used fictitiously. Any resemblance to actual events or locales or person living or dead is entirely coincidental.

Copyright © 2024 Llourettia Gates Books, LLC
All rights reserved. This book or any portion thereof may not be reproduced or used in any manner whatsoever without the express written permission of the publisher.

Llourettia Gates Books, LLC
P.O. Box #411
Fruitland, Maryland 21826

Hardcover ISBN: 978-1-953082-27-5
Paperback ISBN: 978-1-953082-28-2
eBook ISBN: 978-1-953082-29-9
Library of Congress Control Number: 2024901304

Photography by Andrea Lōpez Burns
Cover and interior design by Jamie Tipton, Open Heart Designs

*This book is dedicated to freedom,
the natural condition of the human spirit.*

Contents

Prologue vii

CHAPTER 1 1
CHAPTER 2 8
CHAPTER 3 21
CHAPTER 4 30
CHAPTER 5 42
CHAPTER 6 48
CHAPTER 7 53
CHAPTER 8 63
CHAPTER 9 75
CHAPTER 10 84
CHAPTER 11 91
CHAPTER 12 97
CHAPTER 13 102
CHAPTER 14 106
CHAPTER 15 111
CHAPTER 16 119
CHAPTER 17 132
CHAPTER 18 138
CHAPTER 19 151

Chapter 20	163
Chapter 21	175
Chapter 22	183
Chapter 23	191
Chapter 24	201
Chapter 25	209
Chapter 26	217
Chapter 27	225
Chapter 28	234
Chapter 29	239
Chapter 30	246
Chapter 31	254
Chapter 32	260
Chapter 33	268
Chapter 34	279
Chapter 35	287
Chapter 36	294
Chapter 37	302
Chapter 38	308
Chapter 39	316
Chapter 40	325
Chapter 41	333
Chapter 42	338
Chapter 43	344
Acknowledgments	349
About the Author	351

Prologue

There are many kinds of freedom. Everyone understands the kind of freedom that is granted to those who are fortunate enough to live in a democratic country which has a constitution. That constitution guarantees certain inalienable rights and freedoms to its citizens. Many who live in these countries take their freedoms for granted. Those who live in authoritarian and tyrannical nation states do not enjoy these freedoms.

In addition to freedoms guaranteed by a constitution, there is the freedom one experiences when finally escaping from an intolerable situation. That situation may be a release from prison, getting out of a miserable or abusive relationship, ending a toxic friendship, or leaving a job one despises.

In addition, there is the freedom that an individual experiences when they are able to overcome the shackles of an addiction or find their way forward from the ghosts, either real or imagined, of a difficult past.

Freedom is more deeply appreciated when it has been earned or achieved through sacrifice. Freedom lives in the human heart, even when circumstances dictate otherwise. Those who wish to enslave in any way are on notice. The quest for freedom never ends.

Chapter 1

Rosalind Parsons had worked hard to earn a PhD in computer science from Syracuse University. The red-headed beauty had spent years in an abusive marriage and at last, pregnant with her husband's child, found the courage to leave her miserable life behind. Afraid her husband would hunt her down and kill her and the baby, she made plans to disappear. She spent money she didn't have to buy a fake identity, so she could live her new life as an altogether different person. Then suddenly, Rosalind Parsons was declared dead in a horrendous, bloody triple murder, a domestic triangle gone terribly wrong. But in fact, someone else had died in Rosalind's place.

Rosemary Carmichael had no college degree and no PhD in computer science from any place. The dark-haired beauty was a single mother, struggling to take care of a baby on her own and make a life for the two of them. Rosemary Carmichael had all the brilliance and possessed all the computer expertise that Rosalind Parsons had earned. Rosemary just didn't have the credentials to prove it. Rosemary had a driver's license and a birth certificate in her new name. She had some credit cards and some other pieces of paper that testified to the fact that she was Rosemary Carmichael.

When she ran, she took everything she owned with her in a used minivan.

Rosemary had not intended for Asheville, North Carolina to be her final destination, but Asheville was where she and her newborn baby girl, Christina Rose, had found themselves when Rosemary collapsed from exhaustion in the bathroom of a gas station convenience store. Even though she didn't know exactly where she was, Rosemary knew she was a long way from the seacoast. It wasn't hurricane season, but the rain was blowing sideways in a torrential downpour. Rosemary could barely see the road in front of her as she made her way west on Interstate 40. One of her windshield wipers was practically useless, and she knew it wasn't safe to continue driving in the terrible storm. She'd filled her minivan with gas and bought a cup of coffee, hoping the caffeine would give her the jolt she needed to continue running.

Christina Rose was not yet two weeks old, and that meant Rosemary was not yet two weeks out from an emergency Cesarean section that had been preceded by a long and difficult labor. Rosemary had left the hospital before the doctor wanted to release her, and she'd been on the run ever since. She hadn't had a good night's sleep for days, partly because newborns demand to be fed at all hours of the day and night. And, Rosemary hadn't slept because she'd been trying to get as far away as possible from Syracuse, New York, as quickly as she could get there, wherever there turned out to be.

Rosemary's plan had been to drive to Arizona to begin her new life in the Grand Canyon State, but life's what happens while you're busy making other plans. She was trying to breastfeed Christina Rose, but fatigue and the lack of fluids and regular meals had diminished Rosemary's milk supply. The baby wanted to be fed every two hours, and Rosemary couldn't produce the volume of milk the baby needed. The exhausted new mother was in the bathroom of a gas station convenience store changing her baby's diaper when she suddenly felt weak and lightheaded and collapsed on the floor. As she slid down the wall and lost consciousness, she remembered thankfully that she had belted Christina Rose securely to the changing table.

It was several minutes before the cashier behind the counter found Rosemary. Christina Rose was screaming at the top of her lungs, and the cashier, Marley Kurtz, became concerned when the crying didn't stop. Marley knelt beside the unconscious woman and felt for a pulse. She found a weak one and took her flip phone out of her pocket to call 911. Marley used the phone for emergencies only. Just as she was about to place the call, Rosemary stirred and opened her eyes. She heard her baby screaming and tried to stand up to get to the changing table.

"Hang on there, mom. I'll take care of the little one. You just lie here for a minute until I can help you sit up. I almost called 911, but then I saw you were awake. Do you want me to call for help?" Marley tried to reassure the baby's mother. Something about the situation, not anything Marley could put her finger on exactly, made her think the woman on the floor might not want anybody to call 911. Maybe it was the woman's hair that made Marley hesitate. The black dye job was awful, and the young mother had obviously hacked it off herself, creating a very unbecoming hairstyle, if it could even be called a hairstyle. The young woman not only looked ill; she looked as if she were trying to disguise herself and had done a very poor job of it.

The fear she saw in the young mother's eyes confirmed Marley's gut feeling about not making the call. "Oh, no, don't call 911! I'm fine. Please, don't call anybody. I'll be up and out of here in a couple of minutes. I thought the coffee with caffeine and sugar would keep me going, but I guess I was wrong. I'm trying to nurse her, but my milk seems to be drying up. I'm so sorry. I didn't mean to make a fuss or be any trouble to anybody. Just give me a minute and we'll be gone. I promise."

Twenty-five years earlier, Marley had divorced the husband who was beating her up on a regular basis and made her feel like a worthless piece of crap. She immediately recognized the fear and low self-esteem in this young woman who reminded Marley of herself and the desperation that had characterized her own life so many years ago. The young mother's color was returning to her cheeks, and she was sitting up straight now without swaying from side to side. Marley unbuckled the baby from the changing table and wrapped her in the thin receiving blanket that lay crumpled up beside the screaming infant. She handed the baby to her mother, who sat on the floor of the bathroom. "You two just stay here for a few minutes. I'm going to bring you some hot chocolate and a sandwich. Don't argue with me. I want to help you, and I promise I won't call 911."

The food at the gas station convenience store wasn't too bad, and Marley brought a large hot chocolate and a turkey sandwich with lettuce, tomato, and provolone cheese to the new mother. Rosemary was still sitting on the floor, trying to nurse the baby, but the infant was crying rather than sucking. Tears of frustration streamed down Rosemary's face. It was obvious that this woman was close to the breaking point. Marley took the baby and handed the mother the sandwich and the hot drink. Rocking the baby back and forth, Marley wondered if she dare give this hungry child some formula from the convenience store. Rosemary gobbled down the sandwich as if she hadn't eaten in weeks. She tried to stand up but stumbled. Marley secured the baby onto the changing table again and helped Rosemary stand up. She had to literally lift the woman to her feet.

"Let's go to the office and let you rest in there for a few minutes." Marley unbuckled the baby with one hand while she supported the baby's mother with her other arm. She steered the two of them into the tiny office behind the cashier's counter. There was a not-very-comfortable metal chair in one corner, and Rosemary headed for it as if it were a lifeboat on a sinking ship. She fell into the seat and put out her arms for the baby.

Marley realized she had to take charge of the situation. "I'm going to get something for this baby to eat. We sell infant formula in premixed bottles. It's sterilized and everything—perfectly safe and all. If you don't have enough milk, we need to give your baby some supplemental formula. Lots of nursing mothers do that. We sell all kinds of baby formula here in the store, including for newborns."

Rosemary hung her head in shame and defeat. Then she raised her head and said with tears in her eyes, "Thank you. She's hungry and needs to be fed. I can't do it." She clasped her child tightly and leaned back in the chair. When Marley returned with the premixed formula in a bottle, Rosemary was sound asleep holding the baby in her arms. Marley took the baby from her and settled into the chair behind the desk to feed the infant. The baby finished the bottle of formula in record time. She'd obviously been very hungry.

Fortunately, no one had come into the store to buy anything. All of this excitement, from Rosemary's fainting episode to the successful feeding of the baby, had taken less than fifteen minutes, so Marley hadn't been away from the cash register for very long. She found a clean, empty cardboard box and made a bed for the baby on the floor next to her mother. Marley went back to her job as lone cashier on the night shift.

When Marley's work stint ended at midnight, Rosemary was still asleep and so was the baby. Marley had already decided she was going to try to help this young woman. She was going to try to do even more than she already had for the desperate pair. Marley put on her coat and picked up the stranger's diaper bag. She roused her gently and told her it was time to leave. She didn't give the young mother a choice about what was going to happen. Marley asked her for the car keys and told Rosemary she was taking her and the baby to her house for the night. "I don't usually do this. In fact, I've never done this before in my life, but you can't continue driving, wherever it is you think you're going. I'm Marley Kurtz, by the way. You don't know me, and I don't know you. But you need help right now, and I can give you some help. So come on; let's get going. I'm going to drive you, your baby, and your car to my condo. All of the baby's stuff is in the minivan, so we're taking the minivan. My car will be fine parked here for the rest of the night." Marley lifted the sleeping baby out of the box on the floor and juggled the diaper bag, her own purse, and the baby, as she guided Rosemary by the arm out of the convenience store and into the parking lot. They were all soaked to the skin by the time they made it to the minivan, but Marley was going to make sure this mother and this baby survived.

Marley buckled the baby into her car carrier in the second seat and secured Rosemary into the passenger seat. Marley got into the driver's side and drove the two miles to her condo in Boswell, North Carolina. First she carried the baby into her house. The baby wasn't rolling over yet and would be fine on the couch for a couple of minutes while Marley went back to the minivan to get Rosemary and the diaper bag. She woke Rosemary and asked her which suitcase was hers. Rosemary pointed to a small duffel bag in the back. Marley gently guided the woman into the condo and led her to the small guest room. "I'm going to put your baby in my laundry basket for the night. We can get the port-a-crib out of the car tomorrow. Everybody is too tired to fool with setting that up right now."

Rosemary nodded her head in agreement, somehow trusting this stranger, and fell asleep on top of the bedspread in this kind, Good Samaritan's spare room. Marley made a bed for the baby in a blue plastic laundry basket and settled her next to the bed. She left the bottles of premixed infant formula she'd brought from the convenience store on the night stand. If she heard the baby crying, she would come in and feed the baby. If the mother woke up and wanted to feed the baby, the formula would be there for her.

Marley realized, as she took a shower and got ready for bed, that she didn't even know the name of the woman who was sleeping in her guest room. Marley warmed herself a glass of hot milk with sugar and vanilla in it. There had been a time in the past when half a bottle of bourbon was the nightcap she would have chosen to relax with and to be her comforter, the potion that helped her sleep at night. Now, she was thankful every minute of every hour, that those days were a distant memory. The sweet hot milk tasted so much better to her, better than the bourbon had ever tasted. Marley was in her late forties, and she was tired after her ten-hour shift at the convenience store. She worked two jobs and barely made ends meet. If she wanted to keep her condo, she couldn't ever be sick or late for work

Chapter 2

Rosemary Carmichael slept the rest of the night and into the next afternoon. The baby woke up twice in the middle of the night, and Marley fed her when she cried. Marley was worried about the baby's mother, whose name she still didn't know. Marley might not know the new mother's name, but she knew the woman was sleeping too much. She hadn't seen any evidence that the woman was using drugs, but you never could tell. Sleeping a lot could indicate a person was a drug user, but Marley decided the woman was just exhausted. She would let her sleep as long as she could. It concerned her that the mother hadn't awakened during the night when her baby had been screaming at the top of her lungs. Even if she is exhausted and even if she's very sound asleep, a mother almost always wakes up when her baby cries. Marley was afraid the mother might be seriously ill.

When Rosemary finally woke up, she was disgusted with herself for having slept in her clothes. Then she panicked because she was in a strange house and wasn't immediately able to remember how she happened to find herself in this bed in this bedroom. When she saw Christina Rose asleep beside her on the floor in the laundry basket, it all began to come back to her. She closed her eyes and wondered who had fed Christina Rose during the night. Rosemary knew she hadn't fed her child.

There was a small bathroom attached to the guest room, and when Rosemary looked at herself in the mirror, she was frightened by the appearance of the person she saw looking back at her. Who was that dark-haired woman with the terrible haircut whose face was as white as a sheet? She looked like she hadn't had a bath in weeks. Her clothes were dirty, and she smelled. Rosemary had never before allowed herself to reach such a low point in her personal hygiene. She knew she had to do something about herself, but all she wanted to do was crawl back into this unknown bed and go back to sleep.

Marley heard her stirring in the bedroom and knocked. When nobody said anything, she opened the door, "Good morning, or should I say good afternoon? You were completely exhausted, so I didn't want to wake you." When Rosemary stared at Marley with a puzzled look, Marley continued, "Do you remember me? Do you remember collapsing in the gas station bathroom last night? I'm Marley Kurtz. This is my condo. I brought you and your baby home with me because I was very concerned about you. I didn't want you to get back out on the road because you were in no condition to drive anywhere." Marley continued to look for some kind of a reaction or response from the woman.

Rosemary finally spoke. "Yes, I remember you. Thank you for taking me and my baby into your home. I'm sorry if we were an inconvenience, and I am very grateful. I can pay you for your trouble."

"Don't be silly. You weren't any trouble. I like babies. I had one of my own once, a long time ago. And there's nothing to pay me for. I'll consider bringing you home with me my good deed for the day. I work at the gas station convenience store where you fainted in the bathroom. Do you remember that?"

"I think I remember it, but it's all a little hazy. I must have been really out of it. Where am I? I mean, what town am I in? I remember stopping along the highway, but I don't think I knew where I was when I stopped. I was just driving as fast and as far as I could go."

"You're in Asheville, North Carolina. Actually, you're in Boswell, North Carolina which is a few miles outside of Asheville. You stopped to get gas and a cup of coffee at a convenience store just off route forty. I work the night shift there, at the store. I don't even know your name or the name of your baby. How are you feeling?"

Rosemary didn't know how to answer that question. All she could think about was whether or not the story of the triple murder and the fire would be on the news in Asheville, North Carolina. She was a long way from upstate New York, but with 24-hour cable news channels, it seemed as if sensational crimes and disasters of all kinds, no matter where in the world they happened, made it to the cable TV news. Rosemary was terrified that the triple homicide in upstate New York would be on the news in Asheville and that Marley might recognize her.

There had been a terrible photograph of Rosemary on the Binghamton, New York television news. The photo, showing Rosemary with her own red hair, had been taken years earlier, and she didn't think the old picture looked anything like her. Nevertheless, Rosemary was frightened and wanted to get out of this woman's house as soon as she could. No place was safe; she had to keep on the move.

The panic in Rosemary's eyes gave her away. Marley tried to reassure her. "I know you're running from something. I don't know what it is, but you don't have to be afraid of me. I've seen a lot of people in my day, and I can tell you haven't done anything wrong. I can see you're afraid of someone or something, and I'm sure you have a very good reason for running. But you're not in any condition to run anywhere right now. If you won't think of yourself, think of the health and welfare of your baby. What if you have a car accident because you're so tired or because you're distracted? Is that going to make anything better? You can trust me. Let me get you something to eat, and then we can talk about what you want to do. Do you eat eggs? I make good scrambled eggs."

Rosemary was past being hungry and didn't think she could eat anything. On the other hand, she wanted more than anything to have someone put a plate of scrambled eggs in front of her. She got out of bed and began to gather up Christina Rose's baby paraphernalia. She immediately collapsed again, unconscious on the floor before Marley could get to her. Fortunately, she wasn't very far from the bed, and Marley was strong enough and able to get her back into the small single bed. Marley was ready to call 911, but decided to give the poor thing a few minutes. Sure enough, Rosemary came around. First she began to apologize, and then she began to cry.

Marley decided to take charge again. "I studied nursing for two years before I quit school to marry my former son-of-a-bitch, no-good husband who almost killed me. That's a whole different story, but I know a little bit about medical care. I think your blood sugar is very low, and your blood pressure is also probably low. I hope you aren't bleeding internally, but I'm concerned that might be why you keep passing out. I'm guessing you had a long labor or a C-section or maybe both. I think you're running a fever, so I'm worried that you have an infection. You left the hospital against medical advice, before you were really ready to leave. Am I right? You've been driving in your car for a couple of days, and you've been afraid to stop at a motel to get a room and take a shower. You've been sleeping in your car. Now, tell me what part of the diagnosis I have wrong."

"My name is Rosemary Carmichael. I can't tell you why I'm running, but I think your analysis of my medical situation is exactly correct. I don't even know what day it is today, either the date or the day of the week. You're right. I do need help, but I can't drag anybody else into the mess I've made of my life. I don't want to involve you in my troubles. You've been incredibly kind to me and my baby, and I can't imagine how in the world I can ever begin to repay you. I just know I have to leave here as soon as possible."

"I'll help you get away if you insist, but first let me fix you some eggs and toast. Then you can leave." Marley wasn't going to allow this young woman to get anywhere near the minivan and hoped that once Rosemary Carmichael had some food in her, she might begin to think more clearly.

"I'd love to have the eggs and toast, but I'll stay only if you promise me one thing?"

"What's that?"

"Promise me you won't turn on your television while I'm here. If you really want to help me, that's the one thing that will help me more than anything else."

"I promise I won't turn on the television set while you're here. Do we have a deal? Okay, let me get working on those eggs." Marley couldn't imagine why Rosemary was so afraid of the television set. Maybe she'd guessed wrong. Maybe Rosemary wasn't running from a person but was running from the law. Marley had learned to trust her instincts, and she was certain Rosemary wasn't a criminal. Even if the woman had shot and killed an abusive husband or boyfriend, she would have Marley on her side. Marley had wished a thousand times she'd shot and killed her husband instead of divorcing him. The world would be a much better place without Barry, but that was a long time ago and too late to do anything about it now. Marley was not judgmental in any way. She was into survival, and she wanted to help Rosemary and the baby survive.

When she brought a tray with the plate of eggs into the bedroom, Rosemary had gone to sleep again. Marley had to wake her up to eat. Rosemary turned pale when she looked at the food, and Marley was afraid she was going to be sick. But Rosemary recovered herself and took a tiny nibble of the toast. She ate a little bit at a time and eventually finished the entire plate of scrambled eggs and two pieces of buttered toast. She drank the glass of orange juice and the large glass of ice water Marley had put beside the bed.

"I think I've also been dehydrated. I wasn't drinking because I didn't want to have to stop to go to the bathroom. Of course, getting dehydrated is the worst possible thing I could have done—both in terms of nursing my baby and in terms of getting my head all screwed up. I feel better now. I still don't think I have any milk, so maybe I'll have to go with full-time prepared formula." Rosemary didn't want to tell this woman anything, but because Marley had some training as a nurse, Rosemary felt she could trust her.

"No, you won't. Not on my watch. Breast milk is the best thing in the world for your baby, and I'm going to help you get back to nursing her. For now we'll use a lot of supplemental formula, but you'll be back to providing milk for your baby before you know it. Now, tell me the worst thing you've ever done, and then I'll tell you the worst thing I've ever done."

"I really don't want to get you involved in my problems. They're entirely of my own making, and if I didn't have a baby to think of, I would have already gone to the police. If it was just me, I wouldn't care if they put me in jail, but I can't let that happen for Christina Rose's sake."

"You know, that's the first time I've heard you say your baby's name. It's a beautiful name. Maybe someday you will tell me the story behind her name. Right now, I want to know what you did that could send you to jail."

"I burned down my own house."

"Before I ask you why you did that, I want to tell you that I'm sure there had to have been a very good reason for a person like you to have taken such a drastic step. So, tell me, why did you burn down your own house?"

"To destroy evidence of a crime, to protect a murderer."

"Let's back up a bit. Did you have insurance on the house, and did you file a claim after it was burned down?"

"I just burned it down two days ago. Yes, there was insurance, but no one will ever file an insurance claim on the house. Insurance fraud isn't what I'm afraid of. It's much worse than that."

"You said you were destroying evidence of a crime and protecting a murderer. Did you commit the crime? Are you the murderer?"

"I didn't commit the crime, but someone committed a murder for me. I burned down the house because the person who committed the crime for me had left his fingerprints all over the house. I burned the house down to keep the police from going after him."

"What was the crime he committed, and why did you want to cover up his part in it? Why did you feel you had to burn the house down to protect him?"

"It wasn't just a murder; the crime was a triple murder. Three people might have died because of me, and the man who murdered these people was a priest. Even though I'm not a Catholic, this Catholic priest saved my life and took me in when I was pregnant and homeless." Rosemary paused to catch her breath. "Because I went to the authorities and reported my estranged husband for abusing me, he tried to have me committed to a mental institution. I escaped from the men my husband sent after me to take me away to a psychiatric hospital. He was a powerful person in the community, and I was certain he was going to have me declared unfit and take the baby away from me. If he'd thought he could get away with it, I will always believe he would have come after me himself and killed me and the baby.

"The priest drove with me to Canada so I could have my baby, compliments of the Canadian National Health Service. I was on the run and couldn't use my own health insurance or my real name to get medical care in the United States. I went into labor, and my friend, the Catholic priest, stayed with me during my labor and the C-section until Christina Rose was born. He was with me every step of the way. I had no idea he was mentally unhinged, or I would never have imposed on him. More importantly, I would never have told him anything about how my husband had abused me. I was under the influence of several kinds of drugs during my labor, and I told the priest a lot of the horrible details about what my husband had done to me. My labor was a very long one, so I had plenty of time to tell him all about it."

"So, you are telling me that a Catholic priest committed three murders for you, and you burned down your house to hide his fingerprints?"

"Yes, that's exactly what I'm telling you. He'd intended just to kill my husband, and he did that as an act of love for me and Christina. He said he had to do it, or we would never be able to have any kind of life — if I thought my husband was coming after me and if I always had to live in fear of that. The priest knew I was planning to run away and change my identity after the baby was born. He went to my house with the intention of killing my husband, to protect me, to keep me safe, to free me, to allow me to have a life. But things went very wrong."

"You said he killed three people. Who were the other two people he killed — besides your husband?"

"I don't know who the other two people are who were murdered in my house, and I'm pretty sure the priest didn't kill them. He admits he killed my husband, but I don't think he knows whether or not he killed the woman and the other man. When I went to my house to see if my husband was really dead, I found three bodies, and I know three bodies were found in the ashes after the house burned down. I have my own hypothesis about what might have happened, but I don't have any idea why those other two people were there in my house or who they were."

"What's your hypothesis? I mean, who do you think those other two people were? Did the priest kill them just because they were there when he went to kill your husband?"

"That's the part that will probably always remain a mystery. My husband was a philanderer, and I suspect that one of the people who was at the house was a woman he was having an affair with. I don't know her name or anything about her.

He had lots of women over the years. The woman who was killed in my house happened to be in the wrong place at the wrong time. Two men and one woman died, and I have no idea who the second dead man was or why he was there. One of the dead men in the house was definitely my husband. I saw him on the floor, and he'd been there for several days. It was his house, and it would be easy to identify him through DNA analysis. The woman and the other man haven't been conclusively identified. All the bodies were burned beyond recognition. Maybe a future DNA analysis will be able to identify them, but as of now, the authorities don't know who they are. I only know what I've told you from the news reports." Rosemary thought maybe she shouldn't say any more, but she realized that she felt better after telling Marley about what had happened.

"And I received a phone call from the very psychotic Catholic priest, just after he'd committed the murders. He needed to confess, I think, but mostly he wanted to tell me that I was free, that my husband was dead and wouldn't be coming after me. The priest blabbered something about 'the other two being there by mistake,' and that when he got to the house, 'they were already dead' when he shot them. I'm still not sure I know what he meant by that, and he was completely out of it when he called me."

Rosemary continued, "After he called me and told me three people were dead and that he'd killed my husband, he said for me not to worry because he had left his fingerprints all over the house. The police would be coming after him, he said, not after me. After the priest called me, I was in shock and so upset. I tried repeatedly to call my husband. When nobody answered the phone, I felt I had to go to the house. I had to see if my husband really was dead."

Rosemary paused and tried to breathe. She stumbled over her words as she tried to tell the rest of the story. "It was so horrible there, I can't even begin to tell you what it was like. There were three bodies, and they'd been there for days. They were bloated....the smell....I vomited in the kitchen sink. My husband was definitely dead, shot in the back of the head. I didn't know either of the other two people. Their faces and bodies were so distorted, I doubt I could have recognized them, even if either one of them had been someone I knew. The thing that was so odd was that there was so much blood around the bodies of the two people I didn't know. They were covered with flies and maggots and oceans of black blood that had dried around their bodies. It was unbelievable. I'd never seen anything like it. There was a golf club beside one of the bodies. It looked as if the two bodies I didn't recognize had been bludgeoned to death. My friend the priest said he'd had a gun and shot my husband. I found my husband's body in another room, and he'd definitely been shot. But he hadn't been beaten, like the other two. I was so shaky by that time; I just wanted to get out of there. I'd left Christina Rose asleep in the minivan that was parked a block away. I'd had to verify that Norman was dead, like the priest had said. And Norman was very dead for sure. I left the house, but then I went back inside again. I should have kept on going, back to the minivan. I never should have gone back inside the house, but I was in shock and so confused. I did something I shouldn't have done."

"The priest told me he'd left his fingerprints behind, and I didn't want him to be arrested for the crime. I wasn't thinking straight. It was a very stupid thing to do, setting the fire. I turned on the oven and the burners on top of the stove, and I stuffed the oven full of newspapers. I poured paint thinner around on things. I don't really know what all I did. I honestly had no idea if the place would burn or not. I'd never tried to burn a house down before. There was a gas stove, so I guess that's what did the trick. I was intentionally trying to destroy evidence of who had committed the crime—to protect the priest, and the house burned to the ground. This all just happened a few days ago. It was all over the local news in upper New York State." Rosemary was worn out from her monologue. She got quiet and lay back against the pillows on the bed. She'd completely forgotten that Marley had promised to tell her the worst thing she'd ever done, in return for Rosemary's confession.

Marley was quiet. She wanted to give Rosemary a chance to continue her story, and she was stunned by the horrifying and unlikely tale that Rosemary had just told her. Marley sensed that Rosemary was telling the truth, but there were many questions, things unsaid and unexplained. What had ever possessed the priest to go over the edge? Had he killed all three of the people at the house, or had he just killed Rosemary's husband? Who had killed the other two? Did the priest realize what he had done? What had happened to him? Where was he now? Marley knew there was a lot of the story Rosemary hadn't told her. Marley was a good listener, and she could wait.

She felt like she had to say something to Rosemary in response to this incredible account. "No wonder you're freaked out. Anybody would be after going through what you've been through. Just having a baby is hard enough, especially a C-section. Most people would be bonkers by now if they'd had a triple murder and a crazy priest and all of that other stuff going on in their lives. I'm surprised you are in as good shape, physically and mentally, as you are. You're a strong woman."

Rosemary had fallen asleep, and of course the baby had just started to cry. Marley got a bottle from the kitchen and put the baby on her lap. Things were a lot more complicated than Marley had imagined they would be when Rosemary had collapsed in the bathroom at the gas station. Marley had been thinking she needed to find a doctor for Rosemary. Now she wondered if she ought to also find her a lawyer.

Chapter 3

Rosemary didn't want to stay in Asheville, North Carolina, and she didn't want to stay with Marley Kurtz. She liked Marley, but she felt a tremendous urgency to be on her way, to Arizona or someplace far away from the East Coast. Marley knew some of her terrible secret, and Rosemary wanted to distance herself from this woman who knew too much about her. But Rosemary was too sick and too tired to take the initiative to pack up her minivan, get back on the road, and head out of town. She wasn't able to take care of herself, let alone take care of her baby, let alone make an escape in her car and drive to Arizona. She was forced to accept Marley's hospitality and Marley's kindness—at least for a little while.

Rosemary had identity papers that included a driver's license, a Social Security number, and a passport. The pictures on her license and passport showed her actual photograph which included her very conspicuous red hair. She was a novice at acquiring false papers, and she'd made a mistake by not altering her appearance before she'd had the photos taken for her fake IDs. She had never before tried to disappear, and she hadn't done a very good job of it so far. Rosemary knew her new identity had come with a reasonably good credit report because she had been able to buy a minivan on the basis of that credit report. What Rosemary didn't have in her new name was any health insurance, either for herself or for her baby.

She had gone to Canada to have her baby delivered, compliments of Canada's universal health care system, but she didn't intend to go back to Canada again, ever. She knew that Christina Rose needed immunizations, and she realized she probably needed to have a follow-up visit after her C-section. She knew she wasn't feeling well. She admitted that, ever since she'd had the baby, she hadn't felt like her old self. She didn't have a good explanation for her overwhelming fatigue or her random fainting spells. She wanted to consult a doctor, but all doctors now demanded identification before they would see you. Besides not having any health insurance, Rosemary was afraid to risk using her false identification.

Her dark hair was so obviously fake. Rosemary had bought some hair dye and colored her hair black, and then she'd cut her hair off short, so she wouldn't look like the photo that had been shown on the Binghamton, New York television stations. With the black hair, now she didn't even look like her fake Rosemary Carmichael identification. She'd bought a strawberry blond red wig that looked something like her ID photograph, but it was a cheap wig. Even a casual observer would know it was a wig. She would be suspicious of herself if she presented her driver's license to anybody as proof of who she was. Doctors' offices were always suspicious of people without health insurance, and she didn't want to invite extra scrutiny by being one of those people. She didn't know what to do. Everything was a mess, and Rosemary didn't have the energy to confront her mess and figure out what to do about it.

Marley was worried about Rosemary. She genuinely cared about what happened to the woman, but she was also concerned that Rosemary might be really sick with something and die. What would Marley do with a baby? Marley had to work to keep her condo, and at this stage of her life, she was much too old to raise a child on her own. Marley knew that Rosemary needed to see a doctor immediately. Rosemary told Marley she didn't have any health insurance, so Marley called her own primary care doctor and made an appointment for herself. She would take Rosemary with her to the appointment, and when they all got to the doctor's office, Marley would introduce Rosemary as her niece. Marley would take Rosemary into the examining room with her and explain the switch to Dr. Agarwal when they got there. All Dr. Agarwal could do was kick them out of the office or refuse to see Rosemary. If Rosemary couldn't pay for the visit, Marley would pay. Rosemary had said she had some money, but expensive medical care and prescription medications without insurance would eat into anyone's cash reserves.

Marley made her illness sound like an emergency to Dr. Agarwal's appointment secretary. Marley honestly believed it was an emergency; it just wasn't her own personal emergency. She got an appointment for the next morning and knew it would take some slick talking to convince Rosemary to go to Dr. Agarwal's office with her. Rosemary was a stubborn one who had an agenda fixed in her head. She didn't want to give up her agenda to drive to Arizona or even temporarily put the agenda on hold.

Marley made spaghetti for dinner. She thawed hamburger from her freezer, and made the spaghetti sauce with lots of meat. A salad and garlic bread completed the hearty meal. Marley hoped Rosemary would feel well enough and be hungry enough to eat something. One of her theories about what was wrong with Rosemary was that she was anemic. Marley had called in sick to her day job, and she didn't have to work at the gas station convenience store that night. The breastfeeding wasn't going well, and Marley was feeding Christina Rose most of her calories in the form of prepared infant formula. Marley didn't blame the new mother. She knew lots of new mothers had trouble nursing their infants, and nobody ever wanted to admit how often this happened. Everybody wanted to pretend that breastfeeding was as natural and as easy as pie, and it wasn't.

Marley asked Rosemary if she wanted to eat in her room or wanted to try to walk to the table in the kitchen. Rosemary said she wanted to eat in the kitchen. Rosemary was so weak, Marley had to practically carry her to the table. Marley used the difficult trip from the bedroom to the kitchen to point out that Rosemary wasn't well. Marley served Rosemary a bowl of pasta, and Rosemary ate it all and asked for seconds. When Marley thought Rosemary's blood sugar had gone up a bit, she told her about the doctor's appointment she'd made for the next day. Marley assured Rosemary that if the young mother couldn't pay for the appointment, she would cover the cost. Rosemary argued that she didn't have any health insurance and didn't want to present her dubious identification at the doctor's office. They argued about it, but in the end, Marley outlasted Rosemary who finally agreed she would go to the doctor's office the next day.

Marley had called in sick the day before, and she was off today from her day job. She had to show up for work at the convenience store later that afternoon. She couldn't call in sick to her waitressing job again the next day, and she could never call in sick to her night job. They would fire her. She had to show up at the convenience store to work tonight. She was already planning what in the world she would do about Rosemary and the baby while she was working.

The baby's infant car seat was in the minivan, and Marley's car was still parked in the lot at the gas station. They would drive the minivan to Dr. Agarwal's office. Marley had to dress the baby and then get Rosemary dressed. She carried the baby to the car and came back to get Rosemary. When they got to the doctor's office, she had to do the same thing all over again—get the baby into the office and then go back for Rosemary. The appointment secretary looked at Marley with a suspicious eye when she arrived for her emergency appointment accompanied by a baby and a woman who was obviously very ill.

Although the nurse who assisted Dr. Agarwal objected, Marley insisted that Rosemary and the baby both go into the examining room with her. Everybody knew something was up with Marley's phony appointment, but they decided to go along with it. Some of the office staff had known Marley when she was a drinker, and they were so glad to see her sober, and for so many years, they were willing to cut her some slack.

When Dr. Agarwal came into the examining room, the baby was screaming at the top of her lungs. Bina Agarwal always wore a beautiful floor-length silk sari and always had a Brahman red dot on her forehead. She was an exquisite Indian woman who had been in the United States for decades and spoke perfect English with a touch of a British accent, but she was always true to her Hindu culture. Today her sari was a bright royal blue with gold ribbon trim. Marley was trying to feed the baby, and the doctor looked from one woman to the other. "All right, who's the patient here, Marley? I don't think it's you this time, although when you called, you said it was an emergency. I don't do pediatrics, as you know, but if this baby needs help, I can make a referral. Why didn't you go to the hospital ER?"

Marley tried to make herself heard above the baby's crying. Finally she got the bottle into the baby's mouth, and there was blessed silence in the room. "I'm fine, Dr. Agarwal, and the baby is just hungry, I think. It's Rosemary Carmichael here who is in need of medical care. She's my niece. I know you aren't taking any new patients, so I admit I snuck her in here by telling a fib to your appointment secretary. Rosemary doesn't have health insurance, and I am paying cash for this visit. So you don't need to worry about that."

Dr. Agarwal was clearly unhappy with the situation. "I'm not worried about being paid, but I don't like lying, Marley. You know better than to lie to me, but since you all are here, let me see what I can do to help." Marley put the baby in its infant carrier. She had to help Rosemary undress and get up onto the examining table. Rosemary was barely able to answer the doctor's questions, and Marley wondered how many of the answers were even close to the truth. Rosemary did tell Dr. Agarwal about having had a C-section less than two weeks earlier. Agarwal's exam was thorough, and she said she wanted to get some bloodwork and cultures. Rosemary objected strenuously and said she didn't have any insurance and couldn't afford to pay for lab work. Dr. Agarwal said they could do the tests in the office lab and save Rosemary some money that way.

Dr. Agarwal looked Rosemary directly in the eyes and told her the news, "Under normal circumstances, I would admit you to the hospital. You have a very serious infection, which probably started in the uterus and has now spread throughout your body. It's probably systemic, in your blood stream, I'm afraid. It's called septicemia. I think you are also anemic. You are dehydrated, and you are exhausted. You have no business being out of bed. You are very fortunate to have this wonderful lady, Marley Kurtz, to take you in and help you. I don't believe for a second that you are her niece, and I don't know why she is helping you or why she is lying to me. You are darn lucky, though, young lady. You don't look like a criminal, but I can tell you're running from something. My guess, from the physical examination, is that you are running from the abusive husband who has been beating you. I see the scars—the old ones and the relatively fresh ones. I hope you are far enough away from him by now because you can't run any more now until you get well. That may take several weeks. I'm worried the infection has already involved your lungs, which means you might also have pneumonia. If you don't take care of yourself, you could die. What would happen to this precious baby then? Are you going to leave her in your will for Marley to take care of? Do you have questions so far?"

Rosemary hung her head and didn't say anything. She was clearly frightened by what Dr. Agarwal had said to her. Marley's eyes had grown wide with concern, especially when the doctor had said Rosemary could die and leave the baby with Marley. "What do we do now, Dr. Agarwal? Go ahead and draw her blood. I'll pay for it. If you say we need it, we need it."

The doctor drew the blood herself and said she would call Marley with the results. "I'm going to give you all of my samples of three antibiotics, and I want you to take them exactly as I have written it all down in my instructions. Here are prescriptions for when the samples run out. You will need to take the antibiotics for three weeks. Here is a prescription for a vasoconstrictor for your low blood pressure. Be sure to take everything exactly as directed. I want to see you back here in two days. If you get any worse before then, call me immediately. You need to drink lots of Gatorade and water. You need to eat red meat and broccoli and everything else on this list I'm giving you that has iron in it. You must stay in bed and rest to give the antibiotics a chance to work. I'm giving you a list of vitamins and iron that you can get over the counter to treat the anemia. I will know after I see the results of the tests, if the anemia is being caused by something more serious than just not eating well and neglecting yourself. Lots of women who are trying to breastfeed become anemic. Don't beat yourself up. The lab work is to eliminate your having something like leukemia or mono. I don't think you have anything like that, but I have to check it out. Oh, and by the way, the black hair dye is very obvious and very unattractive. You aren't fooling anybody. Go back to your natural color. Get rid of the black hair. "

Marley thanked Dr. Agarwal who still was not happy about being deceived.

"I have a soft spot in my heart for you, Marley. You've come a long way, and I respect you. I can tell that you have a soft spot in your heart for this woman and her child, but don't lie to me again. I'll see you in two days."

Marley helped Rosemary get dressed and took the paperwork and the samples of antibiotics the doctor had left on the examining table. She told the woman at the reception desk she would be right back in to make another appointment and settle the bill after she got Rosemary and the baby into the minivan. When she came back into the doctor's office to pay, Marley was told that there would be no charge. Marley started to protest, but the receptionist said Dr. Agarwal had been very specific that there would be no charge for the visit. Marley made an appointment for two days hence, at a time when she could bring Rosemary in and wouldn't have to miss work.

Marley stopped by the drug store to buy the vitamins and iron the doctor had recommended. Then she drove to the grocery store and bought spinach, broccoli, steaks, dried apricots, and other iron-rich foods. Then she drove Rosemary and the baby home. Marley would fix everybody something to eat, and then Marley had to go to her job at the convenience store. She had decided she was going to take the baby with her to work. She didn't trust the very ill Rosemary Carmichael to be able to take care of the baby, change her diapers, and feed her. She also wanted to be sure Rosemary didn't try to make a run for it. She would take Rosemary's minivan with her to work, but she really didn't think Rosemary would run away without the baby.

Chapter 4

Father Christopher Maloney was completely psychotic and had to be heavily sedated as well as restrained with a straitjacket and leg shackles. Many hospitals didn't allow the use of straitjackets anymore. But in certain cases where inmates are very violent, the rules are overlooked, and the straitjacket comes out of the closet. Maloney ranted and raved and attacked the attendants. His doctor increased his medication, and he slept for days. He screamed about the Vietcong and the gooks and how he was going to kill them all. Then he would begin screaming about the wonder boy motherfucker who had killed his friends with a golf club. He made references to "Norman the Wood Killer Driver" and said Norman belonged in a chipper shredder. No one paid any attention to anything he said. They'd seen and heard a lot worse in their years working at the Southeast Pennsylvania State Mental Hospital in Chester, Pennsylvania.

Darlene Weber, the priest's "psychiatrist," was in fact not a psychiatrist at all. She was not a physician. She was a former patient in a psychiatric hospital who was pretending to be a psychiatrist. Darlene was very smart. She had an IQ that was off the charts. She was a con artist extraordinaire. She had been able to fool everyone. She had falsified her credentials, and using her computer, she had created the imitation diplomas and certificates that hung on her walls and testified that she had earned an M.D. degree and was a board-certified psychiatrist. An expert internet hacker, Darlene had been able to insert her information into the electronic records of universities and hospitals and professional organizations. If a prospective employer checked up on her via the internet, everything would be in order. Darlene had learned the jargon of the psychiatrist, and no one suspected that she was a total and absolute fraud.

When Darlene was fourteen, she had murdered her geometry teacher. The teacher had given Darlene a detention for acting up in class, and Darlene had poisoned the woman with warfarin-laced cookies. The murder had gone unsolved for a long time, but eventually Darlene was tried for the crime in juvenile court. Darlene was living in California when she killed her teacher. Because she was a minor, she was not sent to a detention facility. She was sent to an institution for the criminally insane.

Because she was manipulative and charming and had a way with people, she was able to earn special privileges in the psychiatric facility. One day, when she thought she had learned everything there was to learn about the place, she just walked away from the hospital...never to be seen again. She changed her name and somehow managed to have some plastic surgery on her face to change her appearance.

Her years as a patient in the psych facility had taught her what she needed to know about psychiatric terms and how a psychiatric hospital was run. She used the information she had learned to set herself up as an M.D. psychiatrist. She traveled across the country to Philadelphia and got a job in a state-run psychiatric facility. Darlene was an operator, a manipulator, a con artist, and a phony psychiatrist. She was very successful and was able to fool her fellow colleagues and her patients alike. She had reached the point in her delusions where even she believed she really was a psychiatrist.

The priest's faux psychiatrist, Darlene Weber, tried to keep the man medicated so he wouldn't talk at all, and she'd overmedicated him several times. He was either a raving maniac or drugged into unconsciousness. She didn't want to kill the man. She'd done that several times when she'd overmedicated her patients so they wouldn't make a fuss or scream or talk. She didn't want to lose this one, though, because she had plans for him and thought she could use him in the future. He was a priest, after all, or at least he'd arrived at the hospital dressed in a priest's clerical garb. Darlene had gone to Catholic schools, and although she no longer practiced Catholicism, she didn't want the death of a priest on her hands. Even the criminally insane, it appeared, had some standards.

It was weeks before the Catholic priest was able to speak coherently. He'd been picked up hiding in a janitor's closet at a shopping mall, and he hadn't had his wallet or any identification with him. He had been completely psychotic and so out of it during the time he'd spent in the state hospital, he'd been unable or unwilling to give anybody his real name. He looked as if he might be old enough to be eligible for Medicare, but he had no Medicare card. There was nothing at all to give the authorities or the hospital staff a clue as to who he was or where he'd come from.

Dr. Weber thought she knew who the priest was but decided she liked keeping her patient nameless. She wanted to control him and his care and everything that happened to him in the future. She didn't want anyone else at the hospital to know who he really was. So far, he'd been so violent and so resistant to any of the medication regimes that none of the other doctors at the hospital wanted to take on the extremely uncooperative patient. She had him all to herself. She hadn't yet been able to find out his name.

Whoever he was, when he had been discovered in the janitor's closet at the Springfield Mall and then had been admitted to the state hospital in Chester, Pennsylvania, someone had made a typographical error on his chart. He'd been found at the mall in April 2001. Whoever had typed up his admission information on the computer had mistakenly entered that he had been found and sent to the psychiatric hospital near Philadelphia in March 2001. Darlene Weber was the only person who had noticed this mistake. She had been the first person to see the priest when he had been admitted to the hospital. She would never forget that day. Darlene Weber had chosen not to correct the error in his chart. She wanted as much mystery and confusion, and as few actual facts as possible, to surround the unknown priest.

Darlene Weber had done some research on her own, and she'd had some of her minions try to get some information out of the Catholic hierarchy in the Philadelphia area. She was interested in local priests who'd disappeared from their parishes. There were none in the immediate area who were unaccounted for, so she expanded her search to include all of Pennsylvania. Still there were no clergy missing from where they were supposed to be. So Dr. Weber put out inquiries nationwide and finally found something.

A priest from Saint Stanislaus Parish in upstate New York, near Auburn, had gone missing a few months earlier. He was an older man, and when he hadn't turned up at his parish church to conduct services, everyone had assumed the worst—that he was dead. Mrs. Martha Riley, the housekeeper who took care of Father Maloney and his residence next to the church, said she'd not seen or heard from him. To fail to appear at services was completely out of character for Father Christopher Maloney. He was always in attendance and was never late. He'd never shown any signs of dementia, but Mrs. Riley had no idea where he'd gone. He'd just disappeared. His old car was also missing.

One interesting thing about the priest in New York was that a woman from his parish thought she'd seen him in the vicinity of a triple homicide, a murder that took place in the woman's own neighborhood. She'd occasionally attended St. Stanislaus and was adamant, when giving her story to the authorities, that she'd seen Father Maloney in her neighborhood on a night around the time when law enforcement thought the triple murder had occurred.

The police are always skeptical of eye witness accounts, and they eventually decided that the neighbor, who thought she had seen Maloney in the area, was mistaken. Because of the subsequent fire, the police themselves didn't know exactly when the murders had taken place. They estimated that the three victims had died on the same day, roughly four or five nights or more before the fire. One of the three victims had never been identified, and the Syracuse, New York police had been able to conclusively identify only one of the three dead bodies with DNA evidence.

The authorities were able to say with certainty when one of the victims, Norman Parsons, M.D., had last been seen alive.

The house in which the three murder victims had been found had burned to the ground. The fire had definitely been set intentionally, and after the horrendous arson blaze, there was little evidence remaining after the fire to test for anything. Only Parsons had been able to be identified through his DNA. The woman who had died in the house was assumed to be Rosalind Parsons, Dr. Norman Parsons' wife. She was not in any DNA database, and everything in the house that might have been used to identify her through DNA had been destroyed. There was no hairbrush or toothbrush to confirm the woman's identity, but because the body was found in Rosalind's home, it was assumed to be Rosalind's. No one had any idea who the third victim was.

The woman who had reported seeing the Catholic priest in the neighborhood was positive about the night she had seen Maloney wandering around, but the fire that burned the house down had not occurred until several nights later. Did the priest have anything to do with the murders or with the fire? It was a very confusing case, and the authorities had dismissed as unreliable the neighbor's sighting of a priest wandering around in the neighborhood.

A few weeks after the fire, to add to the mystery, the priest's old green Buick station wagon had been found in Cuidad Juarez, Mexico with a dead body in the back. There were some papers in the car that indicated the dead man was Father Christopher Maloney, the priest who had disappeared from St. Stanislaus, the small parish outside Auburn, New York. Because the car was registered to Father Maloney and the man found dead inside the car had papers with him that could identify him as Father Maloney, it had been assumed that the dead body was that of Father Maloney. Because the car and the body had been found in Mexico, no substantive investigation was undertaken, and no DNA was collected. The body was cremated, and the ashes were returned to the United States. It was cheaper to ship an urn than it was to ship a casket.

Father Maloney's only family was a sister who had preceded him in death. The Bishop of the Diocese of Rochester in New York State conducted a brief service for the priest at the St. Stanislaus Parish Church and spread Maloney's ashes in the adjacent graveyard. Father Maloney's housekeeper and a few parishioners had mourned their priest. The Catholic Church's records were updated to show that Father Christopher Maloney was now deceased. No one was willing to pay to put an obituary in the newspaper.

Darlene Weber thought the madman who was her patient in the hospital might be Father Maloney. But she did not want anyone else to have that information. The last thing she wanted was for law enforcement to come sniffing around, asking questions about the priest. She considered carefully what she ought to do. She finally made a phone call to the authorities in Syracuse, New York. She gave them the name of one of her colleagues when she introduced herself on the phone. She said she had read the report that someone had claimed to have seen Father Christopher Maloney in Syracuse around the time of the murders. Weber told the homicide detective that Father Christopher Maloney had been a patient in a state psychiatric hospital in March. He had still been a patient during the month of April and for many months after that. He could not have been anywhere in the neighborhood of Syracuse at the time of the Parsons' murders or at the time of the fire. She assured law enforcement that the priest could not have been involved in their case. The officer with whom Darlene Weber spoke over the phone seemed relieved to have the information the psychiatrist had shared with him. As the authorities had already concluded, the eyewitness had been mistaken.

Darlene Weber believed her phone call had cleared Father Maloney. If indeed Maloney was the man who was her patient, the police would no longer be looking for him. She could make him into anyone she wanted him to be. She did wonder, if it was Father Maloney who was in her care, how his car had made it to Mexico. And who was the dead person who'd been found in the car? She was going to have to wait to talk to the man himself before she had a definite answer.

In any case, the man was now completely under her control. Dr. Weber was certain that, whoever her patient was, he was a veteran of the Vietnam War. He made references to "gooks" and "slant eyes." He was always cursing the Vietcong. After looking into his background, she was able to confirm that Father Christopher Maloney was a Vietnam vet, but so were lots of men in their sixties. Because of his language, Darlene wondered if perhaps the man who was her patient might not really be a priest. But who was he?

After many weeks had passed and after much trial and error with his medication, Dr. Weber was able to have a conversation with her patient who'd arrived at the Pennsylvania state hospital dressed as a priest. At first, he refused to tell her his name, but he said he had committed many mortal sins. At one time or another during their treatment, many of Weber's paranoid patients talked about their sins. But until this man had come under her care, not one of them had claimed to be a Catholic priest or had arrived at the hospital wearing the authentic priestly garb to support his story.

Weber asked the man if he remembered anything about his arrival at the hospital or what had happened to make his hospitalization necessary. He said he remembered nothing. When she asked him what the last thing was that he did remember, he started screaming and talking about what sounded to Dr. Weber like Christians and roses and doctors and golf clubs. His ramblings made no sense. Dr. Weber was wondering if this man might be one of those patients that was terminally psychotic and would have to be permanently institutionalized, without any hope of ever getting better. Weber felt she might be able to use this man. He wasn't a homeless street bum or a drug addict, as so many of her state hospital patients were. She intended to put forth an extra effort to bring this man back from the hell inside his mind. She would do whatever it took to be sure this man lived to do her bidding.

Dr. Darlene Weber thought she had her patient where she wanted him. She controlled his medications and could drug him into unconsciousness when he wasn't behaving. She thought she knew all of his secrets, all of his sins. She didn't know if everything he'd told her was the truth or if some of what he'd confessed indicated he had grandiose delusions. Weber had wondered if he was sometimes telling her about his fantasy life rather than his personal history.

She was convinced the man really was a priest, and she had concluded, after extensive inquiries, that he probably was Father Christopher Maloney from upstate New York. She didn't know who had died in Maloney's station wagon in Cuidad Juarez, Mexico, but she was almost one hundred percent certain it wasn't Father Maloney. She'd never shared her conclusions about the priest's true identity with anyone at the state hospital in Chester, Pennsylvania. She hadn't written anything substantive in Maloney's medical chart or ever shared her opinions with the patient himself.

The nameless patient was known in the hospital as John Field. John was for John Doe, and Field was because he'd been found at the Springfield Mall outside Philadelphia. Dr. Weber never told Father Maloney that she knew who he really was, and he had never referred to himself as anything other than John Field. Dr. Weber didn't know whether or not John Field knew his real name. Weber thought Maloney probably remembered his name, but for obvious reasons wanted to remain anonymous or in hiding. This suited the doctor's purposes perfectly. She had plans for his future and wanted him completely under her influence. Denying him his true identify and keeping this information to herself was one way she could continue to control the priest.

He seemed very depressed most of the time, and it was difficult to get him to say anything. Weber considered electroconvulsive therapy (ECT) to try to enhance John Field's functioning. Electroshock therapy had been improved and refined since the old days when it had been considered a brutal form of psychiatric treatment. Its use had been discontinued for decades. Now ECT was back, in a gentler and more humane form, and it had worked miracles for a multitude of depressed patients.

Darlene Weber's reluctance to use the new version of ECT on the priest was not because she was worried that it wouldn't work or because she was concerned it might damage Maloney. She was worried that it *would* work. She was worried it might rid him of his depression and make him normal, or close to normal, again. She was afraid he would remember his real name, if in fact he had forgotten it. She was worried he would be cured and remember his crimes, if in fact he had really committed any, and turn himself in to the police. Dr. Weber didn't want any of these things to happen. She didn't want Father Christopher Maloney to go to jail. She wanted him under her thumb, where she could transform him and rebuild him into her own disciple.

Dr. Darlene Weber had decided to try to brainwash her patient John Field. She didn't know if his old life and his old memories had been completely eradicated by his traumatic experiences and all the psychotropic drugs she'd given him during his years in the hospital. But she decided she was going to do everything she could to make sure that ECT finished the job. Memory loss was sometimes a side effect of ECT. Weber would order ECT treatments for her patient that were more in line with the electroshock therapy levels used on patients in the 1950s. If she'd thought she could get away with a lobotomy and if she thought it would have left most of John Field's mentation intact, she would have used that tool as well. She would have to be careful so that as few people as possible found out she was giving her patient an old-fashioned, huge, 1950s-sized dose of shock therapy.

Weber wanted to wipe out the man's memory completely so she could imprint an entirely new identity, personality, and background into John Field's mind. Darlene Weber had always loved the movie, *The Manchurian Candidate*, and for a very long time, she'd entertained the fantasy that she could brainwash one of her patients to the extent they could be programmed to do whatever she told them to do. John Field offered the best chance for her to experiment with reprogramming, and she set about to create her very own Manchurian Candidate. She thought of him as her "Ecclesiastical Candidate."

Weber provided Field with a new personal background that she hoped he would come to believe was his own. She worked with him to develop an entirely new personality. She wanted him to remain a priest but didn't know ahead of time to what extent he would be able to retain his memory of having once belonged to the clergy and what that might have meant to him. She was taking a big risk, and she didn't know if any of it would work. She would use punishments and rewards to encourage the learning process.

John Field would become Father David Carnahan, and he would be Darlene Weber's very own creature. Darlene would spend three years before she was satisfied that Father David Carnahan could leave the psychiatric institution in Chester, Pennsylvania and function on his own. By the end of the three years, Weber thought she was ready to place Father Carnahan in the hand-picked position at an obscure religious facility. She intended to send him to a very low-profile and little-known retreat for clerics. The position Darlene had groomed him for was to preside as a priest and the man in charge at a religious refuge in St. Mary's County in Southern Maryland.

Dr. Weber was never completely certain that the priest wasn't fooling her. She was not absolutely sure that he didn't remember his old name and his old life —the name and the life he'd lived before he'd ended up in her care. There were moments when she thought he was just pretending to be Father David Carnahan, that all along he knew he was still really Father Christopher Maloney.

Chapter 5

The religious retreat in St. Mary's County, Maryland had begun its life as the estate of a seventeenth-century landowner. He'd grown tobacco on his plantation and shipped it to England on board ships that sailed from the nearby Chesapeake Bay. The tobacco plantation had been handed down through generations of the original landowner's family until the last surviving member sold it off to settle his gambling debts in 1912. The plantation had stopped growing tobacco almost two hundred years earlier. Then it had grown cotton and other kinds of crops. The farmer next door had bought the property at an auction in 1912 and tried to grow wheat on the land. He used the beautiful brick plantation house, which had been built in 1700 with its four tall, magnificent chimneys, as a hay barn.

In 1937, a wealthy woman from New York City decided she needed to get away from it all and purchased the struggling wheat farm. She wanted a historic house in the middle of nowhere that she could restore, and she built a matching brick barn for the horses she intended to ride. Amanda Vanderhof did a first-rate job on the renovation of the house. Money was no object, and she brought the brick mansion back from the brink of oblivion, back from its ignominious life as a hay barn. The gambrel roof was painstakingly rebuilt, and the interior was refurbished with love and care and a great deal of money. Amanda purchased antiques in New York and New Orleans to furnish her country house and lived happily ever after at Bard's Rest until she died in 1976.

Not having any heirs to inherit the property, Amanda left her home to the Catholic Church. But the Catholic Church didn't know what to do with the place, and the Archdiocese of Washington tried to sell the property. Because of zoning issues, the lack of adequate access to a main road, and other problems, there were no takers, and the house and its matching barn languished and deteriorated over the ensuing decade. The fields lay fallow and became overgrown. Mice, bats, and raccoons took up residence in the buildings.

In 1984, another wealthy benefactor, who found the setting on the Chesapeake Bay idyllic and the house an architectural gem, asked the current Archbishop of Washington, who was a personal friend, for permission to restore Bard's Rest and make it into a Catholic retreat. The proposal was that it would serve as a retreat for Catholic priests who had suffered mental breakdowns or were recovering from addictions. Because no organization, let alone any church, wants to admit that their leaders suffer from these maladies that everyone knows afflict human beings in all walks of life, the Catholic Church quietly made the decision to allow the renovation of Bard's Rest for the intended purpose.

But the facility would remain obscure, even secret. Only the Archbishop of Washington would be allowed to decide which Catholic clergy were sent there, and no one would be allowed to visit without his written permission. No one would know exactly what was located on that piece of prime real estate in Southern Maryland beside the Chesapeake Bay. No sign would announce its presence, and the thick brush that had overgrown the locked gates would be allowed to stay and grow thicker in order to increasingly obscure the main entrance to the retreat. A much smaller and well-concealed dirt driveway at the side of the property would provide the actual driving entrance. As far as the neighbors knew, the sixty acres that comprised Bard's Rest were still abandoned. Everyone knew it had belonged to the Catholic Church for quite a few years, and a few clerics were occasionally seen coming and going.

Local workmen, who were called in to repair and renovate the house and barn, assumed it was being fixed up so the Catholic Church could try to sell it again. The gambrel roofs were again repaired and rebuilt, and the mansion and horse barn were restored as functional and monastic style dormitories. There was a chapel in the house, and the kitchen was enlarged. More bathrooms were added, and existing baths were brought up to date. It wasn't fancy, but it was pleasant and cheerful.

It was the perfect place for a broken man of God to rest and restore his soul. Residents would plant, weed, and harvest the vegetables from the large garden. They would cook their own food and make their own beds. They would cut the overgrown grass and maintain the property. Staff was limited to one priest and one assistant. It was a concealed and simple place, intended to provide rest and rejuvenation to the depressed and confused, its presence and purpose known only to the archbishop's inner circle and to those who had received help there.

Darlene Weber wanted to send Father David Carnahan, the priest she thought she had programmed into being her own subject, her own "Eclesiastical Candidate," to manage Bard's

Rest. Darlene actually imagined herself as Angela Lansbury, telling Laurence Harvey to take out his deck of cards.

Darlene had been called on years earlier by the then presiding archbishop of the Archdiocese of Washington to help out with a priest at the retreat. Because the archbishop had believed Darlene Weber really was a psychiatrist, he'd called on her for a consultation. She had spent a few days at the retreat and realized what an opportunity it could provide, should she ever need it.

Unfortunately for the priest, this resident of the retreat whom Darlene Weber was called in to see and treat with psychotropic drugs, had died under her care. There was a cardinal of the Catholic Church in a distant city, or so the rumor went, who was not altogether sorry to see that particular priest pass on. The rumblings were that the priest who'd died had intended to publicly reveal his story of being sexually abused by Catholic clergy as a child. The powers-that-be did not want the impending scandal to come to light. It was all conveniently covered up with Darlene Weber's, perhaps not-so-passive, help. She had, by assisting in this questionable incident, established her credentials and her power and control over what happened at Bard's Rest. When the time came, there was no question that Father David Carnahan would be assigned as director there. The clergy of the church owed Darlene Weber, and only a very few people knew why.

Darlene drove Father Carnahan to Southern Maryland and introduced him to the archbishop who had driven down from the District. The archbishop was there to meet them and to welcome the new priest to Bard's Rest. Father Carnahan behaved appropriately and said everything Darlene Weber had programmed him to say. She and the archbishop left Carnahan in charge, hoping things would go smoothly. In fact, Darlene Weber had no idea whom she had left behind in charge of the retreat. Outwardly, Father David Carnahan was always in control and ran the facility as it should be run. He made no waves. Inside the placid and conforming body of Father Carnahan, however, Father Christopher Maloney still raged on and would not be denied.

Maloney knew who he was. He didn't remember everything about his past, but he remembered shooting three people, including Norman Parsons, in a house in Syracuse, New York. He would never forget the death scene he had walked in on and helped to perpetrate. He certainly remembered sweet Rosalind and the birth of her infant Christina Rose who was named for him. He remembered much of the past three years he'd spent at the state hospital in Chester, Pennsylvania. He knew the electroshock treatments had damaged him. He knew parts of his memory and his mind had been destroyed by the evil Dr. Darlene Weber who had tried to brainwash him into being her operative, her own functionary. He had played along with her and cooperated, pretending to be Father David Carnahan.

He knew it was the only way he would ever be able to get out of the hospital in Chester alive. Father Maloney knew he was guilty of murder. He did not take responsibility for a triple murder, as the Syracuse, New York tragedy had billed itself. The priest did take responsibility for killing Dr. Norman Parsons. He had set out to kill the man, and he was proud that he had succeeded in doing so. But Father Maloney knew that if he were ever caught and if the police were able to establish as truth their own favorite version of the crime, he would be tried for a triple murder. He would probably be found guilty and would go to prison for the rest of his life.

Dr. Weber had tortured him, but she had also provided him with a way to avoid being caught and avoid going to jail. She had crafted for him an entirely new identity. He could live and minister to his fellow priests under a new name and in a new place. Dr. Weber had even found him a new job and a place to live. No one would ever look for Father Christopher Maloney again. Father David Carnahan had taken his place.

And so he did Weber's bidding, and eventually, he was free of her. He'd done everything he'd been told to do to earn the position at Bard's Rest. He loved being there in the quiet countryside, and he would pretend, until the cows came home, that he was Father David Carnahan. He would do whatever he had to do to be able to stay at Bard's Rest in Southern Maryland. He never wanted to see Dr. Weber again, but of course she came to the retreat to check up on him every now and then. When he saw her he felt gut-wrenching nausea and hatred. The rest of the time, he could maintain his cool and be a good priest to his poor recovering fellow priests who came to Bard's Rest for solace. But when he saw Darlene Weber, his inner self threatened to explode. He felt murderous rage, and the killer in him longed to be let lose for one more rampage.

Father Christopher Maloney thought many times each day about Rosalind and Christina Rose. He hoped they were safe. He hoped they were happy. He would have given anything to see them again, to be a part of their lives. But he knew that was impossible, that he would put them in terrible jeopardy if he ever had any contact with them again. He knew he had to keep his distance, but he always kept them in his prayers.

Chapter 6

Nursing **Rosemary back to good** health took many weeks, and it took a toll on Marley. She struggled to make it to both of her jobs, but she'd been able to do it most of the time and still take care of her patient and the baby. She took Christina Rose with her to the gas station, but she couldn't take her to the Grove Park Inn in Asheville, where Marley was a waitress. She thought Rosemary seemed depressed, and it wouldn't be any wonder. Rosemary had insisted on paying for groceries, baby formula, and diapers, and Marley welcomed the financial help. Rosemary also wanted to contribute towards Marley's utility costs because she could see that Marley was barely making ends meet. Rosemary was so grateful for everything Marley had done for her. She hated to be indebted to anybody, but Marley had helped her out of the goodness of her heart and seemed to have enjoyed doing this extraordinary good deed. Rosemary knew she owed Marley in ways she could never repay.

After Rosemary was fully recovered from her illness, Marley asked if she would like for her to try to get her a job where Marley worked at the Sunset Terrace, the main dining room of the Grove Park Inn. It was a very upscale restaurant, open for lunch and dinner. Marley told Rosemary the tips were excellent and worth the long hours on her feet. Rosemary's training was in computer science, and she'd never been a waitress. She told Marley she would need a great many pointers about how to be a waitress, but she wanted to go to work. And who would take care of the baby? Marley said she could arrange their schedules so that one of them would always be at home with the baby, and yes, she would teach Rosemary everything she needed to know about how to be a good waitress.

Rosemary had given dinner parties when she'd been married to her doctor husband, so she had a good grasp of etiquette and knew the way things were supposed to look on a fancy table. Marley was hoping that Rosemary would be less depressed if she had something to do. If she had a job, felt productive, and was earning money, she wouldn't have as much time on her hands to feel sorry for herself.

Rosemary was not yet ready to give up her dark hair and go back to her natural red. She did have a Social Security number for Rosemary Carmichael and could fill out the job application forms. Marley had paved the way for her, and she got the job. The Grove Park Inn gave her a training course about how they did things. Rosemary was smart and learned quickly. Within a few days, she was comfortable waiting tables. She knew how to chat up the customers, and she made the effort to do it, so she got good tips. It was hard physical work and didn't really use much of her brain, but Rosemary was happy to be doing something and earning a little bit of money. She wanted to help Marley with her condo payments, and Rosemary knew that eventually she needed to either move on or get a place of her own in town.

One day when Rosemary was at work at the Grove Park Inn, the computer system in the dining room crashed. Nobody knew what to do. It was early in the new millennium, and cell phones were still something of a luxury. Not everyone could afford to own one. Almost everybody still had their landlines. Lots of people used computers, but the general public didn't know that much about how computers worked. When the computer in the restaurant went down, everything came to a standstill, and customers were unhappy because their bills had to be written out by hand. Credit cards had to be called in over the phone because the automated system didn't work. It was Friday night, and nobody could come to fix whatever was wrong until Monday morning.

This was Rosemary's field of expertise, and she thought she could help. She stayed late after her shift was over and worked all night. She had to access the software in the hotel's mainframe in order to solve the problem in the dining room. The person who usually solved the hotel's computer problems was unavailable, so the hotel manager was happy to let Rosemary try her hand at fixing things. Marley called in sick to her job at the gas station convenience store so she could take care of Christina Rose while Rosemary worked late at the Grove Park Inn. Before Rosemary had come into Marley's life and began helping out with the household bills, Marley would never have called in sick. She was now on a more secure financial footing than she previously had been. She would not lose her condo. Rosemary would be certain that didn't happen.

Finally, about five the next morning, Rosemary had everything up and running again, and the management of the hotel was very grateful. The people in the main office were more than curious about the new waitress who had been able to fix their computer system. If she could work miracles with something as complicated as a computer network, which she obviously could, why was she working as a waitress? The powers that be were also impressed that the waitress had been willing to spend all night on the problem and hadn't given up until she had everything working.

Word got around, and as computers took over more and more functions at the hotel and its restaurants and shops and as the programs became increasingly sophisticated, management made a place for Rosemary in the main office of the hotel. Eight months after she'd started working at the Grove Park Inn, Rosemary no longer waited tables but worked full-time keeping the hotel's computer equipment running smoothly and troubleshooting problems. Working with computers and doing programming was what she knew, and Rosemary was thrilled to be able to earn a living in her chosen field. She now received a salary rather than an hourly wage, and she worked regular hours—no more shifts. As she made herself indispensable to the hotel's management, she received commensurate raises in her salary.

Marley, who was still working as a waitress at the hotel and still working night shifts at the gas station convenience store, was thrilled for her. Rosemary was able to afford to take Christina Rose to a daycare center close to the hotel, so Marley wouldn't have to work her schedule around babysitting any more. Marley had grown very attached to the little girl, and Christina Rose loved Marley. Marley and Rosemary had become close. As she earned more money working in the hotel office, Rosemary was able to give Marley more financial help.

Rosemary told Marley she was thinking of getting her own place. She loved her current job at the Grove Park Inn and had decided she wanted to stay in Asheville, at least for a while. Christina Rose was already walking, and Marley's condo was feeling much too small for the three of them. Marley had known this day was coming. When Rosemary and Christina Rose had first arrived at her house, Marley had hoped they would move out and get on with their own lives, sooner rather than later. But now, the young mother and her little girl had become such an important part of her life, she hoped they would stay forever. Rosemary's plan was to buy a condo of her own in the same building where Marley lived, so she wouldn't be too far away.

Rosemary was thrilled to have a place of her own. She'd lived in a house with an abusive husband for way too long, a house she had intentionally burned down. Then she'd lived briefly in a women's shelter, and then, in her car. Most recently Rosemary had been in Marley's condo for almost a year. It was time she got a life and took responsibility for herself and her child. Rosemary bought a three-bedroom, two bathroom place in Marley's complex, and the two women had fun furnishing it with a combination of items from IKEA and pieces from the antique and second-hand stores in Asheville. Christina Rose had her own room, and Rosemary's first floor condo had a patio and small fenced-in backyard so the baby could play outside.

The main restaurant in a large and famous hotel is a very public place. When she'd been working as a waitress and interacting with the public every day, Rosemary had kept her hair dyed black. She'd had her hair cut and colored professionally at a salon, so she looked much better than she'd looked with her homegrown hairdo. She kept it black because she was worried someone from her past might come into the Sunset Terrace at the Grove Park Inn and recognize her. Now that Rosemary was working in the office and wasn't on display in the hotel's restaurant, she allowed her hair to return to its natural, strawberry blonde color. The black dye job hadn't really suited her, and after her red hair had grown out enough, Rosemary invested in a great looking, expensive haircut.

Chapter 7

As she began to earn more money, Rosemary bought updated and more professional looking clothes. She no longer wore the wardrobe from her student days. With her new-found confidence and success and her new look, she was a very different person than the frightened young mother who had fainted in the bathroom of the gas station convenience store so many months ago. She often wondered what her graduate school professor, Eberhardt Grossman, would think if he could see her now. Since the day she'd heard about Grossman's death on September 11, 2001, Rosemary had silently grieved that this very special man and gifted genius was lost to the world.

Eberhardt Grossman had been a wonderful thesis advisor to Rosalind Parsons. He was brilliant with computers and wanted to share everything he knew with his students. Some academicians were afraid their students might someday know as much as they did or even surpass them in knowledge and ability. Professor Grossman wasn't like that. He'd praised and encouraged ingenuity and creative ideas, and he'd wanted his students to be better than he was and to know more than he did. Rosemary Carmichael didn't think

Rosalind Parsons would ever have finished her PhD dissertation if it hadn't been for Professor Grossman. He always had time for her, always seemed happy to answer her questions. He had treated her with kindness and respect.

Academia is just like every other arena where a small number of men want sexual favors from those they consider their underlings, whether those underlings are students, secretaries, aspiring actresses, or working in some other less-than-powerful role. Professor Eberhardt had never imposed on Rosalind in that way. Rosalind had often wished he weren't such a perfect gentleman. All the creepy professors hit on her. The professor she had a serious crush on was respectful.

Rosalind had been desperately unhappy in her marriage. Her abusive husband had made her afraid of all men. It was not until she'd been lucky enough to have Eberhardt as her dissertation advisor that she'd begun to realize that not all men were monsters. She'd built trust with her professor, and then she'd fallen in love with him, a not uncommon but still a strictly forbidden occurrence in the academic arena. Rosalind told Eberhardt about her abusive husband, and he had told her she had to go to the authorities. Rosalind had told Eberhardt she loved him, and she could tell from the few kisses they had shared that his feelings for her were as passionate as hers were for him. But he was a good man, and he did the responsible, ethical, and moral thing. He told her they couldn't have a relationship while she was his student. She knew that he loved her and that she loved him, but he sent her on her way. He also did the right thing by giving up his role as her advisor and arranged for someone else to oversee the completion of her PhD.

After Rosalind Parsons had received her doctorate and was no longer Eberhardt Grossman's student, she went back to his office and again declared her love for him. This time when she'd approached the man she loved, she was obviously pregnant, and he again did the right, but very unromantic, thing. He refused to become her lover while she was pregnant with her husband's child. He told her they could not have a relationship while she was pregnant and while she was still married to her doctor husband. He again urged her to go to the authorities about the abuse.

Rosalind had wished a hundred times that Eberhardt had not been such a good person. She wished he'd thrown caution to the winds and just made love to her. But she'd known he was right. She had to leave her husband, and she had to report the abuse. Hoping that maybe one day she and Eberhardt could have a chance of happiness together, Rosalind had finally found the courage to take responsibility for her life. She refused to bring her baby into the world of abuse and danger she'd endured with her husband. So she gathered all of her courage and reported her husband's violence to the authorities. She made plans to disappear as soon as she had her baby and live a life far away from Syracuse, New York.

But her husband Norman had other plans. After she had reported his abuse to the police, he'd tried to have her locked up in a state mental hospital, just days before she gave birth to their child. Rosalind's physician husband had the personality of a very successful sociopath, and he could talk almost anybody into almost anything. He had the honest face of a choir boy and a glib and manipulative way with words that was able to fool the world. His superficial charm was seductive and persuasive. He supposedly had been able to convince two of his psychiatrist colleagues, who had never seen Rosalind, to sign papers to commit her to a state psychiatric hospital.

Rosalind was convinced that he would take her child and

have her killed or that he would kill them both. She was certain she would be dead by now if she hadn't escaped from the goons her husband had sent to abduct her from the women's shelter where she was hiding. Life had spun out of control for Rosalind after her escape, and she'd found herself homeless and on the run. A Catholic priest had taken her in and had stayed with her when she gave birth to her baby across the border in Canada.

A few days after Christina Rose was born, it was reported on the news that Rosalind Parsons had died as a result of foul play. Investigators were certain Rosalind was one of the three bodies found murdered in the Parsons' home. The house had been burned to the ground before authorities knew there were dead bodies inside. It was only after the fire had been extinguished that three corpses were discovered in the ashes.

Rosalind Parsons found herself supposedly deceased and on the run at the same time. Rosalind Parsons became Rosemary Carmichael in the early spring of 2001. Rosalind Parsons had been declared dead. She could never see Eberhardt Grossman again.

Everyone in the world was shocked when, later that year, tragedy struck the United States, and the World Trade Center towers in New York City came down, the Pentagon was attacked, and Flight #93 crashed in Pennsylvania. Marley and Rosemary sat glued to their television sets along with everybody else in the U.S. and watched the horrible events of that day unfold. Several months later, Rosemary, who via the internet kept up with the news from upstate New York, learned that her professor at Syracuse University, Eberhardt Grossman, had died on that terrible day. She couldn't get many details, but apparently he'd been meeting with his accountant or his lawyer in one of the buildings that had collapsed when the hijacked planes had hit the WTC.

Eberhardt had been her professor, but he had also been the man she loved. She was silently sad for the loss of the great academic mind, and she knew she would grieve for the rest of her life for the gentle soul she had loved and the man she knew had loved her in return. They'd never had a chance. Fate had conspired against them. The world believed Rosalind Parsons was dead, and now Eberhardt really was dead.

Rosemary was eventually put in charge of all the computer systems at the Grove Park Inn, including their accounting software. It was a big job, but it was fun and relatively easy for Rosemary. She could solve any problem that arose, whether it was hardware or software. One of the people she worked with had his own outside business, and he began to ask Rosemary for help with the computer issues he encountered. He encouraged her to form an LLC and start her own consulting firm on the side. Rosemary had enough confidence by now that she felt she could manage her own business. After living in Asheville for just two years, Rosemary Carmichael started her own computer consulting firm, had business cards printed, and was making more money than she'd ever imagined was possible. She worked with her private clients on her days off and on weekends.

Rosemary was grateful to Marley for so many things. Christina Rose worshiped Marley, and the feeling was mutual. Rosemary asked Marley if she would consider quitting her other jobs and taking care of Christina Rose full time. Rosemary would make it more than worthwhile financially for Marley to give up her two physically demanding part-time jobs to chase one little girl around the house.

Marley was delighted to become Christina Rose's full-time nanny. There would be no more night shifts at the gas station convenience store and no more long days on her feet working as a waitress. Marley was the mother to Rosemary and the grandmother to Christina Rose that none of them had ever thought they'd have. Things were working out well for the somewhat odd family of three women of disparate ages.

Rosemary thought about buying a house, but she didn't want to move too far away from Marley. Christina Rose and Marley had formed a close bond, and Rosemary didn't want to separate them. When Christina Rose was four years old, Rosemary bought an expensive house in Asheville. When the smaller house next door to hers came on the market a few months later, Rosemary bought it for Marley. Rosemary wanted Marley close by to continue to take care of Christina Rose, to drive the little girl to and from her private nursery school, and to take care of her after school until she came home from work.

Rosemary eventually quit her job at the Grove Park Inn so she could focus on her own business. She'd trained an excellent replacement and left the hotel on good terms. She was always available to the Grove Park Inn if they had a problem. Rosemary's computer consulting business was booming, and she now employed six people. She was a very successful young businesswoman in the town of Asheville, North Carolina.

Rosemary was proud of her business and loved being very good at what she did. Rosalind Parsons had done the hard academic work of earning a PhD in computer science from Syracuse University, but Rosemary Carmichael had done the hard practical work of turning that academic accomplishment into something useful and productive. Rosemary had proven that she could provide for herself and her daughter. She'd also established that she was able to offer an important service to her community.

Rosemary was thrilled with the material results of her success. She loved being able to send Christina Rose to the best nursery school in town, and she was thrilled she'd been able to buy a nice house for herself and her daughter, as well as one for Marley. But Rosemary never forgot for one minute that she wasn't really who she said she was and that her whole world could come crashing down around her in the blink of an eye. Rosemary didn't like having a high profile, and she was purposely accessible to others only through her business and during business hours. She didn't have a social life, other than what she did with Marley and Christina Rose. Rosemary didn't want anybody to ask questions about her past, and she didn't want anybody to know too much about her private life.

Life in Asheville, North Carolina had been good to Rosemary Carmichael, to her daughter Christina Rose, and to Marley Kurtz, who had assumed the role of much-loved mother and grandmother. Rosemary's business had prospered, and she'd generously shared her financial success with Marley. Christina Rose attended an excellent private school in Asheville and was a straight-A student. At age sixteen, the beautiful young woman with red hair and blue eyes was a member of her school chorus and the drama club and was already looking at colleges.

Rosemary had bought a beach cottage on Shell Island near Wrightsville Beach in Wilmington, North Carolina, and Christina Rose and Marley spent every summer there. Rosemary traveled back and forth between Asheville and

Shell Island during the summer months and was often able to work remotely from her summer house. The times of their lives had flown by. Marley would be sixty in a few years, but she was a spry and energetic grandmother to Christina Rose. Rosemary was in her mid-forties. She thought every day about Eberhardt Grossman and wondered what things would have been like if he and Rosalind Parsons had been able to have a life together.

Rosemary lived constantly with the vague fear that her past and her true identity would one day catch up with her. She had been safe for many years, but living under an identity that isn't one's own is to live perpetually with risk and uncertainty. From the beginning, Rosemary had wrestled with the problem of Christina Rose's birth certificate. The child had been born in Canada, compliments of the Canadian Health Service. Rosemary had a Canadian birth certificate for her little girl in the name of Christina Rose Carmichael, but of course Rosemary wanted her daughter to have a birth certificate that proved she had been born in the United States.

Children need birth certificates to verify how old they are for many reasons. They need a birth certificate to enter school, to get their immunizations at the right ages, to get a passport, to play softball and Little League baseball, to qualify for all sports teams, and for numerous other reasons. A birth certificate is essential proof that a child exists and is the age he or she claims to be. Historically, the birth certificate was required more as proof of age than as proof of birthplace, but in recent years, having the paperwork to prove one was born in the United States had become the critical documentation every child had to have.

Rosemary's knowledge of computers was extraordinary. If she were so inclined, which she wasn't, she could have been an over-the-top and seriously amazing hacker. She could have entered and exited almost any computer network in the world and remained undetected. She didn't need to do this and had no reason to use her skills for any nefarious purposes. Rosemary had, however, illegally used her hacking skills one time, and one time only, in the summer of 2001, to provide her Canadian-born daughter with a U.S. birth certificate—evidence that Christina Rose Carmichael had been born in the United States of America.

Christina Rose's U.S. birth certificate stated that she'd been born on her own real birthday, at Syracuse University Hospital in Onondaga County New York. Her birth weight and height were all duly recorded. Proof of this birth was on record at the hospital and on file in the Onondaga County courthouse. If anyone ever questioned the documentation at either the hospital or the courthouse, no hospital employee or county worker would have been able to verify or deny the veracity of the information.

With every year that passed, Rosemary felt more confident that Christina Rose's entry into the world would disappear in a morass of paperwork and fade away in the collective Canadian memory. Christina Rose's fake birth certificate had worked to gain her admission to nursery school, to convince the U.S. State Department to grant her a passport, and to satisfy all other official entities where a birth certificate was required. To save her own life, Rosemary had taken on a false identity. She'd done it consciously and willingly and with intent. Rosemary had also made this decision for Christina Rose, and she felt no guilt about representing her own American child as a child born in the USA. Rosemary thought she had covered her tracks well enough. The more time that passed, the less likely it was that her ruse would be exposed.

Rosemary often wondered who had died in her place at her house in Syracuse, New York. Why had no one come forward, looking for a missing woman, the woman whose death had made Rosemary's disappearance so much easier? Why had no one filed a missing persons' report, looking for the mysterious man who had also died in the triple murder? Rosemary also often thought of Father Christopher Maloney, the Catholic priest who had taken her in and stayed with her when she delivered her daughter. He had killed for her…to free her from her monster of a husband. What had ever happened to that kind cleric who had eventually lost his mind?

When Christina Rose began to ask questions about her absent father, Rosemary told Christina Rose her father had been a doctor and had died in a house fire before Christina Rose was born. Rosemary explained that she'd been separated from Christina Rose's father for some time before he'd died. Rosemary had made up the story, and she'd stuck to her lie throughout the years.

Many of Christina Rose's schoolmates' parents were divorced, so it didn't seem odd to her that her father and mother hadn't been living together when she was born. When somebody asked her, Christina told the truth that he was dead. Families were very different now than they'd been in the 1950s. Rosemary wondered if the time would come when she would feel the need to tell Christina Rose the real story about her past and her parentage. It was an ugly part of Rosemary's history, and she hoped she would never have to tell Christina Rose anything about it. Marley knew the truth, but aside from Father Christopher Maloney, Marley was the only other living soul who knew about Rosemary and Christina Rose's journey from the dark side.

Chapter 8

Gimbel Saunders *had spent thirteen* years as a homicide investigator for the New York State Police. He mostly loved his work and was proud of the fact that he had a significantly higher than average percentage of cases solved, a considerably better record than most of his colleagues. When asked, he attributed his success to hard work, but what he admitted only to himself was that he had a kind of sixth sense that forced him to stay on the right track until he'd found the answer that fit the facts.

If he started to follow a false lead, an anxiety alarm went off in his head. It was a signal to recalculate and move in another direction. He sometimes referred to this uncanny ability as his "bullshit detector." He could tell when people were lying to him. Sometimes he thought, only to himself of course, what kept him focused on the right issues was his "women's intuition." As a former major league baseball pitcher who was six feet four inches tall and all muscle, nobody would ever think of him as being anything but male. In spite of his masculine looks and his deep voice, he'd always thought of his gift as women's intuition, and he'd always wondered why the term "men's intuition" was never used.

His analytical mind and his hypervigilant radar kept him on track. He noticed everything, and he remembered everything. He had a college degree in pre-law and criminology, but he credited his native intelligence for having helped him solve many of his cases. Both of Gimbel's parents had been alcoholics, and this had forced him to be the adult in the family, almost from the day he was born. Gimbel was twelve years old when his father, who was drunk at the time, drove his car into a tree and died instantly. Gimbel's mother wasn't as lucky. She had died of liver cancer, brought on in part by the thousands of gallons of gin she'd consumed during her life. Her death had been slow and horribly painful, and Gimbel was seventeen when his mother finally and blessedly passed away.

Negotiating life in a household with two drunks, the little boy had learned that, in order to survive, he had to notice everything and remember everything. The only child didn't realize it at the time, but psychologists would later study hypervigilance and realize it was a critical survival skill for children who grew up in pathological families. Gimbel had, out of necessity, developed the skill of hypervigilance to a very high degree, and it had not only helped him to survive his childhood, it had also given him a leg up in his job as a police investigator. His radar was always working overtime.

Forced to give up a promising baseball career because of a torn rotator cuff that couldn't be adequately repaired, Gimbel had spent three years as an intelligence officer in the U.S. Marine Corps. After a three-year tour of duty in Afghanistan, he joined the New York State Police as a detective. He'd never had time to get married, and he wondered if his excellent bullshit detector might have seriously interfered with his ability to keep a romance going. For whatever reason, he had never met the right woman although many women thought they'd met the right guy when they'd met Gimbel Saunders.

Gimbel belonged to the Y and swam in their pool for an hour every morning. He liked to cook and read and owned two West Highland terriers. He chuckled to himself about his domestic life and wondered if maybe he really did have women's intuition. He'd recently been placed on part-time duty because of a heart murmur. Gimbel suspected he'd had the heart defect all of his life, but it had gone unnoticed and undiagnosed for forty-five years. The truth was that, in spite of being one of the fittest state troopers in upstate New York, he could no longer pass the physical for full-time duty.

Gimbel wasn't thrilled to be on a less than fully active assignment, but at least his boss was going to allow him to pursue interesting cold cases of his own choosing. The full-time guys were swamped investigating drug trafficking and overdoses of heroin laced with fentanyl. Gimbel had seen enough of that scene to last a lifetime. They all had. It was an epidemic, and nationwide, thousands died every day. It was sickening, and Gimbel was relieved to have a break from that kind of constant death and sorrow. He'd grown up with intimate knowledge of what addictions do to people and what addictions do to the people who love the addict. Twenty plus years ago it had been gin. Now it was heroin and fentanyl. The real difference was in the number of people who died. Maybe it was easier to hide an addiction to gin. Maybe not as many people died from drinking gin. Or maybe it just took longer to die from drinking gin.

When he'd been told he was going to work cold cases, Gimbel knew exactly which one he wanted to start with. Although he had been playing baseball at the time, he'd heard about the sensational triple murder in his home town. The case had puzzled and angered him ever since. Gimbel had decided that, for public relations reasons, the Syracuse PD had done only a cursory investigation and closed the case before they'd ever found out much of anything. It had not exactly been a cover-up, but it was close.

A few years later, the Onondaga County Sheriff's Department had pretended to do a follow-up investigation of the same case. For their own reasons, it seemed they'd swept the whole thing under the rug for a second time. The murder and both investigations smelled to high heaven. The needle had registered a ten on Gimbel's bullshit detector. Three people had died in a terrible crime, and nobody seemed to care. He couldn't wait to get his hands on the murder book, the evidence boxes, and the other facts that had been largely ignored for almost fifteen years.

In early April of 2001, not many people were looking for terrorists, and somebody should have paid attention to this triple murder. After September 11th, terrorism crowded out everything else, and local crimes were often given short shrift. The lack of attention given to the murders committed in Syracuse in April of 2001 couldn't be blamed on 9/11. In this particular case, Gimbel knew exactly why nobody wanted to touch it—either back then or now.

The chief surgical resident at Syracuse University Hospital Medical Center, or whatever they'd been calling it in 2001, had been accused by his wife, Rosalind Parsons, of spousal abuse. She'd shown up at the hospital in Auburn, New York, covered with bruises and asked to speak to their local law enforcement to tell her story and file a complaint. She'd laid out a very convincing case about years of physical beatings, as well as verbal, emotional, and psychological abuse. She said she'd come to a different town, Auburn, and another county, Cayuga County, to take legal action because her husband had such a high profile at the University Hospital in Syracuse. Because of who her husband was, she said she was afraid nobody would believe her if she reported the abuse at the hospital where her husband worked.

The doctor husband, Norman Parsons, had of course denied everything. After reading the files, Gimbel concluded Parsons was the perfect sociopath who oozed intelligence and charm and had been able to fool everybody, except for his wife, about the sort of person he really was. Parsons had responded to the domestic abuse accusations with a court order to have his wife committed to a state mental hospital. In other words, he wanted everyone to believe that his wife's accusations against him were not only untrue but crazy, a sign of her mental illness. Gimbel read her statement several times and looked at the photographs of her injuries. He knew Rosalind Parsons had been telling the truth about the beatings she said her publicly picture-perfect husband had inflicted on her.

The husband had supposedly been able to convince two of his psychiatrist colleagues on the Syracuse University Hospital staff to declare Rosalind a danger to herself and others. Even though the two psychiatrists had never seen or talked to Rosalind, on the basis of their written declarations, a judge had issued an order for her mandatory psychiatric hospitalization. Gimbel had not been able to find the statements the two psychiatrists had made that had convinced the judge to have Rosalind committed. He wondered if the psychiatrists had actually written these reports or if Rosalind's husband had generated the reports on his own, signed his colleagues' names unbeknownst to them, and submitted the paperwork to the court. Norman

Parsons was certainly smart enough to write the reports on his own. He was a physician and knew exactly what to say to persuade a judge.

Rosalind hadn't shown up to argue against being committed. She had probably not known anything at all about the court proceedings that were taking place in Syracuse—proceedings that were deciding her fate and condemning her to be admitted to the state psychiatric hospital. At the time, she was in hiding at a woman's shelter in Auburn. There was no paperwork to indicate that she'd been notified that her husband had filed a petition to have her institutionalized against her will. She'd never known there was a hearing being conducted to decide her future. Failure to give her a chance to defend herself in court was just more of the same, more abusive behavior on the part of the man she was married to. She was almost nine months pregnant at the time.

Rather than wait for the judicial system to follow through on enforcing its court order, Norman Parsons had hired two off-duty sheriff's deputies to track Rosalind down, forcibly remove her from the women's shelter where she had sought refuge from his abuse, and drive her to the state mental hospital in Elmira, New York.

The deputies had used their official sheriff's uniforms and an official sheriff's van in this unofficial job to abduct a private citizen. The two were being paid a lot of money for their services to Norman Parsons. Hiring law enforcement personnel during their off-duty hours isn't illegal, but it is illegal to hire them to circumvent the normal judicial process and use a judge's court order to force their way into a secure facility such as a women's shelter in a county where they didn't have jurisdiction. Seizing Rosalind Parsons at the women's shelter had in reality been a kidnapping.

Rosalind, even though she was within days of delivering her first baby, had been able to overpower one of the two deputies who were transporting her in the sheriff's van. She had escaped her captors. Then she'd disappeared completely. Her husband had declared her a missing person, and he had used his considerable influence and connections to convince law enforcement in several counties to search for his pregnant wife. Rosalind Parsons was never found alive.

Norman Parsons had completed his term as chief surgery resident at Syracuse. He had signed a contract to go into private practice with a well-known medical group in Seattle. After he'd officially concluded his residency and said his goodbyes at Syracuse, he was taking a month off to pack up his house in upstate New York, make the move across country, and settle into his new life on the West Coast. Because he was no longer expected to show up for work at the Syracuse University Hospital, he hadn't been missed until he'd been dead for almost a week. No one had suspected he might be dead until his house was torched and his body was found murdered and burned to a crisp.

On the night of April 6th, Norman and Rosalind Parsons' house burned to the ground. The fire had been intentionally set. What no one who responded to the fire had expected to find were the three dead bodies inside, all burned beyond recognition. The Onondaga County Coroner could tell some things from examining the burned corpses, but there were many more things he couldn't tell. One of the bodies was positively identified as that of Norman Parsons. This had been confirmed by means of a comparison with a known DNA sample on file at the Syracuse University Hospital. The other two bodies, one male and one female, were never able to be identified using DNA.

Because Rosalind Parsons had disappeared several days earlier and a woman's body was found in her home, everyone assumed the body of the female who was murdered in the house and subsequently burned in the fire was that of Norman Parsons' wife, Rosalind. The size of the woman's body matched that of Rosalind Parsons. No one had ever bothered to find out where Rosalind had been in the days after her disappearance from the sheriff's van and before the alleged discovery of her body in the burned house. There was no nice, neat DNA sample on file anywhere for Rosalind, and everything she'd owned, her hairbrush and toothbrush, and anything else that might have contained her DNA and could have been used to identify her as the female corpse, had been destroyed in the fire. Everyone assumed the female who'd died in Rosalind Parsons' house was Rosalind Parsons.

Dental records might have been used to identify her body, but the loss of Rosalind's dental records was another of the many odd twists that had confounded investigators about this crime. Her dental records had disappeared from her dentist's office. She'd been at the office in February for her semi-annual teeth cleaning and check-up, but when authorities had gone to the dentist's office in April to get the confirmatory dental records, Rosalind's file was missing. Rosalind Parsons' dental records were never found. No positive comparison of the corpse's teeth with Rosalind Parsons' teeth could be made. The disappearance of her dental records was one of many mysteries that plagued the case.

The identity of the second murdered man, whose body had been found at the Parsons' house in Syracuse, had never been determined. Police and sheriff's investigators had searched missing persons databases nationwide, but they'd never come up with anything that could help identify the third body in the murder house. There was a great deal of speculation about why the man might have been at the house, but no one was ever able to discover who he was or why he was there. The complicated murder case had stumped law enforcement for almost fifteen years.

The bodies had been so badly burned in the house fire that all clothing, hair, and skin were gone. Almost all of the soft tissue was gone. In spite of the destruction of most of the physical evidence due to the fire, the medical examiner had been able to determine that the all three bodies had sustained gunshot wounds. The autopsy had revealed that the female corpse, believed to be Rosalind Parsons, and the unidentified male corpse had both been severely beaten before they'd been shot. The medical examiner believed the bludgeonings both bodies had received before their deaths were so severe, the injuries from these severe beatings would have been fatal, even if they'd received immediate emergency medical attention and even if they'd not been shot.

Both of their skulls had been crushed to smithereens. The blood loss would have been tremendous. When they had been shot, the two were essentially already dead or very close to death. It had been a close call with these two as to what was the actual cause of death. The ME believed in the end that the gunshots had probably put them out of their misery. The fatal beatings followed by the gunshot wounds were very bizarre. In their many years of experience, neither the medical examiner nor the cops assigned to the case had ever seen anything quite like it. The ME thought the beatings might have been inflicted by a golf club. He was able to determine that Norman Parsons, M.D. had died of a single gunshot wound to the back of the head, and his body had not been beaten before he was shot and killed.

Perhaps the most confusing additional finding in the autopsy report was the information that the female victim had been pregnant and had lost the baby a few days before her death. Gimbel found this conclusion on the part of the coroner to be undeniably questionable. If most or all the soft tissues on the corpses had been destroyed by the fire, how could the coroner have possibly been able to determine that the woman had recently been pregnant? The autopsy report on the woman's body was entirely wrong in Gimbel's opinion.

Gimbel wondered if the suspicious part of the report had been made up to fit what was known about the suspected victims. Everyone knew that Rosalind Parsons had been pregnant in the months before her death. She had been missing for several days before she was thought to have died at her house. Had she lost the baby in those few days before she died? How and when had that happened? Gimbel knew something was very wrong with at least part of the autopsy report.

It seemed as if those in charge of the case had been anxious to move on and hadn't wanted to hear about the facts that didn't fit. Rosalind Parsons had been pregnant, and the corpse had been pregnant. Therefore, the corpse was Rosalind Parsons. Several statements in the coroner's report provided Gimbel with red flags that signaled significant irregularities in the facts of this very puzzling case.

There were plenty of other unanswered questions. What had happened to the gun that had shot three people? Why had there been almost a week between the estimated date of the murders and the night of the fire? Had the murderer returned to the scene of the crime several days later and decided to burn down the house? Did somebody else come along after the murders had been committed and burn down the house? Was the woman who had been killed really Rosalind Parsons?

If the dead woman wasn't Parsons, who was she, and why had no one ever reported her missing? If Rosalind Parsons hadn't died in her Syracuse house, what had happened to her? Who was the second man who'd been beaten and shot and died in the house? Why had no one ever reported him missing?

The initial investigation had been cursory at best. Gimbel suspected the reason was because Syracuse University had put pressure on law enforcement to back off and not delve too deeply into the lives of Norman and Rosalind Parsons. One of the star doctors at their hospital had been publicly accused of beating his wife. Then the doctor husband had gone to a judge and obtained a court order, perhaps under less than ethical circumstances, to have her committed to a state psychiatric hospital. Then he hired two deputies from the sheriff's department to illegally drag her out of a woman's shelter. She escaped from the two off-duty incompetents, and nobody could find her. Then the doctor was found murdered in his house, and there were two other murdered people in the house with him. One of those other people had supposedly been pregnant, and both of those other people had been beaten nearly to death as well as shot. Several days after three people were killed there, the doctor's house was burned down.

Of course, the university wanted the whole thing swept under the rug—from the disgraceful beginning of the scandal to its horrible end. Norman Parsons was their golden boy. They didn't want any negative media coverage. If information that might sully their chief surgery resident's reputation became public, it might reflect badly on the hospital.

The sheriff's department was complicit in the cover-up. They were embarrassed by the two rogue deputies. Law enforcement was shamed into treading lightly and saying as little as possible. Of course, the woman at the house was Norman

Parsons' wife. Who else could she possibly be? Who cared about the unknown man found dead at the scene? If no one was looking for him, he must not be important. Case closed.

A couple of years after the murders, somebody at the sheriff's department in Onondaga County had stumbled on the cold case and decided it needed a second look. That review had lasted about a week before whoever it was that had decided to open that particular can of worms got the word that they were to cease and desist, sit down, and shut up.

The two sheriff's deputies, who had been hired by Norman Parsons and who had allowed Rosalind Parsons to escape from the van on its way to the Elmira state psychiatric hospital, had been fired. For a big financial payday, they'd agreed to do Norman Parsons' private dirty work in their off hours. Then they'd illegally entered a woman's shelter and kidnapped a woman. Then they'd allowed this very pregnant woman to outsmart and physically overcome one of them, escape, and never be found alive. How embarrassing is that? No wonder most of the law enforcement community didn't want anybody dredging up that case again. The investigation was sent back into cold cases, this time to the subzero, frozen tundra department.

But Gimbel Saunders wasn't buying any of it. Gimbel could see why, pressured by powerful people at the local hospital as well as by a fellow law enforcement agency, the Onondaga County Sheriff's Department, Syracuse PD didn't want to hear anything more about this case. But it intrigued Gimbel. His sixth sense, his hypervigilance, his analytical mind, his women's intuition, and his bullshit detector—all screamed to him that justice had not been given a snowball's chance in hell of being served in this odd tragedy. When he got the evidence box, it didn't look to Gimbel like the items inside had ever been inventoried, let alone examined. Gimbel had work to do.

Chapter 9

Gimbel read over the autopsy reports several times. The fact that the bodies had all been burned in the house fire complicated everything. The report on Norman Parsons was the most straightforward of the three. His identity had been confirmed with a DNA comparison. The other male who was found at the house had never been identified. Gimbel had to admit to himself that the identity of this man might never be known. But it was the autopsy report on the woman that bothered Gimbel. The conclusion that everyone involved with the case had reached was that this was the body of Rosalind Parsons. Something about the autopsy report triggered Gimbel's radar. Something was not right about this report. He read it over several times but was unable to put his finger on exactly what was bothering him. He decided to make a copy of the report. He would take it home and read it. Maybe what was bugging him would show itself.

He copied the report on the copy machine. It was an older and more cumbersome machine than he was used to using. He had to hunt down paper to put in the copier. Finally, he'd made two copies. As he was taking the pages out of the machine, they slipped through his fingers. There were five pages in each copy, and the pages scattered over the floor. As he was gathering them up and putting the pages back together in the right order, Gimbel's hypervigilance and other skills all kicked in. Something about the way the report was written was not right. It didn't take him long, once he had the last two pages of the woman's autopsy report lined up side-by-side, to figure out what was wrong.

The first thing he noticed was that the last page of the autopsy report on the female body had been typed with a different typewriter or printer than had been used to type the first four pages. By 2001, most computer-savvy law enforcement departments had made the transition to word processing on computers and sending documents to inkjet printers. But old habits die hard, and computers and printers were still expensive. Queen bee secretaries and law enforcement officers who had been around for a long time and typed their own reports were used to their old IBM Selectric typewriters. The first four pages of the autopsy report on the woman who had been tentatively identified as Rosalind Parsons had been printed on an ink jet printer. The fifth page looked to Gimbel as if it might have been typed on an electronic typewriter. It was definitely printed on a different machine than had been used to print the first four pages.

The last page was the most interesting to Gimbel because it contained information about the pregnancy of the woman found in the murder house. He studied the last page of the autopsy report which stated that the female body had recently been pregnant and had suffered a miscarriage. The woman's body was too compromised to be able to tell exactly how long before death the miscarriage had occurred, and it was likewise impossible to tell if the termination of the pregnancy had been a spontaneous abortion or an intentionally induced medical procedure. From the first time Gimbel had read this report, he had found the paragraph about the pregnancy suspicious. Then the report ended. All the proper signatures were at the bottom of the page. It all looked official, except for the fact that the last page had been generated by a different device.

Gimbel could imagine several good and legitimate reasons why a different typewriter or printer might have been used to type the last page of the autopsy report. But he was also able to imagine several reasons why the final page or pages of the official autopsy report might have been deliberately destroyed and why another page might have been fabricated and inserted into the murder book. The most important page in the autopsy report, for Gimbel's purposes, might have been changed. Information that more closely confirmed the narrative that those involved favored might have been substituted for what the coroner had actually found when he did the autopsy.

Gimbel wondered if, after he had written and submitted the autopsy report, the coroner ever tracked down the murder book to check and see if his report had been accurately recorded? Gimbel was betting that had probably never happened. Because almost everyone involved had wanted to relegate this case to the back burner and pretend none of it had ever happened, Gimbel felt it was not a leap to assume no one had followed up on these autopsy reports. It was possible that very few people, if any, had ever read the autopsy report that was in the murder book.

Gimbel had suspected from the beginning that this case had been a cover-up. If it was not an out and out cover-up, at the very best, it had been an extremely poor investigation. He knew there were quite a few reasons why this particular case might have been ignored and buried. He even understood how the evidence could have been manipulated to tell a story that many people wanted told a certain way. Now his gut feeling was that someone had intentionally destroyed the final page of the autopsy on the woman who was found dead at the murder house. He suspected that there was something in the original coroner's report that did not support the prevailing and favored narrative. Someone had rewritten the final page of the autopsy report to keep the real story from coming out.

So many years had passed since the murders had occurred. The case was cold. Gimbel wanted to be able to talk to the coroner who had actually done the autopsies and had written the original reports. Gimbel's memory of Seymour Stephens, M.D. was that he had retired shortly after the tragedy had occurred. He wondered if Dr. Seymour Stephens was even still alive. Tracking down what had happened to the medical examiner would be Gimbel's first priority.

Dr. Seymour Stephens had retired in July of 2001. Gimbel wondered if the triple homicide had been the final straw that pushed the man out the door. Stephens had been sixty-five years old when he'd called it quits. He certainly had put in his time, and many people retired at or around the age of sixty-five. There might have even been a mandatory retirement age back in 2001. Dr. Stephens had moved to Florida in 2002. His last known address was listed as a memory care unit in Naples, Florida. He would be in his eighties now, and the memory care unit thing was of great concern to Gimbel.

Would Seymour Stephens remember the murders that had occurred in 2001? Would he remember the autopsy reports he had written? How serious was his memory loss? Gimbel knew that people with dementia had trouble with short-term memory. They could not remember that they'd just had their breakfast or where they'd put their keys or their cell phone. They might not remember what they'd done the day before. But, sometimes, they could remember things from the distant past with great accuracy and detail. Some of them told stories from long ago over and over again. They often seemed to live in the past, rather than in the present.

Gimbel wondered if contacting Seymour Stephens would be worth the trouble. He wondered if a phone call to the former medical examiner would yield any useful information. Gimbel had no intentions of making a trip to Florida to try to talk to the doctor in person, but he thought he would try a phone call to see if the man remembered anything about the Norman and Rosalind Parsons' case.

It wasn't easy to track down the former medical examiner. It had been fifteen years since he'd retired. When Gimbel finally located Dr. Stephens, he was relieved to find out that the man's mind was sharp. Seymour Stephens, M.D. had indeed moved to a memory care unit in Florida, but that move had been made because Stephens' wife had been suffering from dementia. The doctor had moved to the facility with her in order to care for her. She'd died less than two years after the couple had moved to Florida. After her death, Dr. Seymour Stephens had left the memory care unit and moved into his own condominium in Naples. When Gimbel finally made contact with the retired Medical Examiner, he told Gimbel that he still played golf every day and was dating a woman who lived in his condominium complex. He remembered the Parsons murder case very well. It still haunted him.

Gimbel explained that he had reopened the case and that he had some questions about the autopsy report. He read the entire report to Stephens over the phone.

Before Gimbel could question the doctor about the last page of the autopsy report on the woman, the retired ME interrupted him and took issue with what Gimbel had read. "Young man. There has been a mix up of some kind. There has been a big SNAFU. Someone has mixed up this autopsy report that you have just read to me with the report I actually wrote. I wrote the first part of this report, but the last part you just read to me is not the last part of the report that I wrote."

"I suspected as much, Dr. Stephens, as I noticed that the last page of the autopsy report was printed on a different machine than the first four pages."

"As I recall, there were actually six pages of that report. I gave the facts and then I speculated about what they might mean. I didn't usually do that…speculate about what the facts imply…but this was such an unusual case, I couldn't resist editorializing a little bit. But there were definitely six pages in that report. It was longer than most of my reports."

Gimbel's adrenalin was churning when he heard what the doctor said about the last pages of the autopsy report. He'd known something was fishy, and now the ME who had actually conducted the autopsies had confirmed his suspicions. "Do you remember what was in the original report that you wrote? It's been a long time, but I was hoping you might remember what you had written in those last two pages."

"Of course I remember what was in the last two pages of my report. But I can do you one better than to ask you to trust my memory. I saved copies of every case I wasn't absolutely certain about. The Parsons murder case was a mind bender for so many reasons. I saved everything I wrote about all three of the bodies I autopsied. I can send all of it to you, if you want. There's a fax machine in the office downstairs, and I can send you my original reports today."

Gimbel felt as if he'd struck gold. "I would very much appreciate seeing all of it. I know the autopsy report on the deceased woman was altered. It would be interesting to see if anything in the other reports has been changed."

"Before you hang up, I want to tell you that there is further evidence in this case that you can find in the morgue. The woman who died was pregnant. She had not lost the child or had an abortion like that phony autopsy report says. She and her fetus both died when she died. It was a miracle that the tiny bones survived the fire. They only survived because they were protected by the body of the mother. Only a few bone fragments survived the fire. Everything else burned up. The woman was about four or five months pregnant. It was difficult to be more precise, given the condition of the body. I recovered the few bones from the fetus and preserved them in formaldehyde. DNA was not advanced enough at the time to test the bones to try to find out who the father of the unborn child was. The pieces of bone were so small. However, with recent advances, you can probably submit those tiny bone fragments to be tested and come up with the DNA of the father...and the mother. Of course, we know that the mother of the fetus was the woman who was carrying the baby and who died that night. But, we were never certain that the woman who died in the murder house was actually Rosalind Parsons. If somebody hasn't thrown out my sample that I carefully preserved so many years ago, you can do all the tests you want to on it. You will see the number of the specimen in the final pages of *my* autopsy report. I repeat...*my real autopsy report.*"

Gimbel Saunders felt as if he had struck gold for the second time in one day. He thanked Seymour Stephens profusely. He gave Dr. Stephens the fax number to use and promised to let him know what happened with his reinvestigation of the cold case. He couldn't wait to read the fax from Dr. Stephens and make a trip to the Syracuse city morgue to track down the bones of the baby who had so cruelly died on that night almost fifteen years earlier.

When Gimbel received the fax from Dr. Stephens, he quickly scanned the multiple pages. The other two autopsy reports which had all been printed on the same machine were the same as those Gimbel had found in the murder book. He went to the last two pages of the report on the woman who had been found at the murder house in Syracuse. Gimbel was stunned to read what Dr. Seymour Stephens had actually written so many years earlier. His words were nothing like the last page of the autopsy report that was recorded in the murder book.

Dr. Stephens had stated unequivocally that the dead woman had been pregnant at the time of her death. Her unborn child had also died when the mother stopped breathing and her heart stopped beating. The coroner had been able to recover a few tiny bones from the remains of the fetus. The mother's body had been able to protect the body of the fetus from the fire to some extent.

Dr. Stephens was very familiar with the use of DNA in proving identity. He knew that the state of the technology at the time he did the autopsy was not advanced enough to discover anything of value by testing the few bone fragments he had. But he knew that great advances in DNA technology would continue to be made, and he hoped that one day the tiny bones might reveal who the father of the unborn baby was. If he'd been able to test these fragments at the time he did the autopsy and had found that the father of the fetus was indeed Norman Parsons, this would have added credence to the fact that the woman who had died in the house in Syracuse was indeed Rosalind Parsons.

Dr. Stephens believed it might be possible at some time in the future to test the tiny pieces of evidence he had found inside the body of the dead woman. He took great pains to preserve that evidence. He preserved the bone fragments in formaldehyde in the Syracuse city morgue. He indicated in his autopsy report where the preserved evidence could be found.

Gimbel now knew that someone had gone to significant trouble to falsify the original autopsy report. The facts had been completely changed, and no mention of the preserved forensic remains had been mentioned in the falsified report. Gimbel's imagination ran wild with speculation about possible reasons why someone had not wanted the original report to come to light and who that person or persons might possibly be.

Chapter 10

***J**urisdiction had been another issue* that had complicated the investigation. Rosalind had chosen to go to the hospital in Cayuga County to report her abuse. That was one of the first things that had happened in the chain of events that had ended in a triple murder and a fire. Norman Parsons had gone to court in Onondaga County to get his commitment order to hospitalize Rosalind, and the off-duty sheriff's deputies he'd hired had been from that county. Rosalind had been abducted from the women's shelter which was located in Cayuga County. The Parsons' house was inside the city limits of Syracuse, so the SPD had assumed primary responsibility for the murder investigation. The murder book and the evidence box had been kept in Syracuse.

Gimbel knew from the beginning he'd be making himself very unpopular by looking into this case again, the case that everybody wanted to stay buried forever. It hadn't been easy for him to get access to either the murder book or the evidence box. He had a legal right to see everything the Syracuse PD had, but they'd dragged their feet by not allowing him to have what he wanted. At first they'd told him the evidence box had disappeared, that they couldn't find it. But Gimbel hadn't believed them and had persisted. SPD had finally allowed him to see both the murder book and the evidence box.

Gimbel could only look at the book at department headquarters and could only have access to the box inside their evidence lockup. This was the usual protocol, and Gimbel was happy to comply with the rules. He read every word and made a copy of the pages in the murder book. He did a complete inventory of the evidence box. There wasn't much in either, and Gimbel suspected that a number of pieces of evidence had conveniently disappeared. Nobody had wanted to investigate this murder, and nobody really had.

Because the Parsons' house had burned down, it was understandable that there wouldn't be much physical evidence in the evidence box. When the box was brought to Gimbel, the whole thing smelled like smoke. Even after all these years had passed, the smell of burning was still there. There weren't many things of interest inside. One item was a fraternity ring that had been found on Norman Parsons' little finger. He'd never worn a wedding ring. The woman who had died had not been wearing any rings, either. It was assumed she'd taken them off when she had gone to the women's shelter, on the run from her abusive husband. The rings had never turned up anywhere. There were some interior and exterior photographs of the burned house. The fire marshal's report was in the murder book.

There was a metal rod in the evidence box that looked to Gimbel as if it were part of a golf club—probably the weapon that had been used to beat two of the victims to death. The rod was in a plastic bag, but it was still coated with a dark substance that Gimbel assumed was soot from the fire. No one had ever bothered to wipe the rod clean to see what it was. Gimbel wasn't much of a golfer, but he owned a set of clubs that sat in his front hall closet and collected dust. The dark residue from the fire wouldn't be of any forensic value to the case, so he decided he would come back the next day with some cleaning solution and a cloth to wipe the rod clean. He wanted to know if the metal rod was part of a golf club. And if it was a golf club, what kind of club had it started out to be before the rest of it had burned up or melted away. Gimbel was thankful that somebody had at least thought to keep what remained of the metal rod and put it in the evidence box. The reason it had been kept was probably because it was the piece of metal that had been found on top of one of the bodies. There would have been hundreds of pieces of burned and twisted metal in the house after the fire, but this piece had been bagged and kept—probably because of where it was found. Gimbel would find out all he could from this metal rod. He assumed it came from a set of golf clubs that belonged to Norman Parsons.

A burned golf bag that held the rest of the clubs should have been found someplace else in the house, but there had been no mention of such a find in any of the paperwork. Where were the rest of the golf clubs and the golf bag? A couple of Gimbel's friends, who played a lot of golf, kept a driver in their front hall or back hall closet. If they were going to the driving range, and didn't intend to play the course, they grabbed their driver to hit a few balls and practice their swing. A few times these guys had ended up at the beginning of their eighteen holes without their favorite driver because they'd forgotten to return it to the golf bag with the rest of their clubs. Here was another small mystery—the case of the disappearing golf bag. No one had found the rest of the golf clubs, and Gimbel decided no one had ever thought to look for them. He'd found no new answers in the evidence box.

Gimbel would have looked in the trunk of Norman's car to see if he'd stored his golf bag there, but that car had been parked in a garage attached to the house and had burned up with everything else. In fact, the car's gas tank had exploded, and the explosion had contributed to the fire's intensity. The house, the garage, and the car had all been completely destroyed. There was no record that anyone had ever bothered to look inside the car or its trunk after the fire and explosion. Gimbel assumed the car had been towed away in 2001 and taken to the dump with everything else.

Gimbel knew Norman Parsons had been planning to move to Seattle. When he'd died and his house had burned down, he'd been in the process of packing his household belongings for shipment to the West Coast. Gimbel wondered if any of Norman's things had been picked up by a moving and storage company before the murders and before the fire. It might be worth looking into to see if he could find some of Norman's personal effects that might not have been examined because nobody knew they'd escaped the fire. Maybe they had and maybe they hadn't. Of course, if anything had been left in a storage unit and no one had paid the rental fees, whatever might have been stored there was now long gone.

There were a few remnants of fabric and what looked like the remains of a melted watch in the evidence bags. Each bag was marked with a number, but the list of notations corresponding to each bagged and numbered item was missing. Gimbel had known what the metal rod in the evidence box was because a reference had been made to it in the murder book. Without an inventory, the other items in the evidence envelopes weren't useful evidence, but were additional mysteries.

It was amazing to Gimbel how few interviews had been done with people who seemed important to the case. The

Onondaga County Sheriff's Department had been very anxious to put the whole embarrassing part played by their department behind them. Gimbel couldn't find any paperwork that showed anybody had ever interviewed either one of the deputies who'd been hired by Norman Parsons to take Rosalind to the psychiatric hospital in Elmira, New York. There was no report anywhere that either deputy had been interviewed. Gimbel knew from the scuttlebutt that had gone around the law enforcement community at the time that, as a result of their actions surrounding the events with Rosalind Parsons, the two deputies had lost their jobs with the sheriff's department.

No one had talked to Rosalind's obstetrician to find out exactly when her due date was. Gimbel wondered if anyone had interviewed the psychiatrists who'd supposedly signed the commitment papers that had been used to attempt to send Rosalind to the psychiatric hospital. None of the commitment papers were anywhere to be found either. These events had happened more than fifteen years ago. Were these people even still alive? Had anyone talked to the head of the women's shelter where Rosalind had sought refuge?

There were transcripts of several interviews with one of the Parsons' neighbors who swore she'd seen her parish priest wandering around the neighborhood a few nights before the fire. The only reason, it seemed, that this neighbor had been interviewed was because she'd come to the police department with her story on her own. When the police hadn't shown any interest in what she had to say, she'd called them a second time.

Gimbel vaguely remembered something about the priest in question, Father Christopher Maloney. His dead body had been found months later in the back of his old Buick station wagon in Cuidad Juarez, Mexico, just over the border from El Paso, Texas. As Gimbel remembered it, there'd been a couple of sketchy things about this death, but in the end Maloney's ashes had been buried in the St, Stanislaus graveyard at the church in upstate New York where he'd been the parish priest. No one, except the Parsons' neighbor, seriously believed he'd had anything to do with the murders in Syracuse or that he'd ever been in the neighborhood of the Parsons' home.

Gimbel decided he was going to make an attempt to talk to the doctors involved — the two psychiatrists and Rosalind's obstetrician. Because of Norman Parsons' position at Syracuse University Hospital Medical Center in 2001, it looked as if law enforcement had actively avoided speaking with anyone there. Parsons was dead, and enough time may have passed that Gimbel felt he could ask, even those who'd once been friends of Norman Parsons, what they remembered. Gimbel also intended to try to talk to the two sheriff's deputies who had abducted Rosalind. The women's shelter that had taken in Rosalind Parsons had gone out of business due to lack of funding, but Gimbel would make an attempt to find the woman who'd been in charge at the time.

Cold cases are always difficult, and much of the evidence, even if it's been gathered carefully in the first place, is useless after considerable time has passed. Years had passed since this crime had been committed. People had moved away. People had died. People had forgotten things. But sometimes there was value in talking to people, even years after the fact.

He realized he didn't have the names of any of the doctors he wanted to talk to. The names of the psychiatrists would be on the commitment papers they'd signed, but tracking them down this many years later would be almost impossible. He had no idea who Rosalind's obstetrician had been in 2001, and now there were HIPAA rules that pretty much shut down finding out anything about anybody's medical history without a warrant. He knew Rosalind had been a graduate student at Syracuse University. Maybe he could find out something from one of her professors there. He did have the names of the two Onondaga County sheriff's deputies, so he would start with them.

One of the deputies had left town in 2001, right after he'd been fired. He hadn't had many buddies in the department and didn't have any family in the area. No one was sure exactly where he'd gone after leaving Syracuse. The other deputy, Leroy Jarvis, had been the driver of the van used in Rosalind Parsons' abduction, and he still lived in town. Apparently, he was a very personable guy and had done quite well for himself as a salesman at the local Honda dealership. Leroy Jarvis was successful enough that he might not be too defensive about talking to Gimbel about Rosalind Parsons. Leroy had certainly made more money selling cars than he ever would have made working for the sheriff's department.

Chapter 11

*L**eroy Jarvis was not happy* to see or talk to Gimbel Saunders. Leroy had tried hard to bury the memories of his career as a sheriff's deputy and the embarrassment caused by the Syracuse University doctor's wife's escape from his custody. It had all happened years ago, and most people had forgotten that Leroy had been involved in that scandal. Leroy was doing well financially now and didn't want anybody bringing up his inconvenient past. He made no attempt to hide his hostility at being questioned by Saunders, but the investigator refused to be put off.

"I don't want to cause you any trouble, Leroy. You made a big mistake back then, and you lost your job because of it. I'm not here to drag you through the mud again." Gimbel Saunders looked Leroy Jarvis directly in the eyes to let him know he wasn't going to be allowed to wiggle out from under this detective's scrutiny. "Let's take my car for a ride, and you can answer my questions. Your co-workers here at the dealership don't need to know anything about this. I have some questions, and I need answers from you."

"This has already been investigated several times, and I told all of the people who came around, everything I know. I don't want to talk about it anymore. I want to put it behind me." Leroy didn't want to go anywhere with Gimbel Saunders.

"I understand that, and I'll try not to take up much of your time." Leroy reluctantly climbed into the passenger seat of Gimbel's SUV.

"What do you want to know? I need to get back to work." Leroy was petulant.

"How did Rosalind Parsons get away from you? There were two of you, and she was a pregnant woman. How could that happen?"

"It's a really humiliating story, isn't it? I was driving the van. The other deputy was in the passenger seat, and the woman was in the back. She didn't have a place to sit down, and it was very uncomfortable to ride back there. She had to lie down. It was a van we used to transport prisoners back and forth from the jail to court, so it wasn't built for comfort. We'd borrowed it for the night. She yelled to us that her water had broken. She said she was going into labor. She said that riding in the back of the van was too rough and painful for her, and she needed to ride in the passenger seat. Because she was pregnant and said she was in labor, we were afraid not to let her move to a more comfortable seat. We didn't want her delivering the baby in the van or anything like that, so we decided to make the switch. It was a big mistake."

"So you were in the driver's seat the entire time, and it was the other deputy who let her escape."

"Yeah. I pulled over to the side of the road, and Rodney, that was the other deputy, Rodney Dankers, got out of the passenger seat and went around to the back of the van. That was the only way we could get her out of the van—through the back doors. We'd decided we would let her sit up front, and Rodney would sit in the back. We were going to handcuff her when we had her in the passenger seat, to keep her from getting away or grabbing the steering wheel or doing something else stupid to try to escape. But she was a real tiger, and what we didn't know was that she had a big, heavy barbell hidden under her cape. She was hugely pregnant and had on this tent-like cloak. We couldn't see she had a barbell concealed underneath."

"A barbell? Like for lifting weights."

"Yeah, that kind of barbell. Who could have expected that?"

"You hadn't searched her when you picked her up at the shelter."

"She complained when we first showed up at the shelter and said we were acting illegally. When she realized she wasn't going to get rid of us, she was pretty compliant and came in the van without a fuss. Looking back on it, she was probably just trying to lull us into complacency. We should have handcuffed her from the beginning, and we should have searched her. But we didn't."

"So she used the barbell as a weapon?"

"She sure did! She hit Rodney over the head with the barbell and knocked him down. He fell and hit his head on the bumper of the van and collapsed to the ground. He was out cold. He never cried out or shouted or anything. She took off. I didn't realize anything was wrong until I saw her running across the open field. I got out of the van and found Rodney on the ground. His head was bleeding like crazy. I thought she'd killed him. I called 911 on the radio unit in the van."

"You didn't take off after her and try to catch her?"

"We weren't operating in any official capacity, although we'd tried to fool her into thinking we were. We'd been hired by her husband, but officially, we were off duty. I was more concerned about Rodney bleeding and dying there alongside the road than I was about chasing down a pregnant woman. I called 911 so the EMTs would come and take care of Rodney. I didn't care about the doc's wife. I didn't want a fellow deputy to die right in front of my eyes during this off-the-books assignment."

"You said she was 'hugely pregnant.' Did she look like she might deliver at any time? Did she look like she was nine months pregnant? Or close to it?"

"Yep, she looked like she was ten months pregnant. She was enormous, and I was astounded when she clobbered Rodney and ran away. We totally believed her when she said her water had broken and that she'd gone into labor. She was very close to delivering that kid, believe me."

Gimbel believed Leroy's evaluation of Rosalind's pregnancy. Even if he couldn't find her obstetrician, he had the confirmation he needed that she was more than five or six months pregnant. "Did Rodney have any long-lasting effects from the barbell attack?"

"She gave him a concussion and put him in the hospital for three days. And then he lost his job. And I lost my job! She managed to finish off both of us. Rodney left town and went back to wherever it was he'd come from. Nobody's ever heard from him again. I sulked for a while and then decided I would reinvent myself. No more law enforcement for me. I wanted to make some money. Now you know everything about everything."

"Why did you take on this off-the-books assignment in the first place? You must have known it wasn't kosher—to do what you were doing. Why'd you do it?"

"We were young and stupid. And greedy. The doc offered us a ton of cash to do this for him, and he had a court order from a judge. We read the paperwork, and we believed him.

He was a convincing guy, and we really wanted the money. It was wrong. I know that now. Maybe I even knew it back then. So why do you want to know about all this, so many years later? Aren't all these people dead now?"

"That's what I'm trying to figure out. Dr. Parsons' body was identified with DNA, so he is definitely dead. But we've never been able to officially and positively identify either of the other two bodies that were found in the house that burned down."

"I thought the woman, Rosalind Parsons, was one of the bodies. It was her house. That's what everybody thinks, that she was there with a boyfriend. That was when all hell broke loose, and everybody died. Then the house burned down."

"There are quite a few myths and rumors surrounding this tragedy, and there are a lot of unanswered questions and loose ends having to do with the case. I came to you to try to get some answers."

"Did you get anything useful from me?" They'd arrived back at the dealership, and Leroy was ready to get out of Gimbel's car.

"Yes, Leroy, you gave me an important piece of the puzzle, believe it or not. Thanks for your time." Gimbel waved to Leroy who had a puzzled look on his face as he made his way back inside the building.

Gimbel would redouble his efforts to locate Rosalind's obstetrician, and he would try to get some DNA from the fragile remains of the infant whose few tiny bones had been recovered from the woman's corpse at the Parsons' house. For whatever reason, the medical examiner had thought those bone fragments were important enough to preserve. They had been sitting in the refrigerator in a jar of formaldehyde at the morgue for almost fifteen years. With the advances in

DNA technology, what had been a complete mystery in 2001 might, fifteen years later, have become a piece of important evidence. The unborn infant's DNA might be able to tell him something. At least it was a place to start.

Chapter 12

Gimbel had to hassle with the current medical examiner at Syracuse PD to get the fetal remains tested. The previous ME had been the one who'd worried about the discrepancy between the gestation of the remains of the unborn child found in the dead woman's pelvic cavity after the fire and the anecdotal information that Rosalind Parsons had been close to her due date when the murders and the fire had occurred. The previous ME was the one who'd believed the infant's tiny bones were important enough to preserve. Law enforcement's hypothesis about what had happened in the triple murder was not supported by the facts of the case. The physical evidence of the unborn child's remains was not consistent with the known evidence about Rosalind Parsons' pregnancy. Nobody had ever been worried about that before. Now Gimbel Saunders had taken up the cause.

It was important to Gimbel to find out if Norman Parsons was the father of the baby who had died that night. Great strides had been made in the testing of DNA evidence since 2001. Smaller and smaller samples could now be tested with greater hopes of yielding a successful result. Results from degraded DNA samples, that years before would never have been able to reveal anything and wouldn't stand up in court, were now useful because of advances in DNA technology.

Gimbel didn't know if the fetal remains he had would yield any answers. The sample might be too small. The sample might have been compromised by the fire, or by the years that had passed since the fire. The bones had been sitting in the ME's refrigerator for fifteen years, after all. The current ME had said testing the fifteen-year-old sample was not a high priority. Gimbel didn't trust the lab run by the political powers that be in Syracuse. He had his doubts that those who were so worried about looking bad would do an honest job with the DNA. Gimbel decided to send the remains to an independent lab for DNA analysis. The lab was out of town, and Gimbel paid for the testing out of his own pocket. He was scrupulously careful to maintain strict protocols for chain of custody. If he was able to get some answers and if the case ever went to court, he didn't want there to be any question about the procedures he'd followed.

Gimbel was delighted when he received the news that the infant remains had yielded positive DNA results. Of course, he still didn't have any of Rosalind Parsons' DNA with which to compare these latest results, but he did have Norman Parsons' DNA. He wouldn't have been surprised if the results had come back that Norman's DNA wasn't a match for the father of the baby. Because Gimbel's gut had told him all along that the woman who had died in the triple murder wasn't Rosalind Parsons, he was surprised, even shocked, when the DNA revealed that the father of the child, whose fetal remains had just been tested, was definitely Norman Parsons.

It was a match. Norman Parsons was the father of the dead woman's unborn baby. Norman Parsons was definitely the father of the fetus, and the woman who'd been murdered in the Parsons house was obviously the child's mother.

The question for Gimbel continued to be, who was the woman who had been murdered in the Parsons house? The results of the recent DNA testing supported the assumption that the woman who had died at the house was indeed Rosalind Parsons, but Gimbel wasn't ready to accept that conclusion.

Gimbel believed Norman Parsons had been a womanizer. The hospital where Parsons worked had done everything it could to bury and discredit any evidence that this was true about their star surgeon. But Gimbel believed the report Rosalind had given to the police when she reported her abuse. In the months and years since the murders, a few women and even a couple of men had come forward with stories for the Syracuse police about Norman Parsons' affairs with various females. Two patients had come forward, claiming they had been approached by Norman Parsons. One of these patients had actually begun an affair with Parsons when she was a fifteen-year-old psychiatric patient. Several female hospital staff members had told both the hospital administration and the police about Parsons' proclivities.

Most importantly for Gimbel, the gestation of the remains didn't fit with the rest of the story. Gimbel wondered if Norman Parsons could have been the father of the almost full-term child Rosalind was carrying as well as the father of the child of the woman who had been murdered and was five months pregnant at the time of her death. Considering this possibility, as remote and farfetched as it might sound to others, opened up other possible scenarios for Gimbel Saunders to explain what had happened in the Parsons' house the night three people had been murdered.

Could the woman who had been murdered in the house have been one of Norman's lovers? Gimbel could construct a hypothetical explanation for why she had been bludgeoned to death. Playing out this scenario in his mind, Gimbel put the blame for the bludgeoning on Norman Parsons. What if the pregnant girlfriend had shown up at the house to tell Parsons about her condition? What if she had demanded he do something about her unborn child or demanded financial assistance for prenatal care and child support? Norman Parsons might have reacted to these demands in a negative way and killed her with a golf club. A pregnant girlfriend and another baby were inconveniences Norman Parsons didn't want in his life. He was moving on, to his new job and his new life in Seattle. The last thing he wanted to be forced to do was to have to face the consequences of his own bad behavior.

The fly in the ointment always came back to who in the world was the other dead man at the house, the one who had also been bludgeoned and shot and then burned up in the fire. Was he connected in some way to the pregnant woman? Did he have a connection to Norman Parsons? Or was he just an unlucky bystander who had no relationship to either one of them but happened to be at the house that night, in the wrong place at the wrong time? Why had no one ever reported him missing?

Gimbel could speculate forever on the possibilities about who this poor fellow was and why he had been at the murder house that night. There didn't seem to be any way to find out anything at all about the mystery man. Just as DNA testing technology had improved, missing persons' databases had improved over the past fifteen years. The mystery man had died more than fifteen years ago, and Gimbel had no reason to think a missing persons' search would yield anything now that hadn't turned up years ago. Gimbel ran a missing persons search again for the period of time around the murders in 2001. He sent an email out to a long list of law enforcement people in several surrounding counties. He sent his email to the usual people, but he also included social workers, probation officers, and personnel who worked in the juvenile courts.

Gimbel was interested in children who had turned up without a parent. He was interested in anyone who might not have had a family to report them missing. He wanted to know about the person who had fallen through the cracks and hadn't made it into the official missing persons' databases. It was a long shot, but it was all Gimbel could do. The ME had given the dead man an approximate height and weight and had roughly estimated his age to be between thirty and forty. But the fire had destroyed all hopes of getting any DNA from the man to test for ethnic background. He might remain a mystery man for all time.

Chapter 13

Darnel Phillips had spent the last eighteen years of his life in the Auburn Correctional Facility in Auburn, New York. By deciding to rename it a correctional facility, politicians and social workers have attempted to gloss over the fact that the place is in reality a hard core prison where the worst of the worst are warehoused. Did anything ever really get "corrected" at Auburn or at any other correctional facility, or is the name just wishful thinking?

When he was twenty-five, Darnel had killed two men in a drunken rage. The hot-headed young kid with drug and alcohol addictions had found himself at the Ice Man Tavern in Canandaigua, New York, late on a Friday night. Darnel had consumed way too many beers, and his ego was on very shaky ground. His girlfriend had just told him she was dumping him and intended to marry his best friend. Darnel felt as if he'd been kicked in the stomach twice, and he was loaded for bear. Many sad souls take refuge in alcohol to drown their sorrows when life is cruel, but Darnel was an addict. Even drinking one or two beers inevitably led him into serious trouble. Once he started drinking, he couldn't stop. That night, he was even louder and more obnoxious than usual as he sounded off in the Ice Man Tavern.

Two men sitting at the bar asked him to tone down his filthy language and the volume of his voice, and Darnel's hair-trigger temper erupted into a full-blown anger meltdown. He saw an ice hockey stick leaning against the wall in a corner of the barroom, picked it up, and went after the two men who'd asked him to be quiet. Darnel turned into a madman. No one could restrain him. He kept chopping away with the hockey stick, beating on the heads of the two men and cursing them as their blood gushed out—onto the bar and the bar stools, the floor, and everything in sight. Darnel didn't stop until he'd beaten both of his critics to death.

One of the men was declared dead at the scene, and the other died within a few hours of being taken to the hospital. The bartender had taken refuge behind the beer kegs, and the other patrons of the bar were hiding under the tables, appropriately in fear of their lives. The only reason Darnel had halted his rampage was because another patron at the Ice Man had taken out his pistol and shot Darnel in both his knee caps.

Darnel's trial was short. He didn't get the death penalty because his public defender claimed he was suffering from emotional stress and had addiction issues. The jury hadn't bought any of this whining by Darnel's lawyer, who was working with a pretty sorry customer to begin with. But the judge had been lenient and decided, even though Darnel had viciously attacked and killed two people, the convicted double murderer would be given a sentence of only twenty-five years.

Darnel didn't cover himself with glory while he was in prison. His angry outbursts, that had cost him his girlfriend and put him in prison in the first place, also caused him a lot of grief inside the slammer. He would have been out of prison sooner if he'd behaved better. As it was, he was lucky to be released after serving eighteen of his twenty-five years of hard time.

Darnel didn't have an education, and he didn't have any skills. His future looked grim, but he was glad to be free. He didn't have much of a family. Finding his younger brother Fergus was the first thing Darnel Phillips planned to do when he left the Auburn Correctional Facility. Fergus Phillips was two years younger than Darnel, and he'd been more successful in school than Darnel had ever been. Fergus also had problems with alcohol and keeping a job, but he was able to control his anger better than Darnel could. Fergus hadn't made a huge success of his life, but he'd pretty much stayed out of trouble. After their mother died, the two brothers had lost touch—until Darnel was sent to prison.

When Darnel was incarcerated, Fergus had stepped up to the plate and tried to help his older sibling. He'd visited Darnel in prison every few months, and Fergus' visits had meant a great deal to Darnel. Then all of a sudden, Fergus had stopped visiting. He never came to see Darnel again. At first, Darnel was hurt, and then he was angry that his brother had abandoned him. Then he started to worry about why Fergus had stopped coming to visit. Darnel tried without success to contact Fergus, and he'd even asked men who were being released to look up Fergus on the outside. Darnel had an old address for Fergus, but no one was ever able to find him or give Darnel any news about his younger brother.

Counselors had urged Darnel to learn a trade while he was in prison. They'd tried to convince him to get his GED, but Darnel had always hated school and reading books and taking tests. He was not a good candidate for academic rehabilitation, and eventually even the most committed prison counselors, who wanted Darnel to learn a trade to be able to provide for himself after he was released from prison, gave up. At age forty-six, when Darnel left his institutionalized days and the Auburn Correctional Facility behind, he didn't know how to do much of anything and didn't have a way to support himself.

Chapter 14

***D**arnel Phillips took a taxi* to the halfway house in Auburn where his probation officer had arranged for him to live after he left prison. Anyone who has spent almost two decades of their life in an institution will have difficulty adjusting to living on the outside. The world had changed during that time, and eighteen years in the twenty-first century was ten times that many years of change in another century. Darnel experienced severe culture shock after leaving prison. A halfway house is the criminal justice system's attempt to ease former inmates back into society, to give them a chance to get used to the enormous transformations that have occurred in a world that has passed them by.

Darnel was thankful for the halfway house. He had no place else to go. He'd never really taken care of himself, even before he'd gone to prison, and spending eighteen years as a ward of the state wasn't the best way to encourage a person's self-reliance. Darnel needed someone to take care of him, and the people at the halfway house knew how to do that.

Darnel had been sporadically employed as a construction worker before he was sent to prison. When he was in his twenties, he'd easily been able to handle the grueling physical labor construction work demanded of the unskilled. Lifting heavy sections of concrete and spending hours in the hot sun digging tranches for a new sewer hadn't overly taxed the young man's abilities or stamina. The punishing existence had been a way to scratch out a meager living. But a man approaching age fifty was no longer able to do this kind of strenuous work. Darnel was relatively healthy, but he couldn't return to his former means of earning a living. He was too old. Having refused to pursue his GED or any kind of occupational training while incarcerated, he was destined to remain a member of the underclass. Darnel would probably manage to survive, either scraping by, compliments of New York State's generous welfare system, or by falling into some kind of criminal activity related to drugs or petty theft.

If not for the halfway house, Darnel would be homeless. Living on the streets might still be in the future for the ex-con. Darnel had been put in prison because of his violent temper and out-of-control behavior. It wasn't clear to his probation officer or the people at the halfway house if he had conquered those persistent demons. Darnel's best shot was that he would continue to be a ward of the state, his living expenses paid for, thanks to the generosity of New York State's taxpayers.

Darnel did have one goal on his post-prison agenda, however, and that was to try to find his younger brother, Fergus. Ferguson Phillips had last lived in an apartment in Dydonia, New York, about an hours' drive from Auburn. Darnel had the address from almost two decades earlier, and the first chance he had, he borrowed a car and drove to Dydonia to try to find the place where his brother had lived.

It had been a long time ago, and Fergus had rented the apartment for less than a year. When Darnel arrived in

Dydonia, he found the address no longer existed. Where an apartment building must once have stood eighteen years earlier, an aging Microtel and a run-down Denny's now filled the space along the street. Fergus' old address was no longer there, and no one on the block could remember that there had once been an apartment house in that location. All the businesses on the street were new. In reality, they were all pretty old, but they were new since Fergus Phillips' apartment house had been torn down. No one remembered the building where he'd lived, and no one remembered Fergus.

Darnel didn't understand how a human being could just disappear into thin air without anybody knowing where he'd gone and without anybody missing him. What had happened to Fergus and to his belongings? He'd owned clothes and furniture and stuff. He'd owned a truck, because Darnel had given him a truck. Where had all of that gone? Darnel didn't know what to do next. He'd hit a dead end trying to find Fergus' former home.

Darnel knew Fergus had worked several part-time jobs. Fergus had graduated from high school, but he'd never settled into a stable work life. Fergus had been a bartender, a waiter, a janitor, a security guard, a driver for an airport shuttle bus company, and probably had held other positions about which Darnel knew nothing. Darnel knew his younger brother had worked at these jobs, but he didn't know the actual names of any of the businesses or companies where Fergus had been employed. He didn't know where Fergus had been working when he stopped visiting Darnel in prison.

Darnel was almost certain something bad had happened to Fergus. At first Darnel had been hurt, wounded that Fergus had stopped visiting. They'd not had a falling out, but after a while, Fergus just stopped coming to the prison.

Because Fergus had ended their relationship so abruptly, Darnel thought he was probably dead.

Darnel wondered if anything that had been on Fergus's street still existed in Dydonia from before Darnel had gone to prison. Was there a bar or a restaurant or anything at all that was the same as it had been eighteen years earlier? It was as if the town that had existed before Darnel had gone to prison had completely disappeared, and now he was in an entirely different place. He searched and found a strip joint whose name sounded vaguely familiar. He wondered if he'd ever been drunk in the Polecat Grill. He didn't remember if he had or not, but it looked old enough from the outside, like it had been around for a long time. Darnel decided it wouldn't hurt to have a look inside. He wasn't allowed to drink alcohol, but his parole restrictions didn't say he was forbidden to look at naked women. He paid the entrance fee.

The Polecat Grill smelled like it hadn't been cleaned in twenty years. The stale beer odor that permeated everything in the dark bar was the same as it had been for decades. Thank goodness some things hadn't changed, Darnel smirked to himself. The interior, with its terrible sound system and depressing décor, seemed familiar. Darnel thought Fergus might have worked here, or maybe it was a friend of his brother's who had worked here. Somebody having something to do with Fergus had once had something to do with the Polecat Grill.

He'd be expected to order drinks if he wanted to stay and watch the show. He wondered if the waitress would laugh when he ordered a Doctor Pepper. If he sat down, he'd have to order something, so he decided to wander around the place first. Pretending to look for the restroom, he took his time walking to the back of the bar. Framed pictures of former "dancers" crowded every square inch of wall space in the back hall. The hair styles on the scantily clad women in the photographs dated back to the early 1980s.

Darnel had guessed correctly that the Polecat Grill had been around for a while. Trying to figure out what he was going to do, he used up time examining the photos on the wall. The women all looked the same to him, except for their various colors of hair and various colors of lingerie. Darnel's eyes had begun to glaze over when one picture jarred his memory. He thought he recognized one of the dancers. Something about the woman was familiar. The name scrawled on the corner of the photo was Patti Gaylord. The name didn't ring a bell with Darnel, but her face was definitely one he'd seen someplace before. She was pretty and seemed to be classier than the rest of the strippers, a cut above, if that were possible. He took the picture off the wall. The frame and the glass were dusty and greasy in his hands. The photo had been hanging there for a long time. Darnel knew he'd probably get scolded or fined for touching the picture and taking it down, but he wanted to show it to somebody and ask about Patti Gaylord.

Chapter 15

At the end of the wall covered with the dancers' pictures, there was a room with a sign that said "Office." Darnel knocked on the door. A cranky voice called out, "Who is it? Don't bug me, Vicky. I'll be out in a minute."

"It's not Vicky. My name's Darnel Phillips, and I want to ask you about one of your dancers."

"Go away, Darnel. We don't give out any personal information about our dancers. I'm busy. Goodbye." The door stayed closed.

"I'm looking for a missing person, my brother, and I think I might have known Patti Gaylord." There was silence from the other side of the door.

"Patti Gaylord? What do you know about Patti?" The name had piqued the man's curiosity, and the door opened.

An older, overweight man with beady eyes and Grecian Formula in his hair stared at Darnel. He looked at the framed photo Darnel held in his hand and grabbed it from Darnel. Darnel looked back into the eyes of the man who'd taken the picture from him. "I want to ask you about this woman. I think I might know her. Her face looks familiar, but her name doesn't mean anything to me."

The man continued to stare at Darnel, as if trying to place him among the thousands of former customers and hundreds of former employees who'd come and gone over the years through the doors of the Polecat Grill. "Do I know you? You never worked here, did you? I never forget a face, and yours isn't one I've seen before. How do you know Patti?"

"I've never worked here, although I may have been a customer once or twice, many years ago. I don't know Patti. I think I recognize her face, but I don't remember her name. What can you tell me about her? I'm Darnel Phillips."

The man squinted his eyes and scrutinized Darnel with disapproval and suspicion. Darnel, who was a sketchy-looking person to begin with, was sure the grumpy man standing in the doorway of the office could smell ex-con all over him. "Why do you want to know about Patti?" The man in the doorway wasn't giving an inch.

Darnel was trying to be as polite as he knew how to be. He wanted information and knew if he lost his temper, he wouldn't get any. "Like I said, she looks familiar to me. I'm trying to find my younger brother who went missing more than fifteen years ago. He used to come here, I think, and I think I came here with him once or twice. I used to be a drinker, so I don't remember lots of places I might have been to in the past."

The man in the doorway looked as if he understood what Darnel was telling him, about how he used to be a drinker. "Come on in." The man stepped aside to let Darnel into the office. "I used to be a drinker, too. Drinking lost me my wife and my girlfriend. Lost me my kids and almost lost me the Polecat Grill. I finally stopped with the booze and was able to hang on to this place, for what it's worth. It's a struggle, day to day, but I never promised myself a rose garden." The man laughed at his own joke and pointed to a chair. He sat down behind the battered wooden desk, cluttered with piles of papers and half-filled Styrofoam cups of cold coffee. "I'm Leon Koslowsky. I own this place." He stuck out his hand, and Darnel shook it.

Darnel wondered if Leon meant staying off the booze was a struggle or keeping the Polecat Grill in business was a struggle. He probably meant both. Darnel sat down and tried to explain. "My younger brother Fergus Phillips disappeared fifteen years ago. Fergus and I, we'd lost touch after our mother died. I got into some trouble, and Fergus and I started to get close again. Then all of a sudden he just disappeared, and I never heard squat from him. It's like he dropped off the face of the earth. I went to where he used to live, and his apartment house isn't there anymore. It's a motel now."

"You've been doing time, haven't you? It's okay. I can always tell. You have the look. Not everybody would see it, but I do. Did your brother disappear when you were inside?"

"Yes and yes. I've done my time in Auburn, and Fergus used to come and visit me there. We were getting along real good, and I got so's I looked forward to his visits. Then he stopped coming...for no reason. We didn't have an argument or anything like that. He just never came to see me again. I'm trying to find out what happened to him. He's my only kin."

"Darnel, the reason I didn't send you away and the reason I asked you to come in and talk to me is because you said your brother disappeared about fifteen years ago. Patti Gaylord also disappeared about fifteen years ago. Is there a connection between Patti and your brother?"

"I don't know if there's a connection. I came in here because the Polecat Grill is the only place that still exists around here from before I went into the slammer. Everything else is gone, torn down, something else in its place. I kind of remembered being here, once a long time ago, and I came to the Polecat to ask around, to try to find out if anybody remembered Fergus. I didn't expect to see a photograph of somebody that looked familiar to me up there on your wall of dancers. That was a shock. I don't know why she looks like somebody I've seen before, but she does. The name Patti might be right, but I don't know anybody named Gaylord."

"Patti Gaylord was her stage name. She used that name here when she danced on the pole and stripped. She was a beauty, and classy. Smart, too. I always wondered why she was working here. She seemed like the kind of dame who could have had a better kind of job, like as a secretary or a receptionist or something. Her real name was Patsy Grimes. She thought Gaylord sounded more artistic than Grimes and wanted to be billed as Gaylord." Leon was reminiscing about a woman who'd been one of his favorites.

Darnel didn't recognize the name Grimes either, but he thought the name Patsy was a name he'd heard his brother mention. There'd been somebody named Patsy who'd been a friend of his, somebody who'd worked with him or maybe lived near him. The name Patsy triggered a memory for Darnel, and it was coming back to him that his brother had once-upon-a-time talked about a woman named Patsy. She wasn't Fergus' girlfriend, but she was somebody he knew and liked a lot.

"I think Fergus might have known Patsy. I kind of remember him talking about a girl named Patsy. Did you say she'd also disappeared? Rotten luck, because I really need to find her and talk to her. If she was Fergus' friend, she might know what's happened to him. Can you give me her address? Or anything about where she lived or worked a day job? Anything at all?"

Leon was adamant. "I told you, she disappeared, more than fifteen years ago. She was scheduled to work one night and just didn't show up. That wasn't like her. She was always real responsible, unlike too many of the other girls who've worked here over the years. Patti was never late and never took a sick day. She was dependable. The customers loved her, and she got big tips. That may be why she kept working here. She made good money on tips. I was really angry when she didn't show up for her gig. When one of the girls doesn't dance, the men don't stay, and we don't sell drinks. I had somebody call her house, and there wasn't any answer. Then I started calling her. She was a good draw for customers, and I didn't want to lose her. I left a bunch of messages, but she never called back. Her answering machine was full after a while, and I finally stopped trying to reach her."

"Can you tell me where she used to live? Do you know anybody who was friends with her? If I can find her, she might know something about what's happened to Fergus."

"Or she and your brother Fergus night have left town together! She was seeing somebody, I know that, and it was serious. It was also a big secret, whoever it was she was dating. She wouldn't talk about it with any of the other girls. She'd been going with this guy for a while before she disappeared. The guy had money, I think. I often wondered if she'd run away with this man who had the money. I think she was in love with him, or she thought she was. But she kept any and all information about him to herself. Maybe the guy was your brother?" Leon didn't really think Darnel's brother was Patsy's secret lover, but he threw it out there anyway.

"My brother never had any money, and I'm sure the Patsy he talked about wasn't his girlfriend. I wish I could remember what he said about her. I can't remember much. I didn't even know her last name. I don't think he ever said it to me. Why would he?"

"Just between you and me, there was the slightest bit of a rumor the last few weeks she danced here, that Patsy was pregnant. I don't know if it was true, but a couple of the girls who knew her suspected she was. She didn't want to get rid of it. She was a beauty to begin with, but she'd taken on a kind of special glow just before she left. She'd put on some weight, and her boobs were bigger. I think that's why some of the other girls thought she was knocked up."

"Maybe she ran off with her boyfriend or went someplace to have the baby so no one would know."

"I gave that some thought when she disappeared, but that wasn't like her. If she'd been planning to leave, she would have given me notice in plenty of time. She was considerate, you know, a nice person. And she never came back to get her last paycheck. Most of the money my girls make is from tips, but they get a paycheck, too. Patsy's last check is still in her file."

"You still have a file on her? Do you have her address? I'd like any information you've got, anything that could help me track her down."

It took Leon a while to find Patsy's file. He rummaged through several filing cabinets, and finally found a thin, stained and dog-eared manila folder. An address and phone number were scribbled on the front. Darnel tried to read it, but the writing was too messy. Leon copied the information onto a scrap of paper, folded it, and handed it to Darnel. He opened the file and scanned the information inside. "She didn't have a family, I guess, because she doesn't give an emergency contact or a next of kin on her paperwork. That's all I've got. She didn't fill out anything much on her application form. She was so good looking and had a kind of presence about her, so I just hired her without worrying too much about all the forms. Here's her Social Security number. I don't think it would hurt anything, to give that to you now, so many years later." Leon wrote the Social Security number on another scrap of paper, folded it, and handed it to Darnel. "I've thought for a long time that Patsy was dead. I think she would have let me know, if she could have, even if she was leaving town in a hurry."

"Thanks, Leon. I appreciate you telling me what you know."

Leon picked up the file to put it away in an obscure filing cabinet in a corner of the room, when something fell out of the folder and floated to the floor. It was a tiny photograph, black and white and very faded. It showed a pretty young woman leaning against a not-so-pretty pickup truck. The photo was definitely meant to be of the woman's face. The beat-up truck was just part of the background. Leon picked up the photo and handed it to Darnel, "This is another picture of Patsy. I didn't even know this was in here."

Before Darnel ever had the photo in his hand, he knew the reason he'd recognized Patsy's face on the wall of the Polecat Grill. He'd seen another copy of this small photograph many years ago. Fergus had taken this picture, and he'd shown this photo or a copy of it to Darnel when he'd come to visit him in prison. The truck in the photo was Fergus' truck, and Darnel thought that, with a magnifying glass, he might be able to make out the numbers and letters on the license plate of the 1983 Dodge Ram that had once belonged to him and that he'd given to his brother. "Can I take this photo with me, Leon?"

"Sure, if you think it'll help. It's nothing to me. I've got this big one that's framed that I'm going to hang back up on the wall." He smiled at Darnel.

"I wasn't gonna steal Patti Gaylord's picture, Leon. Thanks for the help." Darnel took the tiny photo and left. He now felt as if he had something. What little he'd learned from Leon might turn out to be a dead end, but it was more than he'd had before he'd walked into the Polecat Grill.

Chapter 16

Darnel had a curfew at the halfway house, so he had to make it back to Auburn before he was late. He'd borrowed a car from one of his fellow halfway house inmates, and he'd promised the ex-con who'd loaned him the car that he'd be extra careful and not get stopped. Luckily, Darnel made it home to the halfway house in time. The man who'd lent him his car hadn't been thrilled about letting Darnel drive it in the first place, and he'd demanded that Darnel pay him to use the car, as well as pay for the gas. Darnel wasn't good at managing money, and he'd probably overpaid for the use of the car.

Darnel had long-term transportation problems. He would have to find a different solution. Dydonia was more than an hour's drive from his halfway house in Auburn. If he was going to do any investigating in the town where Fergus used to live, he was going to have to find a way to travel back and forth.

Darnel's driver's license had expired nearly two decades earlier. This presented a problem, and Darnel had purposely failed to mention anything about his license to the housemate who'd let him use the car. Darnel hadn't told the man he was going to drive the car without a valid driver's license. Darnel often couldn't be bothered with what he considered to be unimportant details. Darnel promised himself he would work on the driver's license thing. Darnel was very disorganized about getting things accomplished and negotiating the practical aspects of his life, but when he had a mission, he could focus.

He'd almost forgotten about the scraps of paper he had in his pocket. Darnel had been rushing to get back to Auburn because of the curfew and knew he wasn't going to have time to follow up on Patsy Grimes any more that night. When he unfolded the scribbled notes from Leon, he was shocked to read that Patsy's last known address was in the same apartment house where Fergus had lived. That's how they'd known each other; they'd lived in the same apartment building. Patsy's unit had been 2C and Fergus' unit had been 2D. Of course they had known each other; they'd been next door neighbors. The little photograph of Patsy standing by Fergus' pickup had probably been taken in the parking lot of their apartment complex.

Patsy's phone would have been disconnected years ago. That was a dead end for sure, but Darnel was desperate to find somebody who had also lived in the apartment house where Fergus and Patsy had lived. He wondered who had owned the building and who had managed the property for the owner. He was going to need a lot of help figuring out how to find these people.

Darnel didn't have a cellular phone. He had never used a computer, let alone a tablet or the internet. He was completely illiterate when it came to the technology of the digital world. So he not only had his own personality problems and his lack of skills and financial resources to deal with, he was way behind in terms of what was happening in the world.

A few people had begun to use cellular phones before Darnel had gone to prison, but they were mostly huge, cumbersome, complicated things business people carried around in their cars or very expensive flip phones rich people used to keep in touch with each other. Of course, he'd known about computers before he went to prison, and he'd even known some people who owned their own desk tops and laptops. But his job as a construction worker and his life as a person without a high school education, living close to the poverty line, had not made learning about computers, let alone owning one, a high priority.

The only way Darnel knew to find out anything was the old-school way, to walk around the neighborhood and ask questions in person. It was almost impossible to find out about anything that had happened eighteen years earlier, even using the latest technology to do research on the internet. Without knowing how to use a computer, Darnel was severely handicapped in any investigation he might undertake.

His ex-con housemate with the car wouldn't let him borrow it again, and getting a new driver's license was going to require Darnel to take a written test. Darnel didn't think he could pass a written test, and he wasn't even sure he could pass the practical part of the driver's test. He decided he would have to learn to ride the bus to Dydonia and back to make his inquiries.

What Darnel didn't realize was that public transportation services had been cut back in the almost twenty years since he'd been trying to function in the world. He'd driven a beat up pickup truck to work before he'd been arrested, and when he'd received his twenty-five year prison sentence, he'd signed his truck over to Fergus. Fergus had been thankful for the gift of the third-hand Ram, which had allowed him to get rid of his even older car. Fergus drove the truck to the prison when he came to visit. Darnel wondered what had happened to that truck. He figured that either Fergus and Patsy had run off together in the truck, or it had been abandoned in the parking lot of Fergus's apartment house. Now the truck was gone and the parking lot was gone.

Even though he'd given the truck to Fergus and the truck technically hadn't really belonged to Darnel for a long time, he wanted to find it. He had the bright idea to report it stolen. He reasoned that if the police found the truck, there might be clues inside about what had happened to Fergus. If the truck had been found in Dydonia, Darnel would know Fergus had never left town. If it had been found someplace else, Darnel would know where to begin his search. He didn't want to get involved with the police in any way, for any reason. But Darnel's determination to find his brother turned out to be more powerful than his fear of interacting with law enforcement.

Darnel decided to report the stolen truck to the Dydonia police. They would have jurisdiction. He rode the bus to Dydonia and was shocked at how much the bus ride cost him. He was also angry that there were so few buses that ran between Auburn and Dydonia. It was going to be a lot of work to ride the bus, and it was going to take forever to make the trip. Darnel was now obsessed, so the fact that all of his spare cash was going for cars, gas, and bus tickets didn't seem to bother him. He wanted to visit the Polecat Grill again and ask Leon more questions. He would walk to the Polecat after he'd reported the stolen truck.

When Darnel finally made it to the Dydonia Police Department, he was exhausted. He told the officer who took the report that the stolen Ram truck belonged to him. This was a lie, as Darnel had signed over the title of the truck to his brother Fergus years ago. Of course, when Darnel was asked for his driver's license, he didn't have one. When the police asked him about the truck's registration and insurance, he had nothing. When he reported the truck had last been seen almost twenty years earlier, the policeman who was taking his stolen vehicle report looked at him as if he were either demented or making a joke.

"We don't have time for jokes here, Mr. Phillips. How is it possible that you haven't seen your truck for almost twenty years? Why didn't you report it stolen earlier? There's not a chance we will ever be able to locate this vehicle. It's way past being long gone. I'll take your report and file it, but no one is going to spend any time looking for a truck that's been missing for two decades. You can file a claim on your insurance, but there's probably some kind of statute of limitations on how much time you have to file after your truck goes missing. I'm certain you're way outside that period of time, like by about seventeen years! Sorry I can't be more help." The policeman studied Darnel closely, and he realized the man had been in prison. Darnel could almost see things clicking inside the officer's head as he began to figure out why nearly two decades had passed without anyone reporting this vehicle MIA.

Darnel thanked the officer and left the station to go to the Polecat Grill to talk to Leon. Maybe he would have better luck there. He couldn't have worse luck. The truck was gone, and it had been gone for a very long time. It had probably been stolen from the parking lot where the little photograph of Patsy Grimes had been taken. Darnel wasn't ever going to find the Dodge Ram.

Darnel was tired and decided to take a taxi to the Polecat Grill. He looked around for a phone booth where he could call a cab to come and pick him up and drive him to the Polecat. It took him a while to figure out that there weren't any phone booths around anymore. He'd seen everybody with a cell phone, staring at them as they rode on the bus from Auburn, but he hadn't put that together with the fact that most of the phone booths in the world no longer existed. He gave up and walked to the Polecat Grill. His shoes were too tight, and his feet were killing him by the time he got to the strip joint.

He paid the entrance fee and walked to the back hall where he knew Leon's office was located. Leon wasn't there, and his office was locked. Darnel was having a really terrible day. He'd already paid to watch the show, so he sat down at a table in the bar and ordered a Doctor Pepper. The waitress didn't laugh; she didn't even bat an eye.

"You look like you could use a little company. What are you so down about?" A woman of about forty-five sat down at Darnel's table. He didn't know if she was just trying to be friendly or if she was trying to get him to pay for her services as a sex worker. He was allowed to look at naked women, but his parole officer frowned on his hiring a prostitute. The woman didn't really look like a prostitute, so Darnel decided it was all right to talk to her.

"I am very down. I'm looking for somebody, and I don't think I'm ever going to be able to find him. Actually, I'm looking for two somebodies, and I'm never going to find either one of them."

"Who are you looking for?" The woman seemed to really want to know.

"I'm looking for my younger brother, but the reason I'm here at the Polecat Grill is because I'm looking for Patsy Grimes. She used to dance and strip here under the name of Patti Gaylord."

"I knew Patsy, or at least I used to know her a very long time ago. I was a dancer here, too. Now I'm a waitress, bookkeeper, part-time bartender, and janitor. I'm Vicky. I don't dance on the pole any more. I'm way, way past my pole dancing days. Patsy was a classy lady, especially to be working in a place like this. She just disappeared one day, never came to work again. She didn't tell any of the rest of us girls that she was leaving, and she never gave notice to Leon. He was real upset to lose Patsy."

"I talked to Leon a couple of days ago, and he told me he'd thought a lot of Patsy."

"She was a cut above the rest of us. I think she might have gone to college, for a few years anyway. Maybe she didn't graduate, but she was real smart and knew a lot of stuff. She had a boyfriend she claimed was going to marry her. He was unhappily married and was going to leave his wife. Isn't that what they always say? And it never happens. At first, she talked about what a great guy her boyfriend was, but then she started to show up with these awful bruises all over her arms and back. I knew he'd been beating her. She had to put on lots of makeup to cover up the bruises when she stripped and danced on the pole. I used to help her put the makeup on her back, where she couldn't reach, you know? She thought she was fooling people about how she got the bruises, but she didn't fool me. I don't think she actually knew how bad she was bunged up on her back. She must have been in a lot of pain. She had open wounds sometimes, bleeding and all. It was terrible."

"Do you have any idea who this boyfriend was? The one who beat her?"

"She kept that under wraps, said he was somebody important. Nobody ever knew who he was or where he was from. He never came in here. Some of us thought she was knocked up, just before she left. She'd gained weight and seemed tired all the time. When she first hooked up with this boyfriend, she was like, on cloud nine. Then towards the end, she was really down. She never smiled and seemed very depressed. I was worried that she was going to do something to herself."

"You mean, like take her own life?"

"Yeah, like that. She had this empty, lonely look in her eyes, as if she'd lost everything and didn't even care anymore. I have to tell you, I wasn't that surprised when she disappeared. I figured the next thing, they'd be dragging her body out of the river. But they never did. She was a nice woman. I wish I knew what had happened to her, but whatever it was, I know it wasn't good. What does this have to do with your brother?"

"Fergus, my brother, lived next door to Patsy, and they were friends. He wasn't her boyfriend or anything like that. I figured if I could find Patsy, she might know something about what had happened to Fergus. Now I guess that's a dead end."

"I wish I could do something to help you. I know when Patsy disappeared, Leon spent a lot of time and money trying to find her. He even went out to the place where she lived and demanded the supervisor in her apartment house let him into her apartment. He was afraid she was dead in there. Finally, the super opened the door and walked around Patsy's apartment with Leon. There was a lot of spoiled food in the refrigerator, but no Patsy, dead or alive. I think they finally figured she wasn't coming back, and somebody boxed up her stuff and gave it away. They painted the apartment and rented it to somebody else. Later, they tore the place down, I guess."

"The apartment house isn't there anymore. I wanted to go there and ask the neighbors about Fergus, when they last saw him and where he was working. I went to the address where his apartment used to be, and it's a motel now with a Denny's next to it. I came back today to talk to Leon. I was hoping he could tell me who owned the apartment house where Patsy and Fergus lived or something more about Patsy's friends."

"You've been in prison, haven't you? I can tell. You're pale; you have prison pallor. Patsy hasn't been around for more than fifteen years. How long has your brother been missing?"

"Fergus has been missing for fifteen years, so I can't help but think their disappearances are connected. What can you tell me about Patsy?"

"She didn't have many friends, kept to herself most of the time. She was a loner. Didn't want to talk about her past, like where she grew up or her family. If she had any family, she never talked about them, and I doubt she'd seen or heard from them in years. She didn't want to talk about what she was up to in the present day either. Definitely a loner. Sorry I can't help you. I was sorry to see Patsy go. She was nice to all of us; she didn't have a mean bone in her body."

"I appreciate you telling me about Patsy. My brother thought a lot of her. I don't know what to do now. Both Patsy and Fergus disappeared into thin air, and I'm afraid I'm going to have to give up and just accept that."

"Did you ever file a missing persons' report? For your brother? I guess it's been a really long time now, since you last saw him. If you've never filed a report, I don't know if the police would even let you file one after this many years."

"I never filed any report. I was in prison, and I didn't know how to do that anyway. Now I wish I had. I was just so bummed at first that Fergus had deserted me. It took me a while before I admitted to myself that something real bad might have happened to him."

"I don't understand why nobody would file a missing persons' report. I tried to talk Leon into filing a report when Patsy went missing, but he wouldn't do it. He said he knew she was being abused by her boyfriend, and he thought she'd probably chosen to disappear to get away from the guy. He thought he was protecting her by not asking the police to look for her. I think he believed one day she would get in touch with him and say she was sorry she'd not given him any notice before she ran away."

"I wanted to talk to Leon about the building where Patsy and my brother lived. It's not there anymore, and nobody knows anything about it. I thought Leon might have the name of the owner or the super who managed it. You said he went over there and made the super let him into her apartment. Maybe he remembers the name of the guy. I thought about trying to find out who owned the building fifteen years ago, but the super would be more likely to know Patsy and Fergus than the owner would be. The only thing is, if I could find the owner, and if he's still alive and living around here, he might be able to put me in touch with the super. I have to tell you, I'm really discouraged. I'm almost ready to give up on my search. The goal of finding Fergus was what kept me going in prison. It was all I could think about, and it was the one thing I promised myself I would do, the first thing I would do, when I got out. Now I have nothing."

"Leon isn't here today, but I happen to know there's one of Patsy's boxes in the basement. I didn't know it was there, and I know Leon's forgotten all about it. I don't know if it's stuff from her dressing room here at the Polecat or stuff he packed up from her apartment. I was down in the basement a few weeks ago, looking for something, and ran across it. It's taped up and marked with the name 'Patsy Grimes.' It's all mildewed, and when I saw that box, I promised myself I would get down there and start throwing things away. There are hundreds of boxes covered with mildew in that disgusting basement. Who knows what's in any of them?"

"Can you show me the box? I don't think Leon would care if I opened it and took a look. He seemed to want to help when I was here before."

"Sure. I'll take you down there. It smells pretty bad, so beware. I think I can find Patsy's box again. It's a mess of stuff. Leon isn't into neat and tidy or cleaning things out. He just exists day to day. I'd like to go down and clean it out, get rid of it all. But Leon keeps me busy doing so many other jobs, I can't ever take the time to do anything like that. Cleaning has never taken a priority in this place, as I'm sure you've noticed. If Leon can stay one step ahead of the health department, he thinks he's the king of the world."

"I'd like to see that box, Vicky, if you can show it to me. Can you show me now? I don't think Leon would mind if I went through the box. I promise I won't take anything. If there's anything in there that looks valuable or interesting, Leon can have it. I don't want anything from the box, I just want to see if there are any clues in there about what happened to Patsy and Fergus."

"I completely understand, but you have to be prepared to be disappointed. There have been several floods in the basement, and the box I think is Patsy's is completely covered up with mildew. I'll go down there with you and show you the box, but I don't think you can bring it upstairs to look through it. I'm afraid it will disintegrate when you pick it up."

They went down into the damp and moldy basement. The smell was worse than anything Darnel had smelled in prison, and there are plenty of bad smells in a prison. It was obvious no one had tried to clean up from the floods over the years, and the subterranean space had been used as a dumpster. Darnel could hear the rats scurrying ahead of them as they made their way toward where Vicky remembered Patsy's box had been left. The smell didn't seem to bother Vicky, but it made Darnel sick to his stomach. They finally found the box, and just as Vicky had said, it was covered with mildew. It had been sitting in water for who knows how long, and the sides of the box had collapsed. Darnel was sure the bottom was completely gone. The cardboard was damp, and the tape came away easily. Even after the box was opened, it was impossible to tell what was inside, it was so engulfed by mold. Vicky looked into the gray morass and declared it a total loss. "I'm sorry, there's nothing in here that can be salvaged."

Darnel didn't agree. This was his last and only clue, and he was determined to pick through the mess piece by piece, searching for the most elusive remnant that might provide him with a lead. The mice and rats had definitely been in the box before him. There were rotten clothes on top. Darnel carefully examined each piece of fabric, even when it fell apart in his hands. There were shoes and makeup scattered under the clothes, and these were too nasty to handle. Darnel found a stick and lifted the shoes out onto the floor. He wished he had some protective gloves. A tin box was the last thing in the cardboard box. The bottom of the tin box was rusted through. The few papers inside the tin box had been soaked in one of the basement floods and were pretty much unreadable. To Darnel, however, these looked like a real find.

Vicky was ready to leave the basement, and she said, "Oh, come on, bring those with you. Bring the tin box, or whatever you can carry. I need to get out of here. The smell is getting to me. Those papers look like a total loss, but you can look at them upstairs. Believe me, Leon is never going to care if you take them with you."

They went back up the stairs, and Vicky disappeared into the ladies' room to clean up. Darnel went into the men's room. He hated to put down his precious find, even to wash his hands. When he came out of the bathroom, Vicky handed him a gallon-size Ziploc bag to hold the contents of the crumbling tin box. Darnel was anxious to go through the papers piece by piece to see if he could find anything. He smiled at Vicky. "Thank you so much. There probably isn't anything here, but at least I will have pursued every possible avenue to try to find my brother. My expectations are very low, as always, and this is my last hope. You have been a big help to me."

"Good luck with your search." As Darnel left, Vicky felt terribly sad. He was such a sad man with such a sad life. He was so desperate to find his brother Fergus, and she knew he never would. Vicky was sad just watching Darnel's back as he left the Polecat. No matter how sad she thought her own life was at times, there was always somebody whose life was sadder. She decided not to tell Leon about Darnel's visit and their foray into the basement. Leon could be moody, and he might not like it that Vicky had allowed anybody go through Patsy's things.

Chapter 17

Gimbel Saunders had run into a dead end when he'd tried to find the two psychiatrists who supposedly had collaborated with Norman Parsons to have his wife committed to a state mental institution in 2001. Their names were buried somewhere in the paper morass of the past twenty years, and Gimbel was never able to find out who they were. But some court records from the past had been digitized, and Gimbel had found one line on the internet that gave him the name of the judge who'd signed the commitment order for Rosalind Parsons in 2001. Unfortunately, that judge had died six years earlier. Gimbel had no idea how to find Rosalind's obstetrician, the person he most wanted to talk to right now. His second best strategy was to try to find somebody at Syracuse University who had known Rosalind when she'd been a student there.

So many years had passed, Gimbel was not very hopeful that he would be able to find out anything useful. He knew Rosalind had received her PhD from the Computer Science Department. At the end of the twentieth century, that department had been relatively new and relatively small. Now it was a huge department. Computer technology had grown to be one of the most popular majors at the university. Gimbel doubted if there was anybody from almost twenty years earlier who was still working there. He made an appointment to meet with the chairman of the department.

The chairman was in fact a chairwoman, and she hadn't lived in New York State at the time of the triple murder. She'd heard the stories about what had happened to Rosalind and Norman Parsons, but she did not have any first-hand information. She agreed to meet with Gimbel and said she was anxious to help. When Gimbel went to her office, she sent one of her administrative assistants to the archives to find Rosalind's academic file.

The file revealed what Gimbel already knew, that Rosalind had received her PhD in computer science in June of 2000. Her advisors were listed. The only new item of information Gimbel learned from the file was that a man named Eberhardt Grossman had been one of Rosalind's original thesis advisors. For whatever reason, he had removed himself from her three-person dissertation committee. Someone else, a Dr. Benjamin Sikirt had taken Grossman's place.

There was no mention of anything about Rosalind's personal life other than the fact that she had listed Norman Parsons, M.D. as her emergency contact person. Gimbel wanted to talk to both Grossman and Sikirt. The current department chairman told Gimbel that sadly Eberhardt Grossman had died in one of the World Trade Center towers on 9/11. Grossman was never going to be able to tell him anything. Sikirt had retired three years earlier and was now living in Ft. Meyers. Florida.

The chairwoman made a copy of Rosalind's file for Gimbel Saunders to take with him and apologized that she hadn't been more help. The visit to Syracuse University had turned out about the way Gimbel had imagined it would. He thanked the chairwoman for her help and decided he would try to track down Benjamin Sikirt, PhD in Ft. Meyers. Gimbel would speak with the man on the phone, if he was still alive, and if he seemed like a promising source of information, Gimbel would fly to Florida to speak with him in person.

Sikirt was an unusual name, and Gimbel easily found an address and landline listed for the man. After three tries, Gimbel finally connected with the elderly professor who spoke English with his British Indian accent. Sikirt had been born in Bombay, which was now Mumbai, and he'd been educated in London before he came to work in the United States. Benjamin Sikirt was happy to speak with Gimbel over the phone, but Gimbel suspected from the way he talked that the man was in the early stages of dementia. The good news was that sometimes, those with memory disorders remember things from the more distant past, even when they couldn't remember if they'd eaten breakfast that morning. This seemed to be the case with Sikirt. He said he remembered Rosalind Parsons from his days as a professor at Syracuse.

"I was one of Rosalind's three thesis advisors, but I wasn't on the original committee. She was assigned to me when her thesis was nearly completed. I was puzzled about why Eberhardt Grossman wanted me to take over from him, really at the last minute, just before she had to defend her dissertation."

"Did you ask Grossman why he was dropping her as an advisee?"

Sikirt was silent on the other end of the line for a while, as if he were trying to recall something. "It had to do with her husband. He was a physician at the university hospital in Syracuse, and he abused her. Eberhardt had told me about the abuse, and he tried to get me to talk to Rosalind about it. He wanted her to go to the police, but she wouldn't talk to me about anything personal. Eberhardt had guided Rosalind through the long and difficult process of doing her research and writing the dissertation. I really didn't have much of anything to do with it. I always wondered why Eberhardt reassigned her to me. Rosalind wrote a brilliant thesis and defended it magnificently. That's all I really remember. I didn't know her very well."

"She wasn't pregnant when she defended her dissertation, was she?"

"No, it wasn't obvious to anyone that she was pregnant at the time, and I never saw her again after she defended her dissertation and was granted her PhD. Of course, I heard about her murder and all of that sad business. What a tragedy, and what a waste. She had a very fine mind and would have made an excellent college teacher."

"Do you have any idea how far along she was in her pregnancy when she died?"

"Like I said, I never saw her again after she got her PhD. I did hear she'd come back to the department in January, several months after she'd received her degree. Somebody said they'd seen her wearing a cape and that she was obviously pregnant at the time. I didn't see her myself. That's all I know."

"Is there anything else about Rosalind that you remember, something that might be important?"

"Like I said, I really didn't know her. One thing about Eberhardt, though, and I don't think this is relevant at all, to anything. He was an albino. He was a handsome man and wasn't odd looking or anything. You had to look closely to be able to tell he was albino, and he did try to cover up his very white skin with some kind of lotion that made him look not so white. We knew he was an albino, so it wasn't a secret. I guess he wore the contact lenses and darkened his skin so he wouldn't stand out so much. We used to laugh about his ultra-white skin and my dark skin. There was a Chinese guy in the department, too, and he would join in. Back in the good old days, we could joke around about the different colors of our skin. That would never be allowed today. Eberhardt was a very nice man and an excellent teacher. He knew more about computers than all the rest of the people in the department put together, including me. His death was a real loss."

Gimbel thanked the professor for his time and the information he'd provided. Gimbel hoped he'd understood everything the man had tried to tell him. There was no reason to go to Florida. Gimbel had gleaned one tiny clue from Sikirt, but it was a critical clue for Gimbel. Rosalind Parsons had been seen wearing a cape in January, and she'd been obviously pregnant at the time. It wasn't scientific confirmation, but combined with the other information he'd collected, it was enough for Gimbel Saunders to conclude that the woman who had died in the fire in April of 2001 was definitely not Rosalind Parsons.

Gimbel had no idea who the pregnant woman was who had died in Rosalind's house, but if Rosalind Parsons hadn't died in the fire, what had happened to her? Where was she? Had she given birth to her child? Had she murdered her husband? Had she murdered the other two people who'd died in her house? There were now more questions than answers, but Gimbel was certain his conclusion about Rosalind was right. She hadn't died in the triple murder. But where did he go from here? There were no more leads. He was at a dead end.

Gimbel moved on to other cold cases, but he remained fascinated with the Rosalind Parsons puzzle. He continued to check databases to see if anyone was looking for a man or a woman who'd disappeared in April of 2001. As the years went by, more and more old police records as well as court records had been digitized and were available on the internet. Computerizing data was not intended to provide more information to police departments or to anybody else. The intent was to save space. Paper records require a lot of storage, so law enforcement agencies made it a priority to computerize their new and old records rather than maintain large warehouses full of paperwork from past decades.

Chapter 18

Gimbel *got a call one* afternoon to report to his captain's office. Gimbel thought everyone had completely forgotten he existed, so a call from Captain Henry Pressor was a surprise. Gimbel knew he hadn't done anything wrong, but he always wondered if his pursuit of the Parsons case had ruffled some feathers or stirred up a new hornet's nest. He was ready to defend his actions when he knocked on the captain's door.

"Gimbel, come in, we have a situation, and I need your help. I know you aren't cleared for regular duty, but I think what I'm going to ask you to do will be all right with your doctors."

Gimbel had moved beyond being angry about the heart condition that kept him on less than full-time duty, so he was able to smile at the captain and ignore the remark about his health. "I feel good, Henry, what have you got for me?" Gimbel was relieved the call to the captain's office had not been about the Parsons case.

"We have a murder in Skaneateles, a very odd situation, and you are the man to take this case. They've not had a murder in Skaneateles in a hundred years or so, and they've called us in to investigate. Their police department is really great at handing out parking tickets and keeping parades under control, but it isn't up to investigating anything very complex, like this two-corpse mess is turning out to be. The Onondaga Sheriff's Department is completely overwhelmed with their latest big drug bust, so Skaneateles PD and the sheriff's office have asked me to find somebody to look into what's happened over there."

"What's happened over there?" Gimbel was anxious for Henry Pressor to stop blabbering and get to the point.

"The cook at the Sherwood Inn found two people dead in a van in the Sherwood's parking lot. Nobody noticed that this seafood delivery van was parked at the back of the parking lot and hadn't moved for a couple of days, until somebody noticed the smell. Employees are supposed to park in the back, to leave parking spaces for the customers closer to the entrance. Two employees noticed a really bad smell coming from the van that delivers seafood to the Sherwood on a regular basis. When the workers noticed the smell, they told the cook the seafood delivery van was still sitting in the back of the parking lot and was stinking to high heaven."

"The cook came out to investigate and found a really grisly scene. The van wasn't locked, and when he opened the driver's side door to investigate, the cook vomited and collapsed in the parking lot. He's overweight and has something going on with his heart, so he was immediately taken to the hospital. Before they took him away, he said he knew the driver of the van. The driver was the guy who always brought the Sherwood's seafood order into the kitchen. He knew the man's name was Dirk, but he'd never heard his last name. Dirk, the driver, is a white guy, and the other dead guy looks Hispanic. He's got brown skin and dark hair."

"How did they die, the two people in the van?"

"I just got the call a half hour ago, and I called you right away. So we don't know much. There's blood everywhere in the van, and the meter maid who's guarding the crime scene thinks both men had their throats cut. She was told not to open the door until you get there, so she only knows what she can see through the windshield and the windows. There's so much blood and so many flies, I think it's almost impossible to see anything."

"You have a meter maid guarding the crime scene?"

"Yeah, crime scene investigations are not usually a top priority in Skaneateles. They don't have any crime scene technicians. They have more threats against the tax assessor than they do actual crimes in the town. They couldn't even put their hands on any crime scene tape. You're authorized to take a whole team with you. I'll send the ME and everybody else you need. This is kind of a weird one, I'm afraid. That's why I want you on it, you and your sixth sense. We may need that voodoo to solve this case."

"Is that all you know?"

"That's all anybody knows at this point. Take the helicopter. There's a landing pad at the fire station in Skaneateles, which is close enough to the Sherwood. I've got a team on standby waiting to go with you."

Gimbel was excited to have an active case. It had been a long time. No matter how weird it turned out to be or how bloody, he couldn't wait to get to the scene and start figuring it out. He was very good at this, and he knew that was why his captain, Henry Pressor, had called him to be the chief investigator. Gimbel grabbed his gear and almost ran to the waiting helicopter. He loved Skaneateles and the Sherwood Inn. He sometimes drove from Syracuse just to have dinner at the Sherwood.

The meter maid had done a good job of keeping the crime scene secure. When Gimbel got out of the squad car that delivered him to the rear of the Sherwood Inn parking lot, he was overwhelmed by the stench. It wasn't just the smell of two dead bodies; it was also the smell of spoiled seafood. The combination was not at all a good one. No wonder the cook had been sick and fainted. Gimbel looked at the meter maid with renewed respect.

Employees at the Sherwood had to know about the murders, but it didn't look as if any guests had found out yet that something bad had happened at the inn. Customers were coming and going from the restaurant as they usually did. That would change once the full CSI team arrived. Maybe the rain that the weatherman said was coming would keep the Sherwood's guests from wanting to see what was going on with a bunch of policemen and the big tent that was going to appear in the parking lot. What were the chances? Gimbel spoke with the manager of the Sherwood Inn and explained what had happened and what was going to happen. The man had been understanding, although of course he hated that a horrible double murder had occurred in the parking lot of his hotel.

They began to set up the tent to keep curious eyes from viewing the murder scene and to keep the rain from destroying any evidence in the vicinity of the van. Gimbel thanked the meter maid and asked her to make herself available for questioning. He opened the driver's side door of the van and the smell was so pungent, bile rose in his throat. Flies were so thick, the bodies looked black and not just from dried blood. One quick look let Gimbel know the two men's throats had been cut. When the van was running and the air conditioning had been turned on, everything in the rear compartment was being refrigerated to keep the seafood at the proper temperature, but when the van was turned off or ran out of gas, no part of the van was being cooled.

Gimbel's eyes scanned the inside of the van, and he knew at once it had been searched. Neither man's cell phone was anywhere to be found. Everything that might have been a clue was gone. Wearing protective gloves so he wouldn't contaminate the scene, Gimbel carefully reached into the driver's pants pockets to extract his wallet. The North Carolina driver's license said his name was Dirk Shannon. Gimbel dropped the wallet into an evidence bag and handed the bag to a crime scene technician. He left the driver's door open and walked around to the passenger door. He found the Hispanic man's wallet with a Florida identity card that said his name was Pedro Ruiz. He put the second wallet into an evidence bag. It would not be difficult to establish the cause of death, but determining *why* these two seafood delivery guys had been brutally murdered would be more challenging. There had to be more to this than seafood. The van's license plates said North Carolina. They'd driven a long way just to deliver fresh shrimp.

It took all night to process the crime scene, and the rain was coming down in torrents by the time the bodies had been driven to the Onondaga county morgue in Syracuse and the contents of the van had been bagged and tagged. The smell had made the work difficult, and even after the bodies had been removed, the rotting seafood in the back of the van kept everyone close to their barf bags. Three days earlier, the seafood had been packed with ice, but after the van had been sitting in the parking lot in the sun for two days, the ice had melted. Soaking wet cardboard boxes of shrimp, crabmeat, fish, and oysters in the shell had spoiled and begun to reek.

Something nagged at the back of Gimbel's neck as he watched the boxes of seafood being unloaded from the van and transferred to a crime scene vehicle. The boxes of seafood were evidence, but something about all that shrimp wasn't computing for Gimbel. A less conscientious investigator might just have thrown the stinking boxes of seafood into the dumpster to get rid of it. Gimbel would not do that, but he wasn't sure what it was that he didn't like about the seafood—besides the terrible stench, of course. He gave orders to refrigerate all the boxes of bad seafood. Every one of them would have to be searched the next day before the contents could be thrown away.

Gimbel and his team searched the van again for cell phones or any paperwork that might indicate where the deliveries of seafood were to have been made. Only the wallets had been left behind, and Gimbel wondered if the men's real names were even Dirk and Pedro. Those could have been phony names they used for the purposes of distributing their wares around New York State and New England.

The next morning, Gimbel was the first law enforcement person to get to the refrigerated boxes of seafood. He wanted the search videotaped in case it turned up anything of importance that could be used in court. Everything had to be documented these days. Trust in law enforcement was low in many places, and Gimbel Saunders didn't want to be accused of either cutting corners or planting evidence. His "women's intuition" was telling him the key to the murders was in the boxes of spoiled seafood.

The seafood had been packaged in ten-pound boxes. Three ten-pound boxes were held together with strong plastic strapping tape. Boxes were clearly marked as shrimp or crabmeat or flounder, etc. Dirk would just have to cut the plastic strapping and pick up the number of boxes he needed to fill an order. There was a dolly in the back of the van, and Gimbel could imagine Dirk grabbing two ten pound boxes of shrimp, a ten pound box of crab, and a box of flounder and piling up the four boxes on the dolly. He would have delivered the four boxes of seafood to the Sherwood Inn kitchen.

Each white box was made of insulated, waxed cardboard, designed especially to keep the seafood cold and to keep the ice that was packed with the seafood from melting. Each box was printed with the Coastal Carolina Seafood name and logo in dark blue. All the boxes in the back of the truck were bound together into stacks of three boxes each. Each was clearly marked as to its contents. A delivery person would have no problem selecting the boxes to be delivered for each order.

Gimbel had to open only two stacks of boxes before he found what he'd suspected would be there. The top container in each stack contained exactly what the box indicated it contained. The top box in all the stacks of three contained some kind of fresh seafood—raw shrimp, or crabmeat, or fish. In many of the stacks, however, the second and third boxes contained not any seafood at all, but held packages of heroin and fentanyl, carefully wrapped in waterproof plastic. Gimbel noted that each of the boxes that contained drugs was stamped with a red star. Dirk and Pedro had been delivering seafood in upstate New York, but more importantly, they had been delivering huge volumes of lethal drugs packed in boxes not very heavily disguised underneath the iced boxes of shrimp and crabmeat. The seafood had literally been the "cover" for the more lucrative product, the killer illegal drugs.

Two more teams were called in to process the boxes of seafood and the drugs, and by noon, the packages of drugs had been weighed and locked away. The offending seafood had been taken to the dump.

Gimbel didn't think the cook at the Sherwood Inn knew about the drugs in the van, but nevertheless, he had to question the poor man about it. The cook had found the bodies, and he'd been buying his seafood on a regular basis from these very bad fellows who had come to a very bad end.

Gimbel went to the hospital where the chef, Dimitri Kouris, was recovering from a minor heart attack and the shock of finding two dead men covered with flies and blood in the seafood delivery van. Dimitri was a gifted cook, but he was also a very emotional Greek man. He could cry or fly into a rage at the drop of a hat. He was difficult to deal with and kept his job at the Sherwood only because of his exceptional culinary skills.

Gimbel got right to the point with Dimitri. "It must have been quite a shock to see your friend Dirk and the other man in the delivery van, dead like that, with their throats cut. And all those flies."

Dimitri turned white as a sheet, and Gimbel almost regretted confronting him as aggressively as he had. "It was horrible, to find somebody dead like that, but Dirk is not really my friend. He just delivers the shrimp and the crabmeat and the other stuff I order. I only know him from when he brings the seafood into the kitchen."

"How often does he bring you fresh seafood? Does he always come on the same day every week?"

"He always comes on Tuesdays. Every Tuesday and only Tuesday."

"I noticed his van has North Carolina license plates. Why do you have your seafood delivered all the way from North Carolina?"

"The arrangement for the seafood has been the same since before I started working at the Sherwood. The previous chef had set it all up. We get the seafood very fresh and at an excellent price. When I took over, I checked around, and I couldn't get a better deal. Dirk is dependable, and his seafood is always the best. It's also the least expensive. I don't know how they do it, bringing it up from North Carolina and all. It's never late, and it is always fresh caught. I have high standards. I wouldn't buy it if it wasn't primo."

"Has Dirk been delivering the seafood ever since you took over as head chef at the Sherwood?"

"It's always Dirk who brings in the seafood. I don't know that he ever took a vacation. He was as regular as clockwork."

"How did you place your orders for the next week?"

"I called Dirk on his cell phone every Monday morning and told him what I needed for the week. I have other sources for lobsters and cod and other kinds of fish, but I always got my shrimp and crabmeat and flounder from Dirk."

"Do you have your cell phone here with you at the hospital? I'd like to have that number you called to place the orders—Dirk's cell phone number."

Dimitri fumbled around and couldn't find the phone. He finally had to call the nurse to come and find it. "Actually, I have a couple of numbers I used to reach Dirk. There is one number I always called him on, but he often called me back from different phone numbers."

Gimbel carefully wrote everything down. These cell phone numbers might be a valuable source of information. They were probably prepaid phones, but he might be able to trace them, unless whoever had taken them from the van had thrown them away and destroyed the chips.

"Thanks for your help, Dimitri. I hope I don't have to bother you again. Try to put this behind you and get well. It's a terrible thing to have to see what you saw, but you can get past it."

Dimitri nodded and sank back in his hospital bed. Gimbel loved eating at the Sherwood and hoped Dimitri would be able to recover enough to resume his position as head chef there. He might be emotionally fragile, but he was a great cook.

The two dead men had no criminal records, as far as the various fingerprint and facial recognition databases were able to tell. Dirk Shannon had a few speeding tickets in New York and in Pennsylvania, but there was nothing worse than that in the computer. The absence of a criminal record was not unusual for a drug courier. Drug couriers were allowed to operate until they were caught. Once they were in the system, they were no longer eligible for the courier jobs. Neither Dirk and Pedro would ever again be eligible for any kind of job.

The question for Gimbel was not that the two had been murdered. The drug world took no prisoners, and in the drug world, death by murder was almost as inevitable as death by overdose. The puzzling part of the scenario was why whoever had killed the two couriers hadn't also taken the drugs from the back of the van. Whoever had slit the throats of the two must have known some of the seafood boxes in the back were stuffed with heroin and fentanyl. Whoever had done the killing had left more than two million dollars' worth of street drugs behind. Gimbel realized he probably would never be able to solve this crime in the traditional sense. The chances were almost nonexistent that he would ever find the individual who had actually killed these two men. What he hoped he could find out during his investigation was information about the drug distribution system the two dead men had been a part of.

Drugs were everywhere in the United States. They were in the small towns in the Midwest, the South, and throughout the country. They were in the big cities in every state. No age group was exempt. No socio-economic strata or occupation was left untouched by the scourge. The patterns of use were similar throughout the country, too. Doctors were being pressured to prescribe fewer opioids. Addicts who no longer had access to these addictive pain killers, turned to a combination of heroin and fentanyl to feed their habits.

As marijuana became legal in more and more states, illegal pot distribution was no longer as lucrative, so drug dealers had turned to the hard stuff. It was almost as if there was no longer any stigma attached to dealing drugs or doing drugs. The picture of two Ohio grandparents sitting in their car, completely zonked out from their drug use, with their toddler grandchild looking confused and helpless in the backseat, haunted Gimbel. People who would never have used drugs in past decades had become addicts as well as fatalities of the current drug epidemic. It was a demand driven industry, and despair and hopelessness, loss of jobs, and any number of other maladies drove the demand. Gin had destroyed Gimbel's childhood. In the present-day, much more potent demons of addiction threatened to destroy an entire generation of childhoods.

Gimbel immediately put one of his people on tracing the cell phone numbers. It was too much to expect that they would find the phones, but they had several phone numbers they now could trace. If they could track the call history of the phones, they might be able to find something.

The only other evidence found in the van was a set of magnetic signs stacked on one side of the rear cargo area. The signs were standing on their edges, between the boxes of seafood and drugs and the side of the van. The signs probably hadn't been noticed by whoever had murdered Dirk and Pedro and searched the van to destroy any useful clues. The magnetic signs were the kind that could be quickly put on and removed from the sides of a vehicle. These signs made it easy to turn one's family car or SUV into a business operation. The interesting thing about the collection of magnetic signs found in the van was the variety of businesses they advertised. The van could, with just a quick change from one set of signs to another, be transformed from "Coastal Carolina Seafood, North Carolina's Best Bounty from the Sea," a truck carrying seafood from a company based in Wilmington, North Carolina into "Sally's Farm to Table Produce" based in Lancaster, Pennsylvania or "Just Like Grandma's Homemade Pies and Cakes" from White River Junction, Vermont.

Gimbel didn't believe for a minute that these businesses really existed. The names on the signs were camouflage, to slap on the sides of the van to hide what the important product was that was being delivered around the country. What surprised Gimbel was the extensive range of this one van, if it really delivered its wares all the way from North Carolina to Vermont.

Someone from Gimbel's office was already working on tracking the van's VIN. The VIN had been filed off in the one place vehicle owners knew it existed, but the VIN could also be found in other more obscure places on all vehicles. This van was older, and Gimbel made a bet with himself that it had been stolen years earlier, repainted, reregistered in a different state, and kept off the street, except for its special delivery outings. Whoever was running this operation was a professional, and they were leaving nothing to chance. So what had gone wrong with this well-planned and lucrative drug business? Gimbel had seen hundreds of drug deals go bad. The dealers were killed, and the drugs disappeared. This was a different scene. Why had two "clean" couriers been ruthlessly murdered and their very valuable contraband left behind?

Chapter 19

G*imbel was in his glory.* He hadn't realized how much he'd missed being in the thick of a complicated murder investigation. He had enough self-discipline to force himself to wait on the evidence before he began to speculate out loud, but in his mind, he was inevitably forming hypotheses about the case. He was stuck on the question of why the drugs had been left in the van. Surely whoever had murdered the two couriers had known the drugs were there. It seemed as if there had been sufficient time and opportunity, for whoever had committed the murders, to transfer the boxes and take possession of the drugs. Were the deaths of the two men more important than the prize of taking away millions of dollars in drugs? Was this a turf war among drug dealers? Were these couriers important as individuals, or had they been murdered in a very brutal way to send a message?

The medical examiner confirmed what Gimbel already knew—that the two men's throats had been cut with a long knife. That was unusual, and the method used in this murder made the hair on the back of Gimbel's neck stand up. He wondered if there was a new gang in town that was skilled in the use of the long knife. It would have been easy to shoot both men in the van, but it would have been difficult to kill them both in the vehicle at the same time with a long knife. The way they'd been murdered, Gimbel thought Pedro must have been killed first, when Dirk was inside delivering the Sherwood's order. When Dirk had returned to the van, he'd been attacked with the long knife and had his throat cut.

Because the case involved crossing state lines, the FBI was going to be brought in. Gimbel wasn't as defensive about having the federal agency butt into his cases as some of the others in his office were. In the past he'd been the one who'd figured things out before the feds figured things out, and the local FBI agents had a lot of respect for Gimbel's investigative and analytical skills. Gimbel welcomed the federal help because they had access to more resources than state level investigators did. But he wanted to move forward as much as he could, as fast as he could, before the feds got involved because everything always slowed down when an additional layer of investigators was added to the mix.

This case had its origins in North Carolina. At least that was where Gimbel believed Dirk and Pedro had begun the journey that had ended with their deaths in Skaneateles, New York. The seafood had been packed in Holden Beach, North Carolina, and Gimbel figured that was probably where the boxes with the drugs had been put into the van. All the white boxes were printed with "Coastal Carolina Seafood" in navy blue ink. The seafood was good quality, and it was fresh. The "cover" of selling high-end seafood to high-end clients was being carefully maintained.

The chef at the Sherwood Inn had said Dirk's deliveries were always top-of-the-line and always on time. The arrangement was also a "good deal" which the chef had not been able to duplicate with any other vendor. This probably meant that the seafood the Sherwood Inn had been buying from Coastal Carolina was being sold to them at a below-market price. Seafood wasn't the profit maker in the business; it was the loss leader. The drug operation was the reason why the Sherwood Inn was able to get such a high grade product at a reasonable cost.

The magnetic signs on the side of the van that said "Coastal Carolina Seafood" listed a phone number to call. Gimbel called and was shocked when a human being answered the phone. That never happened any more.

Gimbel was so surprised, he asked for confirmation from the woman. "Have I reached Coastal Carolina Seafood? Where are you located?"

"Yes, this is Coastal Carolina Seafood. Our business offices are in Wilmington, North Carolina, but our seafood processing plant is in Holden Beach, just south of Wilmington. How can I help you?" The woman on the other end of the line sounded perfectly legitimate. She made the business sound authentic, but of course Gimbel knew better. He knew the boxes that came out of the Holden Beach seafood processing plant were packed with much more than just shrimp and flounder.

"This is Homicide Detective Gimbel Saunders with the New York State Police. I'm calling from Syracuse, New York because we have one of your vans. There's been a murder, and two of your seafood delivery people are dead."

The woman with the soft Carolina accent gasped. "Oh, no. What van is that? What's happened?"

"Your driver Dirk Shannon and his assistant Pedro Ruiz were delivering an order to the Sherwood Inn in Skaneateles, New York, and they were killed in the van three days ago. We found them dead yesterday."

"Murdered? I know we regularly send orders to the Sherwood Inn in Skaneateles. We send seafood all over the East Coast. The Sherwood Inn has been one of our customers for years. They have a delivery every week. Was the delivery made on time? Are you certain it's one of our vans?"

"The delivery was made on time, on Tuesday, but the two men who made the delivery were subsequently killed in the Sherwood Inn parking lot."

"That's just horrible, but you know, I don't recognize the names of either of those men. The names Shannon and Ruiz are not familiar to me. They aren't on our payroll. And I do the payroll, so they must be contract drivers. I'll talk to my boss, Jason Craymer, and have him call you back. My name is Beatrice Randall."

"Thank you, Beatrice. I'll look forward to hearing back from Mr. Craymer. I have quite a few questions. I'd appreciate his calling me back as soon as possible. Thanks for your help."

Gimbel was processing the phone call with Coastal Carolina Seafood in his mind and trying to weigh the upstanding voice who spoke for the seemingly genuine seafood delivery business against what he knew to be the truth about the van that delivered their wares. It didn't make sense. Beatrice had said she didn't recognize the names of the driver or the other man. She'd said they must be contract drivers. But Gimbel knew Dirk had been delivering seafood to the Sherwood Inn for years. More than one thing about this case didn't compute.

Gimbel thought he might have a small piece of good luck with the cell phone numbers the Sherwood Inn's chef had given him. The driver's cell phone was sending a weak signal from Allentown, Pennsylvania. Someone from Gimbel's office was driving there to try to recover the phone. Gimbel didn't expect to find much of anything, but at least he knew where the killers had dumped the phone. He figured they'd tried to destroy the phone, probably with a hammer or a chipper shredder or something like that. He was still waiting on Dirk's cell phone records.

Gimbel was already thinking the investigation needed to go to North Carolina. The two men who had died in Onondaga County, New York were probably just one of several courier teams that were sent out from the base, the seafood packing plant in Holden Beach. Dirk and Pedro were just delivery guys, the middlemen in the supply chain. If Gimbel could find out who Dirk and Pedro's drug customers were and follow the supply chain to every delivery point, he would find the dealers who sold the heroin and the fentanyl on the street. That would be a very valuable find, to be able to pick up and prosecute those drug criminals, society's worst predators.

But, if he went to the source, which he believed was in North Carolina, he might be able to find and take down the people who were packaging and sending out the drugs for distribution. He might be able to shut down the drug supply at its origin. He was already trying to figure out how he could transfer himself to Wilmington, North Carolina. He'd become convinced, in spite of the soft, sweet Carolina accent he'd heard over the phone, that the root of this evil drug trade chain would be found at the place where the fresh seafood was being packed and put on ice. That was in Holden Beach. Gimbel was already thinking about buying a couple of new pairs of swimming trunks. If he rented a house or a condo in Holden Beach, it would have to be a place that accepted dogs. Gimbel never went anywhere for more than a day or two without his dogs.

Gimbel did some research about the seafood industry on the North Carolina coast. He wanted to educate himself because of the case. If he was going to do any on-site investigating, he wanted to be informed. Gimbel found that seafood processing and packing companies throughout the mid-Atlantic and the South were going out of business. Several factors were to blame, and some of these factors might have some bearing on the drugs and the murders.

Atlantic blue crabs produce the finest and sweetest crabmeat available in the world, but picking the meat out of these critters is tedious and time-consuming. In past generations, local women had picked the crabmeat. This was true up and down the East Coast from Smith Island, Maryland to Holden Beach, North Carolina. Over the years, these local crab pickers had aged and retired. The younger generation of local women no longer wanted the jobs picking crabs. They were better educated and had higher aspirations.

To fill the employment void, the seafood industry had turned to immigrant workers who were issued special limited work visas. These workers came to the U.S., not only to pick crabs, but also to harvest all kinds of agricultural products, including apples, grapes, tomatoes, and other seasonal crops. There was a significant cadre of these seasonal workers who came to upstate New York to pick apples and other kinds of fruit in the Onondaga County orchards. These workers came to the United States for part-time work only. Their work permits did not allow them to stay in the United States all year around.

Most of these seasonal workers, who came from Central America and the Caribbean, were hardworking, honest, and law-abiding. But it wouldn't be a surprise if there were a few criminals among them, people who had drug connections in Mexico or El Salvador or Haiti. Gimbel was already seeing a connection, because of where the seasonal workers came from, between the seafood industry and the drug business.

Another factor that was driving domestic seafood producers out of business was the impact of imported crabmeat, mostly from Asia. The imported crabmeat was cheaper than domestic crab. The Asian crabs were bigger, and it was easier to extract their meat. And there was no comparison between the wages paid to those who picked the crabmeat in Asia and those who picked it in the United States. Pasteurization had made it possible for Asian crabmeat to be shipped "fresh" to the United States and all over the world. There was a global demand for crabmeat, and a global supply had responded.

Well-known seafood restaurants in Ocean City, Maryland, in the heart of Atlantic blue crab country, admitted to using pasteurized Asian crabmeat in the off-season when local crabmeat wasn't available in the quantities required. Even during the peak of the season, these restaurants supplemented the real thing, the Atlantic blue crabmeat, with Asian crabmeat to augment supplies and increase profitability. Jumbo lump blue crabmeat is very expensive. High-end steak house chains throughout the country routinely use Asian crabmeat in their crabmeat appetizers and their steaks served "Oscar style," that is, topped with béarnaise sauce, crabmeat, and asparagus. If you ask where the crabmeat comes from, they might tell you it comes from the Philippines or from Thailand. If you don't ask or if you can't tell the difference in the taste, you can pretend that the crab comes from the Atlantic Coast. The spicy cocktail sauces and savory remoulade sauces the steakhouses use on their crabmeat cocktails are usually able to fool even the most discriminating palate.

The Atlantic Coast seafood businesses hire seasonal workers because of their willingness to do the difficult work of extracting crabmeat from the shell. This new generation of pickers no longer had the connections to the local community they'd had in previous generations. Competition from Asian crabmeat was crushing the demand for the more expensive, albeit more delicious, Atlantic blue crabmeat. It was not a stretch to imagine that a seafood business in trouble might turn to the illicit drug trade to supplement the income they were making from the seafood they sold. There was a supply and distribution organization already established to deliver the seafood. Drug deliveries could piggyback on that system.

Things were beginning to make sense in Gimbel's mind. If it was important to disguise the presence of the drugs, packing drugs with seafood was a brilliant combination. The smell of shrimp and fish was pungent, and drug dogs that might be called on to search delivery trucks could easily be thrown off by the fishy odor. It was obvious that Beatrice Randall of Coastal Carolina Seafood didn't know all the seasonal workers or drivers who delivered her company's product. She had mentioned contract drivers, but what exactly did that mean? The administrative offices of the business were located miles away from the actual seafood packing operation. Was anybody minding the store? Did anybody in the business office know what was happening in Holden Beach at the packing plant? Gimbel wondered when Beatrice had last visited the plant in Holden Beach or if she ever had.

Gimbel heard that the chef had been released from the hospital and was back running the kitchen at the Sherwood Inn. Gimbel decided to have dinner there a few nights later. He loved eating at the Sherwood anyway and wanted to check in with the chef. He had his before-dinner drink at the bar, a club soda with Rose's lime juice and lots of fresh lime wedges, while he waited to be seated at his table for one.

Gimbel didn't drink alcohol for obvious reasons. He'd made that decision years ago.

When he was seated in the dining room, he ordered the excellent shrimp cocktail, as he always did, but this time his appetizer came with a lot of history. The shrimp was perfectly cooked, and Gimbel loved the cocktail sauce the Sherwood Inn served with the chilled shrimp. The shrimp cocktail was just spicy enough and arrived on ice with half a lemon to squeeze on the shrimp. This was exactly the right way to serve a shrimp cocktail. He wondered who would be supplying the Sherwood Inn with their seafood in the future. Would they continue using Coastal Carolina or would a new company be able to deliver the same high quality seafood that Coastal Carolina had always delivered. Gimbel ordered the prime rib rare with au jus, mashed potatoes, and Brussels sprouts. Blueberry pie a la mode was his dessert.

When he paid the bill, Gimbel sent a message with his waiter that he wanted to speak with Dimitri. Dimitri sent a message back that Gimbel should come to his office at the back of the kitchen.

"How are you doing? Are you well enough to be back at work?" Gimbel thought Dimitri looked terrible. The man should have taken more time off to recover from his health scare.

"I wanted to take the rest of the week off, but I had to come back. I'm completely exhausted, although all I did was sleep in a hospital bed. How could that have worn me out? It's a mystery. One of my sous chefs has disappeared, and we're short staffed. Curley Davenport didn't give me any notice. He's worked here for years, and just when I need him most, to cover for me while I recover, he takes off. I hope nothing has happened to him, but I'm mostly angry right now that he's let me down."

"Do you think Curley's disappearance has anything to do with the recent murders? That kind of incident could definitely scare somebody away."

"I don't think so, but I wanted to talk to you about that. When you came to see me in the hospital, I didn't know yet that Curley had disappeared. But I should have mentioned to you that Dirk and Curley knew each other. With the shock plus all the drugs they were giving me, I didn't think about it. Curley had some kind of a relationship with Dirk, the guy who delivered the seafood. Curley's worked at the Sherwood since before I came here, and he knew Dirk. They weren't close friends or anything like that. I figured they must get together and go out for a night on the town when Dirk came to Skaneateles. I never saw them really talking, but they nodded to one another when Dirk came into the kitchen. I had the feeling they saw each other later, away from the Sherwood. It's just a feeling I had. I never asked Curley about it, and I never saw them together. Figured it was none of my business, what Curley did on his own time. I might not have bothered to say anything at all about them knowing each other, if he hadn't disappeared. He was a terrific sous chef, and I need somebody immediately if not sooner."

"What was the first day that Curley didn't show up for work?"

"It was the day after I found the bodies. The word spread pretty fast. I went to the hospital about three in the afternoon on Friday. It was Curley's day off, but he was supposed to come in to work on Friday night, the dinner shift. But he didn't come in that night, and he didn't come in the next day either. Friday and Saturday nights are big nights for us, and I was in the hospital. The rest of the staff had to really scramble to get the food out. It was a rough weekend. The Sherwood's manager, of course, was trying to keep things operating normally. Because the word was out about the bodies in the parking lot, he wanted everything to appear on the surface as if nothing bad was happening. But the kitchen was a mess. And Curley's not been seen again since he worked his shift on Thursday night. Somebody went out to his house to see if he was all right. It looked like he'd packed a couple of bags and left in his car. And it looked like he'd left in a big hurry. I guess the murders must have scared the shit out of him."

The news that Curley Davenport had known Dirk Shannon was an important piece of information for Gimbel. He was disappointed that Curley had disappeared, but the fact that the two had known each other gave Gimbel something to hang onto. "Good luck finding somebody to take Curley's place. I love to eat here. The food is the best. Don't change a thing, please, about the menu or the food. I'm sorry you couldn't take more time off to recover. You're a talented chef, and I want you to be around here for a long time."

"Thanks detective. And, I have to find another seafood supplier, at least temporarily. When it rains it pours."

Gimbel had not told Dimitri anything about the drugs that were found in the van. As far as Dimitri knew, the men who had been murdered were delivering only fresh seafood. Gimbel didn't want to tip off Coastal Carolina that the authorities knew about any drugs. "I hope you'll keep using Coastal Carolina as your seafood supplier. Even if you have to use somebody else until they set up a new delivery schedule for you, their seafood is worth it."

"Yeah, I can't get as good a deal with any other company, so I'll probably go back with them when they can guarantee their deliveries again. I always called Dirk, so now I don't even know who to call to place my orders. I'll figure it out. I think

I have a line on another sous chef. She's a woman, though, and I don't work very well with women. I'm Greek."

"Good luck with that. I hope you find somebody. Just don't change anything, okay? I'm like Billy Joel. 'I love you just the way you are.'"

Dimitri laughed a small laugh and went back to the kitchen. Gimbel was heading to Syracuse, but before he even got to his car he'd put in a call to headquarters for an APB BOLO on Curley Davenport and Curley's vehicle. Gimbel requested a warrant to search the man's apartment. He thought he'd identified Curley as one of Dirk's street dealers, but the man had already given him the slip.

Chapter 20

Gimbel Saunders was meeting with two FBI special agents that morning. Local murders, even double murders, didn't usually attract FBI attention, but because of the interstate implications of the operation and the volume of drugs found in the van from Coastal Carolina Seafood, the feds had stepped in to take the lead in the case. Gimbel would brief agents Brandon and Steinmeyer. He knew Brandon from a previous case, but he didn't know Steinmeyer, a good looking female agent who seemed like she was all business all the time. Steve Brandon was glad to see Gimbel again and greeted him warmly. "Great to be working with you, Gimbel. I know you probably already have this figured out, so we're just here to put a stamp on things. This is Carley Steinmeyer. She's new in our office, transferred from Chicago with a specialty in profiling."

"Nice to meet you, Carley. Welcome to Syracuse. We specialize in colder winters and cooler summers. How long have you been here?" Gimbel was trying to be polite, but Carley wasn't smiling and looked like trouble. She was very angry about something that had nothing to do with the current case, and she had "very ambitious" written all over her face and body language. She wasn't into small talk.

"I've been here long enough to figure out the winters are colder and the summers aren't much nicer than they were in Chicago." She was a sourpuss. Gimbel glanced at Steve who gave an imperceptible shrug of his shoulders and remained silent. "Let's get down to business, boys. What have you got, Gimbel? Bring us up to speed." Carley wasted no time and took no prisoners.

Gimbel gave the agents a rundown of everything he'd done so far. He laid out all the facts, and then he gave them his opinions about what he thought had happened and what he thought should happen in the future. Carley wasn't warming up to anybody, even after Gimbel's thorough and professional summary.

"I still don't know why whoever killed the drug couriers didn't take the drugs. Maybe you can give that some thought, Carley. Why would these two guys have their throats cut and their van scrubbed clean of any clues, if the killers didn't intend to steal the drugs? I've thought about a turf war and somebody wanting to send a message. So far it's all speculation."

"Those are good questions. Do you have anything on Curley Davenport? He seems to be the only possible connection in the New York area. I'm assuming we all agree he was Dirk's drug customer, the one who would be distributing the drugs on the street."

"That's what I'm assuming, but at this point it's just speculation. And we don't have anything yet on the APB. The problem is, even if we find Curley, the only person he ever interacted with was Dirk, his contact. These drug operations are highly compartmentalized. Curley wouldn't know about anybody else who sells on the street, or anything more about the source of the drugs. When Dirk died a horrible and violent death, Curley hit the road. He might have just been afraid he'd be next."

"We still need to find him. He's been dealing with Dirk for years and has to know something." Brandon wanted to find Curley.

"I'm thinking somebody needs to go to North Carolina. That's where the source is. Curley and Dirk are just errand boys, small potatoes, really. We want them off the streets and the distribution system shut down, but the big fish in this case, so to speak, are in Holden Beach. What do you think?" Gimbel wanted to get to the origins of the network.

"You're correct. We may or may not be able to mop up this local mess of a double murder. We may or may not be able to close down the street dealers. We probably will never be able to put our hands on the actual killer or killers. But we might be able to find out who is financing all of this and who is procuring and packaging the drugs for distribution with the seafood. The seizure of the van is an important lead, even if it was completely cleaned out. The lead is Coastal Carolina Seafood in Holden Beach." Brandon was on the same page with Gimbel about the direction the investigation should take going forward.

Carley was skeptical, but she was a good agent. She was a good listener, but she was eager to add her two cents. "One of the reasons we are here is because we have a proposal to make. We've just busted a major drug kingpin in L.A. Nobody knows we have the man in custody. We have him incommunicado. He's wetting his pants, he's so scared." Carley Steinmeyer smiled when she said this. "His cronies think he's on vacation somewhere, so nobody suspects he's missing yet, let alone knows that he's in federal custody. We have a window of opportunity. He is singing his head off because he wants to keep some of his drug money. He knows he's going to prison, but he wants to make the deal to end all deals."

"What's this guy from L.A. have to do with what's happening here?" Gimbel wanted her to get to the point.

"His name is Charles 'Chuckie' Petrossi. To explain his disappearance, we intend to put out the story that Chuckie got some bad news from his doctor. It's his heart, and the doc told him he had to take a long vacation, reduce stress, not work for a while, and all of that. He's been ordered officially, to 'get away from it all.' Supposedly, Chuckie is currently on a cruise, and after the cruise, he's going to 'get away from L.A.' for several months. It's been kind of an ad hoc, make-it-up-as-you-go kind of story about Chuckie's whereabouts right now, so we have some flexibility. He's turned his drug operations over to his second-in-command, while he deals with his health issues. He doesn't have a family, just a live-in girlfriend. She's staying at his house and doesn't seem to be all that upset that he's gone on a cruise without her and isn't communicating with her."

"Where is Chuckie, really?" Gimbel wanted to know.

"If we told you, we'd have to kill you. Ha!" Carley had a sense of humor after all. Maybe.

"What do Chuckie and all of his problems have to do with my case?"

"We've known for some time that there was a very big drug distributor working out of somewhere in the South and/or the Mid-Atlantic. We thought for a while it was based in Maryland. Then we decided it was out of Florida. We couldn't pin it down, but we knew it was huge and very bad and operating up and down the East Coast. We think this double murder has narrowed our search and has in fact pinpointed the location of the where the drug-running outfit is based."

"So you've been watching this drug operation for some time? And now you think the two men who were murdered in Skaneateles are part of that? As you know, I've already called Coastal Carolina Seafood." Gimbel wanted all the cards on the table.

Carley responded. "We know you called them, and that's exactly what should have happened. It would have been very odd if someone hadn't called them to tell them their van was in custody and that two of their seafood delivery people were dead. They don't know the drugs were left in the van. Whoever knows about the drugs must have assumed the killer or killers took the drugs. Why wouldn't they? You didn't mention drugs to Beatrice Randall. As far as anyone at Coastal Carolina knows, there are no drugs. They have to be hoping your call about the murders doesn't have anything to do with their drug business."

"So, where do we go from here? Do you have a plan? I didn't know you'd had your eyes on this until just now. Of course we know drugs are a terrible problem here in New York State, just like they are everywhere in the country these days. The boss at Coastal Carolina is supposed to call me back. What do I say to him when he calls me? I don't want to say too much and tip him off, if he knows what's really going on at Coastal Carolina. But I also don't want to make him suspicious by not asking the hard questions I'd be expected to ask."

Steve Brandon took over the discussion. He was clearly in charge of the case. "We'll go over all of that, what to say and what questions to ask. More importantly, we want you to get ready to take on a special assignment for us...immediately. We want you to go undercover down in North Carolina. We know all about your heart situation, and we think the New York State Police overreacted when they put you on disability. We also know you did a lot of undercover work earlier in your career, so you know how to do it. We have a unique opportunity, with Chuckie Petrossi in custody and incommunicado. Chuckie is going to go to take that beach vacation his doctor supposedly recommended, and you're the lucky person who has been chosen to actually take the beach vacation for Chuckie."

"You mean, you want me to pretend to be Chuckie Petrossi and take a vacation in North Carolina?" Gimbel could hardly believe his good luck, that he was going to have the chance to get to the source of the drug operation. But he worried about trying to pretend to be another person. "Do I look anything like Chuckie? Doesn't anybody in North Carolina know what he looks like?"

"Chuckie has never been to the East Coast. He's strictly a California and West Coast guy. We don't think the people who are running the Carolina business have ever seen or heard of Chuckie. If they look into his background, they will find out all about him, and they will also be able to verify that he has taken time off on doctor's orders and is spending his summer at a beach on the East Coast."

"We will give you a complete briefing on everything you need to know about Chuckie's life and his drug operations in California. We'll tell you more about Chuckie than you ever wanted to hear. We want you to be a drug dealer, but a drug dealer who is frightened about his health. You will have to find your own way into the Coastal Carolina Seafood and Holden Beach situation. You've done this kind of thing before."

"I'm willing to take on your proposition, but I have to take my dogs with me. I don't leave my dogs behind when I go out of town. That's my only stipulation. I'm assuming you will tell me what kind of clothes Chuckie likes and will tell me what kind of house to rent. What's the time table for this? Because you didn't waste any time getting over here, you must want me to leave soon."

"We knew you wouldn't leave your dogs behind, and that's okay. The dog thing did limit where we were able to find a house for you to rent. For a day or two, we thought we'd have to buy you a house, but we finally found the perfect place. And it accepts dogs under twenty pounds." Carley had already rented the house and made the plans.

"You've already rented a house for me in North Carolina? And it's one that accepts small dogs? I guess you were pretty sure I'd agree to accept this assignment and go undercover for the FBI. Should I be offended or flattered?"

Steve Brandon jumped in to explain. "Carley's a profiler. She knows people and what they will do, given certain circumstances. We know you've been unhappy working cold cases, and we know you wouldn't leave your dogs. We were pretty sure you'd jump at the chance to take this case to the next level. Tell me where we guessed wrong."

Gimbel didn't like to be so predictable, but his respect for Carley's abilities increased. She certainly had his number. "You aren't wrong, on any of it. Carley, I hate to be such an open book, but hats off to you for your excellent work. So where's my house, and when do I leave?"

"We'd like for you to leave tomorrow. The house is ready for you. You will fly into Wilmington with the dogs and lots of luggage. You'll actually fly private to Wilmington, compliments of the FBI, but your flight history will reveal, if anyone should bother to check on it, that you flew commercial, first class, of course, from L.A. to Charlotte and then on a commuter plane to Wilmington. The airline records will show the additional charges for the dogs and for the extra luggage. Chuckie is a rich drug dealer and has a very fancy house in L.A. He flies first class, wherever he goes. The only place he ever goes outside the U.S. mainland is to Hawaii. The backstory is all covered for you."

"You've thought of everything, haven't you?" Gimbel was used to making his own plans and running his own undercover gigs, so he was somewhat taken aback that the FBI had already made so many assumptions about him and had already planned so much of the operation. "I can be ready to leave tomorrow. What time and where? Where's the house, the dog-friendly one you've rented for me? Holden Beach?"

"The house isn't on Holden Beach. We decided Holden Beach is too close to our hot spot. We found a house in another beach resort, on Oak Island. Oak Island is close to Holden Beach. We wanted to go with Wrightsville Beach, but availability was a problem. People who rent their houses are more particular about pets in Wrightsville Beach. All of these vacation places are pretty close together. You'll figure it all out once you get down there. You will be going out for dinner in all the beach resort towns. That's what we want you to do. Chuckie doesn't cook, and he loves seafood. So you will be visiting every restaurant in the area. You will be wearing your very expensive, very L.A. outfits and some big gold chains! You will stand out and attract a lot of attention. The big boys will hear about you."

Brandon continued. "We've set everything up, but we are leaving the rest up to you. You know how to work your way into places like Coastal Carolina, so it's your job to figure out that part of it. We want you ready to leave by tomorrow at noon. We'll send a car to your house to drive you and your dogs to the airport in Syracuse. Carley and I will be flying to Wilmington with you to bring you up to speed on everything you'll need to know about Chuckie Petrossi. We've already bought clothes for you, like the ones Chuckie wears in L.A. This may be the part of the deal you don't like, but you have to wear this stuff when you leave your house. When you're inside, at home by yourself, you can continue to wear your own boring, comfortable clothes, but when you go out for any reason, we want you duded up in Chuckie-style stuff."

"Is it terrible? Chuckie's style? Does he wear a thong on the beach? I'm not doing that."

"Chuckie goes to a nude beach in Hawaii. He doesn't go to the beach in L.A., so you can wear whatever you want to when you go to the beach on Oak Island. There aren't any nude beaches there, so you don't have to worry about that." Steve was rattling all this information off, but Gimbel noticed that Carley blushed slightly at the mention of the nude beach. Underneath all that anger and ambition, she was a more complicated woman than Gimbel had given her credit for. He fancied himself as a bit of a profiler, too.

"When do I get to see these clothes? Are you packing them for me, or am I supposed to pack them in my own luggage?"

"We've packed the clothes for you, and we have a new set of matching luggage for you, all ostrich skin leather and very expensive. And very a la gangsta, both the luggage and the clothes. You will hate it all, but it's part of your cover. Chuckie is a clotheshorse, and he always travels with lots of suitcases. We will bring most of the suitcases with us to the airport tomorrow. We have two extra suitcases in the matching set. They're empty, and you can use these two suitcases for your own clothes, the ones you're taking to wear inside your house, your underwear and toiletries, and personal stuff like that. When we leave today, we'll transfer the two empty suitcases to your car. We are also leaving you with one suitcase that's packed with Chuckie's clothes. We want you to arrive at the Wilmington airport dressed in a Chuckie outfit, and we want the whole set of suitcases to match. Chuckie is that kind of guy. He's cheesy, and he likes lots of outward signs of what he considers to be respectability. To him a set of matching luggage is respectability. He likes to show off his wealth and success, hence the tacky and very expensive Rodeo Drive wardrobe and the nine pieces of matching ostrich skin luggage."

"Nine pieces of luggage? You've got to be kidding me! What will I ever do with all those clothes?" Gimbel usually traveled light, with his clothes thrown into a waterproof black duffel bag.

"They're not all full of clothes. There's ammunition for your guns and some electronics so you can stay in touch with us. We have to fly you private because of the firearms. We've rented a BMW convertible for you to drive in North Carolina. It's a sweet ride. I wish I could drive it around. All the women will want to ride with you."

"Sounds like I will be all tarted up, ready for serious trouble."

"You're going to have to dye your hair. I almost forgot to mention that. And your eyebrows. Your hair and eyebrows are too light, and your hair has some very handsome gray streaks in it. Chuckie keeps his hair dark brown. He doesn't let the gray show. That's one thing you're going to have to keep up with, dying your hair. I guess I saved that little tidbit for last. Ha!"

"I've had to change my appearance before, so that doesn't really bother me. What about food and cleaning the house and all of that. Does Chuckie shop for groceries? I know he doesn't clean his own house."

"Hired services take care of the landscaping, cleaning the pool, and all of that. That comes as part of the price of the rental. A maid service will clean the house and also wash your clothes, if you want that. You might want to wash your own everyday things and leave the loud and fancy Chuckie clothes for the maid service. Some of those have to be ironed. The maids come once a week. There's a gourmet grocery store near your house, and they deliver. All you have to do is call them or order online. They promise to deliver within two hours of receiving the order. You'll eat out for lunch and dinner, most of the time. I think you are all set."

"Okay, I look forward to hearing all about the infamous and not-so-famous Chuckie Petrossi, on the flight to Wilmington tomorrow. I'll be ready at noon. I will be bringing a dog crate, but the dogs will be on leashes. They will sit on the seats beside me in the plane, just so you know. Now tell me what I'm supposed to say when the boss at Coastal Carolina calls me back. He's going to be calling me on my cell phone. By the way, I will have to have a new cell phone when I am pretending to be Chuckie, and it will have to have an L.A. area code."

"Already taken care of. We have Chuckie's very own phone for you, with Chuckie's very own phone number. You will get that on the plane tomorrow. I don't need to tell you not to use it until you get to North Carolina. Take your own cell phone, too, but we have a third phone for you to use to communicate with us. Don't make any of Chuckie's calls or any of your personal calls on the FBI phone."

"This isn't my first rodeo, you know. But thanks for the phone directions. I feel good about having Chuckie's own phone. He must be going nuts without his phone."

"Believe me, Chuckie has worse things to worry about right now than missing his cell phone."

The FBI agents gave Gimbel a U.S. passport and a California driver's license, both in Chuckie's name but with Gimbel's picture on them. They had several credit cards and other "pocket clutter" for Gimbel to carry around in Chuckie's pockets. "Are these really Chuckie's credit cards? If they're his and he has to pay them, I'm not going to hold back." The FBI agents didn't tell Gimbel who was paying the credit card bills because he didn't need to know that.

The agents discussed with Gimbel exactly what he should say when the head man at Coastal Carolina Seafood, Jason Craymer, returned his call. The feds wanted the detective from Syracuse, New York to sound like he was diligently pursuing a double homicide, but they didn't want him to mention anything about the drugs in the van. As far as Craymer knew, the drugs had not been found. Gimbel thought he might mention to the Coastal Carolina boss that he was giving some thought to coming down to Holden Beach to talk to the guy. That ought to make him very nervous, if he was in on the drug running scheme.

Gimbel was excited to be getting ready for an undercover operation. He knew he was good at this, and he loved being back in the field. He gathered up the things from his office that he would need while he was away and went to the parking garage to pick up the two empty suitcases and the suitcase that held an outfit from Chuckie's L.A. wardrobe. Gimbel and his two Westies, Dilly and Billy, would be ready to go when the car arrived at his condo at noon the next day.

Chapter 21

Gimbel was ready. When he stepped off the plane at the Wilmington, North Carolina airport, the humidity hit him like a Mack truck. He knew it was hot in the south, but he'd forgotten how horribly humid it could be. The private FBI jet had taxied to a remote part of the airport, and the BMW was parked nearby. It was gold. Gimbel cringed, but knew it was part of his cover. He hadn't known BMW made a gold car, let alone a gold convertible. It must have been a special order. Argh! The dogs were anxious to be out of the plane, and Gimbel found a patch of grass for them. Agents Brandon and Steinmeyer were not deplaning and would return immediately to Syracuse. They'd spent the past few hours briefing Gimbel, telling him everything he needed to know about the sleazy life and times of Chuckie Petrossi.

The man who had driven the BMW to the airport was unloading the luggage and the dog crate from the plane and putting it all into the back of the convertible. He never said a word to Gimbel, just handed him the car keys and walked towards the terminal. The address of Gimbel's rented house on Oak Island was programmed into the GPS in the BMW and into his Chuckie Petrossi phone. Gimbel lifted Dilly and

Billy into the passenger seat. They sniffed around a lot and looked at Gimbel with questioning eyes. Earlier that day, they had checked out his new wardrobe and especially his new shoes. He knew they were wondering what the heck they were doing in this new ride. Gimbel told them he was on his way to embrace his life as Chuckie Petrossi, West Coast bad boy with dreadful taste in clothes and cars.

It was summer, but it was midweek, so the traffic wasn't terrible as Gimbel made his way out of Wilmington and south to find his house on Oak Island. When he crossed the bridge onto the island, the sea breeze finally caught up with him, and everything began to cool off.

His house was ocean front, and it was huge. He double-checked the address to be sure he had the right place. He knew Chuckie was extravagant and showy, but this house was ridiculous. It had a luxurious swimming pool and patio and a gorgeous and panoramic view of the ocean. Gimbel would only have to take a few steps on the wooden walkway that went across the dunes, to get to his own almost-private beach. The house must have ten bedrooms. It was silly for Gimbel Saunders to be vacationing in such a place, but it was probably exactly what Chuckie Petrossi would have demanded.

It was after five o'clock in the evening when Gimbel arrived at the house, so he knew he was allowed to take the dogs on the beach for a run. They were only allowed on the beach between five at night and nine in the morning. Dilly and Billy loved the sand and ran in and out of the surf, chasing small tufts of ocean foam. Gimbel breathed the salt air deep into his lungs and decided he could put up with his undercover disguise—the flashy, horrible clothes, the gold chains, and the gold car—in exchange for some time in this paradise by the sea.

After a brief walk, Gimbel gave the dogs some water and put them back into the car. They were going to dinner. He would unpack his multitude of luggage when he got back. The FBI had put a list of local seafood restaurants on Chuckie Petrossi's phone. Gimbel was hungry and decided to go to the top-rated place on Oak Island. It had been a long day, so he would eat close to home that night. This would be his first public appearance as Chuckie, and he psyched himself into the role as he drove to the nearby eatery. The Captain's Galley was rustic but elegant, and it had a nice outside patio. Gimbel asked to be seated outside. He could keep his eyes on his car and his dogs that way.

Gimbel didn't drink, but Chuckie usually did. The explanation for Chuckie being on the wagon was that his doctor had insisted he avoid alcohol for several months. Most of the people eating on the patio at the Captain's Galley were having cocktails or drinking wine or beer, so Chuckie was unusual when he asked for a non-alcoholic drink. He ordered Gimbel's usual club soda with Rose's lime juice and fresh lime wedges.

"I'm under doctor's orders, damn it, to be a teetotaler for six months. Can you believe that? The doc says the lime juice will be good for me. Ha ha! So bring me a double. Ha ha!" The waitress smiled politely and said she would be right back with his drink.

When she brought the club soda, Chuckie asked her what the house specialty was. "I'm from the West Coast, and I know all about the seafood out there. I've never been to North Carolina before, and I want to try the local favorites. What do you recommend?"

"Everybody orders the 'peel your own shrimp,' and our deviled crab is famous. I personally like the flounder served

Oscar style, if you want a dinner. Everything here at the Captain's Galley is good. The shrimp and the crabmeat and all the fish are local. The lobster comes from Maine, but mostly everything else is from right around here." Gimbel noticed that the waitress was checking out his gold chains and flamboyant clothes. Most of the other male patrons were in loose fitting cotton summer shirts and khaki pants or khaki shorts. They all wore docksiders. It was like a uniform.

Gimbel, aka Chuckie, definitely stood out in the crowd. His purple shirt actually had rhinestones attached to the front in a swirly pattern. Great for certain places in L.A....maybe. Not so much on Oak Island. The white leather Hermes driving moccasins had cost upwards of one thousand dollars, but Gimbel felt like the whole world was staring at his white shoes, as if he were a refugee from the 1970s. While he was waiting for his table at the Captain's Galley, all he could think about was hiding his ridiculously clad feet under the table.

Dilly and Billy had hated the shoes. Dogs know shoes. Dogs always pay attention to shoes. Shoes are down on the ground where dogs are, and shoes are harbingers of what is going to happen for the rest of the day. When Gimbel had put on the white moccasins that morning, both Dilly and Billy had sniffed them. They looked up at Gimbel with sad eyes. They knew there was going to be trouble when their beloved best friend put on such terrible footwear. Supposedly dogs don't see colors, but Gimbel hadn't ever believed that. His two Westies knew the shoes he'd put on today were white; he would bet the farm on it. Gimbel knew his dogs were alarmed that the white shoes meant he was going someplace without them. They were relieved when he brought out their leashes and when he loaded them into the car with himself and his thirteen suitcases.

"I don't feel like peeling my own anything tonight, so I'm going to order the cold shellfish appetizer platter with three sauces. Everything on that platter's already peeled, right? I know it's for two people, but I can take some home for lunch tomorrow if I don't eat it all. Then I want an order of the deviled crab and the large fried seafood platter. Bring extra tartar sauce and lots of lemon wedges. I've never had deviled crab. It sounds delicious. I know I'm ordering way too much food, but it's my first night in town. I can have the leftover fried fish for breakfast tomorrow."

The waitress tried to smile when she heard about the fried fish for breakfast. It was an effort for her to listen to the flashy guy's babbling. She had an emaciated look, and Gimbel thought she was probably a vegan who ate bark and twigs for breakfast, no milk and no meat, let alone fried fish!

Gimbel enjoyed his first meal as Chuckie Petrossi. He figured the waitress had found him remarkable enough that she would mention him to her supervisor or her colleagues. Gimbel was establishing his identity as the West Coast gangster who didn't seem to realize how much he didn't fit in with these well-bred southerners who all dressed alike and talked alike. He was a rube with plenty of money, and he was living his best life as if he were still in L.A. If he weren't on such a serious mission, Gimbel would be laughing out loud at his own brilliant performance as Chuckie Petrossi. Gimbel had the waitress pack up his leftovers to take home and left her an enormous tip. If nothing else got her attention, the one hundred dollar cash tip on the one-hundred and sixty-seven dollar tab surely would. Chuckie Petrossi paid in cash, so the big bills left on the table would make the skinny waitress remember him.

It was time to unpack the ostrich skin suitcases and explore the inside of his enormous summer house. He parked his gold car in the five-bay garage on the ground floor. Gimbel walked and fed the dogs and left them in the kennel beside the swimming pool while he got his luggage upstairs. It was more than a notion to have so many material possessions, so Gimbel was glad to find that the house elevator went all the way up and all the way down. The ground level was for parking and storage, and it was convenient to be able to load all thirteen suitcases onto the elevator and take them up to the main floor.

The house was beautiful. It wasn't fancy in the sense of L.A. fancy, but it was elegant in a relaxed and beachy way. It was all white and light blue and shades of pale yellow. An accomplished interior designer had obviously chosen the paint colors and the rugs and furniture. Very tasteful. Very restful. It was way too tasteful for Chuckie Petrossi, but Gimbel had a feeling everything in this area of Oak Island was equally tasteful. There was an enormous master bedroom suite in one wing of the first floor, and Gimbel chose this bedroom. There were two more levels of bedrooms above the main floor. Gimbel knew he'd probably never go up there for any reason.

The walk-in closet in the master bedroom was almost as big as Gimbel's entire condo back in Syracuse. He hung up the many tacky, expensive clothes and stowed the thirteen pieces of ostrich skin luggage. He was a U.S. Marine, so everything was quickly squared away. He was sure Chuckie had never been a Marine and probably was not nearly as neat as Gimbel. It wasn't difficult for Gimbel to pretend to be Chuckie Petrossi, but it was going to be impossible for Gimbel to pretend to be messy.

Someone had provisioned the house with breakfast food. There were several choices of dry cereal and English muffins beside the toaster. There were eggs and bacon, milk, butter, and a choice of preserves in the refrigerator. There was a variety of fresh fruit on the counter. Gimbel had not ordered the breakfast things, but he had ordered the special dogfood that Dilly and Billy preferred. He found the dog food in the pantry. Somebody was paying big bucks for this kind of service. He hoped those bucks were coming out of Chuckie's drug money and not out of the pockets of the American taxpayer. This was a decadent way to live. It could be seductive and make a person lazy.

The dog's beds and bowls were strategically placed, and Gimbel took them out for one more walk. He wondered if he would become fatally bored, living this slothful existence in these self-indulgent surroundings. Gimbel was used to working hard. He needed something to do. Sitting on the beach was not going to cut it for very long.

Gimbel walked the dogs before nine the next morning. Dilly and Billy loved the North Carolina beach. Gimbel threw a tennis ball into the surf, and they raced to see which of them could get there first. One of them brought it back and then made him chase them to get the ball back. Then he threw out two balls, one for each dog, and the game grew in complexity. Billy picked up one ball and ran away with it. Sometimes, when both dogs went for one ball, a tussle ensued. Billy dropped it in the sand, and Dilly picked it up and ran back towards Gimbel. Throwing two balls out for the dogs gave Gimbel some ideas about the Holden Beach drug case.

Gimbel was sure Beatrice Randall wasn't lying about not recognizing Dirk Shannon's name, but he thought it was very odd that she didn't know the name of the driver of the van who delivered the seafood to the Sherwood Inn. Gimbel knew there was no other driver assigned to that route. Dirk always drove the seafood. The chef at the Sherwood Inn had said that Dirk always delivered the seafood and brought it into the Sherwood's kitchen. But what if he didn't always deliver the drugs? There could be two things going on here. Maybe some seafood shipments were packed with drugs and others were not?

What if Dirk wasn't the driver who left Holden Beach driving the van full of seafood? What if somebody else drove the van with the seafood from the packing plant in Holden Beach, and Dirk Shannon took over as the driver at some rendezvous point, some place removed from the packing plant? What if sometimes the van held only boxes of seafood, and sometimes it carried boxes of both seafood and drugs? There could be several variables at play. One scenario could explain why the name Dirk Shannon didn't ring a bell with Beatrice. The other scenario might explain why the drugs hadn't been taken from the van. Maybe the person who had killed Dirk and Pedro really had not known the drugs were packed in the boxes labeled as seafood. Gimbel knew he somehow had to get on the inside of the business to have a hope of answering any of his questions or finding out if any of his hypotheses were true.

Chapter 22

Darnel Phillips treated his Ziploc plastic bag of papers with great care. He waited until he was in his room at the halfway house before he took any of the papers out of the bag. Most of them fell apart in his hands, as soon as he touched them. He'd had unrealistically high hopes that there might be a clue in the box of Patsy's things. These were the only physical artifacts he had from more than fifteen years ago. The clothes and shoes and makeup in the box had yielded nothing, and the papers were the final vestiges remaining from that time. He almost cried when he looked at the fragments he'd laid out on his bed. Water and mildew had made most of the papers unreadable. The ink from a bygone era had run and faded. Bugs had destroyed the rest. Even the mice seemed to have had a go at this pile of what appeared to be bills.

Darnel could make out a few words here and there, and what he was able to read indicated he'd found a stack of Patsy's paid bills. Only she knew why she had chosen to keep these particular bills in a tin box. What little he could decipher revealed that Patsy had paid her drugstore bill, from a local drugstore chain that hadn't existed in the area for more than a decade. There were charges for make-up and toiletries. There was a receipt from a hairdresser, but Darnel couldn't make out any address. The hairdresser was probably long gone by now anyway. Then at the bottom of the pile, something on one of the pieces of paper caught his eye. It was a bill sent from a doctor's office. He couldn't read the name of the doctor, but he saw M.D. after the name. And he could read an address—in Binghamton, New York. His spirits soared, but he tried to keep himself from becoming hopeful again. There had been too many disappointments. He wondered if the doctor could possibly still be in business or if the office still existed at the address on the bill. Or had that building, too, been torn down to make room for a fast food joint or a parking lot or another unnecessary convenience store?

Darnel hadn't been to Binghamton since he was working construction, more than twenty ago, and he didn't know the city. Much would have changed since Patsy Grimes had driven to her doctor's appointment so many years earlier, but the fact that she had traveled more than two hours from Dydonia to Binghamton to see this particular physician, prompted Darnel to pay extra attention. Why had she consulted a specialist in Binghamton? Why not see a doctor closer to home? Why not go to Syracuse, which even back then was an outstanding major medical center and much closer to Dydonia than Binghamton? Patsy had made a significant effort to see the doctor in Binghamton. Darnel was going to try to find him.

Darnel still hadn't bought a cell phone, so, wherever he was, he was always trying to find one of the few remaining phone booths in the world. Phone booths were now almost non-existent. There was a phone in the halfway house, but the residents weren't allowed to make long distance calls on it. Everyone who made long distance calls these days had a cell phone—except for Darnel. He walked to the library that was less than a mile from his halfway house in Auburn. There was a pay phone outside the front door, but more importantly, inside the library, there were phone books. The library seemed to be the only place that had phone books any more. Phone booths didn't have them, and nobody seemed to have them in their homes or businesses. Darnel was definitely a fish out of water in the digital age.

In the library, Darnel found the current phone book for Binghamton. In fact there were seven current phone books for Binghamton. He didn't think any of them were produced by the phone company. What was the name of the phone company these days anyway, and did they still publish a phone book? These phone books were put out by commercial enterprises. Some were all yellow pages. Darnel began to look through the various phone books. He was trying to match the address he had with a doctor's office. It was tedious work. After more than two hours, Darnel found the address he was looking for, but it was no longer a doctor's office. But at least this address still existed. The building where Patsy's doctor used to have his office was now a mini-mall that contained a pizza shop, a "call center," and some other things. There was no doctor's office.

Darnel decided he would try to call the pizza shop and ask if anyone who worked there remembered years ago when there had been doctors' offices in their building. He had to make sure he had enough coins to use the pay phone to call a business in Binghamton, and he went to the library desk to have someone change his twenty dollar bill. Apparently nobody used cash anymore, even to pay their fines for overdue books. They paid their fines with credit cards, and Darnel didn't have one of those. He didn't have any credit.

Consequently, the library didn't have twenty dollars' worth of change to give Darnel. He had to leave the library and walk down the street to a bank to get change for his twenty dollar bill. Life was difficult for Darnel, and he was becoming worn down with the inconveniences of trying to live his 1990s life in the year 2016. It wasn't working for him.

Finally, he had quarters, and he was in the phone booth. He called the number of the pizza shop and asked to speak to the manager.

The man who answered spoke with an accent he couldn't place. "This is Valdez, how can I help you?" Darnel wondered why the manager of the pizza parlor wasn't called Tony or Vinny. That was the way it had been back in the day. Why was somebody called Valdez running a pizza shop?

"Mr. Valdez, my name is Darnel Phillips, and I'm trying to find somebody who remembers when your building used to be a doctor's office. I'm looking for my missing brother, and my search has led me to your address."

There was silence on the other end of the line. "Just a minute Mr. Phillips. I don't think there's anybody here who goes that far back. That's almost twenty years ago. We've only been here seven years." Valdez covered the phone with his hand, and Darnel could hear him yelling in the background. There was considerable shouting and once the phone got dropped or knocked off the counter. Darnel almost hung up. He waited and waited and was sure he'd been forgotten. Finally, a woman spoke into the phone.

"Hello, I'm just a customer; I don't work for the pizza people. I'm here waiting to pick up my veggie pizza with extra cheese, and I heard Valdez yelling at the staff about the old days. Are you the one who's looking for your missing brother? He's been missing a long time, I guess?"

"Yes, I'm trying to find my brother who disappeared in 2001. Do you remember when there used to be a doctor's office located in the building where the pizza shop is now?"

"I remember there were several doctor's offices in the building back then. What doctor are you looking for?"

"I don't know his name. I just know he had an office at this address."

"Sorry I can't help you. If you don't know the doctor's name, you're looking for a needle in a haystack. One of the doctors here used to be my doctor, but he retired years ago."

Darnell knew for sure that he was looking for that needle in a haystack. "What was your doctor's name? What kind of doctor was he?"

"He was Dr. Elias Trimble, and he was my OB-GYN. He delivered all three of my boys. He always promised me a girl, but it never happened. He was a very good doctor. I really loved the man."

"Do you know where he is now? Is he still alive?"

"He'd be pretty old by now, but I've heard he still lives around here someplace."

"He was for sure an M.D.?"

"Of course he was. I wouldn't have gone to anybody but an M.D. Come to think of it, I think Dr. Elias was the only M.D. in the building. There was a D.O. and a group of chiropractors. I wouldn't go to a chiropractor. They can do real damage to your body. There were a couple of podiatrists, too. I wouldn't go to them either. I have to get off the phone now. My pizza's ready. Sorry I couldn't help you. Good luck finding your brother." The voice on the phone was gone.

But Darnel had found out more than he'd hoped for. He had the name of a doctor who used to practice in the building, and the doctor was an M.D. and an OB-GYN specialist. Even if Trimble didn't turn out to be Patsy's doctor, he might be able to guide Darnel to the other doctors who had practices in the building. Darnel was especially excited about what the woman on the phone had said about Dr. Elias Trimble's specialty.

Leon and Vicky had both mentioned that Patsy Grimes might have been pregnant when she was last working at the Polecat Grill. Elias Trimble, M.D. might have actually been her very own doctor. It made a kind of sense to Darnel that Patsy would have chosen to see an obstetrician who was located far away from Dydonia. Why she hadn't gone to Syracuse was still bugging him, but she probably had her reasons.

Darnel was worn out from his investigation. It was a lot of work to make phone calls to people about things that had happened years ago. Many people didn't remember what that had happened a couple of years ago. Darnel tried not to remember anything that had happened to him in the past eighteen years, so his memories were firmly locked onto what had happened in his pre-prison days. He was a dinosaur in so many ways, and he knew it.

His next step was to find Dr. Elias Trimble. The woman on the phone had said Trimble would be by "pretty old by now." Since the doctor was retired, Darnel knew the man had to be at least in his seventies. He was probably in his eighties, and maybe in his nineties. Darnel hoped dementia hadn't set in yet, and he hoped Trimble would be willing to talk to him, assuming he was able to find the doctor. He hoped the man had kept his landline.

Darnel called information on the pay phone. Miraculously, he got a phone number for an Elias Trimble, M.D. He used his last fifty cents to call the doctor's house. A young woman answered the phone. "Dr. Trimble's residence."

"My name is Darnel Phillips, and I'd like to speak with Dr. Trimble. It's important. I am trying to locate someone who's disappeared, and I think Dr. Trimble can help me."

"This is Dr. Trimble's hospice nurse, Verity. I'm sorry to tell you Dr. Trimble is quite ill and not able to talk on the telephone. Family and very close friends are being notified and asked to come by to make their last visits. Dr. Trimble is now in a coma and probably won't know you're here. We are now praying that he passes quietly."

This was what Darnel had dreaded. Trying to find people from so many years ago was almost impossible. It sounded as if Elias Trimble, M.D. was, at this moment, about to meet his reward in the unknown next dimension. It would be impossible for Trimble be able to answer any of Darnel's questions about Patsy, even if he'd actually been her doctor. All Darnel could think of at that moment was what the hospice nurse had said about family and close friends being notified to come to Trimble's bedside. Even if Elias Trimble wasn't able to speak to him, if Darnel could locate an office staff person or someone else who had worked with Trimble, he might be able to find out something.

Darnel was desperate and knew he'd become obsessed. Darnel's manners and social skills were not the best to begin with, but even he realized it would not be appropriate or polite to confront the doctor's family and friends as they were making a last pilgrimage to see the doctor and say their final goodbyes. Darnel, however, had a mission. He was not able to back away. He was going to find Trimble's address, and he was going to try to talk to everyone who came to see the doctor on his death bed.

Darnel had to go back into the library to look for the doctor's address in one of the phone books, and he discovered that Dr. Elias Trimble was now living in the Sunnyside Retirement Village. Darnel wondered if he would be allowed inside, or if he would have to try to talk to people outside the retirement home. It was getting late. Darnel had no idea how he was going to get to Binghamton which was a two-hour drive south. He didn't have any transportation, and he decided there was no point in trying to hitchhike to Binghamton tonight. He wasn't going to get there tonight, and tomorrow might be too late. If the old doctor was already in a coma, he could die tonight. Darnel began to think he should wait for Dr. Trimble's funeral or memorial service, to try to question his family and friends.

Patience was not one of Darnel strong suits, so now he couldn't wait for the doctor to die and for the funeral festivities to begin. begin. Darnel bought the Binghamton newspaper every day and listened to the evening news. Darnel began to make his plans about how he was going to travel to the funeral home or the memorial service. He assumed the doctor's burial would be somewhere in the environs of Binghamton. He'd lived there and practiced medicine there; his family and friends were there. There would be no reason for him to be buried someplace far away, like California or Alaska.

Chapter 23

Gimbel knew what he had to do. He sent an email to Steve Brandon asking for everything he could find out about the people who owned Coastal Carolina Seafood and about the people who ran it. Gimbel needed as much background as he could get. The only way he was going to make any progress on this investigation was to get inside their organization. To infiltrate that business, he had to have the official resumes as well as the dirt, the inside information nobody wanted anybody to know.

Meanwhile, Jason Craymer, the manager at Coastal Carolina, had called Detective Saunders. Gimbel used an app that disguised his voice on the phone. It didn't make him sound weird; it just made him sound different. Gimbel was concerned that during the investigation in North Carolina, Chuckie Petrossi would meet Craymer in person, and Craymer might recognize Chuckie's voice as being the same as Gimbel's voice. Gimbel questioned Jason about the two employees who'd been found dead in the company's van, Dirk Shannon and Pedro Ruiz. Craymer confirmed what Beatrice had said, that neither man was on the Coastal Carolina Seafood payroll. Jason told Gimbel that some of the vans delivering their seafood products were owned by Coastal Carolina, but they contracted with another company, "Leave the Driving to Us," to provide drivers who made the deliveries.

"Why do you subcontract for your drivers? With something as perishable as seafood, I'd think you would want to maintain a close watch over who delivers your products."

"We've been using 'DTU,' that's what everybody calls them, for many years, and they've always done an excellent job for us. We've had very few complaints about deliveries being late or in error. If DTU wasn't dependable, we would have found another company to drive for us. I'm really sorry about the two guys who were killed, but I don't know them. Do you have any idea why they were murdered? If you want to know anything about their backgrounds or anything like that, you'll have to call DTU about it. Neither one of them worked for us."

"Do you save money by contracting out the driving? Is that why you do it?"

"It saves us some money, yes, but it saves us a great deal in the hassle department. In the long run, contracting out does save us money because there's less paperwork. As our operation grew over the years, we had to hire more and more drivers. There were state and federal payroll taxes, Medicare, unemployment insurance, health insurance, liability insurance, the commercial driver's licenses, security checks ad nauseam, and on and on. It was never-ending, and somebody was always quitting or disappearing. We were getting slammed on part-time versus full-time employees. When we had the chance to go with DTU, we jumped on board. They hire the workers, train them, and take care of all that paperwork and government hassle. They provide us with good drivers. We have a few guys from the old days who still drive for us and are actually employed by us. We didn't want to let them go, but they are phasing out. Our overhead costs and the costs of keeping up with paperwork, are much lower if we can contract out as many things as possible."

Gimbel got the picture, and now understood why nobody at Coastal Carolina's headquarters had ever heard of Dirk Shannon. It seemed that Coastal Carolina Seafood was not the business Gimbel needed to get inside of. He needed to get inside of DTU. He'd hoped he was going to have a chance to stay in Wilmington for a while. The FBI had gone to all this trouble to set him up under cover, thinking he would be getting cozy with the people at Coastal Carolina. Now he was going to have to find out everything he could about DTU and get cozy with those people.

It turned out that the address for DTU's headquarters was nearby in Wilmington, North Carolina, so Gimbel figured he might be able to stay on in the area for a while longer. He could hardly get into DTU by applying for a job as a driver. He was a flashy drug dealer from L.A., and a guy like that was not going to be able to get a job as a van driver and delivery person for DTU. Somebody else was going to have to fill that position.

Gimbel emailed Steve Brandon again and gave the FBI agent a quick rundown about the fact that Coastal Carolina did not hire its own drivers. Gimbel told Brandon he needed everything he could find about DTU, and he wanted it yesterday. As much as Gimbel was enjoying the North Carolina beach, he was highly motivated to get to the bottom of whoever was responsible for distributing and selling millions of dollars' worth of heroin and fentanyl.

Gimbel was going to make himself spend one day sitting on the beach, really just to see if he could do it. He found a beach umbrella and a folding chair underneath his rental house, packed a cooler with water and ice, and brought a book he'd been trying to make himself read. He traveled the brief distance down the wooden walkway and across the dunes. He applied sunblock, put on his hat, and set up his beach stuff. The ocean was beautiful, and he decided to go into the water for a swim. The surf was fairly calm today, and he was able to swim way out beyond where they waves were breaking. Gimbel swam every morning in the pool at the YMCA in Syracuse, but a leisurely swim in the ocean was a new experience for him. He enjoyed his time in the salt water and went back to his beach umbrella and chair.

He stared at his book and his cooler and looked around for an idea about what he was supposed to do next. Completely frustrated, he gathered up all the beach gear and carried it back to his house. He washed off the sunblock and the saltwater, dressed in his own comfortable clothes, and called a rental car company to reserve a Toyota sedan. He put on a baseball cap and drove his BMW to the rental car company to pick up the Toyota.

He promised himself he would be Chuckie Petrossi in the morning when he walked the dogs on the beach and in the afternoon, after five o'clock, when he walked them again. He would be Chuckie when he went out in public to a restaurant at night. He would wear the silly purple and chartreuse shirts and the white shoes. But during the days, during working hours, he intended to work. He gave himself a day job. Today he was going to drive to Holden Beach and look over Coastal Carolina Seafood's processing and packing operation. He was going to follow one of the vans when it left the plant. He might even follow one of the Coastal Carolina van drivers when they went home after work.

He'd been in North Carolina for less than twenty-four hours. He was sure that Carley Steinmeyer, if she was as good as the FBI thought she was, would already have figured out Gimbel wasn't going to be able to sit on the beach all day. She knew he would be running his own surveillance and be into his own operation by now. They'd told him they were setting him up, but making contact was up to him.

When he arrived at the car rental place in his gold BMW, a few eyebrows were raised. Gimbel parked the car in their lot and made a comment to one of the attendants. "It belongs to my great uncle. Horrible, isn't it? He really loves it though, so I can't make fun of it." The attendant laughed and watched Gimbel drive off in his baseball cap and the Toyota sedan. Forty-five minutes after he'd put away the blue and white sun umbrella and the folding chair, Gimbel was on his way to Holden Beach.

Coastal Carolina Seafood was not as big an operation as Gimbel had imagined it would be. It was located on the water, and the shrimp boats and fishing boats could pull up to the docks alongside the processing buildings to unload their catches. It looked as if the company had started with one small building. Over the years, they'd added on to it and then added onto it again and again. It wasn't an architecturally coherent place, but it wasn't intended to be. The corrugated metal roofs and collection of ad hoc spaces made it a functional, if haphazard, structure. T1-11 siding was on all of the assorted, strung-together add-ons, and they had been painted the same seagull gray color in an attempt to make the building look more cohesive. This was where the work was done, where the seafood was sorted and packed into boxes, ready to ship out to customers. The sorting and the packing and whatever processing took place had to be done quickly and efficiently. Seafood was delicate and perishable. It had to be delivered fresh, so Coastal Carolina Seafood was not built for looks; it was built for speed.

Gimbel parked and walked into what he thought was the front entrance. The wooden screen door with peeling black paint banged closed behind him. This building closest to the parking lot was a kind of market. There was an old-fashioned refrigerated display case inside that held fish and other seafood. It wasn't fancy, but customers could walk in and buy their own fish fresh off the boat. There were tubs of various sizes of shrimp on display. The heads were still attached. This was the place for hardcore seafood eaters to buy their dinner.

Gimbel picked up a flyer that listed prices for the various kinds of fish and sizes of shrimp. Two of the larger sizes of shrimp were available already cooked without the heads, but you had to peel off the rest of the shell yourself. Gimbel noted that Coastal Carolina also sold flash frozen seafood and fish. Coastal Carolina made their own special recipe for deviled crab and would ship it anywhere in the country…for a price. Gimbel bought two pounds of their largest cooked shrimp, a half-dozen deviled crabs, the delicious seafood concoction that had been stuffed back into empty crab shells, and two pints of Coastal Carolina's homemade cocktail sauce.

He carried his bag of seafood around the side of the display case where there was a swinging door. Nobody was paying any attention to him, so he pushed through the door and found himself in a kitchen of sorts. Women were sitting at long tables with knives in their hands, picking cooked crabs as fast as they could. There were piles of cooked crabs on one side, and a container to hold the picked crabmeat on the other side of each woman. Gimbel could see through into the next room where people were laboring over enormous stainless steel mixing bowls, stuffing empty crab shells with the deviled crab mixture, wrapping them in shrink-wrap packages, and stacking the individual deviled crab servings into shipping containers.

It was an incredibly busy place. There were lots of employees, and it appeared to Gimbel that every one of them was working very hard. He hadn't seen the entire operation, but he'd seen enough. There was nothing nefarious going on here. This was a legitimate and very active business operation, exactly what it said it was. Gimbel was going to have to look elsewhere for the nexus of the drug distribution business. It wasn't at Coastal Carolina Seafood in Holden Beach. This place was the real deal, exactly what it advertised itself to be.

He was glad he'd been able to see the place where the wonderful Sherwood Inn shrimp cocktail had its beginnings. He had always loved the shrimp cocktail, and now it had not only history but geography. Gimbel knew the seafood he'd just purchased would be fabulous, and he would be back for more. He bought a small cooler and some ice and put his purchases into the back of the Toyota.

Gimbel saw several white vans with Coast Carolina Seafood signs on the side, parked at the loading dock behind one of the buildings. He decided to sit in his car until one of them left. He intended to follow the van to see where it went after leaving Holden Beach. He was sure he would have to do this more than once. The vans loaded with seafood would be heading out for restaurants and food stores throughout the mid-Atlantic and the Northeast. Other vans might be on their way to meet up with drug suppliers who would load their wares, which were already packed into Coastal Carolina Seafood boxes, into the vans.

That was how Gimbel would do it, if he were doing it. He would have the boxes of drugs packed in advance in boxes identical to the seafood boxes, so that the transfer of the boxes full of drugs to the seafood vans could happen as quickly as possible. There would be no fuss; it wasn't happening. Nothing to see here. It would be a rapid transfer, someplace out of sight, but not far off the travel route. Gimbel was more determined than ever to find that place.

One of the vans was leaving, and Gimbel followed it. It turned out that the particular van he'd chosen to follow was making deliveries to local seafood restaurants in the Wilmington area. This van wasn't even going to get on the main highway or leave town. When he realized what was happening with the van, he discontinued his search. He would pick another van to follow on another day, and it was time for lunch.

The van was stopped at Susie's Seafood Shop. It was a small café, but there were lots of cars in the parking lot...always a sign the food was good. Gimbel decided this was where he would eat lunch and went inside to check it out. The tables were all filled, so he sat at the counter. He looked around to see what the clientele were ordering. It all looked wonderful, but the shrimp salad was huge and was served surrounded by sections of ripe red tomatoes he was certain were locally grown. He ordered a bowl of creamy seafood chowder and a large shrimp salad. Gimbel had lucked out, and Susie's was his newest favorite restaurant.

After lunch he programmed DTU into his phone's GPS and drove to their headquarters in Wilmington. He didn't have anything back yet from Steve Brandon, but he decided to check out DTU ahead of the FBI report. When he received the information from the FBI, he would have a picture in his mind of what the place looked like. DTU's address was located in an industrial park area of Wilmington. It was in a plain concrete building in a row of other plain concrete buildings. Gimbel couldn't resist going inside. He told himself he should wait until he knew more about the operation, but he couldn't help himself. He parked his car and knocked on the door. The door was locked. No one answered right away. He knocked again. Finally, a grumpy looking older woman came to the door and peered out at him.

"What do you want?"

"I'm looking for 'Leave the Driving to Us.' Am I in the right place?"

"This is DTU, but nobody ever comes here. All of our customers contact us through the internet or over the phone. I can't help you. This is just accounting and paperwork. We don't deal with customers here." She was about to close the door in Gimbel's face.

"If I'm looking for a job, where do I go?"

"If you'd bothered to read what it says on our website, you'd know not to come here. How did you ever get this address anyway? Nobody ever comes here. Go home and look on your computer, or look us up on your fancy iPhone. That will tell you what to do. You look overqualified to be a driver. In fact, you look like law enforcement to me. Contact us over the internet. And don't knock again."

Gimbel went back to his car. At least now he knew where the DTU business office was. This grouchy person didn't look like a drug dealer either, but if she kept the books and did the accounting, she must know something. Gimbel began to wonder if there were two DTUs operating simultaneously, two businesses working in parallel, one legitimate and one distributing drugs. He figured there were definitely two sets of books. It wouldn't be the first time he'd encountered that kind of set up.

His first whole day in North Carolina had been productive. He'd had an invigorating swim in the ocean, a fight with a beach umbrella, a great lunch, a chewing out by an ill-tempered bookkeeper, and now it was time to get back to his dogs.

Dilly and Billy were used to being alone all day when Gimbel was at work, but they were always happy to see him when he got home. They would be thrilled to have another long walk on the beach. Gimbel already had his dinner in a cooler in the car. He'd turned a day he thought was going to be lost to sloth into a day in which he'd taken some small but constructive steps forward in his investigation.

Chapter 24

Gimbel Saunders had heard about a great restaurant in Calabash, North Carolina. Calabash, the sleepy fishing village in Brunswick County, just misses being in South Carolina. Located at the languid confluence of the Little River and the Intracoastal Waterway, its closest neighbor is the protected preserve of Bird Island. Calabash is all about eating seafood—catching it, selling it, and eating it. There are quite a few places in town to indulge in the eating part. The restaurant that got the best reviews, from Gimbel's non-scientific survey, was Waterside, a rustic, all-you-can-eat place that specialized in steamed crabs.

Calabash is almost an hour's drive from Oak Island, so Gimbel planned to leave his house early on Thursday afternoon. Waterside didn't take reservations, and it was impossible to get in on a weekend. Even during the week in the summertime, there was always a wait. Gimbel didn't want to have to wait very long, so he left Oak Island with Billy and Dilly at 3:30 p.m. They would have their walk on the bank of the Little River while Gimbel waited for his table.

Gimbel tried to take a scenic coastal route to Calabash, but all roads to Calabash required him to drive on Route #17.

The drive took longer than he'd anticipated, and the dogs were ready to get out of the car when they finally arrived. The town is a quiet country place, oriented more towards the water than towards the land. Fishermen live here and make their living here. But if the fishing industry is the primary source of employment and income in Calabash, seafood restaurants were a definite close second.

Everywhere Gimbel looked there was a restaurant, but he was headed for the Waterside. He found a spot in the parking lot and put his name in with the receptionist. The restaurant looked exactly as he'd imagined it would. It was definitely a blast from the past. He put the dogs on their leashes and let Dilly and Billy out of the car for their evening walk. All dogs love new smells, so it was a leisurely stroll along the riverbank as Gimbel let his two best friends determine the pace. He hadn't eaten lunch that day, and he was hungry. He gathered up his two canine pals and carried them back to the gold BMW. He checked in at the Waterside, and his table was ready.

His table was in fact, not his alone. The seating at the Waterside was shared, long tables covered with heavy brown wrapping paper, and you sat down wherever there was an open seat. Gimbel's seat was a chair with metal legs and a seat and back upholstered in red vinyl. It was one of several mismatched chairs that lined both sides of the communal dining experience. He was seated across from an older woman and her granddaughter. They had obviously been here many times before and knew the waitress by her first name. Gimbel figured the two would have the scoop on the menu, and he would order whatever they ordered.

The waitress took their drink orders and insisted on leaving them with menus. She gave one to the women across from Gimbel and said something about "a couple of new items."

The two women across the table were looking at the menu, and they burst out laughing. Gimbel was reading the same menu, but he couldn't find anything on it that he thought was funny. It all sounded delicious, and he wanted to order every item on it. But he wasn't laughing. And he wanted to laugh. At the risk of being intrusive, he decided to ask.

"Excuse me, it's none of my business, but I was wondering what you saw on the menu that was so humorous." Gimbel smiled his best smile.

Both women looked at him across the table and burst into laughter again. The older women with steel grey hair, who looked like she was in her late 50s or early 60s, was trying very hard to get her laughter under control. The younger woman with red hair and bright blue eyes was laughing so hard she couldn't speak. She started to speak, then put the menu up in front of her face. "I apologize. It's rude of us to make such a spectacle of ourselves. It's a private joke," and she convulsed in laughter again.

"I love private jokes." Gimbel was now dying to know what they were laughing about.

The younger woman blushed. Her ears were bright red. "It's the crab...." She couldn't get it out and put the menu up to cover her face again. Gimbel started to laugh, too. It was contagious. She finally said it. "Crab balls." She followed her revelation with another paroxysm of laughter. Tears were running down her face. Once she'd finally said it out loud, she elaborated. "Does the order come with a magnifying glass? How many dozens do you have to order to get filled up? How tiny are they, really?"

Gimbel got it and joined in. "Is that the Carolina version of Rocky Mountain Oysters?" Both women screamed with glee.

"I was so afraid I would offend you, if I told you why we were laughing." The waitress approached with their beverages, and nearby customers at their table looked to see what these three were drinking. Their disapproving glances let Gimbel know they were speculating that this group had been hitting the booze before they'd arrived at the restaurant. Otherwise, why would they be so rowdy and laughing so loud? But Gimbel had ordered sweet tea, and so had the women. This was a menu comedy, not a laughing jag brought on by too much to drink.

All three ordered the "All You Can Eat Special." It was a seafood extravaganza that included all the fried shrimp, hush puppies, fried chicken, corn on the cob, and French fries you could eat plus all the hard Atlantic blue crabs you wanted to pick. It was expensive, but it was an endless buffet, served to you at your table. Of course, you could *not* take a doggie bag home.

The women were clearly professionals at eating hard crabs. They explained that "soft crabs" meant soft-shell crabs, crabs that had recently molted or shed their shells. They told Gimbel how soft crabs were cooked and eaten, very different than the way hard crabs were opened and consumed. They showed Gimbel how to open and extract the delicate meat from the hard crabs. Everyone had their own unique way of getting the meat out of these mysterious creatures. The older woman's method was different than the younger woman's. They told Gimbel he would find his own special way of separating the difficult-to-get-to sweet crabmeat from its shell.

Gimbel hadn't laughed so hard in years, and he'd enjoyed talking to these two women. "I'm Gimbel Saunders." Although he was decked out in Chuckie Petrossi's clothes and shoes and looked totally ridiculous, he couldn't bring himself to lie to these women with whom he had shared a slightly off-color joke and crab-picking lessons. "You've obviously been here lots of times, and I've obviously never been here before. Do you live in the area?"

"We have a summer house on Shell Island. That's near Wrightsville Beach. We don't get down here to Calabash that often. It's a pretty long drive from Wrightsville Beach, but we love to come to Waterside." The young woman was talkative. The older woman was not as social.

"You drive all the way down here just to eat crabs?" Gimbel knew these Carolina people loved their seafood, but he was amazed at the lengths to which they were willing to go to enjoy it.

The older woman smiled. "We come for the shopping, too."

"The shopping? I didn't know Calabash was known for anything but seafood."

The young woman was eager to talk about her favorite store. "My favorite clothing store is in Calabash, and we come down here to go shopping there. It's called Au Naturel, and everything in the store is made from natural fibers. There's no polyester or rayon or anything like that in the whole store. It's cotton and bamboo and a few things made out of linen. Scarves are all silk and cotton. Their styles are the best. You'd never suspect that such a great little store would be able to make a go of it all the way down here in the boonies."

The young woman was a breath of fresh air. Gimbel thought she must still be in high school, but she was obviously very bright and had a great sense of humor for someone so young. She was beautiful. She wasn't Goth or anorexic or depressed or angry. She didn't have any tattoos, at least none that the public could see. Gimbel didn't think there were any young people left in the world who were innocent and happy like this girl obviously was. He was curious about the young woman's grandmother. The young woman and her grandmother were obviously very close. Gimbel couldn't help but wonder if there was a mother in the picture somewhere. These two had a close bond, almost as if the older woman had raised the younger woman.

Gimbel wondered to himself if the older woman had ever had a drinking problem. Because of his own childhood, he was very tuned in to the way drunks and former drunks looked. This grandmother looked as if she might have once been into the bottle, but Gimbel could tell she'd given it up long ago. She was into sweet tea now, and obviously had been for a very long time. Good for her. Not everybody could do what Gimbel suspected this woman had been able to do.

"Do you live in Wrightsville Beach, sorry, Shell Island, all year round?"

"We live in Asheville, except in the summer. My mother works all the time, but once in a while she graces us with her presence here at the beach." Gimbel detected more than a note of sarcasm in the girl's remarks, but she was at an age when it was her job to find fault with her mother and assert her own identity. "What about you? You aren't from around here, are you?" The wholesome teenage girl wanted to know Gimbel's story.

Gimbel didn't know what to say. He was supposed to say he was from Los Angeles, but he didn't want to lie to these people who were very real, completely genuine. "I'm from upstate New York. I'm on disability because of a heart murmur, and I'm renting a house on Oak Island." The young woman's eyes grew darker with concern when he mentioned the heart problem. When she became serious, something about her face reminded Gimbel of something, but he couldn't put his finger on what it was. Most of the time, this girl was a ray of sunshine, smiling and laughing. "Personally, I think the doctor overreacted on the heart murmur thing, but I'm taking time off as prescribed. Supposedly, I've had the heart problem all my life, but nobody ever found it before last year. I've been a professional baseball player and spent three years in the U.S. Marines. The newly discovered heart murmur has never interfered with my life until now."

"Sorry your life has been messed up. You look really healthy to me. But what do I know? I am curious about your car." The older woman put her hand on the younger woman's arm, cautioning her to be careful about what she said. "It doesn't fit, Marley. That car does not fit with this nice man's personality. I have to ask. We saw the gold convertible when you were in the parking lot."

Gimbel laughed and told a small white lie. "It was given to me, and it is a BMW. It's ugly and embarrassing, but it's a good car. I want to sell it but just haven't had the chance. It belonged to my uncle." It was just a small lie. The car kind of belonged to Gimbel's "Uncle Sam."

"See, Marley, I told you the car didn't fit."

The young woman was smart about people. She knew the car wasn't his style. He wondered what she thought about his Chuckie Petrossi clothes.

"I saw your adorable dogs when we were walking in. They're Westies, aren't they? I love Westies. That's when I noticed the car." She didn't miss anything.

When the waitress brought the checks to the table, Gimbel picked up the tab for the two women. They protested. "You two ladies have given me the best laugh of the decade, and you have given me professional crab-cracking lessons. How can I possibly ever repay you for those two gifts? Buying your dinner is the least I can do."

"Well, the least *we* can do it to introduce ourselves to you. I'm Christina Rose Carmichael, and this is Marley Kurtz, my grandmother. Will you give me your email address? My mother is a tyrant about thank you notes. She's just now started to allow me send them via email. It used to be all perfect paper stationery and stamps and snail mail addresses. Who even does that anymore? Now I can send you a thank you note for dinner to your email address."

Gimbel laughed and gave her his email. They walked out to the parking lot together, and Christina Rose came over to the gold BMW and stuck her fingers through the open window to let the dogs smell her hand. "What are these adorable little guys' names?"

"Dilly and Billy."

"Too cute. They are too cute. I'll bet they love to run on the beach on Oak Island. I love to run on the beach on Oak Island. Do you have a nice house there?"

"Yes and yes. The dogs love the beach, and I have a very nice house there. It is way too big for one person, but I'm enjoying it."

Christina Rose had a hard time saying goodbye to the dogs. Finally, she and Marley walked to their white Chevy Suburban. Christina Rose turned and smiled at Gimbel. "Good luck selling that car. Have you thought of giving it a paint job—maybe a nice dark navy blue or silver grey?" She laughed. Gimbel laughed and waved. He was sad to see these two women go. He was feeling lonely as he watched them drive away, out of his life.

Chapter 25

Darnel *finally found the information* he'd been watching for in the newspaper. It seemed nobody had just a funeral anymore; it was all memorial services and celebrations of life these days. Dr. Elias Trimble's memorial service, a Celebration of Life, was to be held at Riverside Episcopal Church in Binghamton. It was two days from now, and Darnel had arranged to borrow a car from one of the other halfway house residents. He'd pretty much had to bribe the woman to allow him to use the car, and her Chrysler Neon was sixteen years old and smelled bad inside. The service was at 11:00 a.m. on Thursday, and Darnel wanted to be there in plenty of time to get a good seat.

He didn't have a suit to wear; he'd not been to a funeral since his mother died almost thirty years earlier. He couldn't remember if he'd had a suit to wear to her funeral, but he didn't have a suit now. He had to borrow one from another resident at the halfway house. It didn't fit very well. The pants were too short and too tight, and the jacket was too large. It had big shoulder pads, so it was a relic of the 1980s. Darnel didn't know enough about fashion to know the suit was from the 1980s, but he knew it was very out of style. He knew it looked terrible on him, but beggars can't be choosers. He needed a suit, and the suit with the shoulder pads was the only one available to him.

Darnel knew his life was a mess, but he promised himself, as soon as he found out what had happened to Fergus, he would straighten things out. He would get a driver's license, and he would think about getting a job. He would buy a cell phone, and he would learn how to use it. He didn't think he would bother to buy a suit. Nobody wore a suit any more, unless it was to go to a funeral.

He got lost a couple of times on his way to the church, but the 1999 road atlas he'd found at the halfway house helped him make it to Riverside Episcopal. He arrived in time for the service, but the church was already filled with hundreds of mourners. Dr. Trimble had delivered many babies, and many people loved him. The church was packed, and the service was long. Darnel had not spent much of his life in churches, so he fumbled with the hymnals and didn't know when to stand up, or sit down, or kneel. He watched what the woman sitting next to him was doing, and he did whatever she did. Finally, it was over, and Darnel tried to strike up a conversation with the woman he'd been watching, the one who had guided him through the religious ritual. But the woman was crying and didn't want to talk to him. Darnel couldn't understand why she was so sad. The doctor had lived to be ninety-three years of age. How could anyone expect to live much longer than that? Darnel had a dysfunctional personality, and empathy was not in his tool kit.

Everyone at the church service was invited to a lunch afterwards. Darnel wanted to go. It would be a free meal, but more importantly, it might provide him with the opportunity to talk to some of the people who had known Elias Trimble,

M.D. There was a small map on the back of the "Celebration of Life" program, so Darnel thought he could find his way to the reception. It was being held at the recreation center of the Sunnyside Retirement Village where Dr. Trimble had lived for the past six years.

Darnel helped himself to the finger sandwiches and the coffee. He was not a sociable guy to begin with, and his years in prison had not enhanced his conversational skills. He made several attempts to interject himself into groups who were talking, but he was awkward and always rebuffed. He finally took his plate of food and sat down on one of the metal folding chairs that ringed the perimeter of the room. He was trying very hard, but he just did not have what it took to be a member of a group. He was feeling sorry for himself—sorry that he'd never finished high school, sorry that he didn't have any money, sorry that the world had passed him by. He was a loser, and he knew it.

"Are you all right?" The plump middle-aged woman in a black suit had seen him sitting alone, hanging his head down over his plate of sandwiches. "Did you know Dr. Trimble well? You seem to be taking this very hard."

Darnel was embarrassed to tell the woman that he didn't know Dr. Trimble at all, and in fact had never laid eyes on the man. "My sister was his patient before she disappeared. That's why I came. I wanted to see if anyone remembered Patsy. I'm trying to find out what happened to her."

The woman in the black suit looked Darnel over and came to a decision. "My mother was Dr. Trimble's office nurse for many years. She's eighty-seven now, and she sometimes has trouble remembering things. But, she might remember your sister. She took a great interest in all of Dr. Trimble's patients."

"I would love to talk to her. I have Patsy's picture."

"I'll be right back with my mom. My name is Shirley Dryden." And Shirley was back in a couple of minutes, pushing her mother's wheel chair. "This is my mother, Annette Dryden."

"I'm Darnel Phillips. My sister Patsy disappeared a long time ago. I came to the lunch today, hoping I could talk to somebody who remembered Patsy."

"Shirley said you have a picture of your sister. Maybe it will trigger a memory for me. I used to know all of doctor's patients." The old woman had a nice smile. You could tell she'd been a nurse. She was a kind person, someone a patient would feel comfortable talking to.

Darnel pulled the small snapshot out of his pocket. He handed the black and white photo of Patsy standing beside the RAM truck to Annette. The old woman carefully took the small glossy Kodak print from Darnel's hand. Her arthritic fingers made it almost impossible for her to hold onto the tiny square, and Darnel was afraid she was going to drop it. She squinted her eyes to see the face in the photograph. "Oh, yes, of course I remember Patsy. She said her name was Patsy Phillips. A couple of time, she came to the office with a man named Fergus Phillips. But I don't think Phillips was her real last name. Lots of women came to us using last names that were not their own. They were the ones who paid cash, and Dr. Elias always gave them a break on the charges. People who were lucky enough to have health insurance had to use their real names, so they could use their insurance. Patsy didn't have insurance and always paid cash."

Darnel was speechless. He could scarcely believe his ears. He'd expected nothing, another dead end. He had hoped, but he had not believed he would learn much of anything. "Please tell me everything you know about Patsy. She disappeared before she had her baby, and I've been trying to find her."

"Yes, she stopped coming for her appointments. Dr. Elias was worried about her. Someone had been beating her, beating her very badly. Doctor was sure it was the father of the unborn child. Patsy had been very honest about the fact that she wasn't married. She was happy when she came in for her first appointment, happy about the baby. But as the months went by, she began to show up with terrible bruises and cuts and even burns on her back and legs. She was from upstate, and doctor asked her why she'd come all the way to Binghamton to see him. On her last visit, she told doctor that her boyfriend, the father of the child, was a physician. Dr. Trimble was beside himself being upset about that. He was outraged that a physician could be the one who was beating Patsy. Doctor hardly ever got angry, but he got a little bit angry with her. He told her she would have to call the police and report the abuse. She laughed at doctor and said the father of her baby was too important, too well-known. She said no one would ever believe her story, that the 'golden boy' was beating her. She said he'd promised to leave his wife. Of course he was married. But same old, same old, we'd heard it thousands of times. He's always going to leave his wife and marry her, but of course he never does. Patsy could have had an abortion, but she wanted to keep the baby. She was five months pregnant when doctor saw her for the last time."

"You said she used the last name of Phillips, and she came to some of her appointments with a Fergus Phillips?" Darnel was almost afraid to ask, for fear he'd heard Annette wrong.

"Yes, Patsy always brought this nice young man with her. She said he was her brother, this Fergus Phillips, but doctor didn't believe her. They didn't look anything alike. I think he was just a friend and someone whose name she'd borrowed for her doctor's appointments. She never came back after that last appointment in March. I remember the date exactly because the last time she came to see doctor, it was my birthday, March 30th, a Friday. One of the staff just happened to say 'Happy Birthday' to me as they walked by. I was sitting there taking Patsy's vitals, and she sang the 'Happy Birthday' song to me. She had a sweet voice, and I was so touched that she had serenaded me. Fergus was there, and he loved hearing her sing, too. She was a very nice woman. She was classy and polite. I really liked her and felt terrible that her boyfriend was beating her so badly. Doctor said the beating was escalating. He could tell that because of the bruises she had from one appointment to the next."

"Did Patsy ever mention the name of the father of her child?"

"Oh, no, she kept that very private. She was afraid to tell anybody, I think. She did tell doctor, at that last visit, that she and Fergus were going to talk to him, to the father of the child. They planned to go to his house. I guess he didn't know yet that Patsy was pregnant. She confided in doctor that she was afraid to tell him, afraid of what he might do when he heard about the baby. Patsy told doctor that her 'brother' Fergus was going with her to Syracuse to help her tell her boyfriend she was pregnant. I guess she said Fergus was going along to protect her. Patsy seemed to know from experience how that boyfriend reacted when things didn't go his way. Doctor said Patsy was terrified of telling the father about the baby, but she felt she had to do it."

"Did Dr. Trimble put any of this in Patsy's chart? Would he have written down anything about the abuse or about the father of the child?"

"He would have put in her chart about the abuse because it had to do with her physical condition, but I doubt it he would have written down anything about the boyfriend. I don't have access to the files anymore, but I could call a young friend of mine who's been working on cleaning out doctor's files and digitizing them. If they're available, I can have them sent to you. Give your address and your contact information to my daughter, and I'll see if I can locate Patsy's file. There's all that HIPAA business to worry about now, but since your sister has disappeared, we can't ask for her permission to release her file, can we?"

"I would really appreciate having a chance to read the file, especially since there might be something in there that would help me locate her. I'll give my address to Shirley"

Annette was still on her stroll down memory lane. "When she didn't show up for her next appointment, or for any more appointments after that, doctor said he was afraid the boyfriend might have killed her. I'd never heard him say anything like that before, about any of his patients. Doctor really did think Patsy might be dead. The staff called her home quite a few times. We left messages for her to call the office, but we never heard from Patsy again. Her friend or her brother Fergus or whoever he was, took good care of her. He was very kind and considerate, opened the door for her and helped her on with her coat and all of that. Not all the men who came into our office did that for the women they were with, not even all the husbands did that for their wives. We saw it all in that office, and I loved every minute of it. Now Elias is gone." Annette began to cry quietly. All the remembering and all the talking had worn her out. Shirley took the photograph of Patsy from her mother's fingers and handed it back to Darnel.

"I'm sorry she couldn't help you. It's been so many years. She's probably forgotten a lot or is confused …"

Darnel stopped Shirley's apology. "No, she was a huge help to me. Your mother told me things I didn't know, things I needed to hear. Thank you so much. Your mother was wonderful. Thank you." Darnel grabbed a discarded a program from the Celebration of Life that was lying on the seat of one of the folding chairs and asked Shirley for a pen. He wrote down his address at the halfway house and said he hoped to hear from her. He stuck out his hand. Shirley took his hand and held it in both of hers for a few seconds.

"Good luck, dear. If my mother can find the files you want, I'll send them to you. It may take a while, and it may come to nothing. I know you're on a difficult journey, and I hope you find out what you need to know."

Darnel left the Sunnyside Retirement Village and began the long drive back to Auburn. He was thinking about Fergus and Patsy, about Patsy's baby, about her trips to Binghamton, about what a good guy his brother was to go to Patsy's doctor's appointments with her, about the SOB who was beating Patsy, the man who was so special nobody could hold him accountable. Darnel was distracted and thinking about everything except the fact that he was driving on Interstate #81, a very busy highway. He wasn't a good driver, and he hadn't driven much in the past twenty-five years. He never saw the eighteen wheeler that crossed the median and hit his car head on. The accident wasn't his fault, but if he'd been paying attention, he might have been able to swerve out of the truck's path.

Chapter 26

Gimbel received all the information the FBI had on DTU. It wasn't much. Their tax returns did not come close to reflecting the volume of business Gimbel was certain they did every year. Coastal Carolina Seafood couldn't be DTU's only client. There was something funny going on with the books. He was law enforcement, after all. He could get a warrant to search the Wilmington offices of DTU. Having already been to the place where all the paperwork was supposedly handled, he knew a search warrant of that office wouldn't get him anything. He knew that breaking into the industrial park business office and going through everything that was in there was not going to shed additional light on anything either. Gimbel did not especially want to include breaking and entering in his bag of tricks.

The other paperwork the FBI had sent included the name of an LLC that owned DTU. There was a person's name listed as the representative and a post office box in Wilmington listed as the address of the LLC. This also amounted to a lot of nothing in terms of real leads. The business was owned and managed by ghosts. The accountant he had offended by knocking on her door the other day was just a dupe, a functionary hired to file paperwork for a front company, a pretend business that wasn't the real business. The only bright spot was that Gimbel felt he had at last been able to put his finger on where the funny business was.

Gimbel called Steve Brandon in Syracuse, and Steve, who saw Gimbel's name come up on his cell phone, asked, "Have you burned Chuckie's clothes in a beach bonfire yet? Are you going to sell the car, or are you going to drive it into a ditch?" Brandon was laughing, knowing Chuckie Petrossi's style was anathema to Gimbel.

"I haven't done either one of those things, yet. However, I do need a less conspicuous car to do surveillance, and I need a couple of people to help me follow the Coastal Carolina vans. I need the extra people for a few days, but I need an inexpensive, inconspicuous car for the duration. I rented a car for one day, but the only way to find out where the drugs are being loaded is to follow the vans on a regular basis. I can't do that in the Golden Gas Guzzler. I have a place to hide the unremarkable surveillance car that you are going to provide me with. Have you seen this house? It's enormous. There's room for five cars to park underneath it and out of sight."

"Carley picked the house. She's tuned in to what's convincing and what isn't. I get it that you need an inconspicuous car. This whole thing with Coastal Carolina and DTU hasn't played out exactly the way we'd thought it would, and hats off to you for being able to switch gears and figure it out so fast."

"I don't feel like I've figured anything out yet. All I've done is eliminate possibilities. DTU on paper is a front. Their office address in Wilmington is the business headquarters for the fake company. There's nowhere to go with that. I have to follow the vans. Whoever is getting the boxes of drugs into the seafood vans is very quick on their feet and very elusive.

They also have access to Coastal Carolina's shipping boxes. I haven't been able to figure out how they get those."

"Okay, one inconspicuous car coming up. And two helpers, each with his or her own inconspicuous car, to follow the vans. Gimbel, remember that even eliminating possibilities helps to narrow the field."

"I know that. It's just frustrating for all of this to be moving so slowly."

"What do you mean, 'so slowly'? You've only been on Oak Island for a few days. Give yourself a break. I don't want to be in trouble with your doctor or with the New York State Police for putting you under too much pressure. Your captain was not entirely thrilled when we stole you from him and sent you to North Carolina. He likes you and wants you back. Take it easy. I'm assuming the two helpers I'm sending can stay at your house. Think you've got room? Ha ha!"

"My thinking right now is that some of the vans carrying seafood rendezvous with a vehicle that's carrying the drugs. How and where they transfer the goods is unknown so far. Not all the seafood vans carry drugs; only some of them do. I followed a Coastal Carolina van from Holden Beach the other day, and all it did was drive around Wilmington delivering seafood to local restaurants. I didn't learn anything useful from that except I found a terrific little seafood shanty that makes the best shrimp salad you've ever had in your life. But I have found no drugs, absolutely none. I know they are here somewhere, but they're well hidden."

"Like I said, you haven't been there for a week yet, Gimbel. Don't push yourself."

"Every day I don't shut down this drug ring, more people die. You know I can't live with that. That's what drives me to do what I do."

"By the way, we found Dirk Shannon's phone in a dumpster in Allentown, Pennsylvania. We didn't find a second phone there. Maybe Dirk's homeboy Pedro didn't own a cell phone?"

"Come on, of course he had a cell phone. Everybody and their support peacock owns a cell phone these days. But I didn't think Pedro's phone, if he had one, would lead us to anything very useful anyway. What about the phone records? I don't expect much from that either, but I never heard anything from you guys or my guys about them."

"Dirk called plenty of phone numbers on his phone. Most of the calls were to legitimate customers on the list from Coastal Carolina. Dirk was calling them to say exactly when he'd be dropping off their seafood orders. He was a pretty responsible delivery guy, especially for a drug dealer."

"Didn't he call any of his drug customers? I would have expected him to call them to tell them when to expect their deliveries, too."

"He called some phone numbers that were for pre-paid throw-away phones. But nothing we could follow up on. Sorry Gimbel, I'm afraid the murders in Skaneateles are going to end up in the cold case files. You know all about those. Maybe you'll have a second crack at the case."

"That isn't one bit funny, Brandon. I've never thought we would find the actual killers, or at least not by trying to find them through the distribution end of the drug chain. I'm counting on finding out who killed those two by investigating these people at their origins. I'm certain that's here in the Wilmington area."

"Counting on you, Gimbel. You do good work. Carley was asking if we'd heard from you."

"Is she the one who wanted to know if I'd burned Chuckie's clothes yet?"

"How did you know?"

Gimbel decided to drive to Calabash again that afternoon. He'd enjoyed the Waterside so much the last time; he wanted to go back. It wouldn't be the same without Christina Rose and Marley, but he might actually order the crab balls from the menu. He started to laugh out loud when he thought of his last visit to Calabash. The dogs would be thrilled to be going on a road trip, and they would enjoy another walk along the banks of the Little River.

There was a lot of water, and there were a lot of boats in the area around Calabash. Gimbel's trip to Calabash that evening was not intended to be work related. It was supposed to be just for fun. He wasn't even thinking about drugs when he drove by the Bird Island Reserve and happened to see a white Coastal Carolina van parked in the marsh. The van was out of place. Gimbel always knew when something was off, and this was definitely off. The van was not on the road. When high tide arrived, the van was parked in a spot where it would be easy for a boat to unload something into it. It would be an easy transfer from boat to van.

Gimbel had given a lot of thought to how the fentanyl and heroin were getting into the United States, and he'd planned to track the source of the drugs backwards from the drug deliveries. He'd thought his strategy eventually would lead him to discover how the drugs were coming into the country. But nothing in this case had happened as he'd expected it to happen. Why would he continue to believe his original strategy would hold up?

Gimbel knew that large quantities of drugs came across the southern border of the U.S. from Mexico in a variety of ways. The fentanyl was mostly manufactured in Mexico with ingredients from China and India. Drug interdiction was always playing catch-up to the creativity of the drug dealers who brought drugs into the U.S. via tunnels, mini submarines, drones, and who knows what other ways they had thought of by now.

Gimbel didn't know when high tide would arrive at the mouth of the Little River and around Bird Island. Local people knew all of that—when high tide was, when low tide was. Of course, fishermen would have to know that every day. Gimbel sometimes heard it on the evening news, but he didn't pay any attention to it. Now he was wishing he had. He Googled "high tide for Bird Island today" on his phone. Google said high tide wouldn't be until after dark, around 10:00 p.m. tonight, not any time soon. The van wouldn't be parked in the marsh at 5:00 p.m. waiting for a rendezvous that wouldn't happen for five hours. Gimbel thought about approaching the van but decided against it. He drove on to the Waterside.

He did order the crab balls, and they were delicious. Really, they were the same concoction as deviled crab, rolled into balls and fried rather than stuffed back into the crab shell. Gimbel also ordered Carolina seafood soup and a fried flounder sandwich. The soup was a tomato-based clear chowder with vegetables, spicy sausage, and all kinds of seafood in it. It was so delicious, he ordered two quarts of it to take home with him. The flounder sandwich came with the Waterside's own homemade tartar sauce and an order of hand-cut French fries. There was a dish of delicious coleslaw served on the side. There weren't as many people at the Waterside tonight, and Gimbel didn't meet anybody. He thought about Christina Rose Carmichael and Marley Kurtz and wished he could run into them again someplace.

Gimbel walked the dogs and headed his BMW in the direction of Oak Island. When he drove by the marsh again, the white Coastal Carolina van was still there. Gimbel was driving Chuckie's car, and he was dressed in Chuckie's clothes. But inside, he was Gimbel Saunders, a police detective who investigated suspicious things. This was suspicious, and he decided to investigate. He would use walking his dogs as a reason to get close to the van. If anybody saw him, who would imagine a guy dressed in a pink cowboy shirt with silk fringe on it and walking two fluffy little dogs was a policeman? Gimbel had to admit to himself that FBI profiler Carley Steinmeyer did good work.

Gimbel and Billy and Dilly took a leisurely stroll through the marsh, heading towards the white van. Gimbel was sure his dogs could not believe their good luck, getting a second walk within hours of the first walk. Gimbel went to the far side of the van where no one could see him from the road. He looked in the driver's side window and almost fainted. He didn't know what he'd expected to see, but he'd not thought he would see a dead person. Only the driver was in the front of the van, and he'd had his throat cut. It was a copycat of what the chef at the Sherwood Inn had discovered a few weeks earlier, almost eight hundred miles to the north. How was that possible?

Careful not to touch the van or anything around it, Gimbel picked up both dogs and hurried them back to the BMW. He called Steve Brandon who fortunately picked up right away. Gimbel told him exactly where he was and what he'd found. Brandon told Gimbel to leave the scene immediately, that he would handle everything going forward. Gimbel urged Brandon to keep him in the loop, and he made his way back to Oak Island.

Gimbel wasn't very often spooked, but he was spooked now. He couldn't get past the fact that in both upstate New

York and just outside of Calabash, North Carolina, there had been murder victims left in vans. All these victims' throats had been cut. Gangs in the U.S. sometimes participated in ritual slayings that included cutting their victims' throats, but it was rare. Americans liked to use firearms to kill their enemies; they preferred to shoot people. Gimbel began to think there was a foreign element involved in these murders. Slicing a victim's throat was quiet, but every professional assassin and every street thug in the U.S. had a silencer for his firearms.

One person could easily gun down two people in a car. It would take two assassins or one very skilled assassin to murder two people in a car with a long knife. The autopsy had shown the two men in upstate New York had been killed with a long knife. Who even carried a long knife around with them these days, or ever? Gimbel knew Middle Eastern cultures used the scimitar sword as a death weapon, but this whole thing didn't smell like ISIS or anybody of that ilk. Gimbel's mind was spinning with possibilities.

Gimbel was happy to find that his "inconspicuous car" had been delivered while he was gone. He was surprised it had arrived as fast as it had and wondered how the FBI's delivery service had been able to get it into the garage. He had to admit, it probably wasn't that hard to open the garage doors. Steve had told Gimbel that nobody at the beach drove a sedan, so Gimbel knew they were going to send him an anonymous mid-size SUV. It was a grey Subaru, and it wasn't new. It was just what Gimbel wanted. Steve had told him the SUV would have four-wheel-drive. Most SUVs came with it standard, and Carley said everybody at the beach thought they needed to have 4WD. Gimbel couldn't wait to drive it in place of the gold BMW.

Chapter 27

After he had walked the dogs the next morning, Gimbel drove to Holden Beach in the Subaru. He sat in Coastal Carolina's parking lot, and when the first van pulled away from the loading dock at Coastal Carolina Seafood, he was on its tail. Once again, he ended up at Susie's Seafood Shop. He had the shrimp salad again and returned to Holden Beach after a great lunch. It was frustrating to be following the wrong vans, but there was no way he could tell which ones were going to be running drugs and which ones were running only seafood.

He waited in the parking lot of the packing plant again that afternoon and followed the next van that left the loading dock. It was headed north as usual on a local road out of Holden Beach. Gimbel had been on these roads before—Sabbath Home Road SW, Old Ferry Connections SW, and Stone Chimney Road SW. He thought the number of the road he was on might be #1115. Gimbel had always wondered why it was, the smaller the road, the more digits in the route number. This road was a tiny road, and its route number had four digits. In California, the main road north and south through the length of the entire state was "The Five."

Gimbel would know, when he approached Supply, North Carolina, whether or not this van was headed to the Wilmington and Wrightsville Beach areas for seafood deliveries. He was resigned to the fact that he was following another local delivery van. He expected it would turn north onto Rt. #17, and he was surprised and excited when it didn't. The van went through the Rt. #17 intersection and continued north on a two-lane road, Rt. #211. Gimbel's phone told him that he and the van were headed for the Green Swamp Preserve and points north. Gimbel was hopeful. Maybe something interesting would happen on this trip.

It was a beautiful drive. There was nothing much except scenery between the town of Supply and the Preserve. There were not many cars on the road, so Gimbel kept his distance behind the van. He was trained in how to follow a vehicle, but following in such a desolate area with few cars on the road meant he had to stay farther back. He hoped he wouldn't lose the van. Gimbel didn't know exactly where this van was headed, but he noted on his GPS that it might be headed for Raleigh.

Of course, he had no idea if this van was just delivering seafood to Raleigh or if it would take on a more criminal cargo at some point. But the route this van was taking gave Gimbel hope that it might be intended to carry drugs. If it was going to Raleigh, it was not taking the shortest road. If a van were delivering something as perishable as seafood, he would expect it to take the most direct and the fastest route to its destination. On the other hand, if this van were headed for Charlotte, it might be taking the quickest way.

When he entered the part of Rt. #211 that passed beside the Green Swamp Preserve, Gimbel decided to follow the van more closely. There were turn offs for camping sights and hiking trails. He didn't want to miss it if the van turned off the road for one of these. He thought he was following closely enough, but all of a sudden, the van disappeared from the road. Gimbel hadn't seen any turn off where the van might have gone, but he'd lost it. He turned around and drove back south on Rt. #211, keeping his eyes open for any place the van might have turned off. He couldn't find anything. The van had disappeared into thin air. How could that have happened? But it had happened, and it had happened all of a sudden. He made a few more trips up and down the section of the road where he was sure the van had disappeared. He made a note of the longitude and latitude so he could come back to this exact spot and look again. He checked the mile markers. Finally he gave up and drove back to Oak Island.

He knew the Green Swamp Preserve was a popular place for camping and hiking. Of course, Chuckie Petrossi didn't do any of those things, but Gimbel Saunders could. The next day, he would get together some camping gear and head out for the preserve. There must be something to be found there, or the van would not have gone off the highway there and vanished. Gimbel thought that maybe he was getting close to something.

That evening he received a nice email thank you note on his phone from Christina Rose Carmichael. She thanked him for buying dinner in Calabash the previous week and said she and Marley would like to return his hospitality with dinner at their house on Shell Island. She said there probably wouldn't be any "crab balls" on the menu, but they would fix something good. Christina Rose had inserted a laughing emoji after that comment. Dilly and Billy were invited to come. Was he available a week from next Thursday? If he could come, she would send their address and a photo of the house. She said it was about an hour's drive from Oak

Island. Traffic wasn't terrible on Thursday nights, but it was terrible on Friday nights. That's why they were inviting him for Thursday night.

More than anything, Gimbel wanted to accept the invitation. He would love to spend another evening with Christina Rose and Marley. He would like to see their beach cottage. But Gimbel had a dilemma. He was not here in North Carolina to have a social life or to make new friends. He was here on an under-cover assignment—to look for murderers and drug dealers. How could he possibly go to Shell Island for dinner? Would he drive the BMW or the Subaru? Would he wear Chuckie's clothes or the worn out work clothes of his own he'd brought to wear inside the house, when he wasn't pretending to be Chuckie? He might have to invest in a third wardrobe, just to have something presentable to wear to dinner at the Shell Island cottage.

The next morning he was going to drive to Wilmington to buy camping equipment and a few items of clothing he could wear to hike into and stake out the Green Swamp Preserve. He had all of this equipment and all of these same clothes back in Syracuse, but none of it was going to do him any good while he was here in North Carolina. He had to think about how he was going to respond to Christina Rose's invitation. He hated to say "no," but he knew he should.

The next morning Gimbel took the dogs with him to Wilmington to find a hunting and camping equipment store. Wilmington was a lovely southern town, and he wished he had more time to explore. He knew they had a wonderful historic preservation district and some outstanding architecture from past eras. Maybe he would have a chance to see some of this charming city when his undercover gig was completed. He found the things he needed for the Green Swamp adventure and treated himself to lunch at Crossroads Steak House where he ordered a steak sandwich and onion rings. The rare steak arrived on an oblong roll, toasted and buttered, with lettuce, tomato, and horseradish mayonnaise. After a steady diet of seafood, which he loved, he'd been dying for some red meat.

Gimbel stopped at a grocery store and bought some things he wanted to take camping with him. He was in a quandary about what to do with the dogs while he went on his stakeout. He didn't want to leave them at an unknown boarding kennel, and the Preserve was only a half-hour drive from Oak Island. Gimbel decided he would take the dogs with him on his first foray into the preserve. If he found anything worth exploring further or anything dangerous, he would leave them at home in the future. He'd camped overnight many times with the dogs, so everybody knew what to do.

Dilly and Billy knew something was up when Gimbel began to pack the Subaru with camping gear, and they were relieved when they got to go along. They left that evening for the Green Swamp Preserve. Gimbel planned to make camp on his own, not stay in one of the official camping grounds. He wasn't going camping for the fun of it, after all. He was tracking a killer or killers. He knew exactly where he wanted to set up his tent and make his camp…in the spot where the Coastal Carolina van had disappeared yesterday from Rt. #211.

There wasn't a very good place to pull off the road, but Gimbel had done things like this before. He would never leave an abandoned vehicle on the side of the road to be seen by passing motorists or other campers. He managed to find a place to conceal the SUV. He left the dogs in the car and walked until he found a secluded spot in the groves of long-leaf pine trees where he could pitch his tent. He was camping in an unauthorized area and didn't want to attract the attention of any forest rangers or official law enforcement people. Dogs were probably allowed only at certain designated campsites. Gimbel was sure he was breaking several rules.

It would attract too much attention to cook anything outside over a campfire. Gimbel fed the dogs and ate his own cold rations. They would make an early night of it and begin exploring in the morning. Best laid plans and all of that…in the middle of the night, the dogs began to growl. They sometimes barked, but they very rarely growled. Gimbel was on alert. He grabbed his gun and told the dogs to be quiet. He exited the tent and zipped up the opening so they couldn't get out. He wished he'd left them in the car.

He moved quietly away from his campsite, listening for whatever had set off Dilly and Billy. He heard men's voices and crept closer to try to hear what they were saying. He was expecting to hear English or maybe Spanish, so it was quite a shock when he realized the men were speaking Russian. Gimbel knew it was Russian because he'd take one year of Russian in high school. It had been a disaster. He had been more interested in sports and girls at the time, and the Cyrillic alphabet had done him in. He'd escaped the year by the skin of his teeth with a C minus grade, and the next year he started over again on foreign languages, this time with Spanish. Gimbel was much more compatible with Spanish. What had he been thinking, signing up for Russian? He didn't remember anything he'd learned that year, but he remembered enough to know these men were speaking Russian with each other. What the heck?

It was dark, so Gimbel could hear more than he could see. He moved closer to try to see what the men looked like.

There wasn't much ambient light in the forest, but one of the men had a flashlight. When he got close enough, Gimbel saw two men arguing. They appeared to be of Slavic descent. One was tall, and the other one was shorter. One had dark hair, and one had light hair. Both had broad foreheads and high cheekbones that Gimbel associated with Eastern European or Russian faces. The two were standing beside a pickup truck with a camper top. Gimbel snapped a few photos of the men and one of the truck's rear license plates.

Gimbel turned on his phone to record their conversation. He couldn't understand a word they were saying, but he was sure Steve Brandon would be able to find someone who could translate the recording. There wasn't enough light to record a video. The men were pointing to something on the ground, but Gimbel couldn't see what it was. Gimbel made a note of the exact latitude and longitude, the coordinates where he and the Russians were now standing. He might have to make a run for it at any minute, but he wanted to be able to come back later to this exact same spot. The terrain in this part of the preserve all looked alike to Gimbel, and the grass of the savanna, the dense evergreen shrub land, and the stands of pine trees made it almost impossible to find one's way without a GPS. He was not on any trail or roadway, so if he wanted to find his way back to this location, he would have to have electronic help.

One of the men shook his fist at the other man, got into the truck, and drove off through the pine forest. He knew where he was going, so the man had been here before. Gimbel would never have brought a truck this far into the swamp, but the Russians had shown him it could be done. The second man stalked off on foot through the pine forest. Being as quiet as possible, Gimbel tried to follow him. Gimbel was afraid to get too close, for fear of being discovered. The Russian walked into a thick grove of trees, and then he was gone. This man had disappeared into nowhere, just as the seafood van had disappeared off the road two days before—into nowhere.

Gimbel searched the area, but he found nothing. He knew he was missing something important, but it was almost impossible to find anything in the dark. He knew he would have better luck if he came back during daylight. He wondered briefly if he were in a magic forest where people and vans just disappeared into thin air. He didn't know if he was living in a Harry Potter movie, but he definitely knew he was in the Twilight Zone.

The two men the FBI was sending to help with van surveillance were scheduled to arrive that afternoon. Gimbel had planned to search the preserve in the morning, but he hadn't counted on being up all night chasing Russians. Gimbel was worn out and decided he had to go back to his house so he could get some sleep. Gimbel sent the photographs he'd taken and his audio recording to Steve Brandon. Before the sun finally began to rise, Gimbel packed up the dogs, the tent, and everything he'd brought with him, into the Subaru. His first attempt to track the van in the preserve hadn't yielded anything useful, except two Russian faces and a pickup truck. He would come back another day and try to figure it out. He and his two helpers would follow more vans to see if any of them drove to the preserve.

Gimbel returned to his house on Oak Island and unloaded his camping gear. He intended to go directly to bed, to catch up on the sleep he'd missed watching the Russians in the middle of the night, but he couldn't shut down his brain. He'd made a note on his phone of the latitude and longitude of the place, so he could return and search during the day.

He had a large scale map of the area, and pinpointed the coordinates of the place where he'd found the two men arguing. Gimbel was surprised to discover that where he'd been standing was not inside the boundaries of the preserve. The spot where the pickup and the man on foot had disappeared was right at the edge of the preserve, and it was on private land. When you were stumbling around through the swamp grass and pine trees in the dark, it was impossible to tell where the preserve's property ended and private land began.

It was clear that whatever was going on with the Russians was happening, not on the public property of the Green Swamp Preserve, but on someone's private property. Gimbel sent a quick email to Brandon, explaining what he'd seen and that the longitude and latitude of the meeting he'd observed were not in the preserve. He asked his FBI contact to find out ASAP who owned the acreage adjacent to the public land.

Gimbel would call Steve Brandon later that day. He wanted an update on the man he'd found dead in the marsh on Bird Island, and he wanted to give the FBI a more detailed report about the Russians in the woods. At last, Gimbel went to sleep. The dogs were catching up on their sleep as well. Dogs are good at that.

Chapter 28

"He died instantly when the eighteen wheeler hit the Neon. He didn't have a chance. It was the truck driver's fault; the guy fell asleep at the wheel and crossed the median barrier. We do wonder why Mr. Phillips didn't try to swerve out of the way. He might have been able to avoid the head-on. Phillips didn't have a driver's license. In fact, he didn't even have a wallet." The notification representative from the New York State Highway Police was calling to give Martha, the woman who supervised Darnel Phillips' halfway house, a follow-up on the accident that had proven fatal for the ex-con.

Martha was able to fill in some information for the caller from the New York State Highway Police. "Somebody from your office called here day before yesterday, asking for another one of our residents, Sally Pollitt. She wasn't here, so I took the call. Whoever was on the phone said a car registered to Sally, a white Neon, had been involved in a fatal accident on Route #81. They wanted to talk to Sally. At first, they said they'd thought she might be the driver, but by the time they talked to me, they'd determined that it was a man who'd died. I happened to know that Sally was shopping that afternoon and wasn't driving her car. I also happened to know that Darnel Phillips had paid Sally a considerable sum of money to borrow the Neon. Darnell wanted to drive the car to Binghamton for a funeral that day. Some doctor he didn't even know had died, but the doctor had something to do with Darnel's brother. Darnel had been talking for days about going to this guy's funeral. He was talking about it, even before the man died. I was able to tell that first person who called who I thought was driving the car. I told them it wasn't Sally Pollitt driving. I told them it was probably Darnel Phillips who'd been driving and Darnel who'd died. I also told them I wasn't going anywhere to identify any bodies or anything like that."

"We were able to confirm that the body was Darnel Phillips. Because he was a convicted criminal, his fingerprints were in a database. It was definitely Darnel who died in the accident. We have a few things from the car and from Darnel's pockets that we'd like to drop off. Do you know if he has any family or anyone we need to notify about his death? He was driving without a license. We know that, but we don't know much of anything else about him. His prison records are pretty sketchy, almost nothing in them. His file indicates he has one brother, a Ferguson Phillips, but we don't have an address for him. Would you be able to help us reach Darnel's brother."

"Nobody knows where Fergus is, where Ferguson Phillips is. He disappeared sixteen or seventeen years ago, and nobody's seen him since. He was Darnel's only relative. Darnel was obsessed with finding his younger sibling. He couldn't think or talk about anything else. I tried to make him take the driver's test so he could get a driver's license. But he kept putting me off. I'd warned him about driving without a license. Sally didn't want to loan him her car, but he kept bugging her and bugging her until she finally let him borrow it. Darnel's probation officer and I tried to get him to look for a job or go back to school. He never graduated from high school. I didn't think it was realistic to talk to him about a GED. That was never going to happen. He was a lost and very lonely man. I didn't blame him for wanting to find his brother, but when somebody has been missing for that long, you have to figure they're either dead or really don't want to be found. I tried to get him to give up his search and focus on what he needed to do to live in the world as it is today. He wouldn't even buy a cell phone. A few other residents here at the halfway house tried to teach him how to use their cell phones, but he was very resistant—to everything anybody tried to tell him. He was stubborn and a loner. He didn't like other people. I don't think he even liked himself very much." Martha hadn't liked Darnel very much either.

"Can I come by with these few things we found in the car and in Darnel's pockets? Some of these things might belong to the car's owner. She might want them back."

"Sure bring them by. I have no idea what I'm going to do with the rest of Darnel's stuff that's here, even though he didn't have much. He borrowed clothes from the other residents. I think he borrowed a suit from someone here to wear to the funeral. I guess the suit isn't coming back."

"No, the suit is definitely gone—gone along with Darnel."

"He was such a sad man, and he had such a sad life. He wouldn't accept help from anybody, though. He was a stubborn cuss."

Sally Pollitt was furious, even enraged, that her car had been totaled. She hadn't wanted to let Darnel drive it, but he had kept after her until she gave in and let him borrow it.

She didn't have insurance on the car, and the registration was expired. Nobody should have been driving the Neon, least of all Darnel. Susie knew her car wouldn't pass inspection, and she couldn't afford the repairs the car needed to qualify for her to be able to renew the registration. She was driving the car illegally, but she didn't drive it much. It mostly sat in the driveway of the halfway house, but it was hers. She felt as if Darnel had stolen her car from her.

Like many sociopaths, Sally wasn't able to feel much empathy for others, and she definitely was not sad that Darnel had died. She told Martha that she was going to take all of Darnel's few possessions and sell them. She said she deserved to have them, to compensate her for the loss of her car. Martha didn't argue with her. Darnel didn't have any living relatives, and he certainly didn't have a will. What harm would it be for Sally Pollitt, who no longer had her Neon, to have the few worthless things Darnel had left behind?

Sally picked over Darnel's clothes and other shabby belongings. She boxed up what she wanted and left the rest in his room. Martha took what Sally didn't want to a second-hand store and to the dump. The halfway house needed the room. It had to be cleaned out. The resident who'd loaned Darnel his suit was not going to be able to reimburse himself for the clothing that had been destroyed in the accident. It wasn't worth much anyway, to anybody. No one claimed Darnel's body, and no one cared that he was ultimately cremated and his ashes buried in a public cemetery, in Auburn, New York's version of Potter's Field.

Life at the halfway house stumbled along. Darnel never had received much mail, but a few weeks after he died, he received a thin, brown mailing envelope. It was taped closed and had a return address from Shirley Dryden, who lived in a suburb outside Binghamton, New York. The manager of the halfway house didn't open it. Darnel's probation officer had other clients at the halfway house, and when the probation officer came the next time, Martha gave the envelope from Binghamton to him, along with a few other papers Darnel had left in his room. The probation officer took Darnel's envelope back to his office, unopened, and stuck it in Darnel's file. He forgot about it.

Chapter 29

The two technicians sent by the FBI arrived on Oak Island. As instructed, Jerry and Sam came in separate "unobtrusive" cars. They were big guys, and both were packing. They could take care of themselves. They each had a small duffel bag and were dumbstruck by the size of the house where Gimbel was living.

"It's big, isn't it? Come on in and make yourselves at home." Gimbel told them how to operate the elevator and showed them to their bedrooms on the second floor. They continued to be amazed by the luxurious accommodations and viewed Gimbel with curiosity and some suspicion. What was this man in the flashy clothes and white shoes doing in this enormous house? The two had received their instructions, and they'd also been told not to ask too many questions. They didn't need to know about the wider scope of the operation.

They would run surveillance on Coastal Carolina's vans and follow them when the vehicles left Holden Beach. The FBI had authorized them to place tracking devices on several of the vans. They would watch to see which ones left the designated perimeter, that is, which ones were delivering seafood locally and which ones were heading out of town and out of state. It was a more efficient way of deciding which vans to follow. Gimbel told them about Susie's Seafood Shop and about the shrimp salad. But if the tracking devices worked, Jerry and Sam wouldn't be chasing after the local delivery vans. They would save time and energy and follow only the vans that traveled outside "the perimeter."

"I want to know immediately if any of the vans drive into or stop anywhere close to the Green Swamp Preserve. I want to know if any of them drive off the road in that area." Gimbel pointed out on his paper map the approximate zone he wanted monitored closely. Jerry and Sam punched some information into their phones. "I want to know everything that happens anywhere around there. I'm going out to the preserve tomorrow and have another look while you guys babysit the Coastal Carolina vans."

Jerry had more to tell Gimbel. "Agent Brandon told us to set up video cameras all around that part of the Green Swamp Preserve, the area where you saw the Russians. So when you head out in the morning, we'll be right behind you. Agent Brandon also instructed us to go down to Calabash and set up surveillance in the area where you discovered the body. We could go down there before dark today and take care of that. He told us there's a good place to eat in Calabash."

"Good idea. Waterside is becoming my new favorite spot. You'll love it."

Sam began to unload more heavy duffel bags out of his inconspicuous car. "I've got the electronics in here. Some of it needs to go into your car, and some of it needs to go into the house. As soon as we get all of this sorted out and set up, we can leave." Gimbel had thought he was going to be assigned a couple of guys who knew how to follow cars. In spite of how tough they looked, these two were apparently also very good with video surveillance equipment, GPS trackers, and computer systems. Gimbel was impressed.

"I'm going to walk my dogs, and when I get back, we'll go." Gimbel wanted to call Steve Brandon and speak to him in private. "Set up your computer equipment wherever you want to on the first floor, however it works best for you. Park your cars in the garage under the house, and put the doors down. The neighbors don't need to know I have house guests. We'll be taking the Subaru to Calabash this evening, so put whatever you're going to need tonight in there. I'll be back in thirty minutes."

When he got to the beach, Gimbel called Brandon who must have seen his phone number on the phone and picked up right away. "Gimbel, have you ever stumbled into a hornet's nest! Spasibo!"

"Okay Steve, that's about the only word I still remember from my ill-fated year of studying the Russian language. Why are you thanking me?"

"We've been chasing our tails for more than eighteen months, trying to find out who is behind this massive, and I mean massive, influx of heroin laced with fentanyl. We were looking at Mexican drug cartels and bad boys from Honduras and El Salvador. We were looking at Asian triads, and we'd even began to look at the people sneaking across our southern border from Somalia and Pakistan. These guys tried to fold themselves into groups of Hispanics who were coming across. To be sure, all these folks despise us and want to do us harm. While we were looking for drugs, we picked up a bunch of MS-13 thugs and some al-Shabab and ISIS jihadists who had plans to blow things up and mow things down a la Nice, France. But we were caught with our pants down on this drug epidemic of bad heroin and deadly fentanyl."

Steve Brandon continued. "It wasn't until you turned up that dead guy in the van a few days ago that we were finally able to put it all together. It's Russians! I know that you know, the two guys you tracked in the woods are Russians. All these dead bodies are probably the results of a turf war. The Russian mafia is moving into this area...hot and heavy and very, very fast. They are ruthlessly eliminating anybody who stands in their way. Hacking into everything in the U.S. wasn't working fast enough for them and wasn't having the impact they were hoping it would. Somebody decided that destroying Americans with tainted drugs would be a quicker way to bring us down. And that's what they're doing. Russian fishing trawlers. Guess what they're up to?"

"That's how the drugs are being brought into the country, right?

"Bingo. That's it. You've seen at least three of these people's faces, and I'm sure there are more hanging out around the docks. It's a massive operation, and because of the huge seafood industry that's there, they picked the Wilmington area as their base of operations."

"I guess Chuckie Petrossi can miraculously recover from his heart problem and go home to Los Angeles."

"No, actually, we think Chuckie is still a good cover. It's a way for you to continue to investigate and maybe get into the drug scene. The people running this are Russian mafia, with the backing and total support of Vlad Putin and the Russian SVR. They might want to cozy up to you. They may try to use Chuckie Petrossi for their own purposes. On the other hand, you will have to be extra vigilant. If you get on their radar screen and they see you as competition, you will be sleeping with the fishes."

"So the dead guy I found in the van parked on the Bird Island Reserve is Russian? Why was he there?"

"Yes, he's Russian, and the Russians killed him. We haven't figured out all the details yet, but we think the Russians made a mistake and killed their own man. We think there's a delivery point there, for the drugs, on Bird Island, and that's where we think the trawlers off-load the drugs. They're fishing boats, floating around in a multitude of other fishing boats. They are hiding in plain sight. No one pays any attention to them, except if they try to steal somebody else's catch. It's the perfect place for the Russians to bring in their drugs. We don't know what happened, but we think the wrong driver turned up in the van, someone the people on the trawler didn't recognize. We're guessing the Russians in the trawlers didn't think he was one of theirs, so they slit his throat. Maybe he didn't have the right password. Who knows? We can only speculate about why that one died, but he was a Russian."

"So the Russians have arrived, and they are not bringing gold, frankincense, and myrrh. They intend to undermine us in every way they can think of. I'm not going to point out, as I always do, that the drug industry is demand driven. EKT! Everybody knows that! I am all in to try to shut down this drug ring of Ruskies. Of course, in time, they will be back with a new setup someplace else, but when that time comes, we will once again have to hunt them down and kill them."

"Don't minimize how big this is, Gimbel. You're the one who got the goods on these bad boys. Because of you, we have their pictures, and we know they own the pickup with the camper top. Now we know where to focus our surveillance.

Before we were just farting around—looking in one direction for a while and then looking in another direction."

"Your guys arrived a while ago. They know a lot of stuff. I'm impressed."

"When we realized what you'd gotten us into, I upgraded your help. These guys are tough. Don't doubt that for a second, but they are also very smart. They are both electricians with degrees in computer science. They know how to set up surveillance cameras in no time flat. They are very good at what they do. Be nice to them."

"I'm always nice. I'm so nice, I'm taking them out for an all-you-can-eat seafood dinner tonight in Calabash. I know they have work to do down there, too. Calabash is such a sleepy place, but there are boats of all sizes and shapes coming and going constantly. It is *the* perfect spot for Russian trawlers to be hanging out. Some smart Russian did a good job when he picked this area to bring in the stuff. There is water, water all around, and there are boats everywhere you look. It is beautiful, but there are, literally, hundreds of thousands of places here where small boats can enter the country. And that's just in one small North Carolina county. Gotta go. My guys are hungry."

"Let's talk a couple of times a day. Things are heating up. We're sending more resources to your area. You won't even know any of them are there. This case has now taken on international implications, as you can imagine. Other federal agencies are involved. Don't look for us; we'll find you, if we want to find you. Above all, stay safe, Gimbel. I'd send you back home right now, but I think there are some loose ends that you and I want you to take care of. But I want us to be in closer communication from here on out. I also want you to be ready to leave Oak Island at a moment's notice.

Anything you don't want to leave behind, put in one carry-all bag, so you can grab it and go if we think things are getting too hot for you. I know you intend to go poking around in the preserve tomorrow. Be careful. It's a dangerous place out there. We think the Green Swamp is close to the main transfer point where the Ivans move the boxes of drugs into the seafood vans, but we haven't figured out yet how they do it. Caution!"

"I'm always careful. I will find out how these bastards do their dirty work. I'm not leaving here until I figure it out."

The dogs had given themselves their own walk. Gimbel hadn't thrown any balls for them, and they were a little put out because there were new people at the house. They were excited when Gimbel put them in the Subaru. They were not so excited when Jerry and Sam also climbed into the SUV. Within a few minutes, however, everybody had made friends. They were on their way to Calabash.

Chapter 30

When they got as far as the Bird Island Reserve, Jerry told Gimbel to pull over to the side of the road. "Can we borrow the dogs for a while? We want to give them a nice nosey walk."

"They will love that. They might be a little skittish because I'm almost the only person who ever walks them. If you let them stop and sniff a lot, they will love you."

As it turned out, the men wanted Billy and Dilly to stop and sniff around. Each man had a dog, and if anyone had been watching, the observer would have given them about five seconds' worth of notice. They were two men walking their West Highland terriers. It was after five p.m.; everything was copacetic. In fact, the FBI surveillance geniuses were controlling exactly where they allowed the dogs to stop and sniff. Every time the dogs stopped to check things out, the electricians installed a surveillance device in a tree or in a bush or on the ground.

There was a dilapidated dock-like structure that Gimbel suspected was where the Russian trawlers were dropping anchor and transferring their wares. You had to look quickly, but if you knew what to look for, you might be able to figure out that Jerry and Sam were installing tiny video cameras all over that end of Bird Island. It took less than forty-five minutes for them to be satisfied they had covered the waterfront.

Back in the car, they explained to Gimbel that the tiny cameras were completely weatherproof and virtually undetectable. Jerry loved to talk about the technology they were using. "They're motion-activated and powered by the sun. They can transmit, via a special communications satellite in the sky, wherever they are programmed to transmit, even to multiple places. These cameras have been programmed to transmit to both Sam's and my phones, to our computers at your house, and directly to an FBI communications center in Virginia."

Gimbel knew technology had made great strides, but he was blown away when the techs told him how the cameras worked. They were tiny, no bigger than Gimbel's thumbnail. How could they see or transmit anything? Sam tried to explain about the special lenses in the cameras, but Gimbel got lost in the technical explanation.

"It's a miracle." Gimbel said, and he really believed it was miraculous.

Sam agreed. "Yep, it's a miracle all right. Nothing will happen here from now on that we don't know about. And when the Russians say they know nothing about any of this drug business, we will have the faces of every one of their operatives on camera, incontrovertible evidence that their fishing boats are here delivering the drugs. This operation will catch the bad guys, and it will convict them. They may not be prosecuted and go to jail, in the traditional sense. But they will be exposed for what they are, and they will be vilified in the court of public opinion. The faces of these Russians will be on cable news 24/7. It will be a wonderful thing."

The three made their way to Waterside. One waitress recognized Gimbel and gave them a table with a great view. Gimbel thought he was a pretty good eater, but Waterside did not make any money on the "All You Can Eat Seafood" specials they served to Jerry and Sam that night.

The next morning, three cars left Gimbel's house and drove to the Green Swamp Preserve. Gimbel was in the lead, but the other two had the coordinates and knew exactly where to go. They would separate before they approached the target area. Jerry and Sam would set up their video cameras, and Gimbel would do his investigating of the area he'd had to abandon in the dark the night before last. The two FBI technicians had come prepared with binoculars and bird watching books and clothes. They had used this birdwatching shtick before as a cover, so they could put their cameras in place. Unless you knew what these agents were up to, you'd never know what they were up to.

Gimbel explored the area where he'd seen the Russians and the pickup truck. He poked around and wasn't able to find anything that didn't belong. The Russians were careful about policing their trash. If there had been transfers of drugs from one vehicle to another in this area, Gimbel would have expected to find something. While he was searching in the grass and brush, he occasionally caught a glimpse of Jerry or Sam as they installed their surveillance devices. This place would be well-covered. Whatever nefarious activity was happening here would be recorded for posterity and for the U.S. State Department to use when it lodged a formal protest with Vladimir Putin.

They had agreed to meet at Susie's Seafood Shop for lunch, to discuss what was next on the agenda. The place was small, and Sam led them to a table in the corner, the most private spot in the restaurant. Gimbel's morning had been a bust, but Jerry and Sam were bursting to talk.

"We are definitely in the right place." Jerry was obviously thrilled about something.

"I'm not really sure we are. I would have sworn, given what I saw the other night, that this was the place it was happening, but I found nothing today."

"Maybe you didn't find anything, but we sure did. We have exactly the right place. We were installing cameras so that we can watch that place in the woods and the area surrounding it, but as we were doing our own installations, we found something, too." Sam was eager to talk about their morning.

"*Their* surveillance cameras?"

"Brandon told us you were smart. They have the area covered with cameras. Of course, whenever we go into a place where we think there is even the slightest possibility there might already be surveillance set up, we jam it before we go in. We don't want our faces on their cameras. We don't want to be recorded installing our own surveillance devices, so we always jam first. Their cameras are set up to transmit remotely, just like ours are. Our technology in this department is light years ahead of anybody else's, of course. Our devices can't be jammed. We have permanently jammed theirs, however. They won't be able to tell exactly what's wrong, and it will be a while before they realize all of their cameras are down. We transmit fake pictures and videos through their cameras, so they don't know for a few days that their surveillance isn't working. By the time they figure it out, we may already have everything we need. Ideally, we will be able to retrieve our own cameras and be out of there, before they start poking around to fix things."

"I had no idea we could do all of this." Gimbel was awed and feeling superfluous at the same time. "Do you have any need for special agents anymore?" It wasn't meant to be a joke, but the two laughed.

"If they know electronics and computers, they might be able to retain their usefulness." Sam was telling the truth. The day of the FBI guy who wore a fedora, carried his gun around, and looked tough on the street corner might be done. If Eliot Ness were around today and wasn't up to speed on his technology, even he would be out of work.

After lunch, Jerry and Sam headed for Holden Beach. They were going to put tracking devices on as many of Coastal Carolina's vans as they could. They would follow those that ventured outside the designated perimeter.

Gimbel went back to Oak Island. He prepared his grab-and-go bag, as Steve Brandon had suggested, so he could leave quickly if he needed to. He'd never responded to Christina Rose's and Marley's dinner invitation, and he made the decision that he was going to accept.

He emailed Christina Rose:

Sorry to take so long to respond. Had unexpected company and didn't know how long they were going to stay. Delighted to accept your invitation for next Thursday. Address? Time? Looking forward to it. Thanks, Gimbel Saunders.

Gimbel knew he shouldn't accept the invitation. He had no business mixing work with his personal social life. He was involved in a deadly situation with the FBI, but he couldn't resist. The main attractions were the two fun women he'd shared a table with in Calabash. Besides, he'd heard Shell

Island was very special and wanted to see it. One night playing hooky from his official assignment couldn't possibly make any difference. He would make a quick trip into Wilmington this afternoon and buy a decent outfit that he could wear to dinner. He was not going to show up dressed in a Chuckie Petrossi costume. It was just too silly. It would be embarrassing to wear Chuckie's clothes to dinner with his new friends.

Gimbel listened to the radio as he was driving into Wilmington, and he paid attention when the news came on. The local news was all about the various tracks the latest tropical storm might be expected to take. Having lived most of his life inland in upstate New York, Gimbel's experience with hurricanes was limited. He'd never been in one, and he only knew what he'd seen on The Weather Channel. He loved the reporters on TWC—Mike Seidel, Jim Cantore, Stephanie Abrams—and the others who clung to telephone poles for dear life during the storms and were kept from being swept out to sea by steel cables wrapped around their waists. Their love of weather and dedication to bringing the story to the viewers was legend. At this point it was too early to say when the tropical depression would become a tropical storm or a hurricane or where it might come ashore. Gimbel knew that places along the Atlantic Coast were vulnerable, but he had his fingers crossed that the storm would avoid North Carolina.

Gimbel spent more on clothes than he'd intended. He bought a periwinkle blue linen sport coat and a pair of white linen pants. They'd cost way too much, but when he'd looked at himself in the mirror, he thought he looked so good in the outfit, he had to buy it. He wondered if wearing the Chuckie Petrossi wardrobe had warped his brain. He bought a light blue linen shirt, and, call the cops, a pair of docksiders. Nobody around here wore anything but docksiders or very expensive trainers. Except for Chuckie Petrossi, of course. Gimbel found a few other items at the upscale men's clothing store and put it all on his credit card. He'd needed some new summer stuff anyway, and he hardly ever bought any clothes. He rationalized that this spurge was really a necessity.

He drove past the Green Swamp Preserve on his way back to Oak Island. He parked alongside the road and walked back into the grove of trees, the clearing in the woods that wasn't actually in the preserve but on private property at the edge of the preserve. He tried to visualize the vans coming and going, perhaps changing drivers, and being loaded with boxes of drugs packed in Coastal Carolina's signature white boxes with blue lettering. He knew he was missing something. What was he missing? Why were they operating on private property? Why not just operate out of the Preserve? They were ghosts, anyway. Maybe he would have better luck if he came back at night. Tramping around in the swampy grass during the day had yielded nothing.

He drove home to walk the dogs. He knew Jerry and Sam would have successfully planted their tracking devices on the vans. He would love to have seen them being surreptitious and wondered what ruse they'd used this time to fool observers. He knew it would be clever. He wondered if any of the vans had breached the perimeter, and if any of them had been worth following.

Gimbel was feeling a bit left out. He didn't have the skills these two guys had. If he was going to keep up with the direction law enforcement was headed, he realized he was going to have to learn more about electronics and computers. Maybe he should go back to school? Maybe the answer to his disability issue and his assignment to review cold cases was for him to develop more skills. He might even start his own company and hire himself out to local law enforcement organizations in upstate. After seeing the FBI technicians at work and all the electronics they had that gave them the edge, he was looking at his old job with very different eyes.

Chapter 31

The next few days flew by as Jerry and Sam built their case against the drug-running Russians. They recorded everything and documented everything, but it was Gimbel who discovered the existence of the tunnels under the savanna and the brilliantly obscured entrance where the vans disappeared into the trees and were never seen again. Again and again, Gimbel had watched the video footage the techs had collected, and he knew the only way the vans could be vanishing the way they did was if they were going subterranean. Gimbel went out with Jerry and Sam during the day, and after hours of searching the swamp, they finally discovered the tunnel's hidden entrance.

Additional surveillance cameras were installed, and within two days, they had found where the vans were entering the tunnel. They also thought they'd identified two places where the vans were exiting the tunnel and driving back out onto Rt. #112 to continue their journeys.

Gimbel was trying to figure out how he could get into the tunnel. He wanted videos of the boxes of drugs being loaded into the vans. Being able to show the actual transfer of the drugs was the only way to make an airtight case against the Russians.

Gimbel brought up a couple of his ideas with the technicians. He also ran some scenarios by Steve Brandon. When he introduced his ideas to Steve Brandon, Brandon told Gimbel to back off—in no uncertain terms. The FBI did not want him going anywhere near the tunnel. Gimbel was annoyed that no one would tell him what their plan was for recording the actual drug transfers, the hard evidence, on video. Gimbel began to wonder if they even had a plan to do that.

Thursday arrived, and Gimbel got a haircut. He took the dogs to be groomed. They knew something special was up. They were very curious about Gimbel's new clothes, especially the new shoes. What did the docksiders mean? What was in the future for these shoes? Dilly and Billy were ecstatic when they realized they were going to get to go in the Subaru with their best buddy who was all dressed up.

Gimbel had the address programmed into the Subaru's GPS, and Christina Rose had sent a picture of their cottage. In the photo, it looked exactly like he'd imagined it would, except it was bigger. It was an older house, old school, a real cottage. The wood-shingled siding was stained white with blue gray shutters and a navy blue door. There were hydrangea bushes loaded with bright blue blossoms all around the house. Strands of slender seagrass grew up in between the hydrangeas. There was even a white fence around the cottage. It was thoroughly charming, just like Christina Rose and Marley.

Gimbel had brought a box of caramels dipped in dark chocolate, from a fancy candy store that made their own candy on site. A bottle of wine wouldn't have been the right gift to bring to this dinner party. He was looking forward to seeing his lively dinner companions again, and he was pleased that Dilly and Billy had been invited. He knew Christina Rose loved the dogs, and he wondered why she didn't have a dog of her own.

Gimbel arrived at five o'clock sharp. The sun was still fairly high in the sky, and he knew they would take a walk with the dogs on the beach before dinner. Christina Rose and Marley were outside cutting blooms from the hydrangea bushes when Gimbel arrived. Both women were dressed in blue. Marley had on a navy blue linen dress with pearls, and Christina Rose had on a linen shift that was the same shade as the shutters on the house. She had a gold choker around her neck. They were quite a good-looking pair. Gimbel asked if their dresses had come from Au Naturel, and he'd guessed correctly.

Gimbel brought the dogs out of the car, and they immediately ran to Christina Rose. She put down the galvanized bucket full of flowers, and Dilly jumped right into her arms. Dilly was not a jumper, so this said to Gimbel that the dog was unusually delighted to see Christina Rose again. Billy stood at her feet, looked up at her, and enthusiastically wagged his tail. Billy definitely wasn't a jumper. Much fuss was made over the dogs, and everybody went for a walk on the beach. They picked up right where they'd left off in Calabash, laughing and talking.

When they got back to the house, Christina Rose brought glasses, ice, and sweet tea with mint and lemon out to the wide porch that overlooked the ocean. It was a beautiful setting, and the house had been carefully positioned many years ago when it was first built, to take the best advantage of the ocean views. Marley brought out a platter of shrimp remoulade, piled high on Bibb lettuce and garnished with black olives and cherry tomatoes. The sauce was her own special recipe. It was extraordinary and was just the right amount of spicy.

The women told Gimbel about the cottage, that it had been built in 1922 and then rebuilt after Hurricane Hazel in October of 1954. When Christina Rose's mother had bought the house, they'd completely renovated the inside and added on two bedrooms and two bathrooms. They had kept all the historic charm and everything they could of the original moldings and trim. They gave Gimbel a tour of the entire house and ended up in the kitchen. Everything was ready except for grilling the steaks and sautéing the fish. Gimbel volunteered to do the grilling.

The turf was New York strip steaks grilled medium rare, and the surf was flounder sautéed in butter topped with crabmeat, a light lemony cream sauce, and a few bread crumbs. Tiny, crisp green beans, French potato salad, sliced tomatoes, and homemade buttermilk biscuits with raspberry jam completed the elegant meal. They ate outside on the porch. It was a beautiful evening. Gimbel helped carry in the dishes and put them in the dishwasher. He helped put the food away and wiped off the kitchen counters.

For dessert, Marley brought out a dense, rich almond cake with a bittersweet chocolate glaze. The confection was the perfect sweet ending to the meal. Gimbel groaned and wanted to ask for a second slice, but he didn't. It had been a wonderful dinner, a relaxed and fun time.

As the three were enjoying their after-dinner coffee, everything changed. A beautiful middle-aged redheaded woman with golden streaks in her hair suddenly appeared on the porch. No one had heard her car drive up, and no one had heard her come into the house. All of a sudden, she was just standing there beside the table. She too was wearing blue, a longish linen skirt the exact color of Gimbel's sports coat. Her linen blouse was the same shade as Gimbel's light blue linen shirt. She stared at him, and he stared at her. "Who are you?" The woman, who was obviously Christina Rose's mother, had not known he was coming for dinner. She wasn't being rude, just curious.

"Mom, what are you doing here? We weren't expecting you until tomorrow. This is Gimbel Saunders, the nice man I was telling you about—the one we met in Calabash, the one with the cute dogs."

Gimbel stood up and extended his hand to the woman. "It's nice to meet you."

"I'm Rosemary Carmichael." She shook Gimbel's hand and sat down at the table. Marley got up and went to bring Rosemary a plate of food. "I was able to get away early today and decided I would drive down tonight. I'll get one more day at the beach. I've got my eye on this storm, and I wanted to be sure I had another long weekend here before it's all swept away."

"Mom, you always think the worst is going to happen. Our house has survived so many hurricanes over the years. I'm not worried."

Gimbel felt it was time for him to leave. He didn't want to interrupt the domestic scene that he could see was going to play out between mother and teenage daughter. "I need to be getting back to Oak Island. It's a long drive. Dilly and Billy won't want to leave, but they're coming with me. Sorry, Christina Rose."

"Oh, don't go, Gimbel. Just because my mother arrived unexpectedly and busted up our party, doesn't mean you have to leave."

"I really do have to get back. It's been an absolutely delightful evening. I hate to leave you with the rest of the dishes."

"No worries, you've done more than your share." Christina Rose was obviously sorry the evening had ended.

"Thanks for grilling and for helping clean up. You can come back any time." Marley had enjoyed his company, too.

The dogs were corralled into the Subaru, and everyone said their goodbyes.

"Where's the 'Giant Gold Bug'?" I was thinking you'd be driving it tonight." Christina Rose laughed her infectious laugh that made everybody else want to laugh with her.

"I just drive it every so often to keep it on the road. But I am seriously thinking about a nice dark navy blue shade of paint." Christina Rose and Marley laughed, and Rosemary frowned, irritated at being left out of the jokes. Giant Gold Bug? Nice dark navy blue? What did all of that mean, anyway?

Gimbel waved, and the dogs put their noses out the passenger-side window. Suddenly, the soft sunset's last light caught Rosemary Carmichael's face in a certain way that made her look much younger than her forty-five years. Gimbel was startled, struck by a memory. Where had he seen her before? Or was he merely experiencing an episode of déjà vu? As he drove away, he was haunted by Rosemary's face. She had a very good looking face, but that wasn't at all what was bothering him. He was absolutely certain he had seen this woman before, sometime in the past. But that was impossible. He had no idea where he could possibly have met her. Maybe in another life? Maybe in his dreams? Gimbel was spooked.

Chapter 32

The next day Gimbel made the decision to investigate the tunnels on his own, and he wanted to do it sooner rather than later. He didn't understand why this wasn't the FBI's first priority. Gimbel was a man of action, and he was often impatient. When he saw the end of a case in sight, he wanted to push forward and wrap things up. Get everything you need to take the case to court and win! Why prolong the agony? Steve Brandon sensed his frustration with the pace of the investigation.

"We've decided to try to scoop up a few street dealers while we're at it. We're following the vans that are carrying drugs into towns and cities and neighborhoods. And we're striking gold in terms of being able to pinpoint who receives the drugs and who is selling them on the street. We're working with local law enforcement to track down as many of the drug supply chains as we can. It's important work, Gimbel. We have the Russians cold. It isn't as though we're ever going to get Vladimir Putin in front of a jury."

"But we don't have them cold, Stephen. We don't have a single video frame of the actual transfer of the drugs to the Coastal Carolina vans. We have the vans going into the tunnel and coming out again. But we don't have actual footage of the Russians loading the boxes of drugs into the vehicles. We absolutely have to have that, or we don't have anything."

"Gimbel, you've done all you need to do. Your role in this has been huge. You are the one who cracked the case. It's time to let the rest of us wrap things up, and we have to do it in our own way and in our own time. We have the State Department, the DEA, the CIA, the NSA, the DOJ, and I don't know who all in on this now. It's moved way beyond my control, too. Don't push anymore. You've done more than enough."

"I don't care who is involved in this case. I don't care if POTUS and the Queen of England are personally involved. You have to have video from inside the tunnel, or you don't have anything."

"Leave it alone, Gimbel. Please just back off. It isn't your case anymore. It isn't my case anymore. There are political ramifications that have to be considered, and there are international implications. There's a lot more to this than even you and I know about...."

Gimbel hung up on the FBI special agent. Jerry and Sam, the two extraordinary FBI technicians were packing up their stuff. Their jobs were done, they said, and they thanked Gimbel for his hospitality. Gimbel suspected they didn't realize that the FBI had paid to rent this fancy house for him. Gimbel offered to take them to Waterside again or to the Captain's Galley for dinner that night, to celebrate a successful case, but they insisted they had to leave. They were heading to Kansas City and flying out of the Wilmington airport later that afternoon. Gimbel hated to see them rush off, but he told them in a number of ways what great work they'd done. He said he'd love to work on a case with them anytime, and he was sorry to see them go.

Gimbel sent a snail mail thank you note to the women who lived in the cottage on Shell Island. He'd addressed it to all three of them, even though Rosemary hadn't really hosted him. It was her house, so he thanked her, too. He also sent an email thank you note and invited them to come for lunch on Sunday. He knew it was last minute, but he said he wanted them to see his house before the storm arrived. The technicians were gone, and the cleaning people were coming on Saturday to be sure everything was ship shape. He would call Susie's Seafood Shop and order the food he wanted to serve for Sunday lunch.

He was reciprocating the women's hospitality, but one ulterior motive was that he wanted to see Rosemary again. He wanted to have another look at her face, to try to place her, to remember where he'd seen her before.

They accepted his invitation for Sunday lunch. They'd already planned to take their sailboat out of the Deep Point Marina and Yacht Club in Southport, North Carolina for the day. They would make Oak Island their destination, and they would arrive at twelve noon. Gimbel and the dogs would meet them on the beach. He called Susie's, ordered lunch, and arranged to pick up the food on Sunday morning. He didn't entertain often, but nobody expected too much from a picnic. He would Google "How to Host a Picnic." Everyone was keeping an eye on the storm that threatened the coast. This might be the last chance for a while to have a sail and a picnic on the beach.

He was surprisingly nervous when Sunday noon arrived. He had carried a folding table and four chairs to the beach. He'd located a tablecloth with four matching napkins in one of the drawers in the dining room. He packed plates, silverware, glasses, and serving platters in a picnic basket he found in the pantry. He picked up the food at Susie's and packed it, along with ice for the sweet tea, in coolers.

He set up a small serving table and took two beach umbrellas to keep the sun off the food and off his guests. He knew they liked hydrangeas, so he picked some from a bush in his backyard and put them in a vase. His table looked pretty good, and he knew the food would be delicious. He was sneaking the dogs onto the beach for the day. They were not allowed on the beach between nine in the morning and five in the afternoon, but today Gimbel was going to break the rules. There was never anybody else on his beach anyway. Who would know?

The sailboat arrived off shore. Gimbel saw a dinghy attached to the rear of the sailboat, and it looked as if Marley and Rosemary were going to row the small boat to shore. But where was Christina Rose? He pulled the dingy up onto the beach and gallantly assisted the two women as they disembarked. As they turned to walk toward the makeshift dining table, Christina Rose appeared out of the surf. She said she loved the ocean and never missed a chance to swim in it. Like a Botticelli painting she stood up and walked out of the sea. She had on a skimpy one-piece bathing suit, and her mother immediately handed her a terry cloth cover-up.

They had a delightful lunch. Susie's shrimp salad was the best, and the women loved the ripe tomatoes stuffed with crabmeat Marguerite. The crab salad was light and simple, made with crabmeat, lightly curried mayonnaise, fresh lemon juice, and Old Bay seasoning. Susie's own homemade potato chips were perfect with the seafood, and the restaurant had included cupcakes from a nearby bakery. The women agreed Susie's was a keeper.

Rosemary was in a better mood today. She was not as tired as she'd been on Thursday night, and she was more relaxed.

They'd had an invigorating sail from Southport, and everyone was talking about the tropical depression that had become a tropical storm and looked like it was going to turn into a Category 1 hurricane. All the storm models were predicting it would be coming up the Atlantic Coast. It was still too early for anyone to say for sure where it would make landfall.

Gimbel had not told Christina Rose's family very much about himself. Because he was in North Carolina pretending to be somebody other than who he really was, he was worried that the two lives he was living would collide. It wasn't that he was afraid for these people to know who he was; it was that he found himself in a bind. It was inevitable that Christina Rose would ask him all about himself, and he'd decided he wasn't going to lie to her.

Gimbel had noticed that Rosemary was reluctant to talk about her life before she moved to North Carolina. He got the feeling that Christina Rose's father was either dead or living in Timbuktu. He was definitely not in the picture and had not been a part of her life for a very long time, if ever. Gimbel wanted to know, but he didn't want to pry into things that were none of his business. He didn't want to open a can of worms that would make these women uncomfortable. There were secrets here. He was certain of that. Maybe there were secrets in all families.

Christina Rose asked during lunch, "What do you do, Gimbel, when you aren't hanging out at the beach on vacation and being lazy? I know you are here because of your heart murmur, but what did you do before they made you take it easy?"

"I was with the New York State Police, a detective. I still do that, but they've put me on light duty."

"What does 'light duty' mean?"

"It means I work on cold cases, and I'm not allowed to work active cases. They're afraid I'll keel over and die and then turn around and sue them." Everybody laughed.

"You said you were from upstate New York. Where exactly? It has to be cooler up there than it is in Wilmington." Christina Rose was continuously curious.

"I work in Syracuse, and it's a little cooler there than it is here. The nights are cooler, but we have some pretty hot days. And it's very humid with all the Finger Lakes in the area." When he said he worked in Syracuse, Rosemary's face turned white, and for a moment she looked as if she was going to faint. Marley looked at Rosemary with alarm, but Christina Rose kept on talking, oblivious to the drama that had affected the other two women. Marley tried to change the subject.

Marley was clearly shaken because of Rosemary's reaction when Gimbel mentioned Syracuse. Rosemary's eyes had grown dark, with anger or with fear. Gimbel wasn't sure which, maybe both. Gimbel realized that Marley knew why Rosemary was afraid of Syracuse, but Christina Rose didn't. Gimbel wanted more than anything to find out why the mention of Syracuse had terrified Rosemary, but he didn't want to torture the poor woman. He graciously changed the subject.

It was close to three in the afternoon, and Rosemary stood and said they had to leave. Christina Rose didn't want to go. She was trying to hide it, but it was clear that Rosemary was in a panic and wanted to get out of there, out of Gimbel's presence. Rosemary said they had to get back to the marina, and then there was the long drive back to Shell Island. They were leaving.

Gimbel helped to launch the dinghy and waved goodbye. They'd all been having a great time, until Gimbel had mentioned Syracuse. Rosemary had turned to stone when he'd said he was from there.

He was sad to see them leave. He really liked these people. He was quite certain he had seen Rosemary before, and the pieces were coming together. Christina Rose looked so much like her mother, but at the same time, they looked very different. Christina Rose was happy; her mother wasn't, really. When Christina laughed, the sound was like a song on the wind. When she smiled, she smiled with her eyes. She had an open face, and an open personality. She welcomed everybody. Gimbel hoped no one would ever hurt her and crush her trusting and inclusive heart.

Rosemary on the other hand was closed. She was not going to let anybody in. She had sad eyes. When she smiled, her eyes did not sparkle like Christina Rose's did. Rosemary did not very often smile with her eyes. Gimbel could tell that Rosemary had known great sorrow in her life, perhaps even great tragedy. It could have been an abusive and unhappy marriage, but Gimbel thought it went deeper than that. Many people escape unhappy and terribly abusive relationships, and many seem to bounce back when enough time has passed to allow them to heal and put it behind them. Whatever had happened to Rosemary, she had not been able to get over it and move on. Her past was seared into every part of her psyche. Fortunately, she had not infected her daughter with her sadness, her tragedy, whatever it was. Gimbel was grateful that the mother had been able to raise a happy daughter and not burden her with her own ghosts.

Gimbel gave Marley Kurtz a great deal of credit for Christina Rose's positive outlook on life. He was willing to bet that Marley had raised Christina Rose. Rosemary adored her daughter, but she was a single mom, raising a child without the father and working long hours to support her family. Christina Rose had spent her happy childhood with the generous and loving Marley. Gimbel was thankful the girl had been loved so unconditionally and by such a good person. He wondered what had snuffed out the light in Rosemary's spirit. If he could figure that out, he had the feeling he would for sure know why she looked so familiar to him and where he had seen her before.

Gimbel's sixth sense told him he was just on the verge of remembering where he had seen Rosemary. He put it on the back burner. He knew from past experience that, if he dwelled on it, he'd never get there. All would be revealed if he let it simmer in the back of his mind.

Chapter 33

Gimbel kept an eye on The Weather Channel and began to worry that Hurricane Gregory was headed for the coast of the Carolinas. If Gimbel was going to get into the tunnel at the edge of the Green Swamp Preserve, he was going to have to do it right away. He'd been formulating a plan in his mind, and now it was time to take action. He packed his own clothes and personal belongings, along with Dilly's and Billy's travel crate and beds, into the back of the Subaru and drove the SUV to the Wilmington airport. He parked in long-term parking and left his wallet under the driver's seat. He took an expensive taxi back to Oak Island.

He left the dogs in their outside kennel with enough food and water for two days. There was a very fancy dog house inside the kennel. If it started to rain, they wouldn't get wet. The dogs loved snow, but they didn't like rain. Gimbel expected to be back at the Oak Island house by the next morning, but just in case he was delayed, he left extra food and water for the dogs.

Gimbel drove the BMW to Holden Beach and left it in Coastal Carolina's parking lot. He wore old clothes and had only his two cell phones and his gun in his pockets. He decided to leave Chuckie Petrossi's cell phone at the house. He'd bought his cheap gun at a gun show, and it wasn't registered to him. He hadn't practiced his shooting in a while, but he could shoot straight if he had to. He had nothing on his person that could reveal his identity, and he'd left nothing in the BMW that might be traced to him.

It was easy for him to steal one of Coastal Carolina's vans; they left the keys in the ignitions of all the vans. He took one that was at the back of the parking lot, hoping no one would notice it was missing — at least for a few hours. The next thing Gimbel had to steal were some of Coastal Carolina's signature white packing boxes with the navy blue lettering.

If he was going to be convincing when he opened his van for the Russians to load in the drugs, he needed to have boxes that appeared to be full of seafood already stored in the back. An empty van would be an instant giveaway that he was not legit. The van already smelled like seafood, so that would help, but the boxes in the back had to look and feel as if they actually had seafood inside. If one of the Ivans lifted a box as he moved it around in the back of the van, the box had to weigh approximately what a box of seafood would weigh. Gimbel had decided he wasn't going to steal any of Coastal Carolina's seafood to fill his boxes, but he didn't have a problem stealing their ice.

Gimbel looked in the windows of the various parts of the packing and processing building until he identified where the empty boxes were kept. Some of the boxes in the store room were flat and would have to be taped. Gimbel decided to bypass this step and take the boxes that were already assembled and ready to be filled. He rolled the dolly from the back of the van into the box storage room and loaded it up. It was later in the afternoon, and everyone who worked in this department had gone home. Gimbel realized how easy it would be for anybody to help themselves to the seafood boxes, just as he was doing.

He loaded the empty boxes into the van and pulled up to the ice machine. Again, the workers who manned the ice machine had also gone home for the day. It wasn't hard to figure out how to fill the boxes with ice, but to get the job done, Gimbel had to hang around the ice machine for what seemed to him like a long time. As he was finishing up filling the last few boxes, he saw someone walking towards his van. He quickly stored the last boxes of ice in the back of the van, closed the rear doors, and climbed into the driver's seat.

The man tapped on the driver's side window. "I saw you helping yourself to ice. Sorry there wasn't anybody here to help you out. We were told all the vans were gone for the day." He looked at Gimbel questioningly. He wondered why Gimbel was there when all the vans were supposed to have been loaded and on their way.

"There was a last-minute order that came in from Durham. DTU called me to come over and pick it up. They told me I'd have to put the ice in the boxes myself, that there wouldn't be anybody to help me. I told them that was fine. I'd done it before."

"I don't recognize you. What's your name?"

"I'm Charles Rossi, and I only work part-time. DTU calls on me when they have a last-minute delivery, and if I can do it, I do it. I get overtime pay, so it's a good deal for me…if I'm available."

"Okay, Mr. Rossi. Drive safe."

Gimbel had been holding his breath. He'd come up with a pretty convincing story, but if the guy who'd questioned him asked for paperwork, there wouldn't be any for a Charles

Rossi or a last-minute order for Durham. Gimbel was anxious to get off the Coastal Carolina grounds. Loading the boxes and the ice had taken longer than he'd planned. He had already pushed his luck too far.

Gimbel drove the van to his favorite hiding place along the road by the Green Swamp Preserve. Now he had to do what was the hardest thing for him to do; he had to wait. The vans that entered the tunnel after they'd left the Holden Beach packing plant were already loaded with their seafood orders and already on the road. This happened randomly during the daytime hours. Because Gimbel was an unknown driver, he wanted to enter the tunnel after dark. Gimbel was going into the tunnel as a Russian. He knew some drivers were Americans and some were Russians. He hoped there would only be a skeleton crew on duty in the tunnel tonight when he went in. This was exactly the kind of thing his doctors had told him not to do. This was exactly the reason his captain had taken him off working active cases. But Gimbel was independent and stubborn. He was determined to get the videos, even if it killed him.

Gimbel suspected, from what Steve Brandon had said to him, that for some political or diplomatic reason, the FBI had been forced to pull back their operation. From Gimbel's point of view, this was bullshit. He was determined that the whole world see what the evil Ivans were up to. He didn't give a rip about hurting the Russians' feelings or busting up some delicate international negotiations that might be taking place. These Russians were thugs and criminals. They were operating on U.S. soil, and they needed to be exposed for who and what they were. Diplomatic ties and presidential side-stepping be damned. Gimbel was going into the tunnel tonight! It very briefly crossed his mind that he might have made a rash decision.

Gimbel knew exactly where to find the entrance to the tunnel. It was very cleverly concealed in a grove of trees, and he'd watched the tunnel's access doorway open and close many times on the videos Jerry and Sam had collected. Most of the area around the preserve was flat, but there were a few rises here and there in the savanna. The entrance to the tunnel was located near one of these rises.

A long wooden panel had been planted with grass and scrub, making it indistinguishable from the identical grass and scrub pine that was growing all around it. The panel was similar to a raised garden bed, but this one was fixed with a metal slab floor. And the bed of grass and scrub was not raised. It was at ground level. When it was in place, the panel fitted so neatly and perfectly down into the ground, it was impossible to differentiate it from the surrounding area's vegetation.

When the right signal was sent, the panel quickly and quietly rose a few feet above the ground and slid to the side. A long, narrow, and very steep ramp that traveled deep into the ground below the savanna was revealed. The opening didn't look as if it would be wide enough for the vans to get through, but they seemed to have no trouble as they drove down the almost vertical corridor of blacktop, down into the tunnel where the drugs would be loaded on board their vehicles.

Building a tunnel in a swamp was a serious feat of engineering and called for more than a bit of audacity. One of the FBI techs who'd worked and lived briefly with Gimbel was into landscaping. He had commented, when he'd seen the imagination and the precision with which the entrance to the tunnel had been designed, that he thought a landscape architect as well as a very creative engineer had worked together to invent the system for entering this unique hiding place. The tunnel contrivance was a brilliant and ingenious invention and a thing of beauty.

A security code was required to activate the mechanicals that unlocked and opened the tunnel's entrance. No unauthorized vehicles would be able to activate the system to make the panel rise and then slide sideways and allow the vans to enter the steep driveway that led underground. Jerry and Sam had had no trouble hacking into the Russian's electronics and obtaining the security code. All three men had watched the surveillance videos in amazement as each time, the panel rose slightly and then slid sideways, revealing the tunnel's entrance.

The FBI had not authorized anyone to go into the tunnel to video the actual transfer of the drugs. Gimbel was not able to get his head around why this piece of the investigation had been overlooked, ignored, swept under the rug, or purposely avoided. He fully realized that, once someone who was not authorized to enter had breached the tunnel, the Russians would know they'd been caught. Their operation would immediately be shut down. Maybe that was why the FBI and everybody else was holding off. Gimbel knew it would be all over when he finally broke into the Russian's hiding place and took videos of the drugs being transferred. But time had already run out. The technicians had left town. Gimbel decided it was time to shut down the operation.

Gimbel realized he felt very strongly about drug trafficking. He knew his almost zealous desire to shut down any and all drug operations probably had to do with his own childhood. He had watched his mother kill herself slowly with bottle after bottle of gin. He had long ago acknowledged to himself that one of the reasons he was driven to destroy the heroin and fentanyl networks that were killings kids and others was because he had wished, as a child and as a young man, that he could destroy those bottles of gin that took his mother away from him every day of his life.

Gimbel's van approached the slight rise in the savanna, the spot where he knew the ingenious sliding platform would reveal an opening in the earth and allow him to enter the tunnel. He punched in the code, and the amazing engineering feat that enabled a piece of the ground to slide sideways was repeated right before his eyes. Gimbel drove the van slowly and carefully down the steep ramp. He'd brushed up on a few simple words from his high school Russian. He wouldn't be able to fool these people for very long, but he might be able to fool them for long enough.

There was one guy waiting at the bottom of the ramp. Gimbel rolled down his window and shouted something in Russian about a storm coming and wanting to get out of there as quickly as possible. The acoustics in the underground space were not great, and the guy at the bottom of the ramp looked at Gimbel with a puzzled expression on his face and waved him on. Workers in the underground facility assumed that whoever had been able to get into the tunnel belonged there.

Gimbel drove the van into a wider space that was lined with wire shelving. The ceiling was very low, and the walls that kept back the dirt were made of corrugated metal. It was a claustrophobic's worst nightmare, very cramped. It was, as expected, incredibly damp in the tunnel. It was underneath a swamp. Gimbel could scarcely breathe down here. There were hundreds of Coastal Carolina Seafood boxes lined up on the wire shelves. Some boxes were empty, and some looked packed and taped closed and ready to go. Others were open and in the process of being filled with plastic bags full of drugs. Gimbel tried to get some videos of the open boxes with the drugs sitting beside them on the shelves. The lighting was terrible, and he was worried about the quality of the film footage he was recording with his phone.

Two guys appeared from somewhere, and Gimbel jumped out of the van, ran around to the back, and opened the rear doors. Now Gimbel was going to be an American who didn't understand any Russian. He realized this was his most vulnerable moment, the moment when he gave his drug order to the men who would fill his van with the correct number of boxes full of heroin and fentanyl. He had decided he was just going to say that he was headed for upstate New York and wanted the usual drug shipment loaded into the van.

When Gimbel had been spying on the activity near the Green Swamp Preserve with Jerry and Sam, they'd never been able to figure out exactly how the people in the tunnel knew how many boxes of drugs to load into each of the vans. They didn't know how that was determined. They'd hacked into the system enough to be certain there were no computer invoices, so they concluded the order was either in writing or given verbally by the driver when he arrived for a pick up. Gimbel was going to have to wing it.

Gimbel hadn't said anything specific or given the men any written orders, but he muttered something in English about upstate New York. Whatever he had said must have been okay because two men went ahead and began loading boxes of drugs into the back of the van. Gimbel figured they were loading the van up with the amounts of drugs they usually dispensed for trips to upstate New York. He wondered if they would give him an invoice to sign for the drugs after they were loaded.

Meanwhile, this was the gold he'd hoped to mine, the videos he had hoped to record of the men loading the boxes into the van. He wished he could take his time and get videos of everything, especially close-ups of the partially packed boxes on the wire shelving with some of the drugs inside. That wasn't going to be possible tonight. He turned on his phone to record...audio and video. He scanned the underground space, so the viewer of his videography would get the idea of what this transfer station was all about. Gimbel was able to get what he thought were good pictures of the men loading the boxes into the van. He got close-ups of their faces. He got close-ups of the boxes of drugs. He recorded everything they said to him and to each other. He wasn't able to get everything he wanted, but it was more than anybody else had.

One of the men handed him a sheet of paper. There were some numbers on it, but Gimbel didn't read it. He just scribbled an indecipherable signature at the bottom of the paper and handed it back to the Russian. Gimbel was now very anxious to get out of the tunnel.

Gimbel climbed back into the van. He immediately sent the videos to several email addresses he'd preprogrammed into his phone. He was sending to Steve Brandon at the FBI, somebody he knew at the DEA, CNN, FoxNews, MSNBC, the BBC, and several local TV stations in Washington, D.C., New York City, Wilmington, North Carolina, and Syracuse, New York. Somebody would have a breaking news story in the morning. Then Gimbel realized his phone wasn't sending. There was no cell phone reception down here in this dungeon. No one was going to receive their breaking news story until he could get out of this hole in the ground and find cell service.

Gimbel had brought two of his cell phones, the one given to him by the FBI and his personal phone. He'd recorded the videos on his FBI phone, but what if the FBI or somebody else decided to block that phone? They might decide Gimbel's evidence would never see the light of day. This flash of paranoia motivated him to forward the videos he'd just recorded to his own personal cell phone. He frantically tried to send the videos to some of the email addresses he thought might make them public. There was still no transmission, of course.

Gimbel knew he had to stay cool and couldn't panic, but he was now desperate to get out of the tunnel. He proceeded along the narrow corridor, going faster than he should. He thought he must be close to one of the tunnel exits. He was looking for another steep ramp going up which would be his last hurdle. There was a wide place in the corridor, and he could see the ramp ahead. His impatience was getting the better of him. He'd never suffered from claustrophobia before, but this was ridiculous.

Someone shouted at him in Russian. A man approached the van and pounded on the driver's side window. Gimbel put the window down a few inches and muttered the same sentence he'd memorized and said to the guy at the tunnel's entrance, about the storm coming and wanting to get back on the road ASAP. The man at the window began shouting at him in Russian, and Gimbel didn't have to pretend that he didn't understand a word of what the man was saying. He motioned for Gimbel to get out of the van. Gimbel knew he was in trouble.

Gimbel had a gun, but he was vastly outnumbered down here. He slid the gun under the passenger seat's floor mat and slipped his FBI cell phone under the driver's seat. When the van left the underground bunker, whenever and however that might happen, the phone would automatically send his emails containing the videos. Gimbel was caught, but maybe the videos would find their way out. If he was going to die, he wanted someone to save his dogs.

He played for time with the man outside the van. He pretended not to understand, and he was not really pretending about that. Gimbel quickly composed a clumsy text message that he sent from his personal cell phone to Christina Rose's phone. He wrote:

```
In trouble. Please save dogs. Gimbel.
```

When someone drove the van out of the tunnel, the emails and videos on his personal cell phone and his text to Christina Rose would automatically be sent. He tossed his personal phone into the back seat. It was all he had time to do. He hoped no one would find the phones until after everything was on its way to the intended recipients. He hoped that by then it would be too late to stop the transmissions.

The man opened the door and dragged Gimbel from the van. He began to hit him in the face with the butt of his very large Russian gun, all the while screaming questions that Gimbel couldn't answer. Gimbel didn't try to fight back and finally lost consciousness, blessedly sparing himself the continuing pain of the ruthless beating by his Russian captors.

Chapter 34

Now upgraded to a Category 3 storm, dreaded Hurricane Gregory had moved up the coast faster than anyone had anticipated, and some of the forecasting models were targeting Cape Fear as a possible landfall location. The governor of North Carolina had declared the coastal counties in a state of emergency and was urging residents who lived along the beaches to make plans to evacuate. A voluntary evacuation order had been issued. In a few hours the evacuation would be mandatory. Citizens of coastal towns were warned to secure their homes and businesses and get ready to leave.

Christina Rose had mistakenly left her cell phone on the sailboat after Sunday's trip to Oak Island. She checked her emails from her computer at the cottage, but she, like every other young person of her generation, felt somewhat insecure and at loose ends without her phone. She couldn't get any texts on her computer, and she wanted to get her phone back as soon as possible.

Christina Rose and Marley put down the sturdy storm shutters on the windows and doors of the cottage and brought the porch furniture inside the house. They packed up the things they wanted to take with them. Christina Rose was cleaning out the refrigerator, and Marley was taking both their cars to fill them with gas. Rosemary had already gone back to Asheville the day before. Marley and Christina Rose had prepared their cottage for hurricanes many times. During the years, there had been multiple false alarms as well as real storms. And they'd been lucky. The Wilmington area had dodged more than one serious hurricane threat.

Christina Rose was irritable without her phone, and Marley was lecturing her about dependency and addictions. This only made Christina Rose grumpier. If they'd stopped to think about it, they would have realized that the rapidly falling barometer was probably contributing to their moodiness and their anxiety. They were tired, restless, and out of sorts.

Marley was going to drive to the marina in Southport to be sure the sailboat was properly secured for the storm, and while she was there, she promised to look for Christina's cell phone. Christina Rose was afraid the phone might have fallen under one of the bunk beds. She'd taken a nap on the return trip, after the lunch at Oak Island. Her mother had been in a terrible mood and wanted to talk to Marley in private. This had annoyed Christina Rose who'd retreated to her bunk and gone to sleep. When they'd arrive in Southport, Christina Rose hadn't been completely awake when her mother had hurried her off the sailboat and into the car. She'd left her phone behind, and she wasn't entirely sure where she'd left it. It could be in the bunk bed, or it might be on the floor. It could have slid anywhere, under anything.

The storm predictions were becoming more ominous for the North Carolina and South Carolina coasts. It looked as if Gregory was going to make landfall somewhere close to the boundary between the two states. Evacuation was now voluntary, but would soon be mandatory. Within hours, all lanes of the roads and highways in the area would become one-way, with all vehicles being forced to head away from the coast. Marley and Christina Rose hated to leave their beloved cottage on Shell Island, but they finally completed securing the house and taking care of all the things that needed to be done before the storm hit. The second car they always left in the garage at the beach was a Prius. Christina Rose would drive the Prius to the long-term parking lot at the Wilmington airport and Marley would follow her in the Suburban. She would pick up Christina Rose at the airport, and they would head west to Asheville.

When Marley returned from the marina in Southport, she gave Christina Rose her phone. Christina Rose was delighted that Marley had found her phone, but the battery was dead and needed to be recharged. They were busy packing the car and would soon be leaving the cottage. There wasn't time for Christina Rose to charge her phone at the house. She put the phone and her car charger in the Suburban. These two seaside dwellers had put forth their best efforts to try to keep their home safe. The young woman and the old woman each said a silent goodbye to their lovely cottage and set out for the airport. Hopefully, they would be back here in a few days, putting the wicker furniture out on the porch where it belonged and taking walks in the sand.

Christina Rose parked the Prius in the airport's long-term parking and walked to meet Marley who was waiting in the Suburban. As she headed for the SUV, Christina Rose noticed how much the wind had increased. She had to keep her head down as she walked into the wind. How could things have changed so quickly? As soon as she got into the Suburban, she plugged in her phone's car charger. She turned on the radio. The storm was now predicted to make landfall at Cape Fear. That was way too close to Shell Island for comfort. Christina and Marley looked at each other. Both were very worried.

It was late in the afternoon when they left the Wilmington area, and their plan was to drive as far as Raleigh and spend the night at the Hampton Inn. They would drive the rest of the way to Asheville tomorrow. Christina Rose went to sleep. A falling barometer always did that to her. So did riding in the car. When she woke up, they were almost to their motel. They stopped at a favorite diner on Rt. #40 for dinner and pulled into the Hampton Inn at 9:00 p.m. Christina's phone was charged. While Marley went into the lobby to check them into their room, Christina Rose checked her messages.

She almost missed the text message from Gimbel. She didn't recognize his phone number right away, but when she read his message, she felt sick to her stomach. Gimbel was in trouble and wanted her to save his dogs. He hadn't explained what kind of trouble he was in, but it must have been something really terrible, Christina Rose thought, for him to have left his dogs behind. If he couldn't get to his dogs, he must think he was going to die. Christina Rose ran into the office of the Hampton Inn and showed the text to Marley.

"I wish we had known about this before we found ourselves more than two and a half hours away from Oak Island. We can't go back there now. Have you tried to call him or text him?" Marley also felt terrible that they couldn't help Gimbel. She'd fallen in love with the two Westies, just as Christina Rose had. But she didn't think it was wise to turn the car around and drive back in the direction of the storm.

Christina Rose sat in the lobby of the Hampton Inn and pored over her phone. She called Gimbel's cell phone. She left multiple voice messages. She sent repeated text messages, asking where he was and what was wrong. She sent a few emails, thinking he might have lost his phone but might still have access to his computer. She received no response from anything. Marley was in their room when Christina Rose burst in sobbing.

"We have to go back and get the dogs. I don't know what's happened to Gimbel, but this is an emergency. He wouldn't have sent the text to me, if he'd had anybody else who could have rescued Dilly and Billy."

"I feel terrible about it, too, but we can't go back."

"He leaves the dogs in that outside kennel on the side of the house. If the hurricane hits Cape Fear, Oak Island will be completely flooded, overrun with sea water from the storm surge. The dogs will drown in the kennel. We have to go back, Marley." Christina Rose was already planning how she could steal the keys to the Suburban in the middle of the night and drive back to Oak Island on her own. She'd had her driver's license for almost a year, but she'd not had much experience driving the big SUV on highways or in hurricanes. Could she take the chance of driving by herself into a Category 3 hurricane?

She cried herself to sleep that night, sick about the adorable Dilly and Billy. Gimbel had reached out to her for help, and she was going to fail him. She knew how much he loved those dogs. He didn't have a family, and he seemed to be very alone in the world. Dilly and Billy were his family. She woke up in the middle of the night and began to cry again.

At 4:00 a.m. Marley woke her and told her to get dressed. "We're going back to Wilmington to get the dogs." Marley didn't say anything else, just started putting things into her overnight bag. They were silent as they climbed into the Suburban. Marley filled the car with gas, and they stopped for breakfast at the diner. They still hadn't spoken, but they both ordered extra food for their hearty breakfast, not knowing when they would have a chance to eat again.

The governor of North Carolina had announced that the roads would all be one-way, heading away from the beach as of 8:00 a.m. Anybody who was still trying to reach their beach house would have to make it there by early this morning. Their first glimpse of the beach let Christina Rose and Marley know how bad the storm was going to be. They'd been listening to the radio and knew that Bald Head Island and Oak Island had already been evacuated and were closed to traffic. The waves were dangerously high, and the last high tide had already washed over the dunes.

When Christina Rose heard about the high tide overwashes, she began to cry again. "We're going to be too late. Please hurry, Marley." But they couldn't hurry. They traffic going towards the beach was terrible. Everyone who had put off securing their beach house until the last minute was scrambling to try to beat the eastbound road closures scheduled for 8:00 a.m.

When they got to the bridge that crossed over the Intracoastal Waterway, the only way to get to Oak Island except by boat, it was closed. Gimbel lived about a mile from the bridge, so they were going to have to break the law and walk the rest of the way. There was no good place to leave the Suburban, so they locked it and abandoned it by the side of the road. It was a bad place to leave a car under any circumstances. They hoped it wouldn't be towed or stolen or vandalized or washed away.

The wind was fierce now, and water was washing across the bridge. Both Christina and Marley had to hold on to the side railings to keep from being swept into the Intracoastal Waterway below. They were soaked to the skin as they struggled across. They were lucky there were no law enforcement vehicles blocking their way onto Oak Island. The police must have figured no one would be crazy enough to try to get onto the island now. The streets were flooded. Marley began to think about turning around and going back to the car, but Christina Rose kept on, head down into the wind, determined to get to Gimbel's house. It was slow going with the wind and the flooding. At one point they were wading through water up to their waists.

Finally, they saw Gimbel's house ahead. Built on pilings like all newer houses at the beach were required to be, the house was swaying from side to side in the ferocious wind. Christina Rose tried to run to get to the dog kennel, but the wind was so strong she could barely hold her own and remain standing. It was bad.

Marley was lagging behind but was still heading towards the house. Christina Rose went around the corner of the house and finally made it to the kennel. The kennel was flooded, and the dogs were gone. The water or the wind or both had knocked down one side of the fencing, so the dogs would have been able to escape the rising water. This was a good thing, that they hadn't been forced to stay inside the kennel and drown. But it was a bad thing because they were now on the loose and could have gone anywhere. Christina Rose ran toward the beach, crying. "Dilly! Billy! Where are you?" The howling wind was so loud, they couldn't have heard her yelling, even if they'd been anywhere nearby.

Christina Rose ran up and down the beach screaming. Marley ran after her and pulled her back from the edge of the pounding surf. "If they're out there in that water, in the ocean, we're too late. Come back to the house. Maybe Gimbel has already been here and taken them to a safe place." They both knew this wasn't true, but Christina Rose agreed to go back. Marley put her arm around the girl to comfort her. Christina could not stop crying.

They looked in the garage spaces underneath the house, and both the BMW and the Subaru were gone. Maybe Gimbel had made it back to get his dogs in time. They went around to the back of the house where the pool was located. Christina screamed. One West Highland Terrier was floating, still as a stone, on the top of the water. Already soaking wet, Christina Rose jumped into the pool with her clothes and shoes on and swam to the dog. It was Billy, and he wasn't breathing. He was dead. His heart had stopped. Christina Rose lifted him out of the pool into Marley's waiting arms.

Marley had almost become a nurse. She'd never been to vet school, but she was going to do everything she could to try to bring this little guy back to life. She stuck her finger in his mouth to clear his airway and began to gently press on his tiny chest, trying to restart the heart of this little dog who had stolen her own heart. She kept up her regular rhythm, pressing on the chest, doing her own ad hoc version of doggie CPR. She was about to give up when Billy regurgitated a belly full and lungs full of pool water and sea water. Were these his final death throes, or was he going to begin to breathe again?

As Marley was working on Billy, Christina Rose was looking and calling everywhere for Dilly, but the little dog was nowhere to be found. The storm raged around them. Would they be able to make it back to their car and save themselves, let alone save Gimbel's beloved dogs?

Chapter 35

When Gimbel regained consciousness, he was in terrible pain from the beating the Russians had given him. His clothes had been soaked with blood and were now stiff with it. Although he couldn't touch his hands to his face, he could tell how badly he'd been beaten. His right eye was swollen completely shut. He couldn't open his eyelid, and he knew the eye socket had sustained serious damage. He wondered why the Russians hadn't killed him. There wasn't a sound in the dark place where he found himself, only silence—deadly and total silence. He smelled the dirt and dampness all around him. He was tied to something and couldn't move his arms or legs. It dawned on him why they hadn't killed him. They'd saved themselves some trouble and just left him here to die on his own. He had to free himself. He wondered if he could even walk. Had the Russians destroyed his legs and arms as well as his face?

He struggled with the metal bindings that cut into his ankles, wrists, and thighs. It was going to take Houdini to get out of these restraints. Gimbel had been trained, when he was in the Marines, to escape from situations like this. He called on all of his patience and worked with the metal strap bindings. He cut himself dozens of times, trying to free his hands. He dozed off to sleep now and then, woke up, and resumed working towards his objective. Finally he had loosened the bindings around one wrist enough that he could slip his hand free. From that moment on, he was energized and called on what remained of his inner strength to get away from this place and survive. He freed his legs and thighs and threw the strips of his metal bonds on the ground.

Until he was out of the tunnel, he couldn't allow himself to think about the storm or what might have happened to his dogs. He hoped his text had reached Christina Rose in time. He trusted that if she had been able to do anything to save the dogs, she would have done it. He couldn't think about that now. He had to get out of this underground death trap.

When he'd been watching the videos with Jerry and Sam, they'd had good views of how the vans had entered the tunnel, but the views they had of the exit or exits had not been as helpful. They had identified at least two exit ramps, and Gimbel had wondered at the time if there were more. Multiple exits would have been a smart way for the vans to leave the underground transfer station, rather than to have all of them leaving from the same spot. Gimbel reminded himself that he only needed to find one of those exit ramps to get out of his underground prison.

He was doing all of this in the dark, but he finally found a ramp. He climbed to the exit door, and it was locked tight. Gimbel didn't have any idea how he was going to unlock the door and get out. He figured there had to be some kind of emergency option, a manual opener for the door. He searched and searched, but he couldn't find it. Maybe the exit doors didn't have a manual back-up safety feature, but he was sure the entryway door would. There had to be a way to open the door in case of an emergency, in case something got stuck. If he could find his way back to the entry ramp and if he could find that emergency manual door opener, he might be able to make it out alive.

He worked his way back through the underground corridor, calling on all of his mental breadcrumbs to remember the way he'd gotten himself into the tunnel in the first place. Finally, he found the entryway, and miraculously, he also found a flashlight. Eventually, he found the emergency lever that opened the sliding panel. He slowly and painfully climbed up the blacktop ramp and walked outside into a raging hurricane.

Gimbel didn't know how long he'd been unconscious in his underground prison, and he didn't know what day it was when he stepped outside to face the fierce wind and driving rain. He did know that Hurricane Gregory had arrived in full force. Gimbel had never been in a hurricane before, but he figured the coast of North Carolina was taking a direct hit. He had no vehicle. He could scarcely remain upright when he was walking into the wind. In decent weather, he knew his house on Oak Island was about a half-hour's drive by car from the preserve—if he had a car. He would have to find one.

He didn't know if it was day or night, but it was definitely dark. He didn't have either of his cell phones with their GPS systems, but he thought he could find his way to the highway, Rt. #112. He'd driven around the area enough and hidden his car in the grass and trees enough times that he was somewhat familiar with where he was. After some false starts, he made it to the road. He knew there were a few houses scattered along Rt. #112, and there were vehicles parked at some of those houses. That's what he was looking for. He'd hung on to the flashlight he'd found in the tunnel, but it wasn't much help with the rain pouring down and the wind trying to blow him over. He couldn't see a thing. He was walking along the flooded road, depending completely on his memory of when he had driven on Rt. #112.

It was parked beside a rundown house with two ancient washing machines on the front porch. Gimbel saw what he needed. The F-150 pickup with four-wheel drive was ancient, but it was unlocked. Gimbel was soaked, and it was a relief to climb into the cab of the truck. He felt bad about stealing the guy's truck, but he didn't feel bad enough about it to keep himself from hot wiring it and driving it away.

The road to Oak Island was flooded and completely washed out in places. He fought to keep the truck on the pavement. Gimbel was headed for his house to try to save his dogs. He turned on the radio, hoping to get some news of the storm. But it was an old truck, and the radio didn't work anymore. He still didn't know what day it was. When he got closer to the beach, he saw signs that said cars could no longer drive east towards the ocean. He'd seen this scenario on television in the past, when the governor told the folks they could no longer drive to their houses at the beach. The time had come when everybody had to evacuate and drive west, away from the beach.

The heck with that. Gimbel was going to drive to his house anyway. He didn't care what the governor of North Carolina said. Gimbel wasn't even from North Carolina. He drove against the traffic, slipping and sliding on the shoulder of the narrow road. When he got to the bridge that crossed the Intracoastal Waterway onto Oak Island, there were cones across the road and a sign that said Oak Island was closed. No one was to enter. Gimbel ignored the sign and ran over the traffic cones. No law enforcement people were around to tell him to stop.

The road was completely flooded. Gimbel kept on driving through the high water. He expected the truck to stall out at any minute. He was expecting the worst when he got to the house, and he found the worst. The full force of the storm had yet to hit, but the driveway was already impassable. He got out of the truck and made his way to the house.

At the side of the house, his chest began to hurt. He wondered if he was having a heart attack or if he was going to die right there of a broken heart. One wall of the kennel was down. The kennel was flooded. He wondered if they'd drowned there, before the side of the kennel came down, or if they'd escaped and drowned someplace else. He sat down in the water and cried.

He'd not been functioning very well to begin with. He hadn't had anything to eat or drink for days. For how many days, he didn't know. He had only been able to think about getting to the house and saving the dogs, and he had failed to save them. His only hope was that Christina Rose had been there. He had no cell phone to call her. He had nothing but an old pickup truck that didn't even belong to him. He could drive it to the airport where he remembered that he had left a car in long-term parking.

He stumbled through the water to get back to the pickup. He headed towards the bridge that went across the Intracoastal Waterway from Oak Island to the mainland. It was the way he'd come, just a few minutes earlier. Or maybe it had been a long time ago that he'd driven across this bridge. He was losing track of time and where he was. He was becoming confused, disoriented. He didn't really care. The cones were up again, forbidding him to drive back across the bridge. He was suddenly filled with fury. No one was going to tell him what to do or where he could drive.

He pushed his foot down on the truck's accelerator and kept it there. The cones flew in all directions as he raced through them. He was going like a bat out of hell when he realized a section of the bridge had fallen away. Part of the road was no longer there. The next thing he knew, the F-150 was headed off the bridge and into the water. He was going to die. This was the end. He'd long wondered if God had allowed his mother to have her flask of gin in heaven. He figured he would soon find out the answer to that question.

The pickup landed in the swirling waters of the Intracoastal Waterway. Gimbel was being swept away, and the truck was headed for the open ocean. He'd had his seat belt on when the truck went off the bridge and into the water. In the Marines, he'd been trained how to get out of a vehicle that ended up like this. If he could just remember what he was supposed to do, he would do it. Or maybe he wouldn't. Maybe he would just go down, down, down in the stolen truck, down to the bottom of Davy Jones' Locker. What was Davy Jones' Locker anyway? He'd always wondered what it was. Surviving in a vehicle in this situation had something to do with rolling down the windows and allowing the water to come into the truck. He began to roll the windows down. Could that be right? It didn't sound right. Maybe there was something else he was supposed to do?

Somehow he found himself out of the truck. Gimbel was a very strong swimmer, but he was now swimming in the middle of a hurricane. He thought of Moby Dick, the white whale, and wondered if he would see it in the ocean when he got there. He thought of the word of the day. He always read the WOTD in the newspaper. When had he last read the newspaper? Did anybody still publish a newspaper anymore? The last word of the day he remembered had been "inchmeal." It was like "piecemeal" but smaller, inch by inch. He'd never heard the word before, and he'd never used it. Now he would never have the chance to use it. Somebody from North Carolina was named Randal Radish, and his grandmother had asked if he were pithy. He thought of word cookies. Gimbel found that funny and began to laugh. His mouth filled with water, and choking, he struggled to get back to the surface. He thought of Will Rogers. Was it Will Rogers who'd said "If there are no dogs in Heaven, then when I die, I want to go where they went."? Gimbel didn't want to go to Heaven either, if his dogs weren't there. He started to cry again. The water pounded him down. He fought his way to the surface again. He was thirsty. He turned over and over and over in the rushing water and the pounding surf. He was very, very tired. He wanted to get some rest. The water took him under again and again. Then he was gone.

Chapter 36

"**Somebody called and said there** was a body on the beach. And sure enough, here it is." The North Carolina State Policeman knelt over the body and reached for a pulse. "Oh, my God, this poor soul still has a pulse." The officer took his phone out of his pocket and called for a helicopter and an EMT team. The almost-dead body was face down in the sand. The sheriff's deputy who had driven the state policeman out to Bald Head Island helped him turn the man over on his back. "He even seems to be breathing, but he's lost his pants. I guess we won't be able to look in his wallet and find his driver's license. I wonder who he is and how in the world he ever got here. He must have been in the ocean and washed up with the waves. How could anybody still be breathing after that? This is one lucky guy. It's a miracle he's still alive. Why don't people evacuate when they're told to? It would make everybody's life so much easier. Or, maybe he was on a boat? I'll bet he was on a boat."

The two law enforcement people sat with the half-naked man. When he began shivering and shaking, they brought blankets out of the cruiser and covered him up. They didn't want him to die of exposure before the helicopter arrived.

There was a first aid kit in the deputy's car, but this man was way beyond the help of a first aid kit. It seemed like they sat there for a long time before the helicopter arrived, but in fact it was only nineteen minutes. The EMTs rushed to attend to their victim.

"Is he going to make it?" The state policeman wanted to know. "I almost didn't bother to check for a pulse and called the ME. He sure looked dead as a doornail to me."

The EMT who was putting an IV in the man's arm said, "It's touch and go. He's really beaten up. Look at his face. We don't know how long he was in the water, but he looks like he was in the water for a long time. He washed up here on the ocean side of the island, so we're assuming he was out at sea for part of his journey. He may have washed ashore from a boat that sank out there. He's unconscious, so we won't know until he wakes up, if he ever does, whether or not he has brain damage. His vital signs are not good. He doesn't have much of any blood pressure. He's been suffering from hypothermia for some time; we don't know how long. He may die on the way to the hospital."

The unknown man without his pants was on his way to the New Hanover Regional Medical Center in Wilmington, North Carolina in a helicopter. Maybe it would be his lucky day. On the way to the hospital, the man began to mutter, "Call me Ishmael. Call me Inchmeal." He repeated this over and over again.

"Maybe that's his name, Ishmael...or Inchmeal? Whatever it is he's talking about....Maybe he's trying to tell us his name."

"Maybe."

"It sounds like a Middle Eastern name to me. Do you think he's a terrorist?

"No. And it doesn't matter anyway. A man without his pants won't be causing us any trouble."

The man was unloaded on the helipad at the hospital. He was admitted to the ICU and didn't regain consciousness for three days.

Outside the hospital, the city of Wilmington and the surrounding area struggled to assess the damage and get back to some semblance of normalcy. Gregory had made landfall exactly at the border between North Carolina and South Carolina. As always, the barrier islands had been hit the hardest. Calabash and Myrtle Beach were destroyed, with water everywhere, as far as the eye could see. Cape Fear, Oak Island, and Bald Head Island had been victims of two high tides and a fearsome storm surge. The farther away a beach house was from the Carolina border, the better it fared. Places on Wrightsville Beach had terrible damage, but the island was still standing. Because of the tides, Shell Island had been extremely lucky. High tide had not coincided with the worst of the hurricane, and the myth that God somehow protected that community had lived on through yet another storm. Wilmington itself had sustained a lot of damage, but it would be back.

The citizens of the southern part of the North Carolina Coast were coping with the destruction, grieving for the losses of their homes, and trying to come to terms with the long and expensive road ahead that would be required to restore their lives. A few people had died, but most had taken the storm seriously and had survived.

An aging Ford F-150 pickup truck had been salvaged from the Intracoastal Waterway. Someone had seen the truck go into the water, just before the worst of Hurricane Gregory hit. There had not been the time or the resources to try to get the truck out of the water, or to see if anyone had been in the truck when it had plunged off the bridge from Oak Island. A few days later, the truck was recovered. No one was found inside. The truck's ownership was traced to a man who lived on Rt. #112, near the Green Swamp Preserve. He'd reported his truck stolen the day after the hurricane. He wasn't sure if someone had stolen the truck or if it had been washed away or blown away in a tornado spawned by the storm. No one could figure out how it had ended up in the Intracoastal Waterway. Strange and freaky things happened in hurricanes.

A gold BMW was found in the parking lot of the Coastal Carolina Seafood Company in Holden Beach. The parking lot had flooded, and the expensive car had been partially submerged for several days. It was a total loss, but the registration was found in the glove compartment. The car was registered to a Charles Petrossi. There was no such person living anywhere in North Carolina, but the license plates were local plates. It was puzzling. The car was totaled anyway. Charles Petrossi, whoever and wherever he was, would not be driving it again. No one would ever again drive that gold BMW anywhere.

All the hospitals had been swamped. Power in the city was spotty, and most hospitals were still operating on emergency generators. Medical staff was spread thin. The ICU at New Hanover Regional Medical Center, where the man they were calling "Ishmael" was trying to survive, was understaffed. They were keeping patients alive and tending to their physical needs. No one had even begun to try to find out Ishmael's real identity. He was a casualty of the storm, and he was a damn lucky one. He was going to live. Whether he had a normally functioning brain any more, after his ordeal, was still to be determined. The staff finally got around to giving Ishmael an MRI. His brain looked totally normal. That was a miracle in itself and boded well for the man's recovery. He was still in a coma after three days, and he was hooked up to countless tubes and monitors and other devices. He was being given IV fluids and blood transfusions, and who knew how many life-saving drugs were flowing in his veins.

On his fourth day in the hospital, Ishmael opened one eye. His other eye had a patch over it. The damage done to his orbital socket and to the eye itself was so severe, the ophthalmologist didn't want his patient to use the damaged eye for several weeks. The eye specialist didn't think the man's eye itself had been damaged by his prolonged swim in the ocean or even from being tossed around on the rocks and in the surf. The injuries looked to the ophthalmologist as if the man's face had been beaten with a hammer. When Ishmael opened his one eye, the nurse called the hospitalist.

"Good morning Ishmael. I'm Doctor Robert Samuels. You're here in the ICU at New Hanover Regional Medical Center. That's in Wilmington, North Carolina. You washed up on Bald Head Island, and our excellent first responders were able to save your life and bring you here."

The man in the bed was not able to speak. His one eye just stared back at the doctor.

"When you first came in, you were saying 'Call me Ishmael! Call me Inchmeal!' You said it over and over again. I don't know anything about any 'Inchmeal,' but I had a minor in American Literature in undergraduate school. I read *Moby Dick*. I'd read it in high school, too, so I've read it twice. I know the first line from the book is, 'Call me Ishmael.' So, we have been calling you Ishmael. But I don't think that's really your name. I don't know if you can hear what I'm saying to you, or if you understand any of it. The good news is, you are going to live through this. The bad news is, we don't have any idea who you are. I'm going to leave you to rest now, but I'll be back. We will figure this out."

The man in the hospital bed heard only part of what the doctor said to him. His hearing had been damaged, and he was only able to hear a word here and there. He was so tired. He wanted to go back to the ocean. He had been so sure he was going to die. What had gone wrong? He remembered he was going to see his dogs in Heaven. And he was going to see Will Rogers and the white whale. He didn't think Captain Ahab would make it to heaven. He remembered that the doctor had said his name was Ishmael. What had happened to the Pequod? It had gone down for sure. The man went back to sleep.

Gimbel Saunders gradually began to remember things. But every time his consciousness came close to thinking about the dogs, his brain shut down. It was a hurdle he couldn't seem to get over. He didn't remember why he happened to be in a place called New Hanover County, but he finally grasped that it was in North Carolina. He'd been swept up onto the beach of one of the barrier islands off the coast of Wilmington.

People kept asking him if he'd been in a boat and if there had been other people on the boat with him. He had no memory of being on a boat, but eventually he remembered being in a pickup truck. But how had he driven a pickup truck through the ocean and ended up in the surf, on the beach at a place called Bald Head Island? It was too complicated and too sad for him to think about any of it. He often started to cry. He cried in his sleep, and he cried when he was awake. The doctors were afraid this was a sign of brain damage. Maybe Ishmael would never be right in the head again. Maybe he would have to be sent to a state institution.

Gimbel's memory returned in random and erratic bits and pieces. He was becoming reacquainted with himself in an inchmeal fashion. Inchmeal had been the word of the day, on some day that Gimbel could no longer remember. Gimbel didn't know his name yet. The hospital staff continued to call him Ishmael, but he knew he'd stopped being Ishmael when he'd been put into the helicopter. His name wasn't really Ishmael.

Gimbel remembered he'd been a baseball player. Then he remembered he'd been a United States Marine. Then he remembered he'd been a New York State police detective, but he had a heart murmur. That meant he wasn't allowed to be a policeman anymore. He remembered a woman whose picture he'd found in an evidence box when he'd been a police detective. She had red hair and blue eyes, and then he had seen her again someplace. He couldn't remember where he'd seen her again, but she was older. But she was also younger. No, that had been the woman's daughter. He got confused trying to sort it all out and went back to sleep.

Gimbel was transferred from ICU to a regular hospital room, and he received much less attention after the transfer. He was still hooked up to the IVs because he wasn't eating. His doctor had brought in a psychiatrist and a neurologist to try to help him piece his life back together. Another MRI reassured everybody that there was no physical damage done to his brain. It took a few weeks, but eventually Gimbel Saunders was able to recover his life.

Gimbel remembered the murders in Skaneateles, his undercover identity as Chuckie Petrossi, the house on Oak Island, the dogs he'd loved and lost, escaping the tunnel near the Green Swamp Preserve, and driving the stolen pickup truck off the bridge. That was the last thing he remembered. He also remembered with fondness his friends Christina Rose Carmichael and Marley Kurtz. He hoped their cottage on Shell Island had survived the hurricane without too much damage. Gimbel was emotionally fragile. His loss of memory and his struggle to recover his identity had undermined his confidence.

Once he'd finally figured it all out, he made progress. His doctor told him he was going to be released from the hospital in a few days. First he would try to find his Subaru at the Wilmington Airport. He would buy a new cell phone, and he would call Steve Brandon at the FBI.

Chapter 37

"Gimbel, you have visitors. *Two* beautiful women are waiting to see you. Will you allow them to enter your room? The doctor said you have to okay everyone who comes in."

"Who's here to see me? I don't know anybody."

"Carmichael and Kurtz. They know you, and they say you know them. I've told them you can't remember everything you used to know. But they insist you will remember them."

"Of course I know them. Bring them in." Marley and Christina Rose came through the door. Christina Rose ran to his bed and threw her arms around him. She started to cry. Marley came to the other side of the bed and gently took his hand. Then she put her arms around him and hugged him. She had tears in her eyes.

Gimbel knew he looked terrible. He'd seen himself in the mirror, with his one eye that was working. He thought he looked like a pirate with his eyepatch. He'd lost a lot of weight and still had bruises all over his face. But these two wonderful women were delighted to see him, no matter how bad he looked.

Christina Rose recovered herself first. She began to speak and then broke down in tears again. Each women was carrying a large leather tote bag. Neither one seemed like a large leather tote bag kind of person to Gimbel. He looked at Christina Rose's big bag and frowned. Christina Rose began to giggle. She put her tote bag at the end of the bed. Marley put her tote bag at the end of the bed beside Christina Rose's. Gimbel heard scratching, and then he heard barking. Then he saw his West Highland Terriers' heads, as they peeked over the edges of the large leather purses. Dilly and Billy were here. He couldn't believe his eyes. Christina Rose had been able to save his dogs after all. It was a miracle. The dogs attacked Gimbel with kisses. They'd found their long-lost friend once again, after a prolonged separation. The humans all started to cry again. The dogs were gleeful and just kept wagging their tails. They nosed aside the IV and the other tubes that were attached to Gimbel and nestled under his arms, happy to be home at last.

"We had to smuggle them in. We couldn't come in here to see you and just tell you we had the dogs. They had to be here with us when we saw you for the first time. We will tell you all about it. It's quite a story." Christina Rose was beside herself with the success of her ability to smuggle two dogs into Gimbel's hospital room.

"We know you must have quite a story of your own, Gimbel. We thought for a long time that you were dead. We didn't hear from you." Marley wanted him to know she understood he'd been thorough a lot.

"It was terrible. We knew you'd probably lost your cell phone, but we called all the hospitals and talked to the police and the sheriff and everybody. Nobody knew where you were. They didn't even have a dead body that fit your description." Christina Rose realized she was blabbering too much and became quiet.

Marley took over telling the story. "Rosemary was the one who finally found you. I don't think she would ever do any hacking. She knows that's illegal, but computers are her business. She did a lot of searching online, and she finally found you at the hospital here. At first, you were listed as 'Ishmael Doe.' She thought it was you, but it wasn't until your name was changed to Gimbel Doe and then to Gimbel Saunders that she told us she'd found you. She was actually following your recovery here, before she ever told us she knew where you were. She knew how much we wanted to find out what had happened to you." Marley was more talkative today that she'd ever been. Her eyes smiled when she looked at Gimbel.

"I scolded Mom for holding out on us, but she said she didn't want to get our hopes up. She was afraid Ishmael Doe might turn out to be someone from Abu Dhabi or someplace and might not turn out to be you after all."

"You look tired. We will tell you about how we rescued the dogs, and then we'll leave. Billy and Dilly are staying with us on Shell Island. They are doing fine now." Marley could see that Gimbel was tired. Christina Rose was excited and full of energy and a hundred stories.

"How is the cottage? Did you have much damage?" Gimbel hoped their beach house had survived Gregory's wrath.

"It came through fine. Shell Island is north of where the worst damage was done. We were lucky. Our porch was pretty much destroyed, but there's somebody there this week rebuilding everything. The storm shutters worked perfectly, and we only lost one window in the garage. A few hydrangea bushes were torn out of the ground, but we've replanted them. Most of them will probably make it. Compared to what most people are dealing with, we have very little to show for a Category 3 hurricane." Christina Rose wanted to tell Gimbel everything all at once.

"Tell me about how you saved the dogs."

Christina Rose had to be the one to tell this part of the story. "Marley is the hero here. She saved Billy's life. She studied to be a nurse so she knew how to give Billy CPR. It was the most amazing thing you've ever seen." Christina Rose was bubbling over with the story, and Gimbel was confused. He felt as if he'd arrived in the middle of the movie.

Marley took over. "Let's start at the beginning, dear. Gimbel needs to hear the whole thing. Christina Rose didn't get your text right away. She'd left her phone on the sailboat, and it was a couple of days before we found it. Then her phone wasn't charged, and then we were on our way back to Asheville to ride out the storm. When we finally read your text, we were at a hotel in Raleigh. Of course we wanted to go back to Oak Island. Christina Rose was devastated when I told her it was too dangerous to go back. I thought it was too late to drive back into an oncoming hurricane."

Christina Rose couldn't wait to take over telling the story. "But we did go back. Marley woke me up in the middle of the night, and we drove back to Oak Island. The bridge was blocked off, and we weren't allowed to drive onto the island. So we parked the Suburban and walked across the bridge. We walked to your house, and the water was up to our waists sometimes. The wind was blowing so hard, we could barely stand up straight. It was amazing."

Marley continued. "Christina Rose saw Billy floating in the swimming pool. We thought he was dead. She jumped into the pool, clothes and shoes and all, and got him out of the water. I did CPR on him, although I had no idea how to do CPR on a dog. Thank goodness, whatever I did, it worked. Billy coughed up a bunch of water, and then he started to breathe again. But we couldn't find Dilly."

Christina Rose picked up the story again. "I found Dilly. She was hiding under your porch. Her collar was stuck to some of the lattice work, and she couldn't get loose. She was soaking wet, of course. She was fine physically, but she was so scared. When I picked her up, she cried and cried. I've never heard a dog cry like that before. It was like a really loud whimper, and she just wouldn't stop. When I carried her over and put her down beside Billy, she finally got quiet. The wind was blowing so hard, we couldn't walk very far or very fast. We started back towards the bridge. Marley was carrying Billy, and I was carrying Dilly. They were so cold. We were afraid they would go into hypothermia."

Marley continued. "A policeman stopped and drove us back across the bridge to where we'd left the Suburban. He really wanted to scold us for disobeying the law and going back onto Oak Island. And he didn't like our leaving the SUV alongside the road. But when he saw us, two very bedraggled females carrying two very bedraggled dogs, he didn't have the heart to scold us. He was really nice. He helped us get the dogs into the Suburban. We wrapped them in blankets. Christina Rose sat in the back seat with both the dogs."

"They wanted to be near a person and near each other. They wanted to hear my heartbeat, and I wanted to be sure their hearts were beating. The wind was blowing so hard, and the rain was coming down so hard. We couldn't see a thing out of the front windshield. The nice policeman gave us a special escort to the main highway. He put on his bubble light and his siren, and we passed all the other cars that were trying to get out of town. He knew the places where the road was flooded and where it was passable. We couldn't have done it without him. He escorted us all the way to Supply.

We don't even know his name." Christina Rose was feeling sorry she couldn't find a way to thank him.

"Once we were on Rt. #40, the traffic was moving faster. Christina Rose has some camp friends who live in Raleigh, and she contacted them for the name of a vet. We took the dogs to the vet in Raleigh, and she checked them out. They were dehydrated and hungry. They were wet and cold. The vet told us what to do, and we drove on to Asheville. Billy and Dilly were with us in Asheville through the storm. They came back with us to Shell Island as soon as we were allowed to return to the cottage."

Christina Rose put her finger to her lips. Gimbel had fallen asleep. Marley picked up one dog, and Christina Rose picked up the other dog. The canines were not happy to leave their warm spots next to Gimbel, and they strongly objected to being returned to the tote bags. Finally they were back in the carryalls, hidden from the view of the hospital staff and covered up with scarves. Marley and Christina Rose left Gimbel's hospital room and left the hospital. Nobody knew, except those who needed to know, that there had been an amazing reunion at the hospital that day. Hardly anybody knew that, not one, but two dogs had breached the "NO DOGS ZONE" at New Hanover Regional Medical Center.

Chapter 38

When Gimbel was released from the hospital, Marley and Christina Rose insisted he come to Shell Island to recuperate. Gimbel wondered if they couldn't bear to part with the dogs, or if they really wanted him to stay at the house. Gimbel had arrived at the hospital essentially without any clothes. The few that had survived his time in the water had to be thrown away. He'd been living in a hospital gown since he'd been rescued after the hurricane. A hospital volunteer had gone to Walmart and bought him some underwear and a warm-up suit, so he would have something to wear home from the hospital. He didn't have any shoes, so he wore the throwaway hospital socks. When Christina Rose and Marley picked him up at the hospital, he was using a cane and needed help climbing into the SUV.

They drove to the airport to pick up his Subaru. He owed almost a month's worth of parking fees, but the airport was giving everybody who'd been parked in long-term parking during Hurricane Gregory a break on the charges. Gimbel's wallet was underneath the driver's seat, and he gave Christina his credit card. She took care of making the payment. She drove the Subaru to Shell Island, and Gimbel rode with

Marley in the Suburban. They unloaded his things into the comfortable guest suite at the back of the cottage and told him to take a nap. Gimbel realized that, without the Chuckie Petrossi wardrobe, he had hardly anything at all to wear. He would have to remedy that, but before he could unpack his few belongings, he was asleep on the bed. It would take time for him to regain his stamina.

The next day, Christina Rose took Gimbel to the Apple store in Wilmington to help him buy a new iPhone. She picked it out, kindly taking his input and his needs into consideration. She made sure he had all the apps he needed as well as the car charger and the AC cord for charging his phone at home. He already had an account and a phone number; he just didn't have the phone any more. He also had a couple of email addresses, so Gimbel was all set to be able to communicate with the world again. He wasn't sure that was necessarily a good thing. He thought he'd enjoyed the hiatus from his electronic devices.

On the way home, he charged his new phone. By the time they were back at the cottage, hundreds of new emails and texts were waiting to be read. There were also countless voice mails, many of them from Christina Rose about the dogs. The communications dated from before the hurricane, when he'd hidden his FBI cell phone under the driver's seat of the Coastal Carolina van and tossed his personal phone into the back seat. All of the videos he'd recorded in the tunnel and sent to himself were there on his phone, so he knew one or both of the phones he'd left in the van had made it out of the tunnel. Gimbel briefly wondered where those phones were now.

Gimbel had not seen anything at all on the news about the videos he'd risked his life to get, the videos that would reveal to the American people what the Russians were attempting to do to undermine the United States. Gimbel had never heard a peep about the drug ring the Russians were running from the Wilmington, North Carolina area or its connection to the seafood industry.

He had the videos on his new phone, so he could only assume that the videos he'd sent had been delivered. That had to mean that the FBI or some other government agency had put the kibosh on releasing any of it to the public. The possibility of government censorship made him very angry, but he didn't have any extra energy to expend on being angry right now. That would have to wait. He would save up that anger for Steve Brandon.

Gimbel hadn't heard from either Steve Brandon of the FBI or from Captain Henry Pressor of the New York State Police. Gimbel decided he needed more of a break before he talked to either of them.

He was tired all the time, and even though being reunited with his dogs and with Christina Rose and Marley had cheered him immensely, he was feeling depressed. The neurologist and the psychiatrist who had seen him in the hospital had warned him this would happen. Many people who have suffered serious illnesses or injuries are overtaken by depression, just when they think they are well. The psychiatrist described it as a kind of double whammy, a seemingly unfair kick in the gut when one is finally putting one's life back in order. He said it was one way the body and the mind forced those who are recovering from major trauma to take it easy. The depression will slow them down. They will not be able to throw themselves back into their old lives as quickly as they might wish. They will have to take time to rest. They will have to reconsider and think about things.

Gimbel hated the depression. He realized he wasn't yet ready to talk to either the FBI or the New York State Police, but he thought he should at least let them know he was alive, even if they didn't care. Gimbel thought his boss, Henry Pressor, would care. He wasn't sure about Steve Brandon. He decided the best way to let his New York State employers know that he was still among the living was to have a copy of his medical file from the NHRMC sent to Henry Pressor's office. It would save a lot of time and explanation in the long run. Pressor would eventually have to know everything anyway — why he wasn't back at work in Syracuse and where he had been for the past few weeks. He wasn't ready to talk to Pressor yet, and he knew he wasn't ready to go back to work.

He was grateful to Christina Rose for her help with the phone. She said they would go shopping for clothes the next day. She realized he wasn't able to do more than one big thing in a day, and she wasn't pushing him. When they got back to the cottage, Marley was frying chicken. Gimbel was impressed; he didn't think anyone fried chicken any more. Christina Rose was excited.

"Marley's fried chicken is to die for. She doesn't make it very often, but when she does, watch out! The only thing better than her fried chicken is her creamy chicken gravy. I don't know how she makes it taste like she does, but it's the food of the gods. Are we having mashed potatoes? Marley's mashed potatoes are pretty good, too. Green beans?" When Marley nodded, Christina Rose laughed. Then Marley laughed, too. These women even had a joke about green beans.

Seeing Gimbel's puzzled look, Christina Rose explained. "Marley and I are on the same page with all kinds of food, almost to the extreme. However, when it comes to green beans, we have different opinions. Marley likes her green beans cooked the country way, for a long time with ham and onions. I like haricot verts, the tiny little French green beans, hardly cooked at all, very crisp and served with butter."

Marley explained. "I'm a country cook. I make green beans and fried chicken and chicken gravy and mashed potatoes like my mother made them. Christina loves all the rest of it, but she likes her green beans raw." Marley smiled.

Christina Rose added. "Truth be told, I love Marley's 'stewed' green beans, too, and she loves my 'raw' haricot verts. We just like to tease each other."

The fried chicken dinner more that lived up to its billing. Gimbel had grown very fond of these two friends of his who had taken him into their lives and been kind to him. He insisted on cleaning up the dishes although he hadn't realized how many pots and pans were required to prepare fried chicken and homemade mashed potatoes and chicken gravy. Marley was good about CAYGO, but cleaning up the kitchen wore him out. He went right to bed after he'd started the dishwasher.

The next day Christina Rose and Marley both wanted to help him shop for clothes. They really wanted him to buy his things at Au Naturel, but the storm had flooded their favorite store. It was closed for clean up, and Calabash was too far to drive today. There was a nice men's store in Wilmington. Gimbel wasn't used to paying high prices for his clothes. He had a few nice things he'd splurged on, but for the most part, he bought serviceable stuff online from the Duluth Trading Company. But two wonderful women were taking him shopping today, and he would rise to the occasion and spend some money. He had plenty, and he could afford nicer clothes. He lived frugally and really never bought much of anything. He had plenty of clothes at his condo in Syracuse, so he didn't need to buy too much.

When he thought about the clothes at his condo in New York, Gimbel realized with surprise and some discomfort that he wasn't looking forward to going back to Syracuse or to his condo there. That was his home, of course, and he had a job there. But he was not in any hurry to return. He wondered why. He'd known his gig as Chuckie Petrossi was just a temporary thing and that he would be returning to his real life when his undercover work was finished. Something had changed him. He wondered if it was his two close brushes with death—in the tunnel and in the ocean.

Or was it his frustration with the legal system he'd always been a part of—the legal system he had spent almost his entire life working for. He'd had his share of frustration with the courts and the lenient judges who let the bad guys off with a slap on the wrist, only to have them appear back in court weeks or even days later. Law enforcement caught them, and then the courts released them. He knew he was angry with the FBI. No, this was something different for Gimbel. Was this what a midlife crisis felt like? He would have to think about that later.

Today Gimbel had to focus on clothes. Luckily he had the docksiders to wear. He'd bought them, what now seemed like years ago, to have dinner with Christina Rose and Marley, and he was very thankful to have them. He'd packed them into the Subaru, and they had weathered the storm in the airport parking lot. The throwaway socks from the hospital were gross and had been tossed into the garbage can. Gimbel hoped and prayed the white leather Hermes driving shoes, both pairs of them, had disappeared into Davy Jones' Locker along with the remains of Hurricane Gregory.

The women picked out the clothes, and Gimbel tried them on and paid for them. They were having fun dressing him.

They let him select his own underwear and pajamas. Gimbel wondered if either one of these women had ever spent any time with a man. Was he a curiosity for them? Christina Rose's father had played no part whatsoever in her life. She had never once mentioned him. Marley had never mentioned being married or having a boyfriend. It wasn't his business to ask. It was just that they seemed to enjoy Gimbel's company, and he wasn't sure exactly why.

He spent more money than he wanted to spend, but they'd all had such a good time, it was worth it. Gimbel said he wanted to wear one of his new outfits and go out that night. He wanted to treat them to dinner at a favorite restaurant, a small Italian place on Wrightsville Beach. Gimbel couldn't help but think about Chuckie Petrossi, his Italian alter ego. The Umbrian Table had an Italian cream soda drink that they made themselves and served with crushed fresh fruit. Christina Rose loved the drink; she said it was almost like a dessert, but not as sweet. The three shared a large antipasto platter. Marley had the eggplant parmesan, and Christina Rose had the veal piccata. Gimbel ordered beef braciole. Everybody had the al dente spaghetti marinara. They laughed all the way home to Shell Island. It had been a very fun day. When he was with these two, he could feel his depression lifting.

The next morning, he walked the dogs alone. Christina Rose usually walked with him, but she was sleeping in this morning. Gimbel was sitting on the sand, throwing tennis balls into the water for Dilly and Billy. It was a gorgeous late August morning. Summer was at its peak, with just the slightest hint that fall might be around the corner. The storm had passed. Gimbel thought Shell Island looked like a piece of heaven today. He was lost in thought when he looked up and saw Rosemary Carmichael standing over him. He jumped up and brushed the sand off his clothes.

"Good morning. When did you get into town?"

Rosemary was silent. She looked at Gimbel, and he could see she was debating with herself about what she was going to say. She looked into his eyes, and she saw there what she was expecting to see but was hoping she wouldn't.

"Do you know who I am?"

Gimbel didn't look away. He matched her candid gaze and looked directly back at her. "Yes, Rosalind, I know who you are."

"We have to talk."

Chapter 39

"*How did you find me?*" Rosemary Carmichael sat down on the sand, and Gimbel sat beside her.

"I wasn't looking for you." Gimbel was not going to lie.

"What gave me away?"

"I recognized you from a photograph, from years ago."

"Will you tell me everything?"

"I didn't come to North Carolina to look for you. I came here on another case, completely unrelated to yours. Because I can't work active cases for the New York State Police any more, before I came down here, I was working cold cases. I remembered hearing about your case and didn't think it received the attention it deserved back in 2001. There were many reasons why everybody wanted the whole thing swept under the rug and forgotten. I reviewed everything about the murders. DNA testing has improved in the past twenty years, and I did some additional investigating and talked to some people who had never been interviewed. I came to the conclusion that you were not the woman who died in Norman and Rosalind Parsons' house in Syracuse."

"Who, besides my husband, died there?"

"I still don't know the answer to that question. We may never be able to positively identify the other two. I figured out the woman wasn't you. I never had any intentions of looking for you. After everything I'd learned about you and about the case, I decided you'd finally gotten lucky and were able to leave your old life behind."

"Do you think I killed them?"

"No, I never thought that. I don't know who did kill them, but I never thought it was you."

"Why didn't you think I killed them?"

"You were at least nine months pregnant at the time they were killed. The murders were bizarre in that two of the victims were beaten to death with a golf club before they were shot. They were essentially dead before they were shot. That still belies explanation. A very pregnant woman could not have beaten two people to death with a golf club. I wouldn't have blamed you for shooting your miserable bastard of a husband. But from everything I'd learned about you, I knew you hadn't shot two people who were essentially already dead. Whoever shot the two dead people also shot Norman, or at least we know that all three people were shot with the same gun. So, I knew you hadn't done it."

"Norman used to threaten to beat me with a golf club. He hit me with it a couple of times. It was a driver, wasn't it?"

"Yes. The metal rod survived the fire. It was a driver. You think Norman beat those two unknown people to death, don't you? Do you have any idea why he did that?"

"I have some ideas about why, but my opinions are purely speculation."

"Speculation is all we have, and it may be all we ever have. There are only three people in the world who could tell us what really happened that night, and all three of them are dead."

"I started the fire."

This was news to Gimbel. The surprise showed on his face. "I wouldn't have guessed that. Why did you do it?"

"It's complicated. I will tell you all about it, if you will promise to tell me everything you know."

"I promise. I was planning to tell you everything anyway."

"My husband was a horrible, evil man. He beat me on a regular basis. I usually could tell when he was going into one of his violent eruptions, and I would leave the house ahead of time, to protect myself. I had hiding places all over our neighborhood where I could be safe and wait for his rage to pass. There was a shed in our next-door neighbor's yard that had empty wooden crates stored in it. I hid behind those crates lots of times. One of the neighbors had a pool, and I could climb in between the parts of the pool equipment and hide myself where he couldn't find me. He looked and looked for me, but I became very good at hiding. I had a lot of hiding places."

"What a horrible way to live. I won't ask you why you stayed with him as long as you did. That's a discussion for another day. I know you finally reported his abuse to the authorities and went to a women's shelter. Good for you!"

"I should have done it years earlier, but I didn't have the courage. It's a long story, and yes, it is a discussion for another day. I guess you know what happened as soon as I reported my 'golden boy' husband's abuse."

"He had a judge commit you to a state psychiatric institution, and he hired two off-duty deputy sheriffs to kidnap you from the women's shelter and try to take you to the psychiatric hospital against your will. But you escaped from the two deputies, and then you disappeared. Nobody ever saw you again. Everybody assumed you died in the fire."

"I escaped from the men my husband hired to abduct me. I was within days of delivering my baby. I stayed out all night the night after my escape. I finally found a place to get warm and went to sleep on a gas station floor. The next morning, I called a priest whose name I picked out of the phone book. I told him I was in trouble. I didn't know what else to do. I told him I needed help. He drove to the gas station to pick me up and took me to his house. I stayed there for two days, and he helped me get my clothes and my car from the women's shelter. While I was at his house, I went into labor. I couldn't use my own identity or my own insurance to pay to have the baby. My husband would have found me. So the priest and I drove to Canada. We were taking a huge risk, driving to Canada while I was in labor. I could have had the baby in the car or alongside the road at any time. But we made it across the border into Canada before I delivered. After a very long and difficult labor, I had to have a C-section, and the Canadian National Health Service paid for me to give birth to Christina Rose."

"What does this have to do with the fire?"

"Please, let me tell this in my own way. It's important that you know everything this priest did for me. He had taken me in and let me stay with him when I had nowhere else to go. And then he drove with me to Canada to have my baby. He was with me during my long labor. I was exhausted and drugged, and I revealed much more to him about my marriage and my husband's treatment of me than I should have. I wasn't thinking clearly at that point, and I was blabbering. If I'd known what was going to happen later and if I'd been in control of my mouth, I might have been less candid. The priest supported me all the way, and I'm not Catholic, by the way. I named Christina Rose after him, so every time I look at her I am reminded of what this man did for me."

"You named your baby after the priest? What else did he do for you?"

"He killed for me. He killed my husband so that Christina Rose and I could have a life. So we could be free. I had no idea he was going to kill Norman. The priest had been in Vietnam, and I think he suffered from pretty severe PTSD. He kept it under control most of the time, but he snapped right after Christina Rose was born. He left me in the hospital, and he drove from Niagara Falls to my house in Syracuse where he killed my husband. I think he was completely psychotic by that time."

"How do you know all this?"

"He called me on the phone afterwards, after he'd killed Norman. He was mad as a hatter when he called to tell me he had freed me, that he had killed my husband. He said he'd also shot two other people who were at the house. He hadn't been expecting anybody else to be there, and he said they'd already been beaten to death so he hadn't really killed them. He shot them by mistake, he said. He said he didn't mean to shoot them and he didn't need to shoot them, because they were already dead. But he was very proud of the fact that he'd shot Norman. He said he had killed Norman because he knew that, as long as Norman was alive, he wouldn't stop until he had hunted me down and killed me and my baby. He knew that Norman wouldn't stop looking for us. The priest said the only way for me and Christina Rose to ever have a life was if Norman was dead. And he was right. It was the only way. Norman was smart, and he had charm. He had resources, and he would have used those resources to come after us and kill us. Don't doubt me on this."

"I agree that he would have hunted you down and killed you. There is no doubt about that in my mind either."

"The priest was afraid the authorities might blame me for the murders. He was confused and completely out of his head when he called me. I had just delivered a baby and was still in the hospital, recovering from a C-section when the people at my house were killed. I had a perfect alibi and wasn't worried that anyone would think I was the one who had murdered them. The priest reassured me that he had left his fingerprints all over my house, so when the authorities investigated, they would come after him, not me."

"I was just a few days post-partum, and I wasn't thinking clearly. After the women's shelter, the kidnapping, running away from the two thugs my husband had hired to take me to the psychiatric hospital, being nine months pregnant, driving to a foreign country to deliver my baby, and a long labor and the C-section, I made the decision to leave Canada and drive to Syracuse. I left the hospital early, before the doctor wanted me to leave. That was probably a bad decision, but at the time, I had to find out whether or not the priest had really killed Norman. I'd tried to call Norman many times, but there wasn't ever any answer at my house."

Rosemary paused to collect herself. Gimbel had a feeling the next part of the story would be even more difficult for her to tell than the horrible story she'd already told.

"I had a four-day-old baby and was exhausted. I was trying to breastfeed and wasn't being very successful. I hadn't had any sleep for days. I was still in pain from the surgery. The priest had driven my old car from Canada back to Auburn, New York to the women's shelter. He left the key in the car, and we hoped someone who needed a car would take it. If I was going to disappear, my car had to also disappear. I bought a used minivan in Canada and drove it back to Syracuse. I parked the minivan in my neighborhood, around the corner from my house. I didn't think anybody would recognize the minivan I was driving, and it was the middle of the night. I left Christina in the car and walked to the death scene."

Rosemary paused again. "Every time I think about what I saw when I walked into that house, my stomach turns over. Even after all these years, I feel as if I'm going to vomit. The murders had happened several days earlier, and the bodies had been lying there. So you can just imagine.... I can still see them—beaten to death, covered with blood, bloated and covered with flies and maggots. But it's the horrible smell I can't get out of my memory. It was like nothing I had ever smelled before. I was sick in the kitchen sink. I knew I couldn't let the priest go to jail for trying to save my life. I had to do something, but there was no way I could ever begin to wipe down the place for fingerprints. So I left."

"You left? But you went back?"

"I got as far as the back porch. I was feeling guilty about leaving Christina Rose in the car alone and wanted to get back to her. But I went back inside the house. If I'd been less traumatized or less exhausted and if I'd been thinking straight, I might not have gone back in. But I did, and I decided to start a fire. I wanted to burn the house down. I figured if the house burned down, no one would be able to find any fingerprints, and the priest who had killed for me would be safe. I'd never tried to burn down a house before, so I didn't know what to do. I turned on all the burners on the stove top and turned on the oven. I put newspapers and dish towels and a bunch of other stuff I thought would burn, in the oven and on top of the stove. I found some paint thinner and poured it all over. I left before the fire really got started. Then I ran. I had no idea if what I'd done would burn anything, but it did.

"Once I'd made the decision to leave Norman and go to the women's shelter, I bought a new identity. I bought Rosemary Carmichael. When I left Syracuse after I set my house on fire, I hid out at a motel in Binghamton, New York for a couple of days. I needed to get some rest and recover my composure. I was trying to take care of Christina Rose. When I watched the stories on the news, I realized that, not only was I free of my abuser, my husband, but someone else had died in my place. The authorities had concluded that the woman who had died in my house was me. This was an extra gift. Her death had been my death, and I hoped no one would ever come looking for me again. I was dead. I had died in Rosalind Parsons' house in Syracuse, New York. My body had been burned beyond recognition, and I was really free.

"Then I saw my photograph on all the news channels, and I got really scared. I went to a drugstore and bought hair dye. I cut all my hair off and died it black. The haircut was horrible, and the dye job looked really fake. But at least I looked different. I left Binghamton after one day. I wasn't rested, and I drove and drove and drove. I wanted to get as far away from New York State as I could. I intended to go to Arizona. I figured that would be far enough away so that no one would know me or be able to find me."

Then Rosemary smiled. "But I only made it as far as Asheville, North Carolina. I collapsed at a gas station convenience store, and my angel, Marley Kurtz, saved my life and Christina Rose's life. She wouldn't let me get back in my car, and she took us home with her and took care of us. I was very ill with septicemia and almost died. Marley did everything." Rosemary had not cried or broken down, during the recounting of her horrible saga until now, when she began to talk about Marley. Rosemary wept as she tried to tell Gimbel all that Marley Kurtz had done for her.

Rosemary made herself stop crying. "I'll tell you all about Marley later. I made a life for myself and my child, with constant love and support from Marley, and I have been very successful. I could not have done any of it without Marley. Now you know my story. Now you have to tell me what you know."

Gimbel looked at Rosemary Carmichael. He could see the remnants of a sad Rosalind Parsons in her eyes and in her psyche. He took her in his arms and held her. She let him, and she sobbed. These were the tears of a lifetime, the tears of long ago, the tears she had until now been afraid to let go. Gimbel held her until she cried herself to sleep, and then he held her while she slept.

Chapter 40

"What are you going to do about me?" Rosemary wanted to know from Gimbel who had taken the dogs back to the house. Rosemary and Gimbel were walking on the beach alone. "Are you going to arrest me?"

Gimbel stared at Rosemary. "Why in the world would I do that?"

"I burned down my house. I destroyed evidence in a triple murder. I obstructed justice. I have been living under a name that is not my own."

"Aside from the fact that the statute of limitations has expired on the arson, you have not committed any crime. You didn't kill anybody, and I am assuming, if you went to trial for anything, even murder, your attorney would argue, and rightfully so, diminished capacity. I think post-partum psychosis might even hold up, considering all the things you had going on in your life at the time. There is no case here; there is no crime. Why would I arrest you?"

It hadn't occurred to Rosemary that there might be a statute of limitations for the arson, and she hadn't really thought about what the reality of going in front of a jury would involve. She had rationalized her behavior to herself a thousand times, and she accepted that she'd had no choice about most of the things she'd done. But she had been reliving the tragedy over and over again, and she'd been stuck back in 2001 where she was consumed by guilt and felt ashamed about the cover-up she thought she'd perpetrated. Now that she'd confessed everything to a law enforcement officer, she began to see things differently.

"I would have gone to the police, you know, if I'd only had myself to consider. I would have confessed everything about the fire, but I couldn't take the chance that I would go to prison. I had to think of Christina Rose and what would happen to her if I went to the authorities. Would she end up in a foster home, like I had? I couldn't allow that to happen. More than anything, I couldn't let that happen."

Gimbel would have liked to ask her about the foster home, but now was not the time. "Christina Rose doesn't know any of this, does she?"

"I hope she never has to know. I would break a number of laws before I allowed anyone to tell her about her father and all the rest of my sordid past."

"But Marley knows."

"I would protect Marley with my life, so I don't want her dragged into this, statute of limitations or not. But, yes, she knows pretty much everything."

"You owe her a lot, don't you?"

"I owe her everything. She is the mother I never had and the grandmother I never thought Christina Rose would ever have. She has been our savior, our refuge in the storm."

Gimbel had promised to tell Rosemary everything, and now he hated having made that promise. There was at least one thing Rosemary didn't really need to know, something he knew would hurt her. Whenever she learned about it, it would break her heart. But if she somehow found out about it later, from somebody else, it would destroy any trust she had placed in Gimbel. He could not fail to keep his promise to tell her everything he knew. He couldn't take the chance that she would think he had betrayed her or held out on her. So he went ahead and told her everything, just as he'd said he would. He decided to break her heart now.

"There's something I need to tell you, something you don't know about the case. I promised I would tell you everything. DNA testing has improved a great deal in the past twenty years. We can find things out from samples that used to be too small to test successfully. And, we also can get DNA results from samples that are severely degraded." Gimbel took a deep breath and continued. "The woman who died in your house was pregnant. That information was never released to the public, but it's one reason why everyone connected with the case assumed it was you who had died. It was well-known that you were pregnant, so when the burned woman's corpse revealed a pregnancy, it was a logical conclusion to believe it was you."

Rosemary's face showed her shock that the woman who had died in her place had been pregnant. She took a deep breath and sighed, as if the news meant something more to her than Gimbel realized.

Gimbel continued. "We were able to save from the fire a remnant of what was in the dead woman's womb. Her unborn child was somewhat protected from the fire's destruction because it was inside her body. The ME who did the autopsy felt it was important to save the fetal remains. Those remains were really just a few bone fragments. DNA testing was not advanced enough in 2001 to yield anything useful. But the ME made sure that those bone fragments were preserved in the police lab for almost two decades. I had them tested last year. I did some investigating and knew you were nine-months pregnant at the time of the murders in early April. The remains in the lab were those of a fetus of five months' gestation, and that was the red flag. The evidence didn't compute. When I confirmed that you were at full-term in your pregnancy, I knew it was not your body that had been found in the house. That was when I decided to try to test the fetal remains to try to determine who the father of the unborn child was."

Rosemary looked at him, and it was almost as if she'd guessed what the results of the DNA test had been. It was as if she already knew what he was going to tell her. Gimbel continued. "The DNA showed that the baby who died when its mother was murdered was Norman Parsons' child. The woman who was bludgeoned to death was pregnant with your husband's son."

Rosemary turned white. Even though she had suspected this might be true, hearing about the DNA evidence, the cold, hard facts, the confirmation of her suspicions, hit her hard. She had a difficult time finding what she wanted to say next. She finally spoke again.

"My husband was a womanizer. He had affairs during our marriage, lots of them. He was handsome, and he had a great deal of superficial charm. I'm not as shocked as you might expect me to be, to learn that the woman who was beaten to death in my house was pregnant with my husband's child. I don't know the poor soul's name, and maybe nobody will ever know who she was. But I am quite certain she was at my house that night to tell my husband about the pregnancy. He would not have been happy to hear the news. He would have become enraged. He would have grabbed the golf club, and he would have beaten her to death. I am as certain of that as I have ever been of anything. What I don't know is, who the hell was the other man who died there? Why was he even there? I've thought about this for a long time. I'd already decided the woman who died was probably one of my husband's girlfriends. I didn't know about the pregnancy, but knowing about that further confirms my theory."

"I agree with you that it makes sense, more sense than any of the other theories that have been thrown around about this case."

"Norman wasn't happy that I was pregnant. He became even more cruel and abusive after I told him I was expecting our child. He never wanted to know anything about the baby. A couple of times I tried to show him pictures of the sonograms, and he walked out of the room. He would have been furious to find out that one of his paramours had allowed herself to get pregnant. He would have insisted on an abortion. If the woman said she wouldn't get an abortion, he would had killed her. He hated children. I knew I had to leave him before I had my baby. I couldn't raise a child in a household with that man. That's why I bought the Rosemary Carmichael identity and made my plans to disappear."

"There's one last thing you probably don't know. It's about Father Christopher Maloney." Rosemary started when she heard the name. "He's the priest one of your neighbors said she saw wandering around your house the night the murders are thought to have been committed. Your neighbor attended Maloney's church, St. Stanislaus. She tried repeatedly to tell her story to the authorities, but they blew her off. I didn't pay much attention to her story either, until now. What you've told me today about 'the Catholic priest' who helped you and who says he killed your husband, gives new credence to your neighbor's story."

"Yes, his name was Father Christopher Maloney. I've tried to find him. I've searched the internet, and I've made phone calls. I wanted to get him the help he needed, to treat his PTSD and his mental illness. I owed that to him. I was never able to find out anything about what had happened to him, not even a notice of his death. He just vanished. I finally gave up."

"Father Christopher Maloney died, years ago, in Cuidad Juarez, Mexico. His body was found in his station wagon. The car was definitely his, and his wallet was in the car. It looked like a drug gang had robbed and killed him. It happened in a border town. There wasn't much of an investigation into his death, and no DNA testing was done. The Mexican authorities cremated his body and sent his remains back to the diocese in upstate New York. Somebody held a service at St. Stanislaus, and his ashes were scattered in the graveyard there."

"Mexico? No! I don't believe that for a second. He had a station wagon, for sure, an ancient Buick. It was like a tank. But you've admitted that nobody seriously investigated his death. What if it wasn't Father Maloney who died?"

"You weren't able to find him. Nobody by that name has ever turned up anywhere. I did some searching of my own, too. The only thing I ever found about Father Christopher Maloney was the story about his death in Mexico…and about his being a priest at St. Stanislaus in New York. I'm pretty certain it was Father Maloney who died in Cuidad Juarez. He might have been trying to escape justice. He may have realized he was going to take the rap, not only for the murder he did commit, but for two murders he didn't. He may have decided to try to live south of the border, off the grid, out of the reach of U.S. law. That explanation makes sense."

Rosemary wasn't able to accept right now that Maloney had died so long ago, in such a derelict place and in such a derelict way. Gimbel believed Father Christopher Maloney was dead, and he felt Rosemary would eventually accept that as the truth.

Rosemary changed the subject. "For a long time, I've wanted to legally change my name to Rosemary Carmichael, but I was afraid to get involved with the courts in any way. I had too much to hide. Now, for my own peace of mind and for Christina Rose's sake, I'd like to try to follow through on that. Can you help me? I don't want to be living any more of a lie than I have to. Christina Rose is going to be looking at colleges this fall, and I want everything to go smoothly for her. I don't want any dirty little secrets to turn up in her life."

"I can help you with the name change, but you need to consult a lawyer. It isn't difficult, as long as you're not changing your name for any illegal purposes."

"To say this confession I've made to you has been life changing would be an understatement. At first, I was so resentful of you, the way you butted into my family. I'm so paranoid; I thought you were looking for me and had ingratiated yourself with Marley and Christina Rose to get to me. Then you disappeared, and we all thought you were dead. Christina Rose had grown so fond of you and your dogs. Marley, too. I knew if Marley trusted you, I could trust you. I tried to find out what happened to you, and we finally found you at NHRMC. When did you know about me?"

"I knew at some level the day you sailed to Oak Island, and we had lunch. When I mentioned I was in law enforcement and lived in Syracuse, New York, you totally freaked out. So did Marley. After I saw that reaction, it all came together for me. I'd recognized you the first time I met you, the night at the cottage when you showed up unexpectedly. I knew I'd seen you before someplace. At first, I couldn't figure out where, but I knew it was just a matter of time before I'd remember where I'd seen you or seen your picture. There were also other small things that began to add up. You had a very successful computer business. Rosalind Parsons had a PhD in computer science. The red hair. You were the right age. The absence of any southern accent. There were little clues."

"What will you do?"

"About what?"

"About me, my case."

"Nothing. I've already taped up the evidence boxes and returned the murder book and everything else to the cold case archives. There's nothing more to do. As far as anyone knows, Rosalind Parsons died in Syracuse, New York in April of 2001. In a way, you know, she really did. I can live with that."

"Thank you." Rosemary hugged Gimbel and kissed him on the cheek. You are a good man. We have not allowed many men into our lives during the past sixteen years. Marley and I both had abusive husbands, and neither one of us trusts men very much. For some odd reason, she has decided to trust you, so I think I trust you, too."

"You need to buy Christina Rose a dog."

"Wow, there's an abrupt change of topic. Where did that come from?"

"She needs a dog; that's all. I had to mention it." They were walking back to the house, and that made Rosemary laugh. Gimbel started to laugh, too. Marley and Christina Rose looked at the two of them laughing together. They'd been afraid the long powwow on the beach portended disaster. How could all that have resulted in laughter?

Chapter 41

Lamb chops were on the menu that night. Gimbel had gone to the butcher shop and had them cut to order. He'd heard they were Christina Rose's favorite. He grilled them on the barbecue, and Marley produced twice-baked potatoes, peas, and mint jelly to go with the chops. They had raspberry sorbet for dessert. Marley and Christina Rose noticed the difference in Rosemary. She was worn out from the revelations and the emotion of the day, but she was more relaxed than Gimbel had ever seen her. All of their talking and his reassurances that she would not go to jail, had to be a huge relief for her. She had unburdened herself of many years' worth of worry.

"I think we need to get a dog." Rosemary shocked everybody with her declaration. "What? Is that such an unreasonable thing to say? Gimbel is going to go back to New York one of these days, and we are going to miss those two cute little guys when they go. We might even miss Gimbel a little bit when he leaves." She smiled at her joke.

Christina Rose looked at the woman who was sitting across the table from her and wondered who had stolen her mother. Who was this woman who was being funny and saying they needed a dog?

"I'm voting yes on the dog, and we need to do it right away, before you change your mind, Mom."

"I'm not going to change my mind, Christina Rose. I want a dog, too."

"Does this mean I have to agree to give up applying to Cornell, if we get a dog?"

"Of course not. You can still apply to Cornell. I think Duke is a much better choice, but you want to do that Hotel School thing, I know."

"I graduated from Cornell." Gimbel was thrilled Christina Rose was considering his own alma mater as a possible college choice.

"How did you happen to choose Cornell, Gimbel?" Marley wanted to know how this policeman had been able to afford an Ivy League education.

"I was a really good baseball player. Ivy League colleges don't give athletic scholarships, but they recruit athletes just the same. I had good grades, and I was financially needy. So they gave me an academic scholarship. I played varsity baseball for four years. I was in the College of Industrial and Labor Relations, which is where I studied pre-law. I was going to be a lawyer."

"What happened to that plan? Why didn't you become a lawyer? You would have been a great lawyer." Christina Rose wanted to know.

"I was drafted to play baseball. I loved the game and played professional ball for three years before I was injured. I had a very serious rotator cuff surgery and had to quit. It broke my heart, and I drowned my sorrows by joining the Marines. I was in Afghanistan for three years, and when that was finished, I decided to go into law enforcement. That's my boring story."

"It isn't boring at all. You have done a lot of things, Gimbel. I'm sorry about the baseball. That's a tough hurdle to overcome." Marley knew about tough hurdles.

"Not really." Gimbel was on a role and decided full disclosure was the theme of the day. "I had a terrible childhood. Both of my parents were alcoholics, and both died before I finished high school. Those days, those years of raising myself, were the tough hurdle. Everything since high school has been easy peasy." Gimbel hadn't really meant to say that much. He didn't want to put a damper on the evening.

"Oh, Gimbel, I am so sorry. We will have to talk about that sometime." Marley had once been on the other end of the alcoholism challenge.

"It was a long time ago. I became depressed and had some therapy while I was in college. The baseball coach sent me to a psychiatrist because my game was in a slump and I couldn't get out of bed in the morning. The therapy helped me a lot, and it helped my baseball." He wanted them to know he wasn't still suffering from his terrible childhood, even though he knew he would really never stop suffering from it, no matter how long he lived.

"Here's to new beginnings and the future, with a new dog in it." Christina Rose raised her glass of sweet tea. They all drank to the future and to the new dog.

"So, what do you want for the future, the future we are toasting here?" It was Marley, the oldest of the group who wanted specifics. "Everybody has to say something, and I will start. Years ago, I gave up on my nursing degree, and I have regretted it ever since. I have done some research, and it isn't too late for me to finish my RN. There are programs in North Carolina that will accept an old bird like myself. I also want to get my BS degree, and I will choose a program that will allow me to do both at the same time."

With tears in her eyes, Christina Rose reached over and squeezed Marley's hand. "I'm so proud of you."

Rosemary spoke next. "I'm trying to decide whether or not to open a second office of my business in Wilmington. I have many clients here, and that is fine in the summer. But in the winter, I have to drive or fly too much. If I had an office in Wilmington, that might solve a lot of the problem. I don't know what to do, so I don't know quite what to ask for in my future."

"I want to go to Cornell. I want to go to the Hotel School. I would love to have my own restaurant. But I also love to sing. I want a dog. The Hotel School provides training for the hospitality industry, but its graduates also get a top notch education in business. I don't know exactly what I want for my future. I'm only sixteen."

"I thought, when I came to Wilmington on this last job assignment that I'd be going back to the New York State Police as a detective, relegated to cold cases, because of my health. I was resigned to going back to the same old, same old. I didn't even think about changing course. But after so many things have happened to me in the past few weeks and months, I am reconsidering my options. I can afford to take some time off and go back to school. I'd like to upgrade my skills. I know a lot about computers, but I need to know more. I need to learn more about the technology of the latest security surveillance techniques. I may start my own business, consulting to law enforcement in small towns. I've looked online at the University of North Carolina Wilmington. They offer what I think I'm looking for."

"All of our hypothetical futures include further education and building on existing achievements. I'd say we are a pretty ambitious bunch." Rosemary summed it up.

They talked late into the night. Christina Rose, Rosemary, and Marley would make a trip to look at Cornell. Christina Rose promised to take another look at Duke. Marley expressed her anxiety about going back to school at her age. Rosemary was reluctant to work any harder than she already did. Would expanding her business mean more or fewer demands on her time? Christina Rose decided she needed to include an outlet for her music in her life, even if she went the Hotel School route. Gimbel had pretty much already decided to hand in his resignation to Captain Henry Pressor, whatever he decided to do next.

"I'm going to be leaving soon. I will miss you all terribly. I am sure one of the reasons I'm considering UNC Wilmington as a possibility for my schooling is so I will be closer to all of you. I know you will miss the dogs, even if you don't miss me so much. But you will soon have your own dog to love and care for. I have too much to express to you, to try to say it all in one night. After I clear up some things in Syracuse, I hope to be back soon."

Chapter 42

Gimbel put off his return to New York several times. He'd been in touch with Steve Brandon, and the conversations had not gone well. Gimbel wanted to know if Brandon had received any of the videos he'd sent from his phone. Brandon was distant with Gimbel on the phone and told him in no uncertain terms that he was not at liberty to discuss anything about the "ongoing investigation." He said Gimbel did not have a high enough security clearance for the FBI agent to be able to talk to him, and Gimbel knew this was baloney. Gimbel was being shut out, and he was angry about it. He wondered if Steve Brandon and others at the FBI were secretly disappointed when Gimbel turned up alive. For weeks they'd thought he had died, and that had taken care of all their problems. A difficult loose end had been nicely tied off with Gimbel's disappearance and death. Now the man who "knew where the bodies were buried" was alive and well and not being compliant.

Steve Brandon, not so politely, threatened Gimbel against communicating anything about the Russians or the drug operations to the media. Brandon, however, was treading a fine line. If he threatened Gimbel too severely, Gimbel might get mad and tell all on CNN or Fox News. Gimbel let Brandon know he had all the videos on his own phone, and the FBI agent warned him against talking about the case or showing the videos to anyone. Gimbel hadn't decided what he was going to do with the knowledge he had. He despised the cover-up which was so excruciatingly and obviously going on. But, he had spent most of his adult life supporting, protecting, and working for the justice system. Considering the way the FBI and the government were currently behaving with regard to the Russian investigation, Gimbel didn't know if he could continue to support this recent muzzle. They eventually reached a point where Steve Brandon didn't want to talk to Gimbel anymore, and Gimbel didn't want to talk to him.

Captain Pressor on the other hand was delighted to hear from Gimbel and to know he was alive. He'd been very worried. Gimbel finally returned to his condo in Syracuse. Dilly and Billy sniffed around their old home as if they were exploring another planet. Living at the beach had spoiled them. They were not happy to be back, living in the smallish high-rise condo.

When Gimbel returned to work, his desk was covered with files and phone messages. He'd told Henry Pressor he would clear his desk and then he was leaving. Pressor wasn't surprised Gimbel was leaving the state police. He'd known Gimbel wouldn't be happy working cold cases forever. He supported Gimbel's choices, although he was sorry to lose him. He was surprised Gimbel was leaving New York, but told him he knew someone who wanted to buy Gimbel's condo.

Gimbel began to work his way through the piles of paper. He was anxious to return to Wilmington. He was excited about going back to school and learning new things. Rosemary had asked him if he would be willing to live in the Shell Island cottage during the winter months. She said it would be a huge relief to her, to have someone she trusted staying there when they weren't using the house. They'd been burglarized a few years ago, and Rosemary now hired a service to take care of the cottage during the off-season. Someone from the service was supposed to come by periodically and check to see that everything was okay. Rosemary said she would love for Gimbel to stay there while he was going to school. She knew he would be getting his own place eventually, but it would be a big favor to her if he would be willing to move into the cottage until he bought his own house. It was an offer Gimbel couldn't refuse.

Christina Rose made appointments to visit the Cornell University campus and have an interview at the Cornell Hotel School. The three women would stay at the Sherwood Inn in Skaneateles, New York, on Gimbel's recommendation. Gimbel would join them at the Sherwood for dinner after they'd had their tour of the Big Red campus in Ithaca. He would love to have joined them for the tour but didn't want to intrude where he probably didn't belong. Marley would return to her nursing studies in Asheville as soon as they were back from the college trip. Rosemary had decided to open an office in Wilmington sometime during the next year.

Gimbel tried to focus on the files he had to go through before he could leave town. It was a hodgepodge of cases, and it mostly involved making sure the bits and pieces of information people had sent to him were filed correctly. One file made it to Gimbel's desk by mistake, or at first he thought it was a mistake. A probation officer in Cayuga County, New York had retired. The woman who had taken over the retired probation officer's cases had learned via the grapevine that Gimbel was interested in hearing about missing persons.

When he'd been working on the Parsons' triple murder cold case from 2001, Gimbel had sent out emails to several law enforcement offices and others, asking for names of missing persons, especially those who might never have been officially reported missing. He wanted to know about people who could have fallen through the cracks of officialdom, people who had disappeared and didn't have families to file official reports.

The file contained a mailing envelope and a note clipped to the outside of the mailing envelope. The note said the envelope had been sent to one of the retired probation officers' clients. The client, a Darnel Phillips, had done eighteen years in Auburn Correctional. He had lived in a halfway house in Auburn, and he had been killed in an automobile accident earlier that year. The envelope, addressed to Darnel at the halfway house where he'd been living, had arrived there after he'd died. The woman who supervised Darnel Phillips' halfway house had given the envelope and the rest of his mail to his probation officer. The probation officer had put all these papers and the unopened envelope into Darnel's file. The deceased ex-con's file had gone into a pile designated inactive and headed for the archives.

The new probation officer had been reading through some of her predecessor's old cases and had come across the file and the unopened envelope. After opening it and reading it, she remembered Gimbel's interest in missing persons, and she thought he might like to look at both the contents of the envelope and at Darnel Phillip's file. Gimbel was conscientious and decided he would at least skim through this paperwork. When he read the cover letter from a Shirley Dryden, that was included in the envelope, he knew he was on to something. He read through Darnel Phillips' file and carefully read the contents of the envelope that had been mailed from Binghamton, New York. The envelope contained the medical file of a woman named Patsy Phillips.

After he'd read everything, Gimbel contacted Shirley Dryden. They had a long phone conversation, and Gimbel thanked her for the effort she'd made to send Patsy's medical file to Darnel. He explained to Shirley Dryden that Darnel had died in a car accident. He told her how he, Gimbel, had ended up with Darnel's file and the envelope Shirley had sent. He told Shirley everything about the triple murder. He told her how the file she had sent to Darnel had, at long last, provided the pieces of information that had solved an almost twenty-year-old mystery.

Two people who had been Jane Doe and John Doe for too long now had names and identities. There were no longer any bodies to be given a proper burial, and there were no family members to be notified. But there was closure of sorts. Shirley assured Gimbel over the phone that she would tell her mother the sad story. She said her mother had always wondered why Patsy Phillips hadn't kept any more of her appointments with Dr. Elias Trimble.

Gimbel would now be able to tell Rosemary who had died in her place, the name of the mother of Christina's Rose's half-brother who had died in utero, so many years ago. Patsy Phillips, who was in actuality Patsy Grimes and Patti Gaylord, had died a horrible death. Gimbel assumed that Fergus Phillips had accompanied Patsy to Syracuse to help her tell Norman Parsons that she was pregnant with his child. Fergus, because of this good deed, had faced Norman Parsons' wrath and had been beaten to death in the murder house along with Patsy. Because for so many years, everyone had believed that the dead woman found in the murder house was Rosalind Parsons, Patsy's death had provided cover for Rosemary Carmichael and her daughter Christina Rose to live their lives.

Christina Rose and her family were arriving next week to see Cornell. Gimbel had packed up his Syracuse condo. His desk was clear. He was ready for a new chapter in his life. Gimbel bought a used Range Rover SUV to tow a U-Haul to Shell Island in North Carolina.

Chapter 43

It was a wonderful reunion. Gimbel had missed his North Carolina friends a great deal. They met in the parking lot of the Sherwood Inn. Dilly and Billy were beside themselves with joy to see Christina Rose and Marley again. A new West Highland Terrier puppy from a breeder in Chapel Hill had been born, and it would be ready to leave its mother and join the Carmichael-Kurtz clan in two weeks. The women loved the Sherwood Inn as much as Gimbel had promised them they would. He would join them for dinner at the Sherwood after Christina Rose's interview at the Cornell Hotel School. Although he knew Rosemary wanted her daughter to matriculate at Duke, Gimbel hoped Christina Rose would chose Cornell.

It was an hour's drive from Ithaca to Skaneateles. The tour and the interview had been a success. Christina Rose had excellent grades from a top private school in Asheville. Her SAT scores were in the high 700s. The woman who interviewed her at Cornell told her she would have a place the following year in the incoming class at the Cornell Hotel School. She also told Christina Rose that her academic credentials would guarantee her a spot in a number of Ivy League schools. She told Christina Rose that if Cornell was her first choice, she should apply there for early decision. She warned Christina Rose about the brutally cold winters that Upstate New York sometimes experienced. She very much wanted Christina Rose to attend Cornell, but she realized the young woman was quite talented and extremely smart and had many options.

They gathered in the bar of the Sherwood Inn to wait for their table. There was a hint of a chill in the air, so they sat around the fire with their club sodas and glasses of sweet tea. Rosemary looked radiant. She had survived the visit to Cornell and had to admit she'd been impressed with the campus and with what she'd learned about the Hotel School's curriculum. She just couldn't bear for Christina Rose to be so far away. Gimbel could tell that being able to unburden herself about her past had been a tremendous relief for Rosemary. She seemed lighter, happier. She laughed more. Her eyes smiled now when her mouth smiled. She looked younger and more like her daughter than she ever had. Gimbel realized that Rosemary Carmichael was a very attractive woman, and he had begun to like her very much.

They had a wonderful dinner, and everyone wanted to talk at once. Gimbel insisted that everybody order the shrimp cocktail He said he'd explain at a later date why. They all ordered the shrimp and loved it. They said it tasted like North Carolina shrimp. Gimbel told them that indeed the shrimp was from Holden Beach. Someday, Gimbel would tell them the story of the murders in the Sherwood Inn parking lot and the ensuing investigation. He would tell them about moving to Wilmington to live as Chuckie Petrossi in the big house on Oak Island and why he'd been wearing the weird clothes and white shoes and driving the gold BMW. He might even tell them what he had just learned about Dirk Shannon.

In the end it had been determined that Dirk was an innocent bystander in the seafood and drug drama. All along, Dirk had just been a driver who delivered seafood. He had nothing to do with delivering drugs. The Russians hadn't known exactly what Dirk's role was as a driver for Coastal Carolina, and they had mistakenly thought he was a drug driver who was holding out on them. Dirk had no idea there were drugs packed in with the seafood in the back of his delivery van.

Even Curley Davenport, the sous chef at the Sherwood Inn who had disappeared, had been exonerated. He'd been terrified when Dirk Shannon and Pedro Ruiz were ruthlessly murdered in the Sherwood's parking lot. He didn't know why it had happened, but he decided to get out of town, pronto! Curley was finally located working as a short-order cook at a truck stop in Abilene, Texas. When the Sherwood Inn cook, Dimitri Kouris, called him and offered him his old job back, he couldn't get back fast enough to Skaneateles and the Sherwood's kitchen.

Christina Rose told Gimbel all about her interview at the Hotel School. She was feeling confident and proud of herself after having been guaranteed a place for the following fall. The women laughed a lot. It was late. Gimbel was driving back to Syracuse tonight, and the women were tired and ready to go to their rooms at the Sherwood. They would see each other again the next day for a ride around Lake Skaneateles on the Judge Ben Wiles sightseeing boat.

Christina Rose had left her sweater by the fire and went back to get it. There was a man sitting at the bar, an albino man, an older man, who kept staring at her. This made her very uncomfortable. A young woman of another generation might have just made a quick escape, but Christina Rose was not one to run from adversity. The man looked like a nice guy. He didn't look weird or anything. He looked normal, but he kept staring at her. She was just about to confront him when her mother joined her.

Her mother also saw the man who was sitting at the bar, and she almost fainted. All of her breath rushed from her lungs. She grabbed Christina Rose's arm to keep from collapsing. She knew the man she was staring at had died on September 11, 2001. She was certain it was the same man. He was much thinner than Eberhardt Grossman had been, and his face looked as if he might have had some plastic surgery. Of course he was older. Rosemary was older, too. She was afraid she might stop breathing. Years had passed. Rosemary was sure it was the same person. But how was that possible? He was dead. But then she reminded herself that she, too, was dead. Rosalind Parsons was also dead.

Gimbel and Marley were waiting in the doorway for Christina Rose to collect her sweater. Rosemary approached the man at the bar. He stared at her face, and then he looked at Christina Rose's face. No one said anything.

Finally, the albino man at the bar looked directly at Rosemary and asked, "Do you know who I am?"

Acknowledgments

Many thanks to my terrific readers: Jane Corcoran, Peggy Baker, Nancy Calland Hart, and Robert Lane Taylor. Your feedback and suggestions were great as always. You keep me and my imagination on track.

My editor, Nancy Calland Hart, is the best. Any and all errors that remain in the book, after her excellent scrubbing and suggestions for rewriting, are mine alone. My husband, Robert Lane Taylor, also keeps my feet to the fire with his screening for accuracy and his sharp eyes for typos. I am indebted to both of you.

Jamie Tipton at Open Heart Designs does everything for me. She transforms the ideas in my imagination into fabulous covers. She formats my manuscripts into beautifully printed pages. She puts together all the pieces that go into making my books complete. She is amazing and wonderfully talented and patient. I could not do any of this without her.

Because this book is part of a series, the cover is similar to that of *RUSSIAN FINGERS*. I wanted a pinwheel of matryoshka dolls to replace the chessboard. Jamie, of course, came up with the perfect pinwheel.

Andrea Burns is my photographer. She is exceptionally gifted and creative and always makes me look good. She also does the photographs for my alter egos, and I am eternally grateful that she has discovered the fountain of youth…for me and for those women in wigs who look like me.

A special thanks to Jane and Robert Corcoran who invited me to their home in Skaneateles for the weekend so I could absorb the ambiance of this charming village and gather material for my story.

The first question Elizabeth Burke, M.D. always asked me when I saw her in her office was: "What's new and exciting in your life?" I promised myself that one day I would have a good answer for her. Thank you, Dr. Burke.

About the Author

MARGARET TURNER TAYLOR *lives on the East Coast in the summer and in Southeast Arizona in the winter. She has written several mysteries for young people, in honor of her grandchildren. She writes spy thrillers, stories of political intrigue, and all kinds of mysteries for grownups.*

More Books By
Margaret Turner Taylor

BOOKS FOR ADULTS

Traveling Through the Valley of the Shadow of Death
Based on actual events that occurred in 1938, Traveling Through the Valley of the Shadow of Death is a fictional spy thriller that will captivate the reader with its complex intrigue and deceptions. Travel with Geneva Burkhart through pre-World War II Germany as she deals with an amorous Nazi minder who has been assigned to watch her group of mathematics teachers. The young American woman who grew up on an Ohio dairy farm has adventures that take her to dangerous and frightening places.
Released 2020, 428 pages

I Will Fear No Evil
This World War II thriller, set in neutral Portugal, tells the story of a courageous few who risk their lives to confront evil. The reader will get to know the cadre of international patriots who live at beautiful Bacalhoa in Setubal. Max, who faced death in Traveling Through the Valley of the Shadow of Death, joins other brave souls who have devised an elaborate and secret network to transport Jewish orphans across the Atlantic to safety and freedom in the United States. Max has his revenge on the Nazis and finds love during his journey.
Released 2020, 370 pages

Russian Fingers
Book #1 in the The Quest for Freedom Series
Peter Gregory spent his childhood in a camp for Soviet spies. Sent to live in the United States and uncover its atomic secrets for the Russians, he soon realizes that he loves his adopted country. After the fall of the Soviet Union, Peter disappears and makes a new life for himself. But Russia wants its spy back. Sergei, now a Russian orthodox priest who knew Peter at Camp 27, is forced by Russia's neo-Soviets to try to track him down. Will Peter and Sergei be able to outsmart Putin's henchmen and disappear again?
Released 2023, 354 pages

BOOKS FOR YOUNG PEOPLE

| Secret in the Sand | Baseball Diamonds | Train Traffic | The Quilt Code | The Eyes of My Mind |

Available in hard cover, paperback and ebook online everywhere books are sold.

MORE FROM
LLOURETTIA GATES BOOKS

CAROLINA DANFORD WRIGHT

Old School Rules
Book #1 in the *The Granny Avengers Series*

Marfa Lights Out
Book #2 in the *The Granny Avengers Series*

HENRIETTA ALTEN WEST

I Have a Photograph
Book #1 in the *The Reunion Chronicles Mysteries*

Preserve Your Memories
Book #2 in the *The Reunion Chronicles Mysteries*

When Times Get Rough
Book #3 in the *The Reunion Chronicles Mysteries*

A Fortress Steep & Mighty
Book #4 in the *The Reunion Chronicles Mysteries*

The Wells of Silence
Book #5 in the *The Reunion Chronicles Mysteries*

*Available in hard cover, paperback and ebook
online everywhere books are sold.*

Printed in the USA
CPSIA information can be obtained
at www.ICGtesting.com
JSHW010623070224
56627JS00002B/3/J